REMINISCENCES

REMINISCENCES

BY

Grace Elvina

THE MARCHIONESS CURZON
OF KEDLESTON, G.B.E.

WITH 37 ILLUSTRATIONS

LONDON
HUTCHINSON

Hutchinson & Co. (Publishers) Ltd.

178–202 Great Portland Street, London, W.1

London   Melbourne   Sydney   Auckland
Bombay   Johannesburg   New York   Toronto

First published 1955

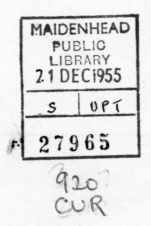
Printed in Great Britain
by The Anchor Press, Ltd.,
Tiptree, Essex

CONTENTS

5

LIST OF ILLUSTRATIONS

7

CHAPTER I

My Background, and My Early Memories

MY paternal grandparents, Simeon Hinds, of Hopkinsville, Kentucky, and his wife, who came from Knoxville, Tennessee, married young and lived in Illinois, where my Grandfather was one of the most considerable stock-breeders and farmers of his county. They had five sons, of whom my Father, Joseph Monroe Hinds, was the youngest. He was born in 1842, and at the age of eighteen he had begun to study Law, when the Civil War broke out. His four elder brothers immediately decided to volunteer as privates in the Northern Army—although they were Southerners—and when my Grandmother went to see them off, my Father turned to her impulsively and said good-bye and went with them. She did not see him again for five years.

My Father joined the Eighth Illinois Infantry, and was in all his regiment's battles. He was commissioned, and transferred to the First Alabama (Federal) Cavalry, a regiment which must have consisted of freed slaves with white officers. They were with General Sherman in his 'march to the sea', and present at the surrender of General Joe Johnston in North Carolina. They were mustered out at Huntsville. My Father was then aged twenty-three. He had seen heavy fighting, had been in the war from start to finish, and was a Captain. When he went home, with a great black beard, his mother did not recognize him. One of his four brothers had been killed in the war, and another had died in hospital.

My Father and his surviving brothers decided to settle at Decatur, Alabama, in a house which had been the headquarters of each army in turn. It was one of the two habitable houses left in a village which had been almost destroyed in the fighting. They bought property there, owned plantations, a line of steam-boats on the Tennessee River, and stage-coaches which served the district.

While still a young man, my Father was appointed U.S. Consul at Rio de Janeiro, which in those days was still the capital of the Empire of Don Pedro. He was promoted to Consul General, and finally to U.S. Minister to Brazil. At Rio de Janeiro he met Lucy Triglia, the beautiful daughter of an English mother and an Italian father, living in Buenos Aires, who was staying with her brother,

John Triglia, in Rio. Joseph and Lucy were married in Rio in 1873, and their two elder children were born there.

I was born at Decatur after their return to Alabama, in the Great House, or Hinds House, as it used to be called. Decatur is named after the naval officer of that name who is responsible for the much-quoted phrase 'Our country, right or wrong!' When I was still a tiny child my Father was appointed United States Marshal for the Northern district of Alabama, and we left Decatur for a time and went to live at Huntsville. We returned to Decatur when his term of office was over, and from then onwards my childhood was spent at Decatur. A certain sense of strangeness and discomfort surrounded us there, Republicans in an area of Democrats, Episcopalians in the midst of Methodists. I was conscious of this feeling even as a child attending the local school, and it may have been responsible for my unauthorized interest in the Revivalist meetings which were always being held in the neighbourhood. It was after my parents had discovered this interest that I was sent away to a boarding school. As a small child I was earnestly religious. When we were living at Huntsville my brother Roe died, and the next year my sister also died, so that I was left an only child until the twins were born—my brother Albert and sister Anita. For years after this I thought that God always gave new babies as a form of compensation when He had allowed a death to occur in a family. In this case there had been two deaths and the compensation had been twins. A year later my younger brother was born, and after that I was very anxious and prayed every night that I might not be taken. I used to implore God to leave me because there was really room for both of us.

Soon after this we returned to Decatur, and I did not leave it again until I went away to school and, later, was taken for a wonderful world tour by my Uncle and Aunt, John and Lucy Triglia.

Decatur, Alabama, as I remember it, was a quiet, sleepy town, although my older friends used to tell me, with great pride, of the wealth and dignity, of the vast entertaining and hospitality, before the Civil War. At one time Decatur had been the very centre of the slave-holding districts; but since the Civil War it had lost a great deal of its wealth with the slaves.

Some of the old Southern houses still remained, mostly built in the Colonial style. The lovely 'Hinds House', where I was born, was one of the best examples of this style, with its vast porch and tall classical columns. Visitors from the Northern States used often to ask to be allowed to look over the house, to see the fine carving, which had been done by the slaves. The garden was enchanting, and typical of the South. There were huge mulberry trees, and masses of roses—real big bushes of them, not the carefully cultivated modern prize-winning roses of to-day. There were lilacs, and catalpas, and both pink and white acacias near the big iron gate. The garden was surrounded by a solid iron-spiked fence topped with iron balls like cricket balls. Many of these balls were missing, and we used to be told that they had been blown or shot off during the war, when the house had been used as the Headquarters of the General of one or other of the contending forces.

Before I left Decatur with my Uncle John and Aunt Lucy, there had been what was called 'a boom', and New Decatur had emerged. It was a rather vulgar place, with a huge modern hotel and many new houses. The inhabitants of Decatur always deplored having this new town so near them, and used to speak of the new-comers as 'carpet-baggers'. The climate of Northern Alabama is both unusual and trying. We had very cold winters, with snow and ice. I remember with what joy, as children, we welcomed the snow. The wheels of the carriage were replaced by runners, and the harness was hung with little bells. This cold spell did not last as long as in the Northern States, but we had very long hot summers. My parents often said it was as hot there as it had been in Brazil.

On the other side of the Tennessee River we had a large plantation, and cotton fields. It was wonderful to watch the Negroes picking cotton in the hottest month—August—the women and girls with their heads tied in bright bandannas, the men and youths in gay shirts, singing as only Negroes can sing. I would gladly go a long way to hear them again to-day.

I remember only two who had been slaves, our 'Aunt' Mary and her son 'Uncle' Odie. Our 'Aunt' Mary had snow-white hair, which in a Negro denotes great age. When slaves, they had belonged to a family called Odie. (Slaves always used the names of their owners.) One sad memory of my childhood is the death of 'Uncle' Odie. I was allowed to visit him in his last illness, and it was pathetic to hear him calling out: "The devil is after me! Don't let him get me, Missie!" Of course I did my best to reassure him in my childish way. Later, and unbeknown to my parents this time, I saw him after death. He had turned dark blue. I still wonder if all Negroes do.

'Uncle' Odie used to tell us frightening stories of the Ku-Klux-Klan—how they terrified the slaves and their children. The mother slaves would rush out and collect their screaming children and lock the doors when they heard the Ku-Klux-Klan coming. Odie would end by saying, "One day the wind blew the white sheet from one of the riders, and I recognized the young master!" Poor, ignorant, superstitious slaves, it must have been a fearful sight—those men and horses enveloped in white sheets, carrying lighted torches and yelling and calling out the names of the slaves whom they wished to frighten.

The Negroes of whom I write were no longer slaves, but they all lived in a part of the town called Niggersville, and they had their own schools, churches and trains, and sides of the streets and pavements on which to walk.

Their religion was mostly hysteria, and, at times, alarming. They used to be baptized in the Tennessee River, wearing their best clothes. The Negro parson would hold them backwards in the river, while their families and friends on the bank were singing 'Hallelujah!' The men, when just baptized, would come out in a state of frenzy, and they had to be held down to keep them from hurting themselves on the stones. I remember hearing a young Negress saying to her friend, "I am going to get Religion on Sunday—will you take care of my new hat?" Since those long-ago days I have seen 'dancing Dervishes' at Constantinople (also many years ago) and their frenzy reminded me of the Decatur Negroes at their baptisms.

As I look back in remembrance to my earliest years, some events stand out, and I can still recall the pain and the utter misery which they caused me. One of these was the wrench of leaving Decatur, when I was fifteen, with my Uncle John and my Aunt Lucy. The train left at two o'clock in the morning, and all my friends seemed to be at the station, as well as my parents, to say good-bye to me. As the train steamed away I thought my heart was broken—I would have jumped off the train had it been possible. Poor Uncle John had a very tearful niece for a companion, and he must have been sadly disappointed. However, I cheered up when we arrived at Washington, where we were to spend a few days with my Aunt Em. She was my Father's sister, and my godmother, Mrs. Griffeth. Auntie Em was a remarkable character, a senior Civil Servant at a time when only in America were there ladies in Government service. She was said to have great influence, and certainly with her as guide we could go everywhere. My Uncle John, accustomed to the Spanish manners of the Argentine, where women were hardly allowed a legal existence, remarked in surprise that never before had he gone through so many doors which were opened at the command of a woman.

I was thrilled with Washington. I thought it a lovely city,

beautifully laid out, with its wide, long and straight avenues. The public buildings did not themselves attract me so much as the way in which they were displayed to the best advantage with lovely gardens and squares round them. We were taken everywhere, including the White House, to meet the President, who at that time was Mr. Cleveland.

From Washington we went to New York, which disappointed me after the beauty of Washington. We stayed only two days there, and then embarked for England in the s.s. *Fürst Bismarck*. It was the ship's maiden voyage.

We had a very rough and stormy crossing of the Atlantic. I can remember almost every detail of this, my first voyage. We could see colossal icebergs and hear the ship's bells clang to alter course as we were almost on them. Great waves dashed over all the decks, we were shut in, all the portholes were closed, and added to this, the fog-horn never ceased. The captain told us that it was one of the worst crossings that he had ever known.

We arrived in England in March, not the best month in which to see London for the first time, and I thought it a gloomy place. Later, when taken shopping, sight-seeing and to some theatres, I liked it better. Jim Corbett, "Gentleman Jim", the well-known prize-fighter, had been a passenger on board the *Fürst Bismarck*, and when the weather permitted I had been allowed to watch him punching the ball in the early mornings as part of his training. He had come to London to take part in a play which had been specially written for him. I was delighted when we received tickets from him for the first night of this play, for I remember that this girl of fifteen thought him an attractive young man.

From London we went to Paris. Being born an American, I loved Paris, although I soon became tired of so much sight-seeing. However, there was no escaping a thorough inspection of the sights at every place we visited, for this tour with my Uncle and Aunt had been undertaken entirely for my education. We spent only two weeks in Paris and then went on to Cairo, where we stayed at Shepheard's Hotel, then in its heyday. Everything in Egypt thrilled me, even the contents of the museums, although I was a little horrified by the sight of the actual mummies of the Pharaohs exposed to view, not merely the sarcophagi—and also by the sight of Rameses II lying in his coffin. I must have had an American accent at this time, because my donkey was always called Yankee Doodle, whereas Uncle John's was called John Bull. I was sorry when the time came for us to leave Egypt, because I had been deeply impressed by the superb temples and the Tombs of the Kings. I have always wanted to go back there.

From Egypt we went on to Constantinople, that most lovely city of palaces and mosques. We stayed at the Pera Palace Hotel, and I remember that as soon as I went out of the hotel I was made miserable by the swarms of stray dogs that filled the streets and thronged the pavements so that one had literally to step over them, and being told that when there were really too many of them they were collected and left on an island to die. I am filled with horror, to this day, at remembering this cruelty. However, that was a Constantinople of long ago, and its beauty impressed me as well as the sufferings of its dogs. I had a frightening experience when I was there. In those days Turkey was one of the very few countries for which a passport was required, and oddly enough in our little party of three we each had a passport of a different nationality. My Aunt Lucy had kept her British passport; Uncle John, who had been born in Montevideo (Uruguay) when it was occupied by the British Navy, possessed dual nationality and travelled with an Argentine passport; I, of course, had an American one. These three different passports caused Uncle John a lot of trouble when he went to get the visas. He left me in an open carriage outside the American Consulate while he was collecting my passport, and soon I noticed with embarrassment that some young Turks were staring at me from a window on the opposite side of the street. A little later I was quite terrified when the three young men came to the carriage and offered me a bunch of flowers, and visions at once flashed through my mind of kidnappings and hidden harems on the Bosphorus. Luckily Uncle John returned at that moment. I was generally acknowledged to be a pretty girl (it is so long ago that I feel I can write this without being accused of vanity), and after the episode of the bouquet I was never left alone again in Constantinople.

From Turkey we went by ship to Greece, where we landed at Piraeus, and took the train to Athens. The railway line ran among cultivated fields which were a mass of red poppies, and Athens—in those days a small, unpretentious, provincial city—impressed me as being a 'fair' town, by which I mean that everything seemed to be white, the houses, the monuments, the ruins, and even the streets were coated with white dust, and left in my mind the effect of the fairness of pale buildings. We saw all the famous sights, the Acropolis and all the temples, but I remember very little of them. I am ashamed that Athens should have made so little impression on me, but I am afraid that I had been made to see too many monuments and museums already. I do remember being much struck by the white kilts of the Evzones.

From Athens we sailed for the Holy Land, and landed at a little port where we had to be let down in baskets because the sea was so rough. I had been more excited and thrilled by the thought of visiting Jerusalem than any other place. I was a deeply religious girl, and I was shocked and distressed by the neglected state of Jerusalem. It made me most unhappy to see the squalor and the disorder in the Holy City. The streets were slimy with filth, the people appallingly dirty, and the flies and every other sort of horror were beyond belief. At that time there was only one hotel, a very primitive one owned by Thomas Cook. We all sat at one long table for meals, and it was crowded with an odd collection of religious cranks. I remember an elderly lady next to me turning to me while she had her soup and asking, with courteous interest, if I believed in a Hereafter. Another unfortunate afflicted lady went to the Mount of Olives every afternoon, taking with her a tea-basket. She used to unpack it and arrange tea for two with the greatest care—a tea-cloth, her best china and silver—and then sit awaiting the Second Coming of Our Lord.

We were in Jerusalem at the time of the Orthodox Greek Church Easter, and we saw many brilliantly coloured processions, as well as the ceremony of the Holy Fire. But I thought that most of the Holy Places were treated with too little respect, and in some cases almost sacrilegiously. It was curious to see the Jewish women, on certain days of the week, wailing at Rebecca's Tomb; and very surprising to meet a Moslem funeral procession on the way to a burial, with the corpse exposed to view and men running beside it who did a kind of turn on reaching a corner of the street.

We drove in an open carriage to Jericho, and outside the walls of Jerusalem we met a group of lepers who came as near to us as they were allowed, begging. Their arms that they held out to us were covered with white rags, and some of the young women were carrying babies. This was a sight that haunted me for many years afterwards. We spent that night at Jericho, and a very dismal place it was. I bathed in the Dead Sea, and waded in the River Jordan.

When we returned to Jerusalem I spent a sleepless and agitated night. I had long, light chestnut-coloured curls reaching to my waist and worn tied back—and my curls had picked up lice, no doubt from the back cushions of the carriage. I was afraid that my hair would have to be cut off, and even perhaps that my head would have to be shaved. However, my Aunt was most resourceful. She managed to get something from a chemist, which smelt quite horrible, and applied it to my head, and I was kept in my room with my head tied up in a towel. When the stuff had taken effect, my head was thoroughly washed, and all was well.

After leaving Jerusalem we went to Naples. I loved being in Italy, and thoroughly enjoyed everything that I saw and did there. No doubt this feeling was due to my Italian blood, for I had an Italian great-grandfather. It all seemed exciting and delightful, and I did not even complain of the smells in the towns and cities, which were certainly very noticeable.

Fortunately for me, our visit to Naples coincided with one of the most spectacular eruptions of Vesuvius which had occurred for many years. It was really a glorious sight, somewhat frightening but most magnificent. The whole sky was lit up by the enormous angry flames pouring out of the towering volcano. I used to watch it, quite fascinated, but decidedly awed as well.

I was charmed by the beauty of the Bay of Naples, and quite agreed with the claim of the Italians that it is one of the loveliest places in the world. The King and Queen of Italy were in residence in their Neapolitan Palace, and while we were there the Queen's birthday was celebrated, with illuminations and fireworks in a wonderful display which vast crowds came to see. We were impressed by seeing the King and Queen driving in their carriage quite unattended along the waterfront through the cheering crowds. It was a great contrast to what we had recently seen in Constantinople, when we had watched the Sultan of Turkey going to attend a service at the Mosque most closely guarded.

From Naples we went on to Rome. This was my first experience of a Pullman car, and also my first sight of the close cultivation of a peasant countryside. The Campagna seemed a garden, and the train ran through the little fields and sunny vineyards as intimately as though we were walking among them.

My memories of Rome would fill many chapters, but I doubt if they differ very much from the memories which everyone cherishes of their first visit to Rome with all its wonders. I will record only one particularly vivid impression—the sight of a large pilgrimage of men which I saw in the Vatican. I do not know their nationality, but they wore tall fur fezes. I saw them as they arrived at the foot of the Scala Santa, and watched them make the long ascent on their knees. Their faces seemed inspired as they said a prayer on each step, many of them bending down to make the sign of the Cross with their tongues. Although they were not of my own religion, I was left with a feeling of the greatest respect for these deeply earnest peasants, and of admiration for their sincerity as they carried out their pilgrimage of worship.

From Rome we went for another visit to Paris, and after that we went back to London to make arrangements for our voyage to Buenos Aires.

So, in the end, I returned to my Mother's home in the New World, where a building a century old is something to be stared at. My youthful mind was crowded with the impressions of all that I had seen. I feel now that this first visit to the cradles of European civilization and culture did a great deal to prepare me for my later life in England.

My first voyage to the Argentine was in April 1894, on board the R.M.S. *Danube*. In those days it took three weeks, as we called at many ports where we would spend a day for coaling and taking on fresh food. This would give us time to spend the day on shore. We sailed from Southampton, and stopped the same evening at Cherbourg to pick up more passengers. The Bay of Biscay was a much dreaded part of the voyage, and I remember many Argentines who would travel overland from Paris to Lisbon to avoid those two or three unpleasant days.

We stopped at Vigo, but too far out for us to be able to go ashore. It looked a pretty, colourful little town from the distance. A large number of immigrants for the Argentine joined our ship in the steerage, and we saw heartbreaking scenes of farewell—young sons and young daughters leaving their parents and their country, and in many cases knowing that they would never see their homes again.

We spent a wonderful day at Lisbon, a place that I was to know so well in later years. Then lovely Madeira, a favourite port of call for everyone—a gay, happy little island, with its bright sunshine and its heavenly flowers, and the exciting toboggan run down the rough stony street, which thrilled me then—as it would to-day, if it still exists. I saw the picturesque bullock carts and wagons, but I was horrified by the way the poor bullocks were prodded along with a long pole with a spike in the end of it, by men who walked beside them. I thought that was horrid.

We then spent a few days without sight of land, on a wonderful calm serene sea, with shoals of porpoises following the ship, which I delighted in watching. My first sight of the Southern Cross was disappointing, for I had expected something more spectacular. It was exciting crossing the Line of the Equator, when we had the usual play which happens at all first crossings in a ship. By this time the heat was almost unbearable. I used to look down at the poor people

B

in the steerage, and my heart ached for them. They were crowded together and slept and had their food on their small deck, and many of them were ill. Late at night when we were all supposed to be asleep, the engine would stop for a few moments—and I knew what that meant—a burial at sea. The thought of these poor Spanish peasants ruined the pleasure of my first voyage. Uncle John allowed me to get up a subscription on board, to raise money to buy better food for them, but this did not go far amongst so many. Thank God the larger ships now have better accommodation for them and I don't believe that so many migrate to the Argentine.

When we arrived at our first Brazilian port we were not allowed to land because there was an outbreak of yellow fever. Two days later we reached Bahia (now Salvador), which I thought dirty and rather ugly. The only thing to be admired was the sight of the wonderful washerwomen, of magnificent physique, who walked like queens, carrying large baskets on their heads, with their arms folded, and looking as if they were made of black marble. At last came the day when we were due to arrive at Rio. I was told to be on the top deck at about five o'clock in the morning, and so I was, in the first light of the dawn. It is hard to find words to describe the heavenly beauty of that morning. The sun was rising in the clearest sky imaginable, and little by little, slowly and proudly, the superb mountains which surround the bay showed themselves to the day. I thought then, and I still think, that it must be the most beautiful bay in the world. The magnificent mountains which almost enclose it were glowing rose pink in the sunrise. I stood entranced, thinking of my Mother, and of the vivid descriptions that she had often given to me of this enchanted place. As a young girl she had come here from the Argentine, which has no natural beauty, and she told me that when she first saw the bay of Rio she stood and cried. I am not ashamed to record that my tears fell, too, at the first sight of it.

I have visited Rio many times since that first moving moment when I was fifteen years old, and I have been filled with the same enchantment every time. Only on my last visit was I pained when I saw tall sky-scrapers against that superb background. Oh, man, to be so vile!

After leaving Rio, we reached Santos one night later. It is a lovely little place, with beautiful tropical vegetation, but after Rio it seemed tame. We went by a funicular railway up a very high mountain to São Paulo, where we went to see a well-known snake farm. There they extract the poison from horrible-looking snakes of every kind, and it is sent all over the world to cure snake-bite.

A week's voyage from Santos brought us to Montevideo, in Uruguay, an attractive place with the wide River Plate dividing it from Buenos Aires. It is a night's journey across the river from Montevideo to Buenos Aires by ship—which gives an idea of the width of the river. When we arrived at Buenos Aires, at that time rather an ugly town, we were met by many of my Mother's relations. They gave me great pleasure by saying that they all thought that I looked like my Mother.

CHAPTER II

My First Marriage. Life in Buenos Aires

THE Argentine has changed so much, and for the better, since my first acquaintance with it in April 1894 that I find it difficult to turn my memory back to those distant days, and to give a true picture of my first impressions on arriving there. The month of April is the beginning of autumn weather in the Argentine. I remember that all the ladies wore their new winter dresses and their furs on May 25th, which is a national holiday. Buenos Aires is an ugly town, although it had some good streets of well-built houses. Avenida de Alvear already existed, and would have been considered a fine street in any city. Avenida de Mayo, also, was a magnificent wide boulevard in the centre of Buenos Aires, but it was mostly commercial. The street that I recall as being the gayest and the most attractive was Calle Florida, a narrow street with the best shops, a kind of Bond Street. There one would meet one's friends for tea at the Agulia. The magnificent Jockey Club building[1] was also in the Calle Florida.

In the afternoon, the Argentine ladies used to drive to Palermo, and there they would drive round and round—a kind of 'course'—bowing to their friends in the most sedate manner. The young men rode, or drove their own vehicles, and they only took off their hats but never descended from their carriages or got off their horses to talk, in those days. It was all very much like what used to take place in Hyde Park every afternoon, only a few years earlier.

The drive would end in the Calle Florida, where the ladies would have tea, but always in each others' company, without any men. The men—that is to say, all the smart young men of the day—would be standing on the steps of the main entrance to the Jockey Club to gaze at these lovely ladies as they drove slowly past.

The Argentine ladies were really beautiful, especially the younger ones, for they were inclined to grow fat in early middle age. The ladies of the Argentine have small bones, beautiful large dark eyes, and black hair. They are most graceful—and, added to all this, they have perfect taste in dress.

I remember the magnificent impression of some of their carriages

[1] Burnt down during the riots of April 1953, it contained the finest collection of books, paintings, and antiques in the Argentine.

and turn-outs—open landaus, with wonderful horses. Young ladies, in light-coloured dresses, would be sitting with their backs to the horses, with rather stout, but handsome, mammas and aunts facing them. They never drove out alone at that time.

Another place to see all the youth and beauty of Buenos Aires was at the Opera. It was a fine opera house, and most of the boxes were open loges, where the 'lovelies', looking their best, sat in front, with their mammas, in this case, in the background behind them. The boxes on the opposite side of the opera house would be filled with young men, with their opera glasses fixed on the girls whom they particularly admired. This did not seem to cause the least embarrassment to the girls in question: in fact, they took it quite for granted as a proper form of attention, for this was their method of courting.

The Argentines are great lovers of music, and all the best singers are engaged, at some time, to sing at Buenos Aires. The great Caruso sang in Buenos Aires before he came to London.

However, I am anticipating, as I took no part in any of these gaieties for the first two years after my arrival at Buenos Aires. I had a governess to teach me Spanish—real Castilian Spanish—and also music. I even had a singing master, but the singing lessons were a dead loss because I had no voice worth training, although I enjoyed the lessons and they helped me to appreciate good singing.

In the meantime, my Mother, my two brothers and my sister had arrived from Alabama, and I became more reconciled to our having pulled up our roots from Decatur. My Father was to join us a few months later.

Whenever I think of the Argentine, my first thoughts at once turn to the camp,[1] and that vast rolling country, and riding on a good horse with the far horizon in the distance all around you, almost as if you were at sea. You canter over the grass for miles and miles, and the stillness and the vastness and the loneliness make an impression that you will never forget. You watch a wonderful sunset dipping into the ground and disappearing, and you ride for home before night descends, for there is no twilight in the Argentine. But I remember wonderful moonlit rides.

My coming-out ball took place when I was seventeen, and after that I had a gay time of dances, balls and picnics. I had many Argentine relations, and of course friends among the English colony. At that time America had not 'discovered' the Argentine.

---

[1] 'Camp' in the Argentine means an *estancia*, or ranch, as it would be called in North America. The word conveys a misleading suggestion of tents, and 'camping out', to English ears.

I met my future husband, Alfred Duggan, even before I came out, because at that time the great passion of the day was roller-skating, and we often skated together. He afterwards told me that long before we met he went especially to watch me skating, and only took up skating himself in the hope of meeting me. At that time he did not even know my name, and he used to think of me as 'Miss Boots'. This name did not please me at all, as I had small American feet, and it sounded most uncomplimentary. However, I discovered that the real explanation was the fact that I wore high, laced American boots, specially made for skating, of a type which had not been seen in Buenos Aires before.

The River Tigre, which is not very far from Buenos Aires, was a popular place for picnics. There were a number of good rowing clubs—I can remember an English, a German and an Argentine Club—and regattas were held there every year. There were a great many attractive little islands in the River Tigre, on which we used to picnic, and where we used to get eaten alive by mosquitoes if we lingered on after sunset. I used to go on the Tigre very often, in our motor-launch, which was one of the first motor launches ever seen in the Argentine, and sometimes I was allowed to steer it. On one of these occasions the launch burst into flames, and I was helped from the burning boat by an Argentine young man. I well remember my annoyance and dismay when I read in a Buenos Aires newspaper the next day, "Grace Darling rescued from a burning launch . . ." etc., etc.

I made two trips to England before my marriage, and loved them both, but I was always quite happy to return to Buenos Aires.

I remember with particular pleasure one heavenly party in the camp with some very dear friends. We were all young, and our host and hostess were wonderful organizers. We seemed to spend most of the day on horses, riding to some distant spot to have an *asaido* picnic. An *asaido* is an Argentine way of roasting a whole lamb in the open air. A fire is made on the ground and when it has blazed fiercely and then burnt itself out almost to embers, the lamb is put on a stake to cook by the embers until it is perfectly done and ready to eat. A picturesque-looking gaucho in his national costume super-vises the cooking, and when the meat is ready, carves it and hands you a piece on the point of his large knife. You eat it with your fingers, and it is perfect. I have never tasted anything anywhere to compare with this delicious dish.

After the picnic we would ride back to our host's home, bathe hurriedly before dinner, and after dinner we used to dance until nearly dawn, to the music of accordions accompanied by the piano, the accordions being played by gauchos. Then we would rush out to see the sunrise, which was always a wonderful sight in this vast, level country with its wide horizons. The world seemed to be glowing—and so pleased with us.

This wonderful house party lasted for a week. I blush to remember that I returned to Buenos Aires apparently engaged to two men. I had promised to marry Alfred Duggan; but another man had proposed to me before Alfred did, and had absolutely refused to take No for an answer, and I suppose that I, being young and inexperienced, did not say No with sufficient emphasis. To my horror this man sent an announcement of our non-existent engagement to the newspapers.

I was married to my first husband on May 1st, 1902. May in the Argentine is the first month of winter—a lovely month. Two days were needed for our marriage, as by Argentine law it is necessary to go before the Civil Registrar before you can be married in church. Our two families, and some close friends, came to the Registrar's ceremony, which took place in the afternoon of the day before the real marriage service. I remember that I wore a lovely white cloth afternoon dress trimmed with white fox fur, and a small white hat.

The next evening the first religious service was the Roman Catholic one. The Duggans were most devout Catholics, and as a mixed marriage could not be solemnized at the High Altar in church, this service took place in the large drawing-room of my home. It was attended by our two families, and my six bridesmaids who were dressed as May Queens because it was the first of May. The drawing-room had been turned into the most perfect chapel, with a beautiful altar, many candles and lovely flowers. Dear old Father Riley performed the marriage ceremony. The same priest had married my husband's parents. After this we drove to St. Peter's Church, Limas de Jamora, outside Buenos Aires. The church was packed, and beautifully decorated with white lilies and white roses. Just below the steps to the chancel was a gate of white roses and white satin ribbon. (I did not approve of this, but it was a present from a kind friend.) The gate was tied across with white ribbon, and no one had been told about opening it, or untying the ribbon. Luckily, Sir William Barrington, the British Minister (for at that time there was still only a Legation, not an Embassy, in Buenos Aires), came to the rescue. He untied the ribbon as he saw me approaching on the arm of my Uncle John, who gave me away because my Father had died.

After the wedding we returned to Paradise Grove for the reception and ball. I was told that the ball would last until the small hours of the morning. The essentials of a good and successful ball are beautiful women, plenty of men, a fine house, a good floor, lovely flowers and good music. These were all provided at my lovely old home, as well as divine gardens, and even though it was the first of May and so the first day of the Argentine winter, it was not too cold to enjoy them.

After spending two weeks at the *estancias*, we returned to Buenos Aires, and then embarked for England for our four months' honeymoon. We had expected to be in England for the Coronation of King Edward the Seventh, but unfortunately it was postponed because of his illness. We stayed for some time in London. It was the height of the Season, and very gay. We went to our first Ascot with the Argentine Minister, Señor Dominguez. I remember still one of the lovely dresses I wore, made in Paris by Doucet. When we left London we travelled in France, Italy and Switzerland. We also paid a visit to Ireland, where we met some of my husband's distant cousins for the first time, this being his first visit to Ireland. (The Duggans were Irish by origin.) We went to the Dublin Horse Show, and enjoyed it very much.

By this time we were due to return to Buenos Aires. We received a wonderful welcome there, and were taken by my mother-in-law to our new home—the house where she had started her own married life, and where my husband had been born.

The house, in Calle Cangallo in Buenos Aires, had been beautifully furnished for us, in our absence, with everything imported from England. Seldom has a bride walked into a house so completely arranged for her, even to such details as the plants and the flowers in the patio. What happy years I spent there! And with what joy I received my first baby, my son Alfred.

One year, not long after we were married, my husband and I were invited to make a trip with a party of our friends who were going to see the great Iguazu Falls. In those days these wonderful falls were not at all well known, for very few people had seen them. We went by boat up the Parana River, and were on board for several days. The Parana is one of the widest rivers in the world. Our boat hugged the coast—near enough for us to see the crocodiles basking in the sun. The scenery was all very wild, and, as I thought, not beautiful. When we arrived at the place of disembarking we found dark, dense forests and wild vegetation, but it was exciting to see wonderful orchids hanging from the forest trees. Men had to go ahead of us in order to cut a way through the thick, luxuriant growth of the forest so that we could reach the hut where we were to spend the night. It was a very primitive hut indeed. It was simply divided into two halves by blankets hung across the middle, and the men slept in one half and the women in the other. I minded no discomfort so long as I could be reassured about the danger of snakes, of which I had an absolute horror. Naturally there was no plumbing, and I must admit that I was terrified of the little walk that we had to take into the darkness. The next morning we went on foot to the falls—one heard the great roar of waters long before they were visible. The beauty of the sight was really breathtaking. These falls cover an enormous area—not like Niagara, which is one colossal waterfall, in a comparatively confined space, but many waterfalls extending almost as far as the eye can see, in a perfect setting. I had never dreamed of such beauty, or of such a glorious panorama. It was an unforgettable sight, beautiful beyond words to describe, and really awe-inspiring.

We had a very gay time in Buenos Aires after returning from our honeymoon. All our friends gave dinner parties for us, and I delighted in giving small dinner parties in our charming house. It was a typical Spanish house in style, being built round two patios. All the principal rooms looked into the first patio, and the second patio was surrounded by the kitchens and the servants' quarters. The billiard room was the most attractive of all our rooms, and had been one of the many wedding presents to Alfred from his father. Alfred was a very good billiard player.

The patios were my special delight. Roses climbed on the walls, and there were tall tree ferns, and every sort of flowering shrub, in tubs, so that the air was always full of the scent of flowers. I particularly remember the heavenly white jasmine, and also a large flowering shrub like a gardenia, and with the same glorious smell. My love of gardens of every sort dates from these days of my early married life, when I took so much pleasure in the flowers that grew in our two patios.

Alfred was a member of the Jockey Club, where ladies were allowed to dine on certain nights, and so we used to give parties there as well as at home. The Jockey Club was a really magnificent building, with a wonderful staircase in the entrance hall made of pink alabaster which was most imposing.

We were both very fond of racing at Palermo, and went there very often. The Jockey Club rooms at Palermo were luxurious, and we could watch the races from comfortable armchairs, after a delicious luncheon. The only drawback to this charming racecourse was that the track itself was a dirt one.

We used frequently to pay visits to the camp, staying with our various friends and relations. Our favourite *estancia* was always San Marcos, which belonged to my father-in-law. We also spent a part of the summer with my mother-in-law at Mar-del-Plata, a gay little place by the sea which used to be considered the Deauville of the Argentine. My mother-in-law had a villa there.

In 1903 my first baby was born—and happiness seemed complete. He was christened Alfred Leo—the second name being after Pope Leo. The christening was beautiful and impressive, every candle alight on the High Altar and the full choir singing. This gave his father great pleasure, and reconciled him to not having been married in his own church.

Alfred was a first-class shot. When we were in the camp I used often to go out with him in the shooting brake. He would shoot from the brake, and we would return home with more partridges than we could use. The Argentine partridge is a much larger bird than the English partridge, but is also a delicious bird to eat. Shooting in the Argentine is never at driven birds. They are all wild.

I remember having an awful shock one morning when I came across a revolver under the pillows of our bed. Alfred had forgotten to remove it when he got up. Every man carried a revolver in the camp in those days—it was most necessary. The sheep-shearing, on an enormous scale, was all done by hand and at shearing time on an *estancia* there would be over a hundred shearers employed as casual labour. It was rather like the hop-picking season in Sussex and Kent, except that the shearers were a good deal wilder than any hop-pickers could be. They came from all parts of the country, some on their own horses, some in a sort of charabanc (of course drawn by horses). Fights were always taking place, and I can even remember a murder. The shearers were paid by chits, not in cash. If they had been given money there would have been far more fighting, and probably more murders.

I used often to watch them working. The best men were wonderful in their speed and dexterity. I should not like to say what was the record number of sheep sheared within the hour, but it must have been remarkable. It was an extraordinary sight to see the sheep in their thousands being driven into the sheds for the shearing—a vast, dirty-white mass of stupid objects, shoving and bleating as they came. I could never admire, or even pity, a sheep—and I always thought I was fond of animals!

One afternoon at Estancia San Marcos I was sitting on the long, low, creeper-hung veranda in the old San Marcos house with Baby Alfred on my lap when I heard a bird making a most unusual fuss just overhead, where there was a nest. I called to Alfred, who came and looked up, and then said that I must move at once to the far end of the veranda. He went and got his revolver from the house, and then, after watching the nest for a moment, he took careful aim and shot. A large snake came crashing through the leaves to the ground. Alfred had seen its head sticking out from the bird's nest. This horrible snake had climbed up the creepers to the nest and had swallowed all the young birds. We could count all the lumps made by the poor little things in the vile snake as it lay dead on the floor of the veranda.

In July 1904 my darling little Hubert was born. As soon as I was strong enough to travel, we left for England, taking the two babies and their nurses with us. We spent three months in England, and loved it: and we returned to Buenos Aires with a strong wish to live permanently in England. In fact, our minds were made up to do everything possible to bring this about, but it was not to be for another two years. In the meanwhile, we were very happy with our babies and our pleasant life in Buenos Aires. My mother-in-law had given me a victoria and a pair of horses, and I used it almost entirely for sending the babies and their nurses to Palermo, because we lived rather far from the park. On one occasion I had taken the carriage myself, and the children had been sent to the park in a cab. Alfred was playing on the grass, and when he saw me driving past he exclaimed, in great indignation, "Oh, look at Mummy in my carriage!" I was told that I spoiled the children!

Two years after our return to the Argentine, we left, as we had hoped and planned, to live in England. We travelled in the greatest comfort, even taking with us a cow, a young calf, a chicken coop full of chickens, and two or three turkeys. All these had been sent on board by my father-in-law for the benefit of his little grandsons. The cow and calf were kept on the open crew-deck, where the children with their nurses could visit them when the weather permitted. Alas, when the cow was milked, it was often found that this had been done already, in the early morning, by one of the third-class passengers. The cow and calf had to be landed at Lisbon, as we were not allowed to take them to England for fear of bringing in foot-and-mouth disease. A dairyman came on board the ship at Lisbon to take them away, and my two little boys stood and watched with tears in their eyes.

We arrived at Southampton on a bitterly cold day, and went to stay at the Hyde Park Hotel in London, and there darling little Hubert developed pneumonia. This was an anxious time, but he soon recovered, and when he was well enough we went to Paris, where we spent Christmas at the Hôtel France et Choiseul with my Mother and sister. Later, we went to Cap Martin, travelling in the Sud Express, and I shall never forget our joy at seeing the blue sky and the dazzling sunshine when we arrived, having left Paris in snow and sleet.

CHAPTER III

Diplomatic Life in London

WE all loved Cap Martin. In the middle of our stay there Alfred and I had to return to London for a short time, for my presentation at Court, and for his at a levee. I should have explained earlier that we had come to England because Alfred had been made an Honorary Attaché to the Argentine Embassy—or, rather, Legation, as it was in those days. I had already ordered my Court dress, and had given fittings for it, while I was in Paris at Christmas time. It was made by Doucet, who supervised every fitting himself. Monsieur Doucet was a most distinguished-looking Frenchman, and he had the manner of an Ambassador. I felt it almost an honour to have him supervising all my fittings. He had a small vandyke beard, and always wore a carnation in his buttonhole. He expressed himself as delighted with the beauty of my presentation dress. It really was a very lovely dress. The long train, which I still possess, was heavily embroidered with silver roses, seed pearls and diamanté, and the whole dress was made of cream-coloured duchesse satin.

I was presented by the wife of the American Ambassador. He was the doyen of the Diplomatic Corps in London at that time. I remember that Nancy Astor was just in front of me. I think that was before her marriage to Lord Astor. Afterwards, at supper—a buffet one—King Edward came to talk to me, and addressed me in German. This took me greatly by surprise, and I had to say that I was sorry but I could not speak German. I then discovered that the King had asked who I was, and had been told that I was an Argentine. The King, however, had misunderstood the reply, and thought that I was an Austrian. He was amused, and so was I, when the mistake had been explained.

Alfred and I stayed for two weeks in London, and I well remember my first dinner party at the American Embassy, and being taken in to dinner by Mr. Ridgely Carter,[1] a delightful man. Later I used to see his lovely daughter, Mildred Carter, at all the balls in London, where she was always an outstanding beauty. She married Lord Acheson, and later, on his succeeding his father, became the Countess

[1] John Ridgely Carter (1864-1944), Secretary at the American Embassy in London 1905-9.

29

of Gosford. Another very lovely American girl who stands out in my memory of those days was Marguerite Drexel. She married Lord Maidstone, afterwards the Earl of Winchilsea and Nottingham.

We returned to Cap Martin, to our children and to my Mother and sister, who had been with them in our absence. From Cap Martin we would often go over to Monte Carlo and spend two or three nights there at the Hôtel de Paris. One night we were at a rather large dinner party given by Charles Mendl at the Café de Paris, when a note was handed to Alfred, who was at the end of the table, asking him the nationality of the lady in the white dress who was one of the guests in his party. Alfred resented this, and his only answer was, 'The lady in question is my wife,' which he scribbled on the card and handed it back to the waiter who had brought it. The sender of the note was Lady Randolph Churchill, who had a dinner party at a table near us, and they had had a discussion as to whether I was an American or a Russian. Dear Jenny, I met her often in London later on, and we became great friends, and used to laugh about the Monte Carlo episode. Writing of her reminds me of a story that George[1] used often to tell of himself in his Balliol days. It will be remembered that the undergraduate verse[2] which dogged him to the end of his days concluded with the line: 'I dine at Blenheim once a week'. George used to relate how on one of those occasions at Blenheim the party went on so long that he was asked to stay for the night. Of course he had brought no luggage with him, and so, by way of night-clothes, he was provided with one of Lady Randolph Churchill's nightdresses to sleep in. (Those were, of course, the days of nightshirts, before pyjamas had been invented, and so perhaps the contrast was not so great as it would have been for a man accustomed to pyjamas. Still, George used to say that he had felt rather ridiculous in it.)

To return to our visit to Cap Martin: one of the acquaintances we made was Rodin, the celebrated sculptor, who was staying in the hotel. He was a funny-looking little man, very crumpled and untidy, and full of strongly held views on almost every subject. He was an ardent vegetarian, and hated the very idea of eating meat. He greatly admired my sister Anita, who was with us, and he used to say to her, "It shocks me terribly to see you sitting there in your white dress,

---

[1] Lord Curzon.
[2] The latest and best-known version of the lines from *The Masque of Balliol* was:

> I am a most superior person,
> My name is George Nathaniel Curzon.
> My face is pink, my hair is sleek,
> I dine at Blenheim once a week.

looking like a pure, beautiful angel, actually eating *meat*—and enjoying it !" He was very anxious to do a portrait head of me, and persuaded us to visit his studio in Paris on our way back to England. It was very interesting to see his big, ramshackle studio on the Left Bank, a wilderness of sculpture of every description, with a pleasant little garden at the back. Alas, neither Alfred nor I were very good judges of modern art then, and of course Rodin was considered extremely *avant garde* in those days, and we did not care at all for his work. In fact Alfred thought it was perfectly horrible, and politely refused to allow me to sit for him, on the excuse that we could not spare the time while in Paris—and said to me afterwards that nothing would induce him to allow me to be caricatured by that terrible fellow. And so I missed having a Rodin head of myself, and now of course I regret it very much.

We took a charming furnished house in Eaton Place for May, June and July. It must have been an exceptionally fine summer that year, because I remember so many delightful out-of-doors parties. We used very often to drive to Hurlingham to watch polo. There were really wonderful international matches, as well as the regimental tournaments and club matches. I met all the well-known American players who had come over for the polo season, and when watching them play I used to cheer them on and encourage them by calling out their names. I was still an American at heart in those days. I also remember a very good polo team which had come from the Argentine. They won all their matches that summer, and were much fêted. Madame de Dominguez gave a ball in their honour at the Ritz. It was a magnificent ball, in that handsome lower floor ballroom. She said to me, "I hope the Argentine team are duly impressed—I have five English duchesses to meet them." And so she had.

Nellie Dominguez was the sister-in-law of the Argentine Ambassador, who was a bachelor, and so she used to act as his hostess when he entertained. He had been *en poste* at the Court of St. James's for many years. Nellie was a wealthy woman; her father was Count Murphy (a Papal Count)—and she was far too well known in London at that time to need any introductory description from me.

The King of Spain[1] was in London that summer. His engagement had just been announced to the lovely Princess Ena of Battenberg. My children's Spanish nurses were thrilled by the sight of the King,

[1] Alfonso XIII (1886–1941), who lost his throne when Spain became a republic in 1931. He married Victoria Eugénie (*b.* 1887), daughter of Princess Beatrice, the youngest child of Queen Victoria.

and always wanted to watch him driving past, but my little boy Alfred did not enjoy this because he hated crowds. One day when I was seeing him leave for the park, he said, "Mummy, please, King of Spain—no!" I took him to the Zoo one Sunday, where in those days the attendants who waited at tea wore red coats. We were just going to have tea, when Alfred saw one of them. He knew what it meant when soldiers wore red coats, and said to me most reproachfully, "Oh, the King of Spain!" He hates crowds to this day.

One of our first country-house visits was to Wroxton Abbey, the home of Lord and Lady North. It is near Banbury, and not far from the famous Banbury Cross. The Abbey is a most beautiful place, and we felt that we had almost stepped back into the Middle Ages. The wonderful dining-room was lit only by candles, and there were long narrow passages lined with armour of every kind. It was all a little gloomy, but interesting and lovely too. Our next visit was to Colonel and Mrs. Cornwallis West at Newlands, in Hampshire. This house could not have been a greater contrast to Wroxton Abbey in every way, both architecturally and in the whole feeling of its atmosphere. We were so gay there—we seemed to laugh all day long, and this was entirely due to the wonderful high spirits of our hostess, a witty and amusing Irishwoman. The Cornwallis Wests' daughters were not there, in fact the only other guests I can remember were my sister Anita and Jack Cowans. There may have been more, but I have forgotten them.

Lady (Arthur) Paget, who had a house in Belgrave Square, gave delightful dinner parties. She gave one specially for us, at which I met the Marquis de Soveral for the first time. He was always a perfect companion at dinner, above all for a newcomer to London, as I was then. He knew all the gossip of the day, and the history of most of the people concerned as well. Minnie Paget also had a charming place at Coombe, where she gave weekend parties that were always the greatest fun. Minnie was a perfect hostess, and took endless trouble over her entertaining, with the result that you could be certain that you would never be bored in her house. Of the balls that I remember that Season, the one that stands out in my recollection was at Grosvenor House, the ball given by the Duke and Duchess of Westminster (his first Duchess, Sheila Cornwallis West). It was a truly magnificent ball, given, I think, in honour of the Crown Prince of Germany. I had never seen so many beautiful women in the same room. The Duchess herself looked wonderful, and her sister, Daisy, Princess of Pless, was a dream of beauty—her fairness

Presentation at Court of King Edward VIĮ

On a visit to the Argentine

Standing : Mr. Albert Monroe Hinds and the author. *Seated* : Miss Anita Monroe Hinds, Alfred Duggan, Mrs. Monroe Hinds, Marcella, Hubert Duggan, Mr. Alfred Duggan, and Mr. Trillia Monroe Hinds

had a pearl-like quality. I remember, too, the beauty of Consuelo, Duchess of Marlborough—of a most distinguished, elegant kind. The Duchess of Portland was of course very beautiful, but of an older generation, as was Millicent, Duchess of Sutherland. The renowned beauty of Lady D'Abernon could never be overlooked. The beauties of the younger generation were the young Duchess of Sutherland (Eileen), Lady Pembroke, Lady Ancaster, Lady Crewe, and, the most lovely of all, Viscountess Curzon, the daughter-in-law of Lord Howe. She is in a class with Lady D'Abernon, only of course of a much younger generation. I consider these two the greatest beauties I have ever seen. I am not certain that the whole of this galaxy was present at the ball at Grosvenor House that night—it is so long ago, and I have seen them all at different times at other balls. I can remember watching the first procession in to supper, and I know that all the older beauties of their day were there: and I know, too, that I shall never see such grace, dignity, and perfect carriage again. The 'lovelies' of to-day do not move with the same ease. They lead such different lives, most of them have what they call a 'job' and they are not brought up to gracious living, or in the Grand Manner —and from what I hear of them, I gather that they have no wish to change. I admire them, for they are not lacking in courage, but I also think that they have missed a lot.

I always regret that I did not come to London in time to have attended the wonderful balls in Devonshire House. I am such an old-fashioned admirer of dignity and deportment that I know I should have been thrilled with those great, formal parties. No doubt the Grosvenor House ball that I have just described was very much like those stately entertainments of an earlier day.

At the end of July we left London for a house that we had taken, between Sevenoaks and Tonbridge. It had a small park which our little boys loved to play in, and enjoyed themselves far more than they did in London, for now there was no longer any need for them to 'be in parks', as little Alfred disapprovingly described their walks in London. Our nearest neighbours were the Cazalets at Fair Lawn. I remember a dinner party with the Cazalets—dear Victor Cazalet, who met with such a tragic death in the last war, was at home from his private school for the holidays—and at this party I first met Clemmie Churchill. She was Miss Hozier then, and a very beautiful girl. After dinner we were all taken to a ball by our hostess, Mrs. Cazalet. I forget whose ball it was, and where it was, but I remember being much amused by my partner at supper saying, "There is a young man here who says he is an Argentine, but he speaks very

c

much like an Irishman—I don't know his name." Of course the man was Alfred, my husband, who, although he had never seen Ireland until we went there on our honeymoon, did have rather an Irish intonation. My father-in-law had always employed Irishmen as far as possible on all his *estancias* in the Argentine, many of them straight out from Ireland, and no doubt Alfred had picked up this slight Irish intonation from hearing them speak ever since his childhood. Each *estancia* had a school, and a small church with a Catholic priest. Alfred spoke beautiful Spanish, and also French, with no trace of an Irish accent.

We stayed at Foxbury, the house we had taken, until after the birth of my third baby, in November, my lovely little Marcella. I was thrilled by having a daughter, after having already had two boys. We returned to London for Marcella's christening; the Argentine Ambassador was one of the godfathers, and we had a rather large party at the Hyde Park Hotel after the christening. For the next Season we took another furnished house, this time in Chesham Place. My Mother had bought a house in Eaton Place, where she lived with my sister and brother.

When the Season was over we took the children to the Argentine on a visit to Alfred's parents, and on our return we went to live at Burfield, Old Windsor.

No one seems to live now in the same comfort—or luxury, as it would be called to-day—as we did in those years at Burfield. It was not a large house, but our staff of servants, compared with present-day standards, was large. We had a butler, footman, hall-boy, two in the kitchen, two housemaids, two nurses (and, later, one nurse and a nursery governess), a lady's maid, chauffeur, groom and stable boy, and two gardeners. I know that the great houses which are still lived in are properly staffed, but lesser houses, of the Burfield class, are mostly run with daily help nowadays, or with perhaps a married couple who live in, if the owners are very lucky.

On looking back to my life at Burfield, all the days seem to have been glowing with happiness. Perhaps this is because I was not yet thirty, and my children were still very young. I have had what would be called a wonderful life since then; but, whatever the cause, all my happiest dreams are generally of the Burfield days.

Alfred and I went to Biarritz for six weeks, leaving the children behind at Burfield. It was in the early spring, and we both loved Biarritz—it was so gay and happy then, a very different place from the great, shabby, overgrown resort that it has since become.

We met many Argentine friends, and some Spanish ones from London. Alfred played a lot of golf, and I enjoyed motor drives through the beautiful Basque country.

We often drove to San Sebastian. I shall never forget seeing my first bull-fight there. It was at Easter time, or just after, and we had paid a large sum of money for one of the best boxes. I remember thinking the *Entrada* very wonderful, colourful and most spectacular —and that was about all I saw, as for most of the rest of the time I sat on the floor of the box, not daring to look at the arena again, after my first sight of a poor horse being badly gored by the bull. On looking back, I realize that all my sympathy was for the horses and the bull—I cared nothing for the fate of one of the most cele-brated bull-fighters of that time, who was being wildly cheered by the crowd after he had killed his bull. I was once told by a very great lady who lived in Spain and was expected to take an interest in this Spanish national spectacle—which she absolutely hated—that she had pasted paper on the lenses of her opera glasses, so that she might seem to be watching it all intently, while seeing in fact nothing at all.

I enjoyed watching pelota,[1] a game played with great skill in the Basque country. I had seen pelota played in the Argentine, and I understood the game and was able to appreciate the brilliant play. I would choose to watch a first-class game of pelota every time in preference to seeing a bull-fight.

From Biarritz we went to Paris, where I had to go into a nursing home for two weeks, to be looked after by dear old Dr. Marrange. The nursing homes in Paris at that time were not very good, and so I pleaded with him to be allowed to move to the hotel. We had chosen the Hôtel Mirabeau in the Rue de la Paix, and I shall never forget my arrival there. I was brought in an ambulance from the nursing home, and taken out on a stretcher. Then it was discovered that my stretcher, naturally, would not go through the revolving doors of the hotel. So the stretcher was put down on the pavement of the Rue de la Paix while the revolving doors were removed. I was wearing a dressing-gown, and my hair was hanging down my back and tied with a pink ribbon, and this happened at about two o'clock on a lovely sunshiny day. I lay there, with my eyes closed, hoping desperately that none of my friends would pass and recognize me, and feeling terribly embarrassed and conspicuous. I wished with all my heart that we had gone to a hotel in a quieter part of Paris, but

[1] Pelota or jai alai, a fast wall game in which the players use long narrow curved wicker baskets strapped to the hand to catch and hurl the ball.

we had chosen one in the Rue de la Paix in order to be near my dressmakers, so that they could come to me for my fittings as I was not well enough to go to them.

Another winter visit that remains a happy memory is the six weeks that we spent at Cannes one year. Our boys, Alfred and Hubert, had by this time gone to their private school, Wixenford. I went on in advance to Paris to order my dresses, as usual, and Alfred was to come on later and join me at Cannes, bringing little Marcella and her Nannie. I was amused and rather horrified when told by Nannie that Alfred had taken little Marcella, aged four, to dine in Paris at the Café de Paris, while the train was on the way round the Banlieu from the Gare du Nord to the Gare de Lyons, where they were to join the train again. In those days the Café de Paris was considered a distinctly 'fast' establishment. Little Marcella talked of this wonderful event for days.

Minnie Paget was also staying at the Carlton Hotel at Cannes, and I had been persuaded to take part in the great Pageant which she was organizing for the Versailles Ball at the Albert Hall. She helped me to choose the dress I was to wear, and it was made by Worth of Paris. I represented Madame de Montespan, and the dress was copied by Worth from one of her portraits. It was a truly beautiful dress of cream satin embroidered in small gold wheat-sheaves and pearls, having a lemon-coloured silk velvet overskirt with a long train, also heavily embroidered with pearls. This over-skirt opened in front as I walked, to show the cream satin dress underneath. On my head I wore a tall hat made entirely of white ostrich plumes standing straight up, and I carried a tall silver staff. (So lovely and timeless in fashion was this embroidered satin dress that I wore it under my Peeress's robes at the Coronation of Queen Elizabeth.)

Many of those taking part in this pageant dined with Minnie Paget before going on to the Versailles Ball at the Albert Hall. I remember Mary Curzon (Viscountess Curzon) looking a dream of beauty as Louise de la Vallière. Lady Dudley represented Queen Maria Theresa, to whom we each made a curtsey before forming our little court in a sort of tableau.[1] When this was over, we had to walk with great dignity the whole length of the Albert Hall. We had had many rehearsals, and they had been the greatest fun.

That Season in London was a very gay one. We went to Ascot

[1] King Louis XIV was the Grand Duke of Mecklenburg-Strelitz, and Prince Paul of Serbia represented the Dauphin.

on all four days, motoring down from London; and often to the Opera at Covent Garden as well as to the wonderful Russian Ballet which we both loved. There were many Argentines visiting London, which meant a great deal of entertaining at the Argentine Legation, at which Alfred and I were always expected to be present.

The Legation was in Palace Gate, a large house with a good ballroom and other good reception rooms. The Argentine Minister, Señor Dominguez, was no longer young, and he had two unmarried sisters living with him. He had been *en poste* in London for a great many years. He gave many large dinner parties, at which the food was excellent, but the parties were not exciting. We preferred those given by Nellie Dominguez at her charming house in Tilney Street, where we met all the most attractive ladies in London, and the most amusing men. Madame Dominguez did not go in for entertaining the diplomats very much, but she adored giving parties to a very gay set. Señor Vicente Dominguez, her husband, was a charming man, and most distinguished-looking—a *grand seigneur*. I remember a delightful ball at the Knightsbridge Barracks given by the Blues (Royal Horse Guards). Colonel Gordon Wilson was their Colonel at that time; his wife, Lady Sarah Wilson, was a sister of the Duke of Marlborough. I have always found soldiers perfect hosts. So, too, are most bachelors! In those days it was pleasant to walk in Hyde Park in the morning, where one would meet friends and often lunch at the Ritz, which was then the great place for luncheon.

That Season I attended my first Court Ball. I thought it very wonderful—such beauty, and jewellery! I find that when an English lady is smart, she is the smartest in the world—she is smart herself, and it does not seem to depend on her clothes.

One very good ball that I remember that summer was given by Mrs. Cornelius Vanderbilt. She had taken Spenser House, which of course was perfect for a ball, being one of the most beautiful houses in London. The last ball that we enjoyed that Season, before leaving for a visit to Scotland, was one given by Mrs. George Keppel. Dear Alice was always gay and charming, and a very good hostess, and her ball was delightful.

In Scotland we stayed with Princess Dolgorouki at lovely little Braemar Castle, for the Braemar Games. This little castle seemed to me just like something out of a fairy tale, so small and perfect—in fact I felt that if only I could reach up to stroke the round towers, it would positively purr with contentment. Our fellow guests were Lady Irene Dennison, Lady Theodora Davidson and her son, Colin Davidson, and Seton Gordon, who would play the bagpipes beautifully under our windows most mornings. He taught me to throw a fly, and how thrilled I was when I killed my first salmon!

When we left Scotland we took our children on a visit to Buenos Aires to see their grandparents. Alfred and I were thankful for the rest that the voyage gave us.

CHAPTER IV

Old Windsor

OUR visit to Alfred's parents in the Argentine lasted for two months, and we all enjoyed it very much. We spent most of the time at Estancia San Marcos, where a delightful new house had been built, since our last visit, by an English architect. My youngest brother-in-law, Bernard Duggan, was the manager there at that time, and we were all most comfortable. Our boys loved the camp life, as they were old enough to ride, and to take an interest in all the working of an *estancia*.

We had no regrets, however, when the time came to return to Old Windsor. I think Burfield was one of the happiest houses I have ever known. I don't only mean that we were happy there, but that the house itself, and the lovely gardens, seemed to be smiling. The Burfield atmosphere was perfect. I am very susceptible to the atmosphere of a house, I feel it as soon as I enter the front door, and I always found a welcome at Burfield. We had taken it on a lease from Sir William Carrington. It was a delightful house, rather like a villa in the South of France, and it had a charming garden which was cleverly laid out in perfect keeping with the house. It was a formal garden, with long rows of clipped hedges, and lead figures standing on stone pedestals in niches of green yew at intervals along the walks. I have always loved gardens, and I can look back upon many—formal gardens, wild gardens, my patio gardens in Buenos Aires, and simple, haphazard English gardens—but nowadays I find that my memory takes me back to those sunny green alleys at Burfield with the happiest recollections of all. I can always see the children in them. My children were very young then—my sons, Alfred and Hubert, were aged four and three when we went to Burfield, and my daughter, Marcella, was only a few months old. They were good and delightful children, and Alfred adored them. I remember how often he used to slip away when we were entertaining people, and would be found romping with the children when he ought to have been helping me with the guests in the drawing-room!

After we settled at Old Windsor we did not take another house in London. We used to stay at Claridges for parties in London, and it was near enough for us to motor up when our presence was

39

required at the Argentine Legation. We had begun to find Alfred's duties as an Honorary Attaché to the Minister a little irksome, and when we had been at Burfield for some time he resigned his post.

I used to take my sons out riding with me in Windsor Great Park every morning. In the afternoons we used often to watch polo, also in the Park. There was always so much happening at Windsor. I remember my first view of the magnificent sight of the open landau drawn by four horses with postilions, the portly but distinguished figure of King Edward, and the exquisite figure of Queen Alexandra, still looking really young. I was standing with my two little boys on the pavement near Queen Victoria's statue when they drove past. To my delight, Queen Alexandra saw us and pointed us out to the King. We went to our first Garden Party in the grounds of Windsor Castle. It remains in my memory as one of the loveliest of the Royal Garden Parties. The ladies of that time dressed beautifully in flowing summer dresses with flower-trimmed hats and lacy parasols. They no longer have the time or the leisure to be as beautiful as they were in the early days of this century.

Windsor was a very gay place in those days. The Life Guards always had a regiment there and the Foot Guards a battalion, and many of the married officers used to take furnished houses in the neighbourhood while they were stationed at Windsor. We always had a large house party for Ascot Races, and all our friends had people staying with them too, and there were dinner parties and balls every night during Race Week. These full days of gaiety involved frequent rapid changes of dress. We wore chiffon and lace dresses at Ascot, with large and becoming picture hats. We would rush home from the racecourse and change quickly into linen or cotton dresses in order to go on the river, enjoying the late afternoon sunlight on the cushions of punts, or sculling-boats, or small steam-launches, until it was time to change for dinner. We always spent Ascot Sunday at the Guards' Club at Maidenhead, which was a very gay spot. The Life Guards used to give a ball in their barracks during Ascot week, and there were many other excellent dances. Every house was full, and there was a vast amount of entertaining, in an agreeable, leisurely manner that few people now remember. Motoring was not very common then, and the pace of pleasure was far slower than it is to-day. We enjoyed ourselves light-heartedly, and loved every minute of our lives. In retrospect, the summers seem to have been real summers then—the river always sparkling in the sunlight, the sky always blue. When I write now of those light-hearted and enjoyable times it all sounds frivolous and trifling—but we were young then, and the shadows of this century had not yet fallen across our lives. The 1914 War, with all its horrors, had yet to come.

I always gave a children's party on my birthday. It was rather a large party, because many of the married officers of the Household Cavalry and the Foot Guards had young children. Since then I have met distinguished soldiers who have told me how much they have enjoyed my children's parties! One summer stands out in my recollection as especially brilliant and gay. For our Ascot house party we had Count and Countess Wedell; Inga Wedell was an addition to any party, always beautifully dressed and distinguished-looking. Count Wedell was Danish Minister to the Court of St. James's at that time. They had lived in England for some years, and had many friends. Our party included also my sister Anita, and another lovely girl, Valerie Glover (now Mrs. Tempest); Sir Richard and Lady Musgrave, Lord Herbert Hervey, and the Roche twins. (At that time it was quite impossible to distinguish between them, and to tell which was Maurice and which was Frank. Now, however, the elder twin is Lord Fermoy.) I gave what I thought was a successful dance. It was a pleasant change to see the officers of the regiments who were stationed at Windsor wearing their dress uniforms at these parties—although I can remember having a long ball dress badly damaged by a cavalry officer's spurs!

Of course we often went to parties in London. Minnie Paget organized another great Ball at the Albert Hall in aid of charity. It was called the Hundred Years Ago Ball, at which we danced stately quadrilles. I took part in these, and before the ball I gave a large dinner party at Claridges of, I think, between thirty and forty guests, who were taking part in the quadrilles. We dined in an oak-panelled room lit only with candles, and we were dressed in the costume of a hundred years before. The waiters in attendance also wore the dress of the period, with powdered wigs; and the food was copied from a menu of the same date. I seem to remember great rounds of roast beef. It was a good party.

At Windsor we were full of activity. We rode, and danced, of course, and also we played games—lawn tennis, and croquet, and especially golf. We used often to play at the Stoke Poges Golf Club, which was quite a new golf club then. There were many varied amusements in the evenings. I remember a most successful entertainment in Windsor Town Hall, organized for charity by Lady Edward

Churchill,[1] who lived at Windsor. (These were the days when
pageants and tableaux were popular and enjoyable ways of raising
money for charities.) In the course of this particular entertainment
a minuet was danced, in eighteenth-century costume, in which I
took part. I was carried on to the stage by my two footmen dressed
in the costume of the period. Donough O'Brien escorted me from
the chair, and we led the minuet, which consisted of six other couples
—they included my sister, and other girls whose names I have
forgotten, but I remember that most of the young men were from
the different embassies in London, and dancing a minuet seemed to
come more naturally to them that it would to the average young
Englishman, who is usually a little self-conscious when called upon
to perform a formal dance in public. Lady Edward Churchill had
written a sort of Review of the British Empire in many scenes, and
in this I represented India, wearing eastern costume, with a long
gold train carried by my two little boys dressed as tiny maharajahs.

I was a little disconcerted when we were greeted with roars of
laughter on our entrance, and I only discovered afterwards that as
we went on to the stage Hubert was hanging back and Alfred had
given him a most noticeable shove. My sister Anita represented the
West Indies, and looked lovely, draped in a beautifully embroidered
Spanish shawl belonging to my Mother, and carrying a basket of
tropical fruit and flowers on her head. She received great applause,
because, in spite of this burden, she made her entrance with a little
rush and fairly shot forward from the wings on to the stage—it was
a nice change, after so many stately and dignified entrances made
by the other members of the cast, including myself. The whole
entertainment was the greatest fun.

The Household Brigade races at Hawthorn Hill each spring were
always most enjoyable. We would have a party at Burfield for that
week, and I also remember giving a small dance.

I arranged a concert for the benefit of The Queen's Nurses (I am
still a member of The Queen's Committee). The concert took place
on a lovely summer afternoon, when the garden was at its best.
Lady Cunard[2] found for me two professional singers; one was the
great Isidore de Lara, and the name of the other I have forgotten.
Miss Vacani brought some of her pupils to give a display of dancing.

[1] Wife of Lord Edward Spencer-Churchill (1853–1911), son of the 6th Duke of
Marlborough. She was Commandant of the Windsor Detachment of the Red
Cross, etc.

[2] Maud, née Burke, the American-born wife of Sir Bache Cunard, 3rd Bt.
(1851–1925). She later adopted the first name of Emerald, and was one of the most
brilliant hostesses of her time. Nancy was her only daughter.

I also had the full band of the Life Guards to play, Maud Cunard had arranged for a bevy of lovely girls to sell programmes—Lady Diana Manners,[1] Nancy Cunard, Phyllis Boyd, one of the Tree girls, and several others. Princess Alice came to the concert, and at that time she had never seen Lady Cunard. I was much amused to see her, with Lady Arthur, looking through a gap in the hedge to get a better view of the famous Maud.

All the lovely programme sellers stayed to dine, and when I discovered that we should be thirteen, I sent to the nursery to ask one of the boys to come down. They were on their way to bed when they received this message. Little Alfred, who disliked parties, refused, but Hubert, who already had social gifts, came down in his pyjamas, wearing a pale blue dressing gown, and he did not appear in the least embarrassed. He made us laugh the next morning, when he complained that he had been made to sit between two of the plainest girls!

The dinner table looked wonderful, being almost smothered in heavenly red roses. The whole house was filled with their scent. The Burfield dining room was the best room in the house. The walls were decorated with plaster trophies of flowers and fruit, and there were two large paintings by Snyder framed in the panelling. The marble chimney piece had been made for Queen Marie Antoinette. At the end of the room were large folding doors opening into a square hall hung with eighteenth-century French tapestries. During dinner these doors were thrown open, disclosing the Band of the Life Guards, which seemed to fit so perfectly into the picture as they played to us, their scarlet tunics blending with the mass of red roses on the dinner table.

After the Christmas holidays, which were always spent with the children at Burfield, my sister and I joined a party going to St. Moritz. To my joy, I soon became quite good on skis, and especially enthusiastic about ski-joring, and in fact before I left St. Moritz I actually won a tandem race round the frozen lake. (But I expect that the credit for winning this race ought really to be given to the pair of excellent horses. It was an exciting experience, and I enjoyed it immensely.) We were staying at the Palace Hotel, where many of our friends were staying too. The Duke of Alba was there, with his lovely young wife, who had an exceptional elegance which was entirely individual; Marquesa Casati; the Marquis de Jocquet, who

[1] Lady Diana Manners, daughter of the 8th Duke of Rutland, who married in 1919 Alfred Duff Cooper (1890–1954), who became Viscount Norwich in 1952. A celebrated beauty, she appeared with great effect in *The Miracle*.

later married a very pretty Argentine; Marthe Latallier, then at the
height of her great beauty; Prince Gorgil de Festedicz; Baron
Gourgeaud; the Roche twins; and Donough O'Brien. We were
having a wonderful time, when one day we went for a long ski-joring
run—so long that it took us right into Italy—and although I had
started out feeling perfectly well, I returned to the hotel in positive
agony. A doctor was called in, and he diagnosed acute appendicitis,
and said that I would have to be operated on at once. This was done,
the next morning, in my bedroom, as they did not dare to take the
risk of moving me. The operation was performed with only a local
anaesthetic. My hands and feet were strapped down to the operating
table, and a small screen was fixed in front of my face. I felt no pain,
but only the strange and rather sinister sensation—and on a much
greater scale—that one feels when a frozen gum is cut by the dentist.
The operation was most successfully carried out by a well-known
Swiss surgeon, Dr. Bernhart. Sir Stanley Fripp was on his way over
to me, having been sent from London, when he was stopped by a
telegram at Calais, because the operation was already over. Poor
Alfred came out in great haste, to find me well on the way to
recovery. I recovered so rapidly, no doubt largely as a result of the
wonderful air of St. Moritz, that I was allowed to go down to a
luncheon given in my honour ten days after the operation.

Soon after our return from Switzerland we received the sad
news of the death of old Mr. Duggan. We had only recently come
back from a visit to the Argentine, and felt that we could not under-
take another voyage so soon with the children. It was decided that
Alfred should go to Buenos Aires without us, to take over his
inheritance. We were indeed thankful to think that we had taken
the children to see their grandfather so shortly before he died.

My father-in-law was a charming old man, very handsome (the
Duggan good looks came from him), courteous, generous, and in
every way a very great gentleman. At the time of his death he
possessed eighteen large *estancias*. By Argentine law each child
inherits an equal share of the property—daughters taking an equal
share with sons. No doubt it is a fair law for so new and so vast a
country.

Alfred remained in the Argentine for some time, for there was so
much to be arranged in taking over his property. At the end of July
1913 I took Grey Walls, Mrs. Willie James's house at Gullane, and
went there with the children. It was a charming house built by
Lutyens, with a lovely garden, close to the sea, and overlooking the
golf course. We thought it quite wonderful to find strawberries, and

all the spring vegetables, in August, as well as other fruit. I had many friends to stay, and they enjoyed the excellent golf—we were surrounded by first-class golf courses. Most of them were on their way to shoots farther North. Among my other guests, I remember my future brother-in-law, Francis Curzon, Colonel Gordon Wilson and his son, my sister Anita and her fiancé Ambrose Dudley, my brother Trillia, Captain Sam Ashton and his sister Nellie Ashton.

The time came all too soon for our return to Burfield, as the boys were to go to their private school, Wixenford. It was their first term. This was a terrible wrench for me. I shall never forget leaving little Alfred and Hubert—only thirteen months apart in age—on the front steps at Wixenford. All three of us made desperate efforts to be brave. I motored back to Burfield feeling that I had been cruel and heartless, and haunted by those two little woebegone faces. However, they were soon very happy at school. I used to motor over to see them play cricket on most Saturday afternoons. I grew to love their cricket ground, and watching all those nice little boys in white flannels wearing, on very hot days, 'land and water' hats. Sometimes on my arrival I found it quite difficult to distinguish my own two boys among so many other little boys all of about the same age, and all looking very much alike. I once received a little note from Mr. Morton, the Headmaster, suggesting that I should not visit my boys quite so often as he thought it was unsettling for them. No doubt he was right, and so I reluctantly complied, and went less often.

In the late spring Alfred returned from the Argentine. He was not looking well, and soon I began to be most anxious about him. Later that year he became very ill, and had to enter a nursing home. His long illness left me with all the responsibility for our home and our children. I had to make the plans, and take the decisions unaided, for he was too ill to be worried by such things. I wanted the boys to go to Eton, but as they were Catholics, and as their names had not been put down, there were difficulties in the way. My letters on the subject were met with various objections, and I could not get a definite answer. So one day I drove over to Eton and myself saw the Headmaster, Dr. Alington.[1] He was charming, and promised to discount the difficulties and take my sons. When the time came for them to leave Wixenford, they both went to Eton.

Of course they were still at their private school when the 1914 War broke out. It was a heartrending time—a time of endless farewells to all one's friends who were leaving for one or other of the

[1] Cyril Argentine Alington (1872–1955), Head Master of Eton 1917–33, later Dean of Durham.

fronts. I was kept very busy, I am thankful to say, with various forms of war work. Windsor was full of troops, and I organized a Recreation Centre for them at the Town Hall—a most necessary work, which was greatly appreciated. Then there were the wives and families of soldiers who were not 'on the strength' of their regiments, for whom no official arrangements could be made, and who would have come off very badly if I and some of my friends had not exerted ourselves on their behalf. I am glad to think that our efforts made some of these little families comfortable and happy during the last weeks that they were together—for so many of their husbands never returned from the front and their wives and children did not see them again.

My principal war work, however, was raising money for the Red Cross, by means of appeals, and various entertainments, and other methods. I went on doing this all through the war, and altogether I managed to collect the very satisfactory total of over a hundred thousand pounds. (I hope that I do not sound boastful when I record this—I do so largely because I remember that work with real thankfulness. It was such a comfort to me in those anxious days to feel that I was doing something practical for the country that I had come to regard as my own.)

I lived at Burfield during the early stages of the war, but when our lease of the house expired, I did not renew it. My Mother was living in Eaton Place then; my brother Trillia had contrived, in spite of his American nationality, to be commissioned in the British Army; and my sister Anita had married Ambrose Dudley, a regular soldier who commanded the Chestnut Troop of the Royal Horse Artillery; she herself was working as a V.A.D. The English blood in my Mother's family seemed to have asserted itself strongly, and long before the United States of America entered the war, we three were wholeheartedly involved in England's desperate struggle.

CHAPTER V

The War Years

DURING the early months of the war, I took a house in Grosvenor Square, and moved there in the course of the winter. It was a sad day for me when I left my smiling and lovely little Burfield, but sadness in one form or another had come to all of us with the 1914 War. I was kept busy in London with the many new obligations I had undertaken. I had joined Elizabeth Asquith's[1] 'depot' in Bond Street, where we collected silver plate and jewellery and objets d'art for the Red Cross. I was a member of Queen Mary's Sewing Guild at St. James's Palace; and I had my own Convalescent Home for Belgian Officers, and also for Belgian soldiers. I seemed to be always selling at different bazaars, and organizing concerts. Thanks to my friends in the City, and most especially to dear Alfred de Rothschild, I was fortunate in collecting a substantial sum for the Red Cross.

32 Grosvenor Square, which I had taken on leaving Burfield, was a most adaptable house for entertaining. I still had my good cook (Mrs. Owen) and my old butler. Food was difficult at that time, of course, but I managed to give little luncheons and dinners for officers on leave from the front. I always had politicians and writers to meet them. I recall one never-to-be-forgotten dinner—the Prime Minister (Asquith) and Margot, George Curzon, W. B. Yeats, and Maud Cunard. The talk on that occasion was memorable, but Yeats shocked us all by suddenly telling, in outrageously blunt terms, a story of his past life that struck a jarring note. I remember also Jack and Anne Islington, Arthur Balfour,[2] George Curzon, George Moore, Pamela Lytton, and Muriel Beckett at one of these little dinners. The one officer on leave who remains in my memory is Francis Grenfell, of the 9th Lancers—a dear and valued friend. Once, when I went to the theatre with Francis when he was on leave from the Front—it was soon after he had been awarded the V.C.—he was recognized as we entered the theatre, and the entire audience

---

[1] Elizabeth (1897–1945), daughter of Henry Herbert Asquith, Earl of Oxford and Asquith. She married Prince Antoine Bibesco, and was well known as a novelist and poetess.

[2] Arthur James Balfour (1848–1930), who was created Earl of Balfour in 1922, and is often referred to by his initials as A.J.B.

stood up to cheer him. It was an embarrassing moment, but very moving. He had received the first V.C. of the 1914 War.

I have a happy memory of Marcella's party on her eighth birthday. We had the usual amusements for children's parties—a conjuror, and a small orchestra. Jennie Churchill brought her young grandson, Randolph—I can see him now, a very pretty little boy, of about Marcella's age. The conjuror's performance was evidently not to the liking of little Randolph, and, in the middle of it, he suddenly jumped up on his chair and exclaimed: "Man, stop! Band, play!" How delightfully Churchillian! And the man did stop and the band played.

I sometimes missed my sunny home, Burfield, in those days in London. I used to wonder what had happened to our horses, which of course had been taken soon after the war broke out. Gertie Millar, a lovely little thoroughbred mare, would have been of little or no use to the Army, I felt. St. George, my special hack, was not easy to ride, but our two Argentine horses were strong and fit for anything. The boys' ponies had been left to us, and little Marcella's Shetland pony, as well as my own high-stepping hackney, New Gal, a present from Alfred de Rothschild, which I delighted in driving. They were still stabled at Old Windsor, and I sent for them when I took a house in the country for the children's holidays.

The first time Lord Curzon ever saw me was at a ball given by Lady Londesborough at St. Dunstan's, the house in Regent's Park which is now the headquarters of the wonderful work of rehabilitation of men blinded in the wars. On that occasion we did not meet, but he always retained a vivid recollection of seeing me, in a pink ball-dress, standing against a tall pillar. (Afterwards, when we were engaged, he insisted on my putting on that pink dress again and going with him to the house and standing against the same pillar, so that he might re-live the sensation of seeing me for the first time.) Our first meeting was at a luncheon party given by the Duchess of Rutland in Arlington Street. She was a great friend of George's, and in her note of invitation to him she had said, "I have asked that pretty Mrs. Duggan." (I confess that I have always felt slightly aggrieved by the word 'that'!) It was a large luncheon party, and George and I were nowhere near each other at the table. However, the man next to me had to leave early, for some urgent appointment, and as soon as George saw the vacant place he came round the table and sat down beside me. Almost the first thing he said was, "Why are you in mourning?" I explained that I was not in mourning at all and that my dress was not black, but very dark blue. (For once

Alfred

Hubert

Portrait of the author by F. M. Bennett

George's excellent eye for colour had misled him.) We talked until it was time for me to leave, and when I rose to go, he asked if he might call on me one afternoon. I said that he might, and told him that for the time being I was staying at Claridges. He said that he would come on a certain afternoon, two or three days ahead, and I said good-bye and went away—and, I am sorry to say, promptly forgot all about it. On the appointed day I was out for most of the afternoon, and on returning to my suite at Claridges I was surprised and conscience-stricken to find that he had been waiting in my sitting-room for over two hours, patiently playing the piano to while away the time until I came in. I doubt if anyone had kept George waiting, for years past; and I suspect that my unintentionally cavalier behaviour was one of the reasons for his determination to get to know me better.

After that we met quite frequently, at the houses of our friends, and sometimes dining together. He used to come to see me at Claridges, and once I dined with him at the Royal Automobile Club. George was so much in the public eye that it would have been unwise for him to be seen dining with a woman in a restaurant— the gossip-writers would have seized upon it with glee. He felt that at the R.A.C. we should be perfectly safe from observation.

George had never seen Burfield, and he asked if he could spend a night there on his way to Windsor Castle, where he had been invited to stay by the King and Queen. My Mother and my sister were visiting us at the time. I have often smiled since when I recall this, his first visit. I invited quite a number of my friends to meet him, mostly his own contemporaries who were living at Windsor—Lady Edward Spencer-Churchill, Lady St. Leonards, Sir William and Lady Carey. As I know him now, I realize that this cannot have been his idea of a party!

On one occasion when George was to make a speech in the City —at the Mansion House, I think—Minnie Paget asked me to go with her to hear him. On my return to Claridges, where I was staying, I was surprised to find a note from George, telling me of his delight at seeing me in the audience, and thanking me for coming.

In the autumn of 1915 Alfred's long illness ended, quite suddenly, in his death on November 5th. He died of pneumonia in a nursing home, and I was with him when he passed peacefully away, holding my hand and murmuring '*Mujesita*', which was the Spanish pet-name by which he called me. Later, when I went to say farewell to him in a little chapel where he lay surrounded by candles and

D

flowers, I thought I had never seen anything more beautiful than the perfect serenity of his face in death. He was very good-looking, and his calm features seemed scarcely altered at all from the young man I had first met sixteen years before. I sent for my little boys to come at once to my house in Grosvenor Square, but I thought it best not to tell them what had happened when they arrived late in the evening; so I kissed them good night without giving any explanation for having sent for them. The next morning, when I broke the news to them, they said, "Oh, Mummy, we guessed that that was what had happened, but we thought that you didn't want us to know last night." I consider myself very fortunate in having two of the most loving and sensitive sons that any woman could wish for.

I wanted to have my children in the country for the Christmas holidays and so I took a short lease of a house called Sunninghill Park. It was a very pleasant, charmingly furnished house, and as soon as the holidays started Alfred and Hubert came from Wixenford, their private school near Wokingham. Members of my family, and a few close friends, used to come for a few nights at a time, thankful for a brief rest from their various forms of exacting war work. My sister, Anita Dudley, whose husband was in France, came for Christmas. She was working as a V.A.D., and had been given short Christmas leave. I had intended that she and I and the children should spend a very quiet Christmas, with no guests, when Lord Curzon suggested joining us for a few days. I was glad to welcome him, and hoped that he would benefit from a short, restful visit in the midst of his arduous duties and responsibilities. He was then Lord Privy Seal[1] in Mr. Asquith's Coalition Government.

He seemed to be very tired and strained when he arrived—and, indeed, the Christmas of 1915 was a time of the greatest stress and anxiety for everyone, and of course above all for members of the Government. The enormous casualty lists made one dread to open the newspapers, the Battle of Ypres was raging, and there was the constant fear of what might be happening on the Gallipoli Peninsula. It was not surprising that George looked troubled, and worn out, and seemed hardly able to make the effort to join in the conversation. At dinner he made a pretence of eating, and scarcely spoke at all, and appeared to be deeply preoccupied. Towards the end of dinner he was called to the telephone, and he followed the butler from the

[1] Lord Curzon was Lord Privy Seal from the formation of the Asquith Coalition in May 1915 until its fall in December 1916.

room so slowly and so heavily that I felt he dreaded hearing some exceptionally grave news.

He returned after a few minutes, looking quite a different man, walking rapidly and lightly, and beaming with happiness. The change was quite extraordinary. And then, as he sat down, he suddenly began to sob, and could not restrain his tears, so great was his relief and thankfulness at what he had been told. He said to me: "That was Arthur Balfour. Gallipoli has been evacuated without a single casualty!" He repeated this several times, as he tried to overcome his emotion. "Without one single casualty . . . and we had feared the most terrible massacre . . . all those gallant men!"

This was the first time that I had ever seen George deeply moved about anything, and it gave me an insight into the extraordinarily emotional side of his complex character. It was an affecting moment for all of us, and it endeared him to me very much.

When the boys went back to Wixenford I returned with Marcella to Grosvenor Square, and resumed my war work—with the addition of a night service of helping at a canteen at Waterloo Station for soldiers coming home on leave from the front. I was going through a most anxious time with little Marcella, I was worried, and Dr. Still was puzzled about her, as she was losing weight. Then it was discovered that she had caught an infection from the milk of an untested cow. An operation was necessary, and it took place at 32 Grosvenor Square early one morning. Acting on the surgeon's instructions, I went into my darling little girl's room and asked her to take a good sniff at my handkerchief—which she did, but said, "Mummy, I would rather have Eau-de-Cologne, I don't like that scent." It was chloroform, of course. I then waited through one of the most anxious hours of my life. The operation was a great success.

Marcella was always rather an original child, and when her Grandmother (my Mother) went in to see her the next day and asked her how she felt, she answered, "I am quite well to-day, Grandma, but the day of the operation I felt a perfect wreck." George's thoughtfulness, affection and care throughout this critical time—one of the worst crises of my life—can never be forgotten, and he always remained truly devoted to Marcella.

When, in the spring of 1916, my boys were due from Wixenford for their Easter holidays, I had to find a country house. I took Ratton, Eastbourne, from Lord Willingdon. While I was there I had a rather surprising caller—some kind of 'official person' who asked to see me. He said, "I understand that you are not English, and in that case you should not be here in a house so near the coast, as this is a Prohibited Area." I replied that I was sorry, but I had not known about this regulation. He said, "You should have known—there is a notice in every Police Station." I apologized for not knowing, explaining that I seldom saw the inside of Police Stations. As Alfred's widow, I had an Argentine passport. He was entitled to a British passport as well, being the third generation born in the Argentine of British parents. However, as an Honorary Attaché to the Argentine Legation, he had used the Argentine one. George, on his next visit, called on the 'official person', and explained matters to everyone's satisfaction.

I liked Ratton, and the children and I were happy there. I wished that there had been less mauve predominant in the colour scheme. My bedroom was mauve, my boudoir was mauve, most of the flowers in the garden were mauve, including a long herbaceous border in many shades of mauve, and even the dinner service we used was mauve as well. It was Lady Willingdon's favourite colour.

My boys enjoyed their holidays, and Marcella was quite recovered from her illness. I was always at my happiest with my children. But only too often we were reminded of the war that raged on the other side of the Channel by the sound of the not far distant guns. My young brother was then in the trenches.

George often came to Ratton for a restful Sunday. My Mother and sister were frequent visitors, and others whom I remember being glad to spend a day or two away from their war work were Belita Hollway, a dear friend of my girlhood who had been one of my bridesmaids, Sarah Wilson, Anne Islington, Pamela Lytton, Richard and Nora Musgrave, George and Kate Arthur, Lord Colum Crichton-Stuart and Jack Cowans.

Ratton was by no means a 'spooky' house—very much the reverse, standing on the top of a hill, with its many small, sunlit reception-rooms overlooking the lawns and flower-beds of the garden, to the sea. Nevertheless, one evening there my guests became enthralled by Planchette, which was then very much in vogue. The fine, sunny afternoon had been spent in walking round Beachy Head, and in the course of the walk Belita Hollway had lost a valuable diamond ring, an heirloom. We were all very sympathetic about her loss, but in spite of it dinner was most cheerful. After dinner Belita, who had been a convinced Spiritualist for years, fetched the Ouija board that she had with her. I fancy this was done more in the hope of getting some guidance about her lost ring than to gratify the curiosity of the other guests. She and my sister Anita put their fingers lightly on the small triangular printer while the rest of us sat round them in silence, waiting for possible answers to Belita's questions.

I don't remember that there were any helpful replies about the ring, but soon the pointer was moving steadily from letter to letter, in answer not only to Belita's questions but also to Sarah Wilson's about the war. When someone asked whether Lord Kitchener would remain long at the War Office as Minister for War, the pointer moved so quickly that we could not spell out the words. Then it stopped completely. At first we thought that was the end. But Belita repeated the question, saying "Please move more slowly, we can't follow such speed." Then the pointer began again, and moved with great deliberation, pausing at each letter while an unmistakable sentence was spelt out. "Kitchener will be drowned."

This seemed to all of us such an absurd prophecy, with Kitchener obviously safe and well inland at the War Office, that we lost interest in what Planchette had to tell us.

The next morning Belita insisted on returning to Beachy Head to continue the search for her ring, but on the way my sister Anita had the happy idea of enquiring at the ticket office. There they were told that a London banker had in fact found the ring—he had seen it sparkling in the sunlight on a piece of gorse—and had taken it to London with him for safe-keeping, leaving his name and address. Belita joyfully wrote to him, describing her ring, and in due course she had it returned to her.

I am by no means a believer in the messages received by means of such methods as Planchette, but I could not but be profoundly impressed afterwards by the extraordinary forecast of Lord Kitchener's strange end. I remember one other prophecy almost equally curious. I was once tempted by a friend of mine, Edith Clark, to go with her to a fortune-teller somewhere in St. John's Wood. It was the only occasion that I ever did such a thing in my life. This woman looked into a crystal and told me that I would be a widow, that I would marry again, and then she said: "It is all most puzzling, the man you are to marry is a king, and yet I see that he is not a king. And he is surrounded by snow—or else it could be sand—quantities of white sand. . . ." I thought I had never heard such nonsense in my life, and I forgot all about it. About a year after my marriage to George, Edith Clark, who was an American, came to England again, and came to see me. She said: "Do you remember that wonderful fortune-teller I took you to see? Lord Curzon was then Viceroy of India!"

Back in London from Ratton, I began going out to small dinner parties again. I remember dinners with Jack and Anne Islington which were most enjoyable. Maud Cunard (she had not yet become Emerald) lived at the Ritz Hotel, and gave many luncheons and dinners there, often in the large private room next to the restaurant. I seemed to be a frequent guest of the Duke and Duchess of Rutland in Arlington Street. I also remember wonderfully entertaining luncheon parties at 10 Downing Street with the Prime Minister and Margot Asquith. On one of these occasions I was arriving for a luncheon party and walking through that well-known long narrow entrance hall when I recognized Lord Kitchener, whom I had never met. He was coming away from a Cabinet Meeting (as the Prime Minister told me at luncheon). When he had passed, I turned to look at him, and to my great embarrassment I found that he also had stopped and was looking back at me. We exchanged a momentary stare. I suppose I was rather noticeable, as I was still wearing my very formal widow's weeds.

The Planchette message about Lord Kitchener had made no very great impression on me, or on my sister either, although she had helped to operate the Ouija board—neither of us believed in these strange prophecies, and the recollection of that evening at Ratton was soon crowded out of both our minds by the war news, and all the events of our busy lives. One day at the end of the first week in June, it happened that both of us were selling things for some charity at a huge bazaar that had been organized at the Caledonian Market. We were not together—we each had separate stalls quite far apart at this big charity bazaar. I remember that it was a very hot, sunny day, and we were both very busy. Late that afternoon newsboys came dashing in with the evening papers, calling out the news because newspaper posters were forbidden then on account of the paper shortage. They were shouting: "The *Hampshire* sunk! Lord Kitchener lost! Drowned in the North Sea!" I was shocked and distressed by this very bad news, but still it never aroused any recollection in my mind of the Planchette prophecy. I just thought, how dreadful—and how unexpected. Dot (my sister Anita) told me afterwards that her thoughts had been just the same, and that she, too, had forgotten the prophecy and did not remember it or connect it with the news. That evening, however, Sarah Wilson rang me up, greatly excited and moved, and reminded me of what had been written on the Ouija board at Ratton, and pointed out that we could all bear witness to the message that had been foretold by Planchette. It was a very strange thing, and I do not pretend to understand it.

I wished to have my children with me in the country for the summer holidays, but I was tired of taking a different country house for each holiday period and returning to London in between, and so I took Trent Park, in Hertfordshire, from Philip Sassoon, and decided to give up 32 Grosvenor Square and live altogether at Trent. While I was still at Grosvenor Square, George and I met very often, both in London and staying with our various mutual friends in the country at weekends. I remember staying for a weekend at Coombe with Minnie Paget. The fellow guests were George, Flora and Lionel Guest, Harry Cust, Mrs. Paul Rubens, Evelyn Fitzgerald, and Jack Cowans. On Sunday morning we were told by Jack Cowans that news had been received of the death in action of one of the Grenfell brothers, son of Willie and Ettie Desborough. George left by motor at once for Taplow to see his oldest and dearest friends, and while he was with them King George and Queen Mary arrived to pay a personal visit of condolence. The Desboroughs were a wonderful couple, and they stood the loss of their two brilliant sons[1] as only such characters as theirs would. "Valour was theirs." George returned to Coombe that evening very much saddened, and all the light-hearted joy had gone out of the Coombe party.

I was seeing a lot of George at that time, and he often tried to talk of marriage, which I always did my best to ward off. I was much younger than George. I was truly fond of George, but my children were still very young and they needed me. I also confess that I had begun to love my freedom, which I did not wish to lose; and the thought of grown-up step-daughters was a little alarming, no matter how charming they were. I remember well my first visit to Hackwood. I motored down with Minnie Paget. Irene, Cimmie, and Baba[2] were all there, and the other guest that I remember was Jack Cowans. We spent a delightful weekend, and I thought George's daughters charming. The next weekend I spent at Hackwood was for a very large party, and his daughters were away at Broadstairs at that time—he owned a house there.

Diana Cooper (as was to be expected) was the loveliest bride I have ever seen. How well I remember her walking up the aisle of St. Margaret's, Westminster, looking a perfect dream of beauty. I was in mourning for my first husband when I attended this wedding. As the congregation walked out of the church through the

[1] The eldest was Julian Grenfell (1888–1915), the poet, author of the famous poem 'Into Battle'.
[2] Lord Curzon's daughters by his first marriage: Irene, Cynthia (often called Cimmie or Cim), and Alexandra (Baba).

great doors, at the end of the service, we were photographed by a Ciné camera. (Later, after my marriage to George, we were on a visit to Belvoir Castle, the Duke and Duchess of Rutland's lovely home, and after dinner one evening we were shown the cinema picture of Diana's wedding. I was much amused to recognize myself among the wedding guests leaving the church, and George was thrilled to see this photograph of me in my widow's weeds. One of his favourite jokes was to say to me, "I know you have kept that becoming little bonnet, and you will get it out and clap it on as soon as you are a widow again.")

George often talked to me about Bodiam Castle, which he had recently bought from Lord Ashcombe. He had been trying to buy this wonderful castle ever since the first time he saw it, when he had been staying with Violet Cecil (as she then was) at Great Wigsell near by, and Violet, who knew of his great love for ancient and beautiful buildings, had taken him to see Bodiam. Unfortunately for George, nothing would induce the Lord Ashcombe of that day to part with Bodiam Castle; however, after his death, George again made an offer, to the next Lord Ashcombe, and he then succeeded in buying the castle.

One day in the summer of 1916, just before I was leaving 32 Grosvenor Square to move to Trent Park, George asked me to motor with him to see Bodiam Castle. As we approached the hill leading down to Bodiam village, the chauffeur was told to drive very slowly while George looked for an opening he remembered between the trees by the roadside. Suddenly he told the chauffeur to stop and we got out; and turning to me he said, "Now give me your hand, and climb up this bank, with your eyes closed, and don't open them until I tell you." He helped me up the bank, and then said, "Now, look!" I have that picture in my heart for all time. Looking down on the castle was like looking into another world, I can find no words to describe the beauty. It was a heavenly summer morning, and I felt, as I looked at this divinely inspired picture, that I dared not take my eyes off it, for fear that when I looked again it would have disappeared in a mist or a cloud—it could only be a fairy castle.

We drove into the grounds, and spent an hour or more while George, more excited than I had ever seen him before, described all that he hoped to do to restore Bodiam to its original magnificence, so that its beauty might last for ever. We then had our luncheon, which we had brought with us, in a small room at the Castle Inn, opposite the castle. Afterwards, George suggested that we should drive to Winchelsea, as he wanted me to see a church there which he considered one of the best of its period.

We arrived, we entered the church, George led me to a pew, and we sat down. Then in the most solemn manner possible, he asked me to marry him. I write this with the greatest humility. I, too, was greatly moved, and I marvelled at George's deeply thought-out plan and the sacred setting he had chosen for so serious a moment. I again asked for time, for I was still afraid of all that would be expected of me if I became his wife.

CHAPTER VI

Engagement to Lord Curzon

IN the late summer, at Trent Park, I felt that at last my doubts
were resolved, and George and I became engaged. George at
once went to see my Mother, with whom he had already become
great friends. My Mother had decidedly Victorian views about some
things, and she earnestly advised us to wait until my year's mourning
was over before announcing our engagement. We both felt that she
was right; and I decided that I ought to go out to the Argentine
and tell my Mother-in-law about it myself before the announcement
was made, for she had always been most kind to me and I had a
great affection and respect for her. I felt that she was entitled to this
consideration from me, and George quite understood and appreciated
this decision. I arranged to sail for the Argentine at the end of
September; and in the meanwhile we remained privately engaged,
and George came to see us constantly at Trent Park during the
summer holidays.

The children and I loved Trent. It really was a perfect place,
although the house itself I considered rather ugly, and of no architectural merit, but quite comfortable to live in. The gardens were
a dream of loveliness—there was a large lake, and a perfect little
Japanese garden with a tea-house. Philip Sassoon, who owned Trent,
had a large collection of every kind of water fowl, as well as black
swans, pink flamingos, and tall storks, which were a great delight to
watch by the lake. We spent such a happy summer there. The joy of
Trent was being so near London—about fifteen miles—and still,
looking out on the beautiful park from the wide terrace, we seemed
to be in the very heart of the country. There was a wonderful kind
of colonnade of beautiful Greek pillars, with a lattice roof simply
covered with the most divine roses, and here, most mornings, we had
our breakfast brought out to us, and were almost able to forget the
war.

Since Trent was so near London it was easy for visitors to motor
out to us, and the house was always full.

It was a pleasure to receive large groups of convalescent soldiers,
who would arrive in two or three motor-coaches, wearing their
hospital blue, and looking cheerful and happy, brought by various
women friends of mine who undertook to bring these men two or

58

three times a week. They would be given a substantial tea on arrival, and then their delight was always to go on the lake—those who were strong enough—in boats they found ready for them. I well remember the happy picture they made in their bright blue. I felt that I just could not do enough for these brave uncomplaining men.

Maud Cunard was a frequent guest, and also her daughter Nancy. It was while staying at Trent that Nancy became engaged to Mr. Fairbairn. Maud did not approve of the engagement. Unhappily we—the house-party and the children—were unwilling listeners to a rather acrimonious dispute one afternoon at tea. Maud, who had little self-control when annoyed, started to find fault with the newly engaged couple, who were there too. It became so heated that I finally said to the children (who were having tea at a separate table, with their tutor), "I think you will have finished your tea and you can go." The poor boys told me afterwards that they had barely begun their tea, but that they were glad to go all the same. George Moore often stayed at Trent. Naturally, he was an amusing guest, but his conversation often made me a little anxious when my boys were present. One morning I received a note, brought to my room before breakfast, from him, saying, "I am sorry to leave without seeing you, but I can no longer stand the love-making of the doves by my window."

At one of the largest weekend parties at Trent, we had a most exciting and anxious experience. The party consisted of Diana Manners, Mrs. George Keppel and her daughter Violet,[1] Maud Cunard and her daughter Nancy, my sister Anita, Osbert Sitwell, George Moore, Mr. Fairbairn, and others whose names I do not now remember. We had all gone to bed, when a Zeppelin was heard flying low over the house. The anti-aircraft guns put up a tremendous barrage, and bombs dropped all round us. We all rushed out of our rooms in dressing-gowns, the younger people perfectly calm, but some of the older ones decidedly nervous. My first thought was for little Marcella, who was still not strong enough, after her operation, to be allowed to walk up or downstairs. Osbert Sitwell dashed up to her room and carried her down to the hall. I was thankful that Alfred and Hubert were safely at school at Wixenford. We all sat on the floor in the hall until the raid was over—I don't quite know why we sat on the floor, but I suppose it was to be out of the way of flying glass if the windows had been blown in. My stately old butler

[1] Now Violet Trefusis, author of the autobiography *Don't Look Round*, and other books.

walked round serving drinks and coffee, wearing his dress coat over pyjama trousers! At dawn, the Zeppelin was brought down, in flames, quite close by. The raid was over, and Osbert Sitwell kindly carried Marcella up to her room again.

The next morning we learned that it was the first Zeppelin to be brought down in the war—it was in July 1916. It crashed at Cuffley, and all the crew were killed—many of them burnt to death. Some of the members of my house-party motored over to Cuffley that day to see the remains of the wrecked and charred Zeppelin, but I did not go with them. I felt that I could not face it, and also it seemed to me a little like gloating.

Apart from my Mother, my sister and my brother, only one very old friend of mine had been told of our engagement before I sailed for the Argentine. This was dear old Alfred de Rothschild, whose friendship for me and devotion to my children had been one of the greatest and most peaceful pleasures of my busy life since I came to England. This distinguished and courteous friend had been kindness itself to me and to the children in a thousand unobtrusive and considerate ways. His devotion to my children was extraordinary, and touched me very much. (When he died he left each of them a most generous legacy, and to me he left four beautiful pictures—a Boucher, two Greuzes, and a Reynolds.) I had come to regard him almost as a member of the family, and when I said to George that I wanted to include him in the tiny number of people who were told of our engagement three months before the official announcement, George at once concurred. In fact, George suggested that I should go and tell him, as a joint communication from both of us—a gracious gesture which Alfred de Rothschild appreciated very much. This is the letter which he wrote to George the next day.

"19 September, 1916.   1 Seamore Place,
                                                        Mayfair.

My dear Curzon,

    I received yesterday afternoon an extremely kindly visit from Mrs. Duggan, who called to tell me that she was engaged to be married to you and that the marriage was to take place immediately after her return from the Argentine.

Mrs. Duggan communicated this to me not only in her name but likewise in yours, and I cannot tell you what pleasure this joint message gave me, and I must offer you at once my most sincere and heartfelt congratulations, for you have succeeded in winning the greatest prize which can fall to the lot of man, namely to have found

'Perfection' in the lady who is to be your future companion of your life—unusual beauty, a refinement and delicacy of character which could not be surpassed, and the most gentle and tender of natures. I think therefore, my dear Curzon, I am justified in saying 'Perfection'. I am convinced that you will vie with each other in making your 'future' the happiest and brightest in every respect. I wish you both with all my heart a continuance of perfect health—the rest, you possess. I can only repeat how touched I was by being told what gave me unfeigned joy and pleasure—and I rejoice all the more as Mrs. Duggan will have found in you a future companion of whom she will be justly and fully proud.

Believe me, my dear Curzon,

Your most sincerely,

Alfred de Rothschild."

I had arranged with my sister that she should tell my children of my engagement to George just before the announcement was made public. Both the boys wrote charming little letters to George, from Wixenford. Hubert writes gaily that he hopes "you and my darling Mummie will be very, very happy always, and I am sure you will be", and then goes on to describe rehearsals for the school play, in which he played the part of Mrs. Cluppins in the trial scene from Pickwick! Alfred, as befits the elder son, strikes a more serious note, and says ". . . how glad I am to hear that my darling Mummie is going to be so happy, and I am sure you will be happy too, and will help us to take care of her always". The rest of his letter discussed the results of the Common Entrance Examination, which he was anxiously awaiting, and whether he would take Upper Fourth at Eton, or Remove—the latter he thought unlikely, "because I do not learn Verses".

I sailed for the Argentine from Southampton on September 22nd, 1916, in the R.M.S.P. *Araguaya*—not without some slight trepidation, which I did my best to conceal; because of course a voyage then was attended with all the hazards and discomforts caused by the U-Boat menace—sailing without lights, a rigorous black-out, and the ever-present chance of a torpedo or a mine. However, my mind was made up, and I had to take this step looking forward to the future. I planned my voyage so that I could be in Buenos Aires in time to be present at the great Mass which was to be sung for Alfred on the anniversary of his death; and only when that was over would I tell my mother-in-law of my forthcoming marriage to George. My brother Trillia accompanied me. He had been badly gassed at the

Front, and was on sick leave. We hoped that the sea voyage would
do him good.

George came to Southampton to see me off, and left a letter with
me which I read as soon as he had gone ashore. I sat down to answer
it the same night. I wrote to him almost every day, but of course the
letters could only be posted when we reached a port, and so I give
extracts from them telescoped together, because they were in effect
a journal despatched at intervals in batches.

". . . I thank you for the most wonderful letter that has ever been
written. . . . Who else would have done all that you did for me to-day?
I adore you for having come to see me off. And I thank you with all
my heart for your books, your flowers, your fruit—I shall never
forget seeing you arranging my cabin. . . .

Saturday. We got well on our way about 11 o'clock last night.
Rather creepy with no lights on deck—my heart jumped two or three
times in the great stillness of the night when I heard the man on the
bridge call out 'Ship Ahoy!' We would slow down a bit and then
steam ahead faster than ever. I was surprised to see the coast of
Ireland all to-day—in fact we are not yet in the Bay. You will be
pleased to hear that I have got the little sitting-room, and have had
one of the beds taken out of my cabin. Your flowers look too lovely . . .
I am wearing some of your lilies-of-the-valley.

Sunday. Too sad, no service to-day, no doubt as we are still in the
danger zone and the men cannot leave their posts. I read my prayers
on deck and thought of you reading the lessons in your beautiful
chapel. . . . We are having the most wonderful weather, but even so
Vinson (my maid) has managed to be ill every day. Trillia and I are
both very well.

Monday. Vigo. We arrived here at four o'clock to-day after one of
the roughest and most miserable nights and mornings I have ever
spent. Everyone on board was ill—I still feel too stupid to write
much. We only stay two hours here, no time to go on shore. I don't
remember if you have ever been at Vigo. It is most picturesque from
the ship—quite a wonderful harbour. I was delighted to see a
number of German ships in harbour going to ruin—they have been
here for two years. . . . I was disappointed at hearing nothing from
you here. I had counted on getting a telegram. . . . I sent you one as
soon as we arrived. I am so anxious to hear news of the air raids.

I wonder if all is well at Trent. I am advised not to post this until we get to Lisbon as it will reach London sooner from there.

Tuesday, 26th. We expect to get in to Lisbon in an hour's time. We had a very rough night again, the Captain tells me it is the worst he has seen for over two years. I will write to you again later on from on shore, where I hope to go for luncheon. . . . *Lisbon.* We are just leaving here, and I am still without a word from you. I am quite sure it is not your fault but it is most disappointing. I am told that even cables from England now take three days to get here, as they must all be censored. When on shore to-day I went to the Royal Mail Agents myself hoping to find a cable. I was again disappointed, although Trillia found *two* from a friend of his. We shall be at sea for seven days, as you know our next port is St. Vincent. We had a nice afternoon on shore to-day—a lovely day, quite hot. We took a motor and drove for three hours all over Lisbon. We also went to the Palacio de St. Vicente and saw all the Familia Real as well as Mother's friend Dom Pedro of Brazil—I must write to Mother and tell her how wonderful he still looks. As you know, the Portuguese embalm all their Kings, even when they assassinate them first. We just escaped a mine this morning as we were coming into Lisbon. The captain fired at it and as you can imagine there was great excitement for a time on board. I shall be anxious to know if my letters to you are censored, please let me know. . . .

September 28th. I have not written for two days because it has been very rough and quite impossible to do anything. To-day is a divine day and I wish I could send you some of the sunshine. The sea is the most glorious blue. . . . I love to remember that you have been in these rooms. Some of your flowers are still quite fresh, and your books are as you arranged them. I am reading *The Brook Kerith*, I like some of it very much. It amuses me to recognize George Moore and his little understudy Maud's view of life. This afternoon we passed quite near the peaks of Tenerife. I have never seen it look more beautiful—in fact I have never passed so near before.

September 29th. I have started playing bridge so the days are not quite so long. I play with Mr. O'Driscoll, who plays a very good game. You remember you spoke to him on board. Captain Phillips (in the Navy) also plays with us. He is quite a nice little man, and the only gentleman on board; unfortunately he leaves us in a day or two to join his ship. . . . I shall write to you again to-morrow, before we arrive at St. Vincent.

October 1st. We had church service this morning. Many of the Brazilians came in, and I am sure they thought it was a concert. The last two days the weather has been beautiful, and I am sure this slack life is good for me, although one day is merely a repetition of the other.

October 2nd. I was very delighted to receive your telegram, at St. Vincent. It seemed such an age since I had a word. . . . I hope you receive all my letters, this will be the fourth I have posted to you. We arrived at St. Vincent (Cape Verde Islands) too late to go ashore.

October 3rd. The heat is very trying to-day, with little or no breeze. I am reading the Memoirs of the Duchesse de Dino, 1831–1835. I love memoirs, and feel that they are always such human documents. The Earl of Durham was then Lord Privy Seal.

October 4th. The usual sports and games have been started to-day, and it is almost impossible to find a quiet corner on deck, and my cabin is so hot, even with the electric fan. . . .

October 5th. We crossed the Equator this morning. The weather has greatly improved, there is quite a cool breeze. . . . The Captain very kindly sends me the Marconi telegram every morning. (I can't think why it is not posted up for all to see.) All seems to be going well with us, but I *hate* the many air raids in England.

October 6th. Two weeks ago to-day I left England. I shall never forget your noble and touching farewell words. There is always something solemn and peculiarly painful in doing a thing for the last time, in departure, in absence, in saying good-bye, especially when one *loves.* I said good-bye to you with a heart-sinking as great as if I was not going to see you again in three months. . . . We expect to get in to Pernambuco late this evening. I shall post this to you, and shall hope to find a telegram there from you.

Near Bahia. October 7th. I was so delighted to receive your telegram yesterday at Pernambuco. Pernambuco, or Recife, as the Brazilians call it, is the first port of the South American continent at

Author with her sons at a Windsor pageant

Photograph of the author by Lallie Charles

which one calls again, going south. Owing to the heavy swell that is usual, landing is somewhat difficult, passengers having to disembark by means of a basket suspended to one of the ship's cranes and lowered into a large passenger lighter. This operation, as you can imagine, is much more amusing to the onlookers than to the occupants. We should arrive at Buenos Aires in a week's time. I shall not be sorry to say good-bye to the ship. . . .

October 8th. We arrived at Bahia this morning, where we only stayed a short time. We did not go ashore, as there is nothing to be seen there.

October 9th. The weather which had been wretched for two whole days improved yesterday, and a veritable sun of Brazil pierced the clouds. We expect to arrive at Rio to-morrow.

October 10th. We are all looking forward to arriving at Rio in time to go on shore and dine, one gets so tired of the ship's food. I am getting rather anxious as I get nearer to Buenos Aires, and I dread all that is before me. I will always keep in front of my mind the great happiness that is waiting for me—and then I am sure of my courage not failing me. . . . I shall send you a long cable this evening from Rio. . . . Forgive this untidy letter—the ship is pitching and it is most difficult to write.

October 12th. I wish you could have been with me yesterday at Rio. It really is the most beautiful place that I have ever seen. We arrived about six o'clock in the evening. As soon as we landed we went for a divine motor drive along the sea front. A beautiful half-moon shone down on the heaving water and the sky was studded with stars. The wonderful dark, grand mountains in the background completed such a perfect picture. . . . The Italian taste predominates in the construction of the villas, the gardens and the arrangements of the flowers recall England. The frame of the picture alone is Brazil, and it could not be more grandiose.

October 13th. We went on shore at Santos for a drive. It comes too soon after the grand beauty of Rio to be quite appreciated. I was delighted to receive a cable from you. . . .

October 14th. This will be my last letter to you from the ship, as we expect to arrive at Montevideo to-morrow morning, and at

E

Buenos Aires to-morrow night. Our voyage has been uneventful. I am glad to have reached the end. . . .

October 16th. Plaza Hotel, Buenos Aires. First of all I must thank you for your two dear telegrams to me at Montevideo. We arrived here last night at 7.30. You will be pleased to hear that I received a very affectionate welcome from all the Duggan family. It is always a great event for me to get back to Buenos Aires. . . . All my past unrolls itself before me, and awakes so many memories. . . . I sent you a telegram telling of my safe arrival. I hope to hear from you to-morrow.

October 17th. I have quite enjoyed to-day. I found many old acquaintances and had some agreeable meetings. Buenos Aires has changed very little since my last visit about four years ago. I am staying here until next week, and then go to my camp.[1]

October 23rd, 1916. I am still anxiously looking forward to receiving a letter from you. I have been here over a week, and as yet no mail has arrived from England. It seems an eternity to me since I left you. I have had to postpone my visit to the camp as they are not ready for me out there. I hope to go next week. I find Buenos Aires very dull. Old Mrs. Duggan does not approve of my going to the opera, or to the races, until after the 5th of next month. All my business is going slowly, and not too well—big death duties, as well as fat lawyers' fees! I hope to be in a position to write you more details after my visit to the camp. I have been so worried and unhappy about you since receiving your cable saying you were in bed suffering with your poor back. I have not told my in-laws about our engagement. They asked me about Lord Grey. In fact even the newspaper reporters worried the Hotel Manager for news. I am told the Duggans heard the rumour of my engagement to you, but so far they have not spoken to me about it, and I think it wiser to tell them later, just before I leave. The weather is divine. The air is full of feeling—and I am well, very well. . . .

October 29th. Estancia San Miguel. I wish you could see the lowly chalet which now shelters me from the storm, and I'm afraid— unless I perish earlier!—that it's got to go on doing so for a week longer. The house is small, clean, pretty, and well looked-after. My

[1] See note, p. 21.

Manager here is a curious, absurd, and absent-minded person who puts himself about for nobody—but I am told he is a good Manager. The weather is very hot and trying and makes me long for cool peaceful England. The country is flat and ugly, with little stubby trees that stand here and there like bushes. The *estancia* is ten leagues —about 81 miles—and we have about a thousand horses, ten thousand head of cattle and fourteen thousand sheep. An English railway runs the length of the place. We had the first good rain here yesterday since April! This rain has saved us much loss, but unfortunately we now have thousands of locusts which will, I fear, do a lot of harm to the wheat—too sad, as we have never had such big prices for our wheat as this year. I lost ten thousand pounds in the month of September alone through so many of the cattle dying— all due to the dryness of the camp and want of rain.

I hope, darling, you will forgive this vulgar business letter. I cannot help being interested in all these details when I am out here —and I only hope they do not bore you. I return to Buenos Aires in a few days, about a week, and I then go to 'Duggan' to stay with my mother-in-law at one of her places. I look forward to finding letters from you. . . .

November 1st. Estancia San Miguel. I return to Buenos Aires to-morrow, and I look forward to finding my first letters from you. We have had more rain so everything is more promising. I think darling I should die if I had to live much longer in this flat uninteresting country. . . . The weather has been so bad we have not been able to stir out of the house, so that you may suppose we have been comfortably dull. I wonder how you are pleased with your Air Board?[1] What a different view I take of everything; not merely that which concerns you, or will concern you—but my whole view of life is a new one. . . . I wonder if I shall ever see the Argentine again after this visit. . . . I often try to imagine you in Buenos Aires, and somehow I cannot see you in the picture. . . .

November 4th. Plaza Hotel, Buenos Aires. I arrived here last night and was delighted to find *four* dear letters from you. I hope you have received some of mine by this time. I dined last night with the British Minister. He offered to send some letters home for me by the mail going to-day in the bag from the Legation. . . . I have been

[1] In May 1916 Lord Curzon became president of the Air Board, which had been established in order to decide the conflicting claims of the Admiralty and the War Office for aircraft.

having many worries—some things out here are not easy, and the law is all for the people living in the country. . . .

November 7th. I find I still have time to send you a few lines by this mail. I have had a horrid cold and spent two long days in bed. We had a very beautiful Mass on the 5th for my husband. The music was wonderful and most impressive.

I have talked to old Mrs. Duggan about our engagement. I had the courage to tell her the truth, which is always right when dealing with people of great age. I think she is pleased. Her manner is restrained, as always. I have only two weeks and a few days left before leaving here. . . . I have still much to do, and spend my days seeing lawyers and other dull people. I have had a terrible time dodging newspaper reporters. I only got rid of them by promising to send them a notice about myself when I had anything to tell them. Unless I hear from you to the contrary I shall have our engagement announced here as arranged on December 11th. . . .

November 14th. I returned here from Hurlingham yesterday, and found a cable from you. I at once sent you an answer saying that all is well. I have just returned from lunching with the American Ambassador. Sir Reginald Tower[1] was there, and members of most of the other Legations. I dine to-night with Sir Reginald. I have found it necessary to tell him of my engagement to you! The weather here is getting very hot, and I long to get away. I see by the cables to-day that you had a very dense fog in London yesterday. I wonder if you remember a fog in London about a year ago, when you dined with me in Grosvenor Square?

I can't tell you how disappointed I am at arriving home five days later than we had expected to do. The *Amazon* should arrive on December 20th, a Wednesday. I think darling we shall have to wait until after Christmas—don't you? Of course as you know I am only too anxious to do as you wish and think the best plan. . . ."

When our engagement was announced, it was amusing to read the various descriptions of George in the Argentine newspapers. *La Argentina* called him 'Lord Curzon, *distinguido caballero perteneciente a la alta nobleza Britanica*'; and *El Diaro* referred to him as '*el ilustre aristocrata Jorge Nathaniel Curzon, uno de los hombres mas autorizados de la nobleza y la politica britanica*'.

As I had arranged with George, the announcement was made

[1] Sir Reginald Tower (1860–1939), Envoy Extraordinary and Minister Plenipotentiary to the Argentine 1910–19.

simultaneously in London and in Buenos Aires, while I was on my way home in the R.M.S.P. *Amazon*. George wanted me to leave the ship at Lisbon and to make the rest of the journey overland, but I would not do this, and stayed on board until we reached Southampton. George's new position in the Government—Lord President of the Council[1]—was announced at the same time. The Captain of the *Amazon* told me that he considered that the ship might well be a special target for U-Boats, in view of George's prominent position and the publicity given to our engagement. This was not a very cheerful notion to have in mind during the last, uneasy, blacked-out stages of the voyage. However, we arrived without mishap, and George met me at Southampton.

[1] Asquith fell in December 1916, and when Lloyd George formed his ministry, Lord Curzon became leader in the House of Lords, Lord President of the Council, and one of the four Ministers composing the inner war cabinet which supervised the daily conduct of the war.

CHAPTER VII

Marriage to Lord Curzon

I ARRIVED at Southampton most thankful to have got over the last stage of our voyage, for we had not had a very happy time after leaving Lisbon on our return journey. I regretted more than once that I had not taken George's advice about returning through Spain and France. The Bay of Biscay had been at its very worst, rough beyond belief, and there was fog as well—and of course the black-out was the strictest possible. I was told later that our embassies both in Madrid and Lisbon had expected me, and had made all arrangements to help me on my journey. However, I was impatient to get back to the children and to George—I had been away for three months. Trillia and I were thrilled to arrive at Southampton, where George was waiting to welcome us. We went by train to London, and then motored to Trent, where the boys, Marcella, my Mother and my sister were assembled. It was a wonderful homecoming, and it made up for the bad time we had had in the Bay. George arrived two days later, bringing with him his three daughters, Irene, Cimmie, and Baba, who all spent Christmas with us. We had the usual large Christmas tree. I cannot remember a Christmas in my life without a Christmas tree, even in the difficult times of both the wars—and Christmas would never seem the same without one. It was a very happy Christmas, we were all together for the first time, and I was thankful to have these few days of domestic peace and rejoicing after my travels. Our marriage was to take place only a week or so later, and the complete family house party at Trent made a joyful preparation for it.

One of the great pleasures during these few days at Trent between my return and my marriage was reading all the letters of congratulation which George and I received. They were full of kind thoughts, praise, and encouragement, and it was a delight to read them. Alas, I did not preserve the ones I received, when I had answered them—how I wish that I had!—but George, who preserved everything, kept his and put them away. I have a great pile of them before me now, and many of them are most interesting, for the writers went on from their congratulations to express their views about various aspects of the war. It so happened that George had made one of his brilliant and effective speeches in the House of Lords just before our engagement was announced, and this, with his new post as Leader of the House of Lords, was made an additional matter of congratulation by many of his correspondents. It was quite amusing to compare the order in which the various writers assembled these points.

King George wrote a personal letter of congratulation to George when he had informed him of our engagement.

Dec. 10th, 1916.   Buckingham Palace.
"My dear Lord Curzon,
          "The Queen and I were most interested to hear the good news which you were kind enough to give me.
"We heartily congratulate you on your coming marriage to Mrs. Duggan and trust that it will bring you both all possible happiness. I know how lonely your life has been in the past years, I rejoice to think you will now have a partner who will bring brightness into your home and thus help you in the discharge of your many and heavy duties and responsibilities, important additions to which you have now undertaken.
"Hoping to make your future wife's acquaintance before long,
          "Believe me,
                    "Very sincerely yours
                              "George R.I."

Some of the letters of congratulation which George received put our engagement first, and others, his post as Leader of the House of Lords. It is quite entertaining to compare them. Lord Dartmouth even contrived to place me as a bad third.

15 Dec. '16.   37, Charles Street,
                                                   Berkeley Square.
"My dear George
          "A line to offer you a triple congratulation.
"Firstly on the Leadership of the House of Lords.
"Secondly on your speech on your first appearance in that capacity, which if you will allow me to say so, seemed to me to be admirable in every way.
"I hope the criticisms that emanate from the somewhat over-crowded Opposition Front bench will be helpful and not destructive, and
"Thirdly on a recent announcement in the Press, and though

that is matter of more private concern, you will know that you carry
with you the best of good wishes of your many friends.

"Yours sincerely,

"Dartmouth."

The Archbishop of York[1] wrote:

"My dear Curzon,
        "I am reluctant to inflict a letter upon you at a time of
manifold stress: but an impulse of old friendship compels me to
send you a word of twofold congratulation—on the prospect of your
marriage, and on your place in the War Cabinet. As to the former,
with all my heart I wish you every happiness and blessing. Even a
confirmed bachelor can well understand the relief which this
renewal of home life will bring to the burden and strain of public
affairs.
        "Next, the Cabinet. I am sincerely glad that you have your place
in the influence and direction of the war. It is an immense responsibility: and I pray that a full measure of counsel and strength may be
given to you. I am sure that the great mass of your fellow-country-
men will support decisive action and are only waiting to be told
clearly what part they must play and what sacrifices they must be
ready to offer and endure.

"Your ever

"Cosmo Ebor."

Sir Douglas Haig—as he then was—cared nothing for politics,
and wrote only about our engagement.

"Tuesday, Dec. 12, 1916.   General Headquarters,
                                  British Armies in France.
"My dear Lord Curzon,
        "I have just read of your engagement, and so write at
once to congratulate you most heartily, and to wish you everything
that is good.

"Yours most truly,

"Douglas Haig."

Sir Rider Haggard sounded a faintly dubious note.

[1] Cosmo Gordon Lang (1864–1945), Archbishop of York 1908–28, and of
Canterbury 1928–42, and created Baron Lang in 1942.

"11th Dec., 1916. Thomsett,
Budleigh Salterton.

"My dear Curzon,
"I send you my heartiest congratulations on the double event announced this morning.

"May your success be complete in your high public office (never were men such as you more needed in England!) and your private happiness as perfect as human conditions will allow—is the earnest wish of

"Yours most sincerely,
"H. Rider Haggard."

Dr. Spooner,[1] the Warden of New College, left me out altogether.

"12 Dec. 1916. New College,
Oxford.

"My Lord and Chancellor,
"I hope you will not take it amiss, if I write you a line of congratulation on your having so leading a place in the new cabinet. It is a great thing to be called at such a crisis in our History to take so leading a part in the direction of our affairs. Yet what a dreadful burden too! I trust that you and Lord Milner[2] may have much wisdom and skill given to you for you will need all that you can have. What problems there are to solve! What difficulties to face! Yet I think the country looks forward with confidence and hope to the part you and your colleagues will play, tho' realising very keenly how great and formidable are the difficulties you are called upon to surmount. That you have the good wishes and confidence of the members of the University I feel confident.

"A year ago you were good enough to congratulate me on my progress to recovery. I am thankful to say I am now quite well.

"Believe me, my Lord,
"Yours very sincerely,
"W. A. Spooner."

Sir Robert (then Mr. R. C.) Witt,[3] who was associated with George

[1] William Archibald Spooner (1844–1930), originator of 'spoonerisms' such as: 'Kinquering Congs their titles take.'
[2] Also a member of the small inner war cabinet, and largely responsible for the civilian conduct of the war.
[3] Sir Robert Witt (1872–1952), chairman of the National Art Collections Fund 1920–45, which he helped to form in 1903; trustee of the National and Tate Galleries; and collector of the Witt Library of photographs of works of art, which he bequeathed to the Courtauld Institute.

in his concern with pictures and the national collections, framed his congratulations with charming tact.

"12 Dec. 1916.   27 Connaught Square,
                                                          W.
"Dear Lord Curzon,
          "May I congratulate *you* on the personal news in the newspapers and the nation on the public announcement of your position in the War Council in its new form. It is indeed good to think that at last the men who are prepared to act will be free to do so. I am just a little disappointed that you did not accept the Foreign Secretaryship which is the post that so many of us hope to see you fill, but at the moment perhaps it is better so, if only, when the War is over, and things assume their regular course, you will take it then. I sometimes wonder whether you can be aware of how strong the feeling is that it is in foreign politics you stand for all that we believe counts and will count.
          "We met at the National Gallery to-day and discussed the Bill.[1] The Director has cold feet—as he would—and counsels surrender to Claude Phillips.[2] I am trying to encourage him but it is no easy task.
                              "Yours very truly
                                        "Robert C. Witt."

The Archbishop of Canterbury's letter was full of his own personal difficulties about his availability to officiate at our wedding.

"Sunday, 17 Dec. 1916.   Lambeth Palace, S.E.
"My dear Curzon,
          "This afternoon for the first time, I am up for a few hours. I have had a very severe bout of influenza, with great pain, hence my failure in correspondence.
          "First: let me from the bottom of my heart wish you every possible joy and blessing in the new home life which lies ahead. May you have many years of renewed happiness and of enhanced strength.

[1] A Bill introduced in 1916 on behalf of the Trustees of the National Gallery, to extend their powers for the sale and loan of superfluous pictures. It was largely prompted by the knowledge that certain very valuable paintings were about to be sold to the United States, and was defended by Lord Curzon, and opposed by Lord Burnham and others.
[2] On November 23rd Sir Claude Phillips (*d.* 1924), who had been Keeper of the Wallace Collection 1897–1911, attacked the Bill in the *Daily Telegraph*, and Robert Witt was among those who replied in its defence.

"As to the Marriage Service, I need hardly tell you how anxious I should be to further your wish in every way. Unfortunately things are not easy for me. After this illness we must get away for a fortnight's change and quiet. On Thursday Dec. 28th, I have to consecrate Ld. W. Cecil to the See of Exeter, and to marry Sir Herbert Plumer's daughter, if he can get leave from the Front, so that will keep us here for the great part of next week. If it suited you to be married here on Wednesday morning, Dec. 27, we could I think arrange it. I realise that you wish it to be absolutely quiet—without fuss or special preparation, which indeed would be impossible for us at present, and this facilitates things. Very likely, however, that morning will not suit you. If it does, what would you wish to be done? And would you like to come here quietly this week and arrange any details that require settlement?

"I should deem it a privilege to be in that way a contributor to your new happiness.

"I am,

"Yours very truly

"Randall Cantaur."

Dr. Randall Davidson wrote another letter to George on the same day.

"Dec. 17, 1916.
"My dear Curzon,
        "I have said nothing (in my other note) about public affairs or the developments which each day brings. I need not assure you how much you have been in my thoughts in connexion with the Central Bureau which will be yours, and the Leadership of the House, and other things.

"I am, from having been ill for eight days, quite uninformed about public affairs save what the Press gives.

"If it is devolving upon the Government to send a formal message of some sort in reply to Peace proposals(?) I very earnestly hope that it will not be in the mere unvarnished form of a curt negative, unaccompanied by explanations or constructive words.

"I feel intensely that we shall be putting ourselves needlessly in a false or misunderstood position if we simply say 'No peace at present', and are thus liable to be quoted as having merely scouted the offer made, without showing what is *our* side. If, as I suppose is certain, we say NO, do let it be an explained NO—'You profess to offer Peace. You do not so offer it as to make acceptance of your offer thinkable.

We as Allies went into the War against our will, for a purpose. That purpose must be secured. Give us security for it, and then we want peace as much as you do. Till then, NO. But, when you do that, Yes.'

"Pardon this lucubration, which needs no reply.

"I am

"Yours very truly

"Randall Cantaur."

I have included this letter from the Archbishop because, although it has no connection with me or my life with George, it is an important expression of the views of a great man and has not hitherto been published.

One letter from a total stranger is such a touching tribute to George that I cannot leave it out.

"12.XII.16.   Marseilles.

"My Lord,

"No more welcome gift could have been given to a very large class of men like me than your nomination and appointment to the War Cabinet. You represent to us 'action', 'determination to win the War'.

"With the deepest patriotism and love of our beloved KING and Empire we say reverently 'God give you courage and strength and force to do your great share.'

"The papers also mention your approaching Marriage. May I also add my congratulations and wishes for a very happy life for both of you?

"I am and have been for $2\frac{1}{2}$ years Deputy Assistant Director of Railway Transport at Marseilles to which place I was posted owing to my knowledge of Indian language and people after 6 months most strenuous service up at the front.

"I am my Lord

"Your most sincere servant

"A. W. Pope."

Lord Grey wrote:

". . . I called in the hope of seeing you just before 6 but you were not at home. I wanted . . . to give you a double handshake on

(1) Cabinet
(2) Marriage

—also to congratulate you on having beaten your own great record in the Lords the other evening. I wish I had heard you. I am told you were magnificent. If I had not been so wet and dirty, having tramped thro' snow and mud to call on you (D—n these Taxiless Days) I wd. have presented myself to Madame to whom I shd. have much liked to offer my heartiest congratulations . . ."

I have quoted only a few of the many kind and charming letters written to George at this time. My great regret is that I destroyed the ones I received myself, for I remember that there were many that would have been well worth quoting if only I had kept them.

One letter survives of all those which George wrote to thank the senders of wedding presents. It is typical of his ability to express gratitude gracefully in a phrase or two. It was written to my brother.

"Dec. 18th, 1916.   1 Carlton House Terrace.
Dear Trillia,
        That you should have dreamed of giving me a present never occurred to me. But that when you generously decided to give it you should select a gift so attractive and valuable (a first edition) adds tenfold to the charm and the intention, and leaves me a very grateful and happy man.

You know well how warm a welcome you will find in our home when we are married.

                    Yours affec.
                        G."

On New Year's Eve George and his daughters returned to London. My Mother and sister and brother went back to Eaton Place, taking with them the boys and Marcella.

On New Year's Day, 1917, I went to the Ritz, to be in readiness for my marriage to George on January 2nd. Our wedding took place in the morning, at Lambeth Palace. The Archbishop of Canterbury was to have married us, but owing to his convalescence after an illness, he was unable to do it. And so George's old Balliol friend, Cosmo Lang, the Archbishop of York, took his place. George had prepared every detail of the ceremony himself, and had chosen all the hymns. Lambeth Palace Chapel was a perfect setting for a marriage service.

George told me afterwards that he could not leave by the front entrance to Carlton House Terrace that morning as there were so many reporters there. He and his daughters left by walking the length of the terrace overlooking the Mall, and down the steps at the foot of the Duke of York's Column, to his waiting motor. His brother Francis Curzon was his best man. My Mother and sister had gone in advance to Lambeth Palace, taking with them Alfred, Hubert, and Marcella. My brother Trillia came for me at the Ritz and we drove together to Lambeth, as he was to give me away.

The great Charles Worth of Paris made my dress for my marriage. It was of cream chiffon velvet trimmed with Russian sable, and I wore a long sable cape, also made by Worth, and a small brown velvet hat from Reboux.

I had realized by this time that George was very emotional by nature, but even so I was not prepared, when I arrived at the altar, to be met by George with the tears pouring from his eyes. He told me afterwards that he was overcome when he saw me walking up the aisle and thought of my willingness to marry him. He sang all the hymns, in his truly delightful voice, and this too caused me some surprise, but it gave me a feeling of great happiness.

After the ceremony we motored straight to Trent. We had tried to keep the marriage as private and as unpublicized as possible, as we had asked no one to be present except our two families. Afterwards we learned that various friends of ours had noticed that both families were lunching together at the Ritz, without either George or me, and had therefore rightly guessed that our marriage must have taken place that morning.

CHAPTER VIII

Trent Park

AFTER my first marriage we had had a wedding journey of four months. How differently did my second marriage begin! —for George's great responsibilities in those anxious times in the third year of the 1914 War obliged him to be always hard at work without even a day's respite. Some of the letters which he had to deal with directly after our wedding lie before me now, and reflect the varied and arduous work on which he was engaged.

This letter from King George is typical of the King's deep concern with every detail of the war, and especially of His Majesty's especial interest in all that affected ships.

"January 3rd, 1917.   York Cottage,
                                                                        Sandringham,
                                                                              Norfolk.

"Dear Lord Curzon,
            "The King is much concerned about the number of women and children travelling at the present moment in the Mediterranean on board British and French ships.

"His Majesty thought, with the Prime Minister away, I might write to you on this important question, especially as you had so much to do with the Shipping Committee.[1]

"The King hears that it is quite astonishing to see the crowds of small children, women, and girls, travelling on nearly every ship that comes and goes through the Suez Canal.

"His Majesty feels that a Commander, who has women and children and babies on his decks, cannot take risks in fighting submarines which he would be inclined to take with only men on board. It might shake the nerves of any man to have so great and unfair a responsibility, and, moreover, it must impair the efficiency of the service.

"His Majesty has also been informed that many people who are obliged to travel, have some difficulty in obtaining passages to or from ports in the Mediterranean.

                                                        "Yours sincerely,
                                                        "Clive Wigram."

[1] Early in 1916 the Shipping Control Committee had been entrusted to Lord Curzon.

A letter from Lord Sydenham[1] on convoys at sea shows a clever anticipation of the system which was to save lives and ships in both the wars, and is especially interesting for its lesson learned from history.

"19.2.17   101 Onslow Square, S.W.
"My dear Lord Curzon,
          "I can well understand how terribly overworked you must be in these difficult times. I must not worry you: but I wanted to ask whether the Admiralty has sufficiently considered organized convoy, which was largely resorted to, in the French wars. The drawbacks are manifest: but in one way the system is more easily worked than in the 18th century. Steamers can keep station. If a convoy of 10 or 12 ships bringing only essentials could be guarded by cruisers and met in near waters by destroyers, one way of overcoming our difficulties would be opened up.
          "A convoy has the advantage that its route can be changed at any time by wireless.
          "In the old days, neutrals took our convoy. There is no reason they should not do so now.
                              "Yours very sincerely,
                                        "Sydenham."

Sir Ian Malcolm, an old friend of George's whom I knew already, wrote about a War Museum.

"20th February 1917.   5 Bryanstone Square, W.
"My dear George,
          "In the midst of our occupations and responsibilities, do find time to look at my article 'A National War Museum' in to-day's *Times* (page 11). I feel sure you will agree that we ought to be starting something of the same kind as this, and I should love to be one of the humble instruments to push it along, if you could indicate the right direction, though I quite realize that you will probably be unable to help.
          "I wonder if I might come and lunch one day from the Foreign Office to be re-introduced to her ladyship and to talk over this thing?
                              "Ever yours,
                                        "Ian Malcolm."

[1] George Sydenham Clarke, Baron Sydenham (1848–1933), author of a standard work on fortification, and works on naval history.

Lord Curzon in his robes as Viceroy of India

Portrait of the author by Speaight

Mr. St. Loe Strachey[1] writes, rather surprisingly, on the subject of war-time diet. There must have been an uncommonly good cook at the hospital he visited!

"Thursday, April 5th, 1917.   Newlands Corner,
                                                Merrow Downs,
                                                        Guildford.

"My dear Curzon,
        "As a member of 'The New East' Committee, I have just received a copy of your message to Japan for our first issue. In the ordinary way I should not have worried you about it, but I am so immensely struck by the message that I must tell you what I feel in regard to it. It says the right thing in exactly the right way and says it with a dignity and impressiveness which is worthy of the occasion and will, I am sure, be greatly appreciated by Japanese readers. It is a piece of true political eloquence, worthy of Wellesley at his best.

"The American situation seems to me to be developing on the very best possible lines. I hope everything is being done to get us the use of the 700,000 tons of German Shipping. I am very happy as to everything connected with the War except the food shortage question, which haunts me. I cannot think why we have not accumulated a store of rice in these Islands. Food experts repeat like parrots that the British people will not eat rice, but that is pure nonsense. I saw 35 patients in our hospital here the other day eating risotto with the very greatest contentment, and discussed the matter with them as I discuss lots of political and economic questions. They were good samples of the new British Army and so of the British people—coming from Wales, Ireland, Scotland, London, everywhere—and they laughed to scorn the notion that our people would not eat rice, pinch or no pinch. If the rice is left unpolished it has all the best elements of food. My Mincing Lane friends tell me that there is any amount of rice to be got at Rangoon and that the price has not risen there though of course it has risen here. I know some rice is being brought in but only for current needs and with no idea of creating a reserve store.
                        "Yours very sincerely,
                                "J. A. St. Loe Strachey."

Letters about the situation in Russia since the Revolution have a

[1] John St. Loe Strachey (1860–1927), proprietor and editor of the *Spectator* 1897–1925.

F

perennial interest. This is one from General (now Sir Alfred) Knox, then our Military Attaché in Petrograd.

"14th Sept., 1917.   Shelbourne Hotel, Dublin.
"Dear Lord Curzon,

"I stopped here a night on my way to Ulster. If one can believe the telegrams from Petrograd, which of course give only the Kerensky[1] version, Kornilov[2] is finished. I am afraid this may be true. He may have been manœuvred into a premature attempt by Kerensky or he may have risked everything on an attempt to restore discipline at once, which he knows is necessary if Russia is to make any pretence of continuing the War.

"Kornilov is a big patriot. I stayed with him at Chernovitse in June. When we were discussing the situation one day he said: 'If the Government makes peace with Germany, I want you to take me as a private soldier in the British Army for I will never be a party to such a peace.'

"Kornilov and his handful of supporters have been playing the Allies' game. If they are hung, as now seems likely, our slackness and lack of moral courage in failing to tell Kerensky and his satellites their duty to the Alliance will be largely to blame.

"Kerensky has now 'got a chance', as the papers say. We should point out to him in unmistakable terms what we demand of the Russian Government. All the Allied representatives should be told to point out that the War has been prolonged a year by the weakness of the Russian Government, and that the cause of democracy in the world, which Kerensky professes to champion, will be put back a generation unless definite steps are taken to restore the Russian Army to its fighting efficiency. There is a danger that there will be a Bolshevik reaction, and if there is God help us and Russia.

"The Russians are orientals and only want a strong hand. Kerensky himself is half a Jew.

"As you know I pressed this course of action when I was called before the War Cabinet, but Mr. Bonar Law did not like it. I do not know on what grounds, for if you consult any of the people at home

[1] Alexander Kerensky (b. 1881) had in July 1917 become Prime Minister in the second Provisional Government, and on the 16th September proclaimed a republic. In November his Government collapsed before the Bolshevik revolution and he fled the country.
[2] Ivar Kornilov (1870–1918) was appointed Supreme Commander-in-Chief by Kerensky, but when he wanted to discipline the demoralized army, Kerensky saw this as an attempt to establish a military dictatorship. A revolt of the 8th–12th September was quashed and Kornilov was imprisoned.

now who know anything of the Russians—Professor Pares, Lockhart (our Consul in Moscow), or Young of the Committee of Imperial Defence, you will find they agree.

"I remained a fortnight in London but could make no headway, so came over here for a week's holiday. I will be a few days in London on my return, before going back to Russia and will come to see you.

"I think the main point is that we should do something *at once*.

"I am so sorry that my writing is so bad. I normally type, but have not got my machine here.

"Yours sincerely,

"Alfred C. Knox.

"P.S.—I believe the Prime Minister would agree if you were to tell him."

This letter from General Sir Charles Townshend, the gallant defender of Kut,[1] is moving, for it was written from a Turkish prison.

"26/December, 1916.   Constantinople.
"My dear Lord Curzon,

"I am so glad to see you are in the new Cabinet and to lead the House of Lords, and at last you have your proper chance in England, which the nation should have given you long ago when you returned from India home. I am glad with all my heart and so much the more so as I am so grateful always for that manly and encouraging letter you wrote me when I was holding the gate of Kut. I pray now, how I pray, to be exchanged. I hope Government will not forget my work and at least try to negotiate with the Turkish Government for my exchange. They had treated me so honourably and I am sure they all like me. *You* can imagine that I am eating my heart out because my career is at stake, there is no man of 30 stronger and more energetic than I am. What do you think of my being able to swim from the island of Halki to Prinkipo! Well I can do it easily, it must be 2 miles—it is more than my swim round St. Michael's Mount in Cornwall in 1895 in a rough sea and that was a record down there at that time.

"Do try and help me, you have always been my friend and you

[1] Kut-al-Imara, town of Iraq on the Tigris, which was besieged by the Turks December 8th, 1915–April 29th, 1916. After the British surrender General Charles Townshend (1861–1924) was held by the Turks until released in October 1918 to make terms with Britain. He was created a K.C.B. for his services, but although he was regarded as a popular hero, his conduct of the siege met with criticism elsewhere and he received no further command.

know I was so grateful for your kindness to my wife while I was shut up in Kut.

"All good luck to you in the New Year. The situation now reminds me of 1801 when Napoleon made his second offer of peace to England after 8 years war in which time we had doubled our commerce, doubled our Navy, and doubled our Colonial possessions including the whole of India!

"It is interesting to remember that Treaty of Peace and the conquests yielded up by both sides.

"I am, my dear Lord Curzon,
"Yours very sincerely,
"Charles Townshend.

"When I do get home I shall offer to go to India again I think if they would give me a good command there, much as I should like a command at home and fond as I am of my 'turnups' in Norfolk. But I have claims on India now, and as sound experience of Indian troops as most men, I fancy, and so I think my knowledge there would be of most use to the State.

"It is not for me to throw asparagus as Arthur Roberts of pious memory used to say, but I should like to observe that a lot of what I saw there in the past three years might be summed up as where the bustle of confusion was mistaken for the authority of business.

"C.V.F.T."

A letter from Oscar Browning[1] is interesting with reference both to the Government, and to the Eton War Memorial scheme, to which George had subscribed. He wrote from Rome on February 27th, 1917:

"My dear George,
        "Your speeches in Parliament are splendid. I am delighted to see how they impress people more and more and are gradually becoming more quoted both in English and American papers than any others. You are virtually the Prime Minister of England. David could do nothing without you and Balfour. He is a genius but not a statesman, and no great country can be well governed except by statesmen—also, a statesman is born and not made. Bismarck once said that the good fortune of England was to be full of *Königliche Persönlichkeiten* which were lacking in Germany.

[1] Oscar Browning (1837–1923), Master at Eton 1860–75, when Lord Curzon was a pupil, and author of numerous historical studies.

Kingly personalities, that is people who take to government as if they were born to it, and who indeed are born to it. I am as you know a Radical and a Democrat but we should get on badly without the blood of the Curzons and the Cecils. Thank Heaven we have it.

"It is very noble of you to give £500 to the Eton Memorial Fund and of your brother Frank whom I take to be the finest character in England, to give £250. But I hope that one effect of this munificence will be that those who contribute so generously will also be allowed to reform the school, and to make it again a nurse of English Statesmen, as it used to be. It has got into a terrible state, but I believe that Reform would never be popular. I don't know whether Allington [sic.] is the man for it, Edward Lyttelton[1] was not. The first thing is to reduce the expenses. The education ought to cost at least £100 a year less, and would be all the better for it. £100 a year for a thousand boys would just make the £100,000 you want. Then hard work, intellectual interest, and a sense of public duty—the education of a statesman. If all were educated like you, George, England would indeed be different. I have heard it said, I think with truth, that Warre[2] had a passionate hatred for intellect, Hornby[3] never had a passionate hatred for anything, except O.B., but he had a mild abhorrence of it. I never worked so hard for anything in my life as I did to make Eton a proper place of education for the Governing Class, and you know the result.

"I am busy writing the History of the World which is both amusing and edifying. I have just killed Gustavus Adolphus and hope this morning to despatch Wallenstein. I send you a poem. Why have you never sent me a copy of your poems? You always used to. . . ."

Reading through the personal letters addressed to George at this time—unlike me, he was a great preserver of documents, of every sort, and kept thousands of letters carefully put away and docketed—I am impressed once more by the terrible toll of young lives exacted by the first war. There was scarcely one of our friends who did not lose a son, a husband, or a brother. Among George's correspondence there are countless letters written in reply to the condolences he had sent to his friends on the loss of their sons. There are letters from Lord Shuttleworth, Lord Albemarle, Lord Falkland, Lord Barnard, Lord Denbigh, Lord Treowen, Lord Kinnaird, the

---

[1] Edward Lyttelton (1855–1942), Head Master of Eton 1905–16.
[2] Edmond Warre (1837–1920), Head Master of Eton 1884–1905.
[3] James John Hornby (1826–1909), Head Master of Eton 1868–84.

Bishop of Derby, Dr. Pember the Warden of All Souls—to mention only a few. In every one of these letters the grief is tempered by pride in their gallant sons who fell fighting for what they felt was a just and righteous cause; and many of them refer to other members of their families, sons and brothers, who were serving in their ships or with their regiments. One, a man in his sixties, records that of the eight male members of his family, only he himself and his nephew of seven years old were not engaged in the fighting. Truly England lost the flower of her young men in those terrible days: and the noble resignation of their parents, as reflected in these letters, is infinitely touching and inspiring.

When George and I returned to Trent after our marriage we had the pleasure of having our six young people with us for the rest of the Christmas holidays. My sons were schoolboys, and my daughter in the nursery; George's eldest daughter was grown up, the second had just left school, and the youngest had a governess. The first party that George and I gave together was a 'coming-of-age' dance for Irene. It was in no sense a ball, as we were then still at war—I don't think that there were more than 150 people altogether. I enjoyed giving this party, and it was great fun. The house was packed with guests, almost to overflowing, and all our friends within motoring distance brought parties. I remember a party of the Salisburys from Hatfield, and one brought by the Desboroughs from Panshanger; and one or two crowded motor coaches brought other guests from London. I remember that Cynthia Hamilton, Lord Lascelles, Lord Spencer, Dick Curzon (now Lord Scarsdale) and many others were staying in the house. Irene was dressed in white, and wore a wreath of green leaves in her hair—she looked lovely. George and I stood and watched her waltzing with Willie de Greune from the Belgian Embassy—Irene waltzed with closed eyes, and they danced beautifully. The next day George and I motored to London, and we were shocked and pained when we saw a placard on a newsboard displayed in Piccadilly—'Curzon's Dance While Europe Burns'. It was distressing to find that our simple little party for Irene's coming of age had been so greatly exaggerated.

The little dinners that I remember with the greatest pleasure were small ones at Trent, of not more than six people. Usually they consisted of Arthur Balfour, Evan Charteris, and Harry Cust—and of course of wonderful women like Ettie Desborough and Mary Wemyss. To dine with George and Harry Cust was a delight—*such* wit! They so thoroughly understood each other, they played into each other's hands, and the ball was always tossed back. I think that if I had wished George to be at his most brilliant, I would have chosen Harry Cust as a guest for the occasion.

Irene had brought her horses to Trent, and Alfred and Hubert had their horses there. They started hunting for the first time, being given a lead by Irene. I don't think it was very good hunting country, in fact the first time the boys were out they killed almost on the tram-lines—but they all three seemed to think it great fun. At the end of the Christmas holidays Alfred went to Eton, and Hubert returned to Wixenford. I began to realize that my boys were growing up, and, like most mothers, I still wished to be needed by them.

Hubert went to Eton a year later than Alfred, being thirteen months younger. Alfred had entered Mr. de Haviland's house, and Hubert Mr. Goodhart's. I always enjoyed my visits to Eton. It was wonderful having both boys there together. I remember an occasion when the Derby meeting clashed with the Fourth of June, and, to George's surprise, I chose to go to Eton. George said to me more than once that I was certainly a devoted mother but he wondered if I was a very wise one!—and he sometimes remarked that I spoiled the children. He thought that I arranged too many theatre parties for them during their holidays. Later, both boys went to Oxford— Alfred to Balliol, Hubert to Christchurch. Hubert, who had always hankered for the Army, left Oxford very soon, as he decided that he wished to join the Life Guards.

When we were living in Carlton House Terrace, where all my rooms overlooked the Mall, I would rush to the window as soon as I heard horses approaching, hoping to see Hubert on the way to the Changing of the Guard at Whitehall—and indeed I was sometimes rewarded, and did recognize him as he rode past.

I kept Trent on for a little over a year after my marriage to George. It was so near London that George could motor up for his Cabinet Meetings. Carlton House Terrace was still closed.

At the time of my marriage my portrait was painted by Mr. Philip de Laszlo.[1] It was a full-length portrait of me in a white evening dress, wearing a tiara. It was thought a good likeness, and generally admired, but George never cared for it. He was extra-ordinarily critical about my portraits, almost unreasonably so, because he could never prevent his personal feelings from interfering with his artistic judgment on this one subject. Before our engagement had been announced, however, Mr. Laszlo had painted a sketch portrait of me in my widow's weeds—the very becoming

[1] Philip de Laszlo (1869–1937), Hungarian painter who became a naturalized British subject, and painted many portraits of the Royal Family, etc.

black bonnet edged and lined with white, which was then *de rigeur* for correct mourning, black draperies, and a big sapphire pectoral cross. George adored this picture, and had a special case made for it, so that he could take it with him wherever he went. He very seldom moved for more than a few days without it, and always had it in his room where he could see it.[1]

Soon after my marriage, my portrait was painted by Sir John Lavery. Again I was wearing white evening dress, and a tiara. When George saw it he was disappointed, and said so. Sir John Lavery seemed to see all his women sitters as elongated and narrow—perhaps because Lady Lavery, whom he often painted, was so tall and thin—and George objected to this version of me, and exclaimed, when he saw the finished portrait, "But what have you done with her curves?" He refused to have the picture, and it now hangs in the National Gallery of Art in Edinburgh, where it is known as The Lady in White.

Some time after we were married, George, who knew Mr. Sargent very well, wrote to ask him if he would paint a portrait of me, although he knew that Mr. Sargent had announced that he would accept no more commissions for portraits. He received a reply regretting that this commission could not be undertaken. However, soon after this, Evan Charteris wrote and asked me to dinner—without George, because he said that he needed only a woman to complete his dinner party. When I arrived, I found that there were only four of us!—Lady Desborough, and Mr. Sargent, as well as myself and our host. The next day Sargent wrote to George, saying, in effect, "Now that I have seen your wife, I have changed my mind, and I do agree to paint her." I gave him many sittings, and George was never allowed to come, much as he wanted to see the progress of the picture. Sargent was adamant on this point, and I did my best to co-operate with him in persuading George to stay away from the studio. When at last the portrait was finished, George went with me to see it. Sargent and I waited in some trepidation for his verdict—at least, I did, because Sargent was a somewhat prickly character who did not care for criticism, and I dreaded some crushing comment from George. George stood for a long time gazing at the portrait, with his back to us as we stood in silence behind him. Then he suddenly turned round to us with the tears running down his face and seized both of Sargent's hands in his own, exclaiming, "But it is ideal—I could not wish for anything better!" My relief was enormous, and Sargent seemed genuinely pleased, as indeed he

---

[1] This portrait is reproduced as the frontispiece of this book.

might be by so spontaneous and heartfelt a tribute. Poor man, he died very soon afterwards, and this portrait of me was hung in the Royal Academy Exhibition of that year with a wreath of laurel leaves as a memorial to this great painter whose last exhibited picture it was.[1]

As well as the Laszlo, the Lavery, and the Sargent portraits of me, there is a portrait by an artist called Bennet, who was a discovery of Alfred de Rothschild's, and became a fashionable Edwardian portrait painter. This again is a picture of me in a white evening dress—it sounds a little monotonous, but on the whole it is preferable to the portraits of women in jodhpurs or djibbahs[2] which succeeded them at Burlington House—and is very large indeed; it now hangs at Kedleston. At about the same time he painted a charming portrait of Vita Sackville-West, Harold Nicolson's wife, in the character of Portia, and they were exhibited at the same Summer Exhibition of the Royal Academy.

Not long after my marriage to George I went with my daughter Marcella to have our photographs taken by Alice Hughes, who was a fashionable photographer of that time. She was struck by the beauty of Marcella—who was a most lovely child—and exclaimed, in raptures, "Oh, Lady Curzon, those wonderful Mary Leiter[3] eyes!" I was somewhat amused, and explained that Marcella was my daughter, and that the lovely blue eyes were a Duggan feature.

At about this time, or soon afterwards, I went with George to a great dinner at which there were a number of Indian Maharajahs. I was placed between two of them, and the one on my right was a charming old man who had become a little shortsighted and forgetful. He said to me at the very beginning of dinner, "How delightful it is, Lady Curzon, to see after all these years that you look just the same, and have not altered at all." I was quite taken aback by this, although of course I did not betray my surprise to my neighbour, and while talking to him I managed to scribble a note to George and sent it to him. I received a note from George in reply, saying simply "Do not undeceive him." So I talked away to the old Maharajah for the rest of dinner, and he remained happily under the impression that I was Mary, George's first wife whom he had last seen many years before, in India.

---

[1] A reproduction of the Sargent portrait appears between pages 184–185.

[2] *Djibbah* or *jibbeh*, the long cloth coat with sleeves worn by Egyptian Mohammedans.

[3] Mary Victoria Leiter (*d.* 1906), daughter of the American millionaire Levi Leiter, whom Lord Curzon married as his first wife in 1895.

CHAPTER IX

The Belgian Royal Family. The End of the War

GEORGE, and Mary, his wife, had met King Albert and Queen Elisabeth of the Belgians in the South of France, and they had become friends. This was on their return from India. When Belgium was overrun by the Germans in 1914 George had sent a telegram to the King of the Belgians, putting Hackwood at his disposal. The King had accepted the offer with gratitude, and he and the Queen sent their three children to live there, with their governess and their nurse. Docile Prince Leopold went to Eton; naughty, merry Prince Charles went to Wixenford, and they spent their holidays at Hackwood, where their flaxen-haired little sister Princess Marie-José remained with her governess. George's two younger daughters were there, too, with a governess of their own. The King and Queen of the Belgians used often to come over for a brief visit to their children during the war. They stayed with us in London, too.

On one occasion, not long after my marriage to George, I answered the telephone, and asked, "Who is it?" A voice replied, "The King of the Belgians." It never entered my head that it was really the King—I merely thought it was one of my friends attempting to be funny, and so I cheerfully answered: "Is it really? And this is Queen Anne!" However, I quickly realized that it was in fact King Albert, whose aircraft had developed some defect when he was about to fly back to Belgium, and who wanted to stay with us for the night. He and Queen Elisabeth always stayed with us on their frequent visits to England to see their children. It was a considerable anxiety to have the King as a guest in London, because he objected to any arrangements being made for his security, and insisted on going about quite by himself and walking for miles on his own. Often, when he had been absent for some hours, we were almost in a panic by the time he returned. He was very conspicuous and an easily recognized figure, being immensely tall, and of course his appearance was well known to the public because his photograph had appeared so frequently in the newspapers. However, nothing untoward ever happened to him in the course of his rambles about London, but we were always very uneasy when he was out of the house.

One of Queen Elisabeth's many kindnesses to me was to send over an orchestra from Belgium to perform at a concert which I organized at the Albert Hall at the end of the war in aid of the Red Cross. This was the Orchestre Symphonique de l'Armée Belge en Campagne, and consisted of a hundred and nineteen Belgian soldiers. They arrived by air—all the hundred and nineteen of them—and in those days this was considered quite a remarkable feat of air transport. The concert was a great success. It took place on the 10th of July, 1918, and three Queens were present at it—Queen Mary, Queen Alexandra, and Queen Elisabeth of the Belgians. Sir Henry Newbolt wrote a poem specially for the occasion, which was printed at the beginning of the programme; and, between the two parts of the performance, George made a speech on the Glory of Belgium. It was an excellent speech, in which he surveyed the progress of the war— he was then a Member of the War Cabinet—and was much applauded. The orchestra played the César Franck Symphony in D Minor and the Egmont Overture of Beethoven; and Madame d'Alvarez and Mr. Basil Radford sang. The Red Cross benefited very substantially from this concert, and I felt most grateful to Queen Elisabeth for her airborne military musicians.

The King of the Belgians did not go to the concert, but he and the Queen were staying with us at Carlton House Terrace, as a most interesting ceremony had been arranged to take place on the following day. This was the presentation of the Honorary Degree of D.C.L. to the King of the Belgians by a Deputation from the University of Oxford. This consisted of Dr. Blakiston, the Vice-Chancellor, Mr. H. A. James of St. John's, Dr. R. W. Macan the Master of University College, Mr. C. Lenzedorf the University Registrar, Mr. F. H. Hall the Senior Proctor, Mr. Rowland Protheroe the Member for the University—and George, the Chancellor. I was fascinated by the dignified ceremonial, and deeply interested to see, for the first time, George in his role of Chancellor of the University. The ceremony took place in our large drawing-room on the first floor, overlooking the Mall. The Queen of the Belgians and I watched it all from the doorway of the Empire Room, next door to it. (This most charming small room, octagonal in shape, was devoted entirely to George's remarkable collection of Napoleonic relics. The bookshelves contained his collection of books on Napoleon, the furniture was all French of the Empire period, and the walls were hung with prints and framed documents of great historical interest. The whole contents of this room were left by George in his Will to the University of Oxford, and are now in the

Bodleian Library, assembled together as one unit, in accordance with his wishes.)

When the ceremony of conferring the Honorary Degree was over, the Queen turned to me and said, most unexpectedly, "Now there is something to be given to you." To my complete surprise she decorated me then and there with her own special Order, the Order of Elisabeth of Belgium. I was naturally delighted.

The King and Queen of the Belgians were very simple, cheerful guests when they stayed with us at Hackwood and in London, quite informal in their tastes and habits, always making jokes and ragging the children at luncheon, and both of them liked everything to be as unceremonious and natural as it could be. I was therefore immensely surprised to find how completely different they were, in manners and behaviour, at home in their Palace of Laeken. George and I were asked to pay them a visit there in 1920, on our way to the Conference at Spa.[1] A rather comic incident occurred at the beginning of that journey. We were about to embark at Dover in the Ostend boat, when we were forestalled by a large and rowdy party of men, who turned out to be Horatio Bottomley[2] and a lot of his boon companions. George and I were politely requested by some officials to stand back and allow them to precede us on board, Bottomley then being regarded as quite a power in the land. George, who was merely the Secretary of State for Foreign Affairs, had not been recognized. This amused him enormously.

At Laeken, everything was formal and ceremonious to the last degree. The royal children were never allowed to utter a word at meals unless they were addressed by one of their parents, etiquette of the most elaborate kind prevailed, conversation was solemn and serious, and yet it was a completely domestic occasion, with no other guests except ourselves. Long, formal meals, formal conversations, formal walks and drives—it was all rather like a grave and stately minuet that went on from morning until night. It made George very restless, but it was impossible to escape from it for a moment. One afternoon when we were having a breather in the sitting-room which had been given us, tea was brought in—and immediately afterwards

[1] Spa Conference, July 5th–16th, 1920, between the representatives of the Allies and Germany, at which it was attempted to put into effect the provisions of the Versailles Peace Treaty.

[2] Horatio Bottomley (1860–1933), company promoter and journalist, who exposed public and private scandals in his journal *John Bull*. He was expelled from the House of Commons on August 1st, 1922, following his conviction for fraudulent conversion.

there was a tap on the door, and the kind Queen appeared, saying that she had come to pour it out for us.

I have always followed, with much interest and concern, the lives of those three children of the King and Queen of the Belgians who spent so much of their childhood at Hackwood. Prince Leopold, always a serious, quiet boy, became King, and abdicated after the Second War in favour of his son. Prince Charles, the gay and irresponsible younger brother who was such a merry child, became a splendid and popular Regent during the minority of King Leopold's son; and the little golden-haired Princess Marie-José married the Prince of Piedmont,[1] who was to succeed for so short a time to the throne of Italy. Now she lives in Portugal, a Queen in exile with her husband, and her daughter has lately married a son of Prince Paul of Yugoslavia—another old friend of ours. In imagination I can still see them all playing happily with my step-daughters in the sunny gardens at Hackwood.

Just four months after the concert with the Belgian orchestra at the Albert Hall, the end of the First War came—the unforgettable day of the Armistice, in 1918. It so happened that on November 11th George and I were staying with Lord Derby[2] at our Embassy in Paris. We had gone there for a short visit, and it was only by chance that we were there on the dramatic day when the war ended. I had travelled to Paris a day or two in advance of George, and stayed at the Ritz until he joined me and we went to stay at the British Embassy. A letter to my sister about this journey shows how comparatively easy it was to travel from England to France during the First War.

"November 7th, 1918.   Ritz Hotel, Paris.
My dearest Dot,
        I have written to Mother, and asked her to send the letter on to you. Mr. Lord, the Station Master at Charing Cross, secured me the end coupé in the Pullman and saw me off. I was met by Captain Brooke Greville at Folkestone Harbour Station, who passed me through the Home Office Bureau and saw me on board the transport ship. I had a very good cabin but stayed on deck the whole time. I was met at Boulogne by M. Troc, the Belgian Sûreté Agent,

---

[1] Umberto II (*b.* 1904), the last king of Italy, who succeeded on the abdication of his father Victor Emmanual III on May 9th, 1946, and himself abdicated on June 13th and left the country. He married Princess Marie-José in 1930.

[2] Edward G. V. Stanley, 17th Earl of Derby (1865–1948), British Ambassador in Paris 1918–20 and Secretary of State for War 1916–18 and 1922–24.

and by the British Reception Officer, and taken in their car to the
Folkestone Hotel, where we dined. Ambrose must know this hotel,
as it was crowded with our officers. I had a sleeping berth on the
night train to Paris, but the line was very rough and I could not
sleep. I arrived at 7.30 this morning. Everyone in Paris is very gay,
and seems to think the War is over! The streets are still very dark at
night, much more so than in London. You have never seen anything
so short as the dresses!—small hats, and only dark colours. . . ."

Lady Derby was in England at the time of our visit to Lord
Derby, but their daughter Lady Victoria Primrose was staying at
the Embassy. (She was the widow of Lord Rosebery's son, who had
been killed in Palestine two years before.) George and I were the
only guests. I shall never forget the excitement that prevailed in
Paris on November 11th. At eleven o'clock that morning the guns
began to boom—it was Victory, and everyone at once poured out of
houses and shops and offices into the streets. Soon all the main
thoroughfares were completely blocked with the crowds, and traffic
was practically at a standstill. Lord Derby had to go to the Chambre
des Députés to hear Clemenceau make the official announcement of
Victory, and his car could scarcely move through the cheering
crowds that packed the Faubourg St. Honoré outside the Embassy—
they were, however, largely a crowd of English people in Paris who
had come to catch a glimpse of the British Ambassador, for the
French were not in the least concerned with anyone's contribution
to victory except their own. This was the one aspect of the Paris
rejoicings that we all found very galling. When Lord Derby returned
from the Chambre des Députés he told us that in his speech
Clemenceau had made no reference at all to England, Belgium,
America, or any of the Allies—he had simply concluded with the
words, "*La France à remporté la victoire.*" It was the same wherever one
went. The tricolor was everywhere, naturally—but not a single
British flag was to be seen among all the vast display of bunting.
(Lord Derby had sent for some, but they had not arrived, and the
French had not produced a single one.) The King of the Belgians
was in Paris—he had come to discuss the Armistice terms, and had a
talk with George about them—and he, too, must have been grieved
by the absence of any Belgian flags. In spite of this, however, we felt
that in a way we were fortunate to be in Paris when the war came
to an end—we felt closer to it all than we would have felt in London.
It was an intensely moving occasion. George and I went out into the
streets that night, and the scenes of gay rejoicing were unforgettable,

with people dancing in the street, and singing and cheering. The feeling of relief was overwhelming.

The next day there was a gay little episode at the Embassy which I am afraid rather annoyed Lord Derby. He had gone to Elysée Palace to visit the President, when a huge crowd of British soldiers turned up in the Embassy courtyard in very good spirits, clamouring to see the British Ambassador in order to have some real English rejoicing in victory. They came from the Leave Club which was run by Miss Decima Moore, a member of a distinguished theatrical family, who was afterwards Lady Moore-Guggisberg. She accompanied them, and obviously they all adored her, their fairy-godmother of the Leave Club. In the absence of Lord Derby, George, who happened to be in when they all arrived, went out to greet them as he felt that they ought not to be disappointed. He stood on the steps leading up to the Embassy front door from the courtyard and made a speech to them about the victory—a longish speech, and a very good one, which they wildly applauded. Miss Decima Moore was so delighted that she warmly embraced George, and the Tommies burst out spontaneously into "For He's a Jolly Good Fellow!" At this point Lord Derby returned from his call at the Elysée Palace, and was not best pleased when he realized that the men probably all thought that George was the Ambassador! However, Lord Derby's well-known good humour was never disturbed for long. He gave luncheon parties and dinner parties at the Embassy while we were staying with him, and we met many old friends, and some new ones. I remember Helen D'Abernon, Malcolm Bullock (then an Honorary Attaché, who afterwards married Lord Derby's daughter Victoria), the Pembrokes, the Lyttons, General Sir John Du Cane (Chief of the British Staff to Marshal Foch), and Admiral George Hope.

The King of the Belgians was to make his State Entry into Brussels on the Saturday after Armistice Day, and he had invited George and me to be present on this occasion which meant so much to him, and to drive in the procession. It was difficult for us to accept this invitation, for George's Cabinet duties required his return to London, and, much as we longed to see the King return triumphantly to his Capital, in the end it proved impossible. The Belgian Government had sent a car to take us from Paris to Belgium, and the French Government also provided a car for us to go up to the Front line and have the unique experience—for English civilians—of seeing the trenches and the battle area where the fighting had only just stopped. We stayed the night at Lille, in a hotel which had been used as their

Headquarters by the German Army until only a short time before—I was actually given the room that had been occupied by the German General commanding that area, and felt that it was haunted by his hateful presence. We were driven up to the silent trenches, and indeed it was a most moving, terrible, and unforgettable experience. It was so soon after the Cease Fire that the guns were still hot—I felt them with my hand—and we saw at last the trenches and the dug-outs that had occupied so much of our thoughts for four years. In some of them still lay the bodies of the dead that awaited burial. In a way perhaps it was just as well that we had to return straight to England and could not go to Brussels for the triumphal entry of the King of the Belgians—for after what we had seen it would have been hard to change to a mood of gaiety.

At the end of the war my brother Trillia was very ill, as a result of his war service. He had been badly gassed, and had never recovered in spite of long periods of sick leave—in one of which he accompanied me to the Argentine in 1916. He had served in France with the Northamptonshire Regiment—with evident enthusiasm, as this letter to my Mother shows. It was the first letter that he wrote to her from the Front.

"17th June, 1915.   2nd Battn., Northamptonshire Regt.
24th Brigade,
8th Division.

My dearest Mother,
        Here I am at last! We entrained yesterday from Havre and arrived at our last railway station at 4.30 to-day. The journey was not over comfortable as it was so frightfully hot in the day and cold last night, but the scenery was lovely. Since about 2 p.m. to-day I have heard the firing, and now that I am less than two miles from the trenches I am going into on Friday, I have all the old keenness I had before getting my Commission. I am writing in a billet (the dirtiest little hut I have ever seen!) and firing is going on like thunder. Some building or something had caught fire near by, and the sky is all lit up. I have met several friends here and am *quite* happy, so please do not worry about me. I shall be in the trenches for six days, then, come out for six days. When in trenches, I shall sleep in a 'dug-out'. I have had very little sleep lately, Mother, and it is now half-past ten and I must be up at 5.30., so please excuse this . . ."

Trillia never recovered from the effects of the gas. He spent many months in a sanatorium at Leysin, in Switzerland, after the

An Alice Hughes portrait of the author

Lord and Lady Curzon at Balliol College, Oxford

The author with King Albert at the wedding of Lady Cynthia Curzon to
Sir Oswald Mosley

war, with my Mother at his bedside. I often visited him there, and I was with him in the autumn of 1919 when his illness had taken a desperate turn, and stayed until the doctor pronounced him to be out of danger. My letters from Leysin to George contain nothing but anxious accounts of his illness. George was full of sympathy for my brother, and used to write amusing letters to him in his desire to cheer up the poor invalid who was cut off from the rest of the family life. This is one that he wrote to Leysin from Cannes, where George and I had been enjoying a short holiday in the spring of 1920—at any rate, *I* had enjoyed it, even if George did not, as his letter shows!

"Feb. 2, 1920.   Le Grand Hotel, Cannes.
My dear Trillia,

This is our last night at Cannes, and we are packing up. I put this along with some photos sent you by Gracie. We have had some dull chill days here, but about 5 days' glorious sunshine and are returning much the better. Gracie likes the Casino and dancing and polo and Cannes social life much better than I do. I feel rather like a Bishop in Regent Circus at midnight. In the crowd that dance the greater part of the day and night at the Casino and in the Hotels it is difficult to distinguish the professional dancers (into whose hands ladies squeeze 40 francs) from the amateur, or the lady pleasure seeker from the cocotte. All rub shoulders together and affect a frivolity which few in reality feel.

Ambrose[1] is a great local success, his tennis being excellent, his dancing good, his manners unimpeachable and his silence unbroken.

Gracie and I have driven about the neighbourhood and looked for villas which are not to be found except at a ruinous outlay. She is in the top of her form and looks amazingly well.

We often think of you and Mother. Gracie will be with you before long, bringing a breath of good spirits and affection.

How I loathe returning to the worry and fatigue of Office and Parliament and the eternal round.

All love to you both.

Yours affectionately,

G."

Ever since the original Armistice Day celebrations which we had chanced to see in Paris, George had been meditating and planning a great formal celebration of victory to take place in London. His

[1] My brother-in-law, Colonel Ambrose Dudley.

G

imagination had been fired by the impromptu decorations that the gay, talented Parisians had produced at a moment's notice, and, with his great instinct for showmanship and stately display he worked out the details of a splendid piece of pageantry for London. The result of all this thought and planning was the Victory March in July 1919, that historic parade of the Forces and the leaders and the statesmen of the Empire and the Allies. I watched it from my seat on the stand, which had been erected as a saluting base for the King, and it was impressive indeed.

It is to George's imaginative genius for ceremonial that we owe the annual Armistice Day service at the Cenotaph, with the roll of drums, the two minutes' silence, and then the guns. Few people realize that this moving ceremony, so much a part of our national life after all these years, originated in his mind. Alas, I was unable to be present when it was inaugurated in November 1920. My brother Trillia was dying at Kedleston, and my Mother and my sister and I were with him. He died on the day that I had planned to go to London for the Cenotaph ceremony.

CHAPTER X

Entertaining, in London and at Hackwood

TOWARDS the end of the war we started entertaining at George's London house, 1 Carlton House Terrace. This charming house, the corner one at the eastern end of the Terrace—it is now the Savage Club—was ideal for giving big parties and receptions, with its fine hall and staircase, its large rooms with the excellent proportions that Nash's designs had provided, and its wonderful outlook over the Mall to the trees and grass of St. James's Park. Of course, when we first started to entertain there it was looking decidedly shabby and badly in need of doing up, as it had been used all through the war as the offices of the Belgian Relief Fund, and the ballroom had been used by George for the meetings of the various important committees over which he had presided. I tackled the problem of redecoration the moment it was possible to do this after the war—it was much easier then than it was after the Second War to have such things done, as there were no restrictions such as coupons for curtain material and 'quotas' for decorators' bills—and, room by room, the house took life and became a really delightful place in which to entertain. One of the first rooms that I had redecorated was the ballroom, which had lovely proportions and four long windows overlooking the entrance, and opening on to a balcony. I very much enjoyed planning and supervising the colour schemes for the various rooms—George, of course, had beautiful furniture, and so it was only a question of doing up the rooms in order to make a fresh and more cheerful background—and I was helped by a clever young decorator whom I employed, called White Allom.

Once the house was in order, I concentrated on important details such as flowers, food, music, linen—everything that makes for comfort and a gay, charming, welcoming atmosphere for one's guests when one entertains. I have a strong feeling for the personality of a house and I have always tried to make my houses welcoming and, as far as possible, beautiful. I don't in the least regret the amount of time that I have spent in my life on the arrangement of houses, and on the flowers, the menus, choosing lovely linen in Paris, working out schemes to ensure that each party was, as far as possible, a

99

success—because a pleasant and well-run house gives a great deal of pleasure to a large number of people, as well as being a source of delight to those who live in it.

George was almost as much concerned as I was with the details of organizing our houses, although in a rather different way. His passion for detail extended to the most trivial domestic matters. He was never content to leave to our secretary, our housekeeper, and our excellent butler the matters that would ordinarily have fallen on them to decide, but insisted on dealing with many small household arrangements himself. For instance, he once sent for me to join him in the hall at Carlton House Terrace to help him to choose footmen from a number of young men who had been recommended for the position. The candidates were made to walk up and down while we observed their gait with critical eyes; their deportment was noted, and we even inspected their hands, with a view to what these would look like when holding plates and dishes. (I must admit that the candidates did not appear to resent this inspection, or to find it in the least derogatory, but that was thirty years ago. If anything of the sort happened to-day, there would be letters to Members of Parliament and the Press, and it would be considered almost justifiable grounds for a revolution.) I remember that one detail of our Carlton House Terrace and Hackwood arrangements of those days was the footmen wearing knee-breeches if there were fourteen or more guests to dinner, and trousers when there were less than that number. I don't know why George fixed upon fourteen as the size of a party that called for the formality of the knee-breeches—I suppose he felt that a dinner party of twelve was a domestic sort of occasion, and that anything larger amounted to serious entertaining.

George had strong views about food, which were rather different from mine, and he was not easily satisfied, except when he was given certain very simple things which he was fond of. One of these was a dull pudding with jam inside and a meringue top, called Queen of Puddings, which he would have liked me to order for dinner parties. Another was seed cake. He complained that he never had proper seed cake, until my Mother, who was living in Eaton Place, happened to get a cook who made it to perfection. She used to send a seed cake to George every week, and he ate it with butter, which he said was an old North country custom, and evidently enjoyed it. He liked all the teatime food—cakes, and jam, which I never cared for—and insisted on vast quantities of jam and marmalade being made every year in the still room, and used to go and inspect it in the dark cupboards where it was stored. (He had, after all, written from Wixenford as a small boy to his mother to send him from Kedleston "several pots of superior jam, including, *mark me*, apricot, etc.")

He used to complain quite often that our French chef did not cook ordinary English dishes properly. 'Greasy French cooking' was a favourite term of contempt which he used to describe poor Chambon's best efforts. However, on one occasion when Chambon was away and was temporarily replaced by the Granards' chef, he complained even more, and himself telegraphed to Chambon to return immediately, because in his first three days the Granards' chef had given him noisettes, tournedos, and custard. One of the things that he particularly objected to was the temporary chef's kedgeree. I was not at home when all this happened, but I can quite imagine that if the chef made the kedgeree into a 'greasy French dish'—like a risotto, perhaps!—George would have disliked it intensely.

He used to go into every detail of the household accounts, and sometimes these were presented to him by our secretary in a misleading form that made him suppose our expenses to be insanely extravagant. For instance, he wrote to me when I was travelling to the Argentine in the autumn of 1923 that "during July the cost of each person in this house, servants included (for food alone), was £5 each per week! Yet if they were on board wages they would get 16/- each week". George had of course failed to realize that Wyliman—the secretary—had simply added up the food bills for the month and divided the total by the number of people actually living in the house, without taking into account that in July we had had numbers of big luncheon and dinner parties, not to mention suppers for receptions and a ball. No wonder it averaged a startlingly large sum per week!

One of George's particular dislikes in the way of food I discovered by chance, the first time that I went to Kedleston. He was showing me the house, and when we came to the old schoolroom in the 'family wing' he told me how much he had hated tapioca pudding, and how, when they had it for luncheon, he would scoop up his plateful into his handkerchief when nobody was looking and conceal it until they had all finished eating. Then he would dispose of it, handkerchief and all, by stuffing it into a hole in the wall. We looked for the hole in the wall, but repairs had been carried out since those days, and the hole no longer existed. Of course all children do positively loathe tapioca pudding, and with good reason—but I always felt that this was a rather touching little story of poor George's grim schoolroom days. They had all been dreadfully bullied by an ogress of a governess, who seems to have been almost maniac. When little George fell into the pond and was pulled out cold and soaked, she beat him mercilessly all the way back to the house, and said, "You should thank God you have been saved from a watery grave!" I do so hate children to be made unhappy or even uncomfortable, and I hate to think of George's childhood.

One final example of George's concern with details of household management has only just come to my notice. In reading the letters which I wrote to him from my voyage to South America in 1923, I find, written in pencil on the back of one of the envelopes in George's writing, the words 'Bacon. Marmalade'. They must have been written at breakfast, when he had finished reading my letter. Now one thing that George—for all his passion for detail—never had to make was a shopping list of groceries! So I assume that he had not liked the bacon and the marmalade that he had had that morning for breakfast, and had made an instant note to remind him to speak about it. He was extremely fussy about his breakfast food. Often, when I was having my breakfast in bed at Carlton House Terrace— reading my letters, talking to my maid about my clothes for the day, and probably having my nails done at the same time—George would appear, in his dressing-gown, holding a plate and saying reproachfully, "Look, Gracie, my egg is again far too hard,"—or, alternatively, "quite undercooked." Remembering these occasions, I can see him in imagination making a note on my envelope about the bacon, which must have been either hard, or undercooked. But I wonder what can have been wrong with the marmalade?

George's taste in drinks was even more restricted than his tastes in food. He did not care for spirits, except brandy-and-soda occasionally—whisky he had a positive horror of—and he did not like port, or sherry. He never drank anything at all at luncheon, but at dinner he drank champagne, which he liked. He had a quite remarkable head, and could drink any amount of champagne without it ever having the slightest effect on him. When he sat up late at night dealing with the Foreign Office boxes he was always provided with chocolate and a bottle of champagne. I used to get a special kind of chocolate that he liked from Rumpelmayers' in St. James's Street, the fashionable tea-shop that once existed where there is now Prunier's Restaurant. (Eventually I noticed with amusement that the packets of the chocolate that I ordered for George were labelled "as supplied to the House of Lords"!) George used to sit up very late dealing with the Foreign Office boxes, and would never go to bed until he had been through every one. They used to arrive in a tall pile, fastened together with a strap, and he would settle down to deal with them no matter how late it was. (I thought of George's conscientious habits in this matter when, soon after his death, I met the Stanley Baldwins at Aix-les-Bains, where, in deep mourning, I was staying with my daughter Marcella. Mrs. Baldwin told me that she was determined that her husband should not be troubled by anything unnecessary when he was having a holiday that he greatly needed, and that she would never let him see the red boxes until she herself had looked through them to see which contained anything of real importance. It was at this time that Mrs. Baldwin asked me to tell her where I got my hats, and I told her that they came from Reboux, in Paris. Afterwards Mme Caroline, of Reboux, who always attended to me, told me that Mrs. Baldwin had been to her but that it had been difficult to provide her with the triumphant kind of hats that she wanted.)

At Carlton House Terrace we used the ballroom for all large official dinner parties. One of the first that we gave there was for members of the House of Lords, George being the Leader of the House. We had returned from Cannes two days before this party, and I had brought back boxes and boxes of mimosa, which had been beautifully packed and remained fresh and fragrant. I had the mimosa banked all over the house, and its delicious scent filled the hall and greeted the guests as they arrived. The curtains in the hall, and the furniture, were of old-gold brocade, and so the effect of the mimosa with this background was perfect. This great dinner took place the night before the opening of Parliament, and was the first I had arranged since my marriage to George. I received the guests with George, but I had to go out for dinner, as this dinner was for peers only, and George read the King's Speech to them afterwards. It was a charming sight to see them arriving in court dress with their cocked hats—one of the picturesque things that I remember with pleasure. The next day I received kind notes of thanks and praise from many of the guests—and also a complaint that some of the small gold chairs were damaged by the weight of those who had sat on them! They were small chairs, and some of the peers were very large. We had been obliged to hire the chairs, as so many had been needed. Before we gave another very large party we had bought our own chairs.

At Carlton House Terrace we always used the ballroom for large dinners. The room on the ground floor where we had small luncheons and dinners could accommodate twenty-four at most. It was a very pleasant room, looking out to the front of the house, and was hung with lovely black and white velvet curtains from Italy, and a fine collection of prints which George had made when he was still up at Oxford. I had two round tables in it—the malachite one that I was very fond of, and another one of mahogany—that held twelve people at each. But when we had one of our big dinners, sometimes of sixty people, the ballroom had to be used. I used to arrange these dinners at separate tables for small numbers of guests, and at first I had different coloured roses arranged on each table, and the guests were told that their places would be at the 'red rose table', or at the 'yellow rose table'. At these big dinners, I had a table plan displayed in the hall where all our guests could see it when they arrived, and when they received their 'take-in-to-dinner' cards, they found a table plan printed on the back of them, with an X to mark their own place at the particular table where they would sit. I had to give up the idea of different-coloured roses to distinguish each table when the parties were so large that there were not enough varieties of roses to meet the occasion, and so I had the tables described as 'between the first and second windows', or 'on the left of the fireplace'. These arrangements made all the difference when moving a mass of fifty or sixty dinner guests from the drawing-room to their proper places for dinner, and saved endless delay and confusion.

1 Carlton House Terrace was always an 'open house' to our friends on the occasion of the State Opening of Parliament, the Trooping of the Colour, or any other great processions down the Mall. I would have a cold buffet in the small dining-room, and have chairs and rugs arranged on the terrace overlooking the Mall. It was a perfect place from which to watch these wonderful processions.

I always thoroughly enjoyed a State Opening of Parliament. The scene in the House of Lords on the entrance of the Sovereign is one of the most impressive that I have ever witnessed. Alas, I no longer have this privilege, as there is now no room for dowagers. I am not exactly a dowager, but the widow of a peer—the name of Curzon of Kedleston dies with me, and the peerage becomes extinct. However, I had my place with others of my rank in the Abbey for Queen Elizabeth's Coronation. Being a Grand Dame of the British Empire, an honour which I am proud of having received from King George V, I was accorded my seat in the Abbey. I never expect to see again so moving, so inspiring a ceremony. As I watched our beautiful young Queen in all her touching dignity I was moved to the heart, and found tears in my eyes.

One of my greatest pleasures was to attend the House of Lords when George was to speak. He was the best speaker I have ever heard. His voice, his diction, the natural ease of his remarkable vocabulary, always enthralled me. George succeeded Lord Lansdowne as Leader of the House of Lords on Lord Lansdowne's retirement. This was at the time of Mr. Asquith's Coalition. George remained Leader in Mr. Lloyd George's Coalition Government, Mr. Bonar Law's Government, Mr. Baldwin's Government, and was Leader of the Opposition in the House of Lords when Mr. Ramsay MacDonald came to Office; and he was again Leader of that House when Mr. Baldwin was returned as Prime Minister for the second time. I can remember a few occasions when I suffered for George in the House of Lords. I think the Member who caused me most distress on George's behalf was the late Lord Carson, when he attacked George on an Irish question. Lord Carson had not long been a Member of the Upper House, and I thought his manner rather violent. George, however eloquent, never became heated. Even to hear him give an order to one of the staff was for me a real lesson in elocution. I suffer from poverty of language, and to listen to his wonderful rich flow of words always delighted me.

My social activities in those days were not always confined to our own houses. I remember a Ball that I organized at Lansdowne House in aid of the Queen's District Nurses. Lansdowne House in Berkeley Square, designed by Robert Adam, was a masterpiece of English eighteenth-century architecture, with its tall porticoes and classic pillars. The beautiful rooms were perfect for a large ball. It belonged at that time to Mr. Gordon Selfridge, who lent it for the ball, and who also generously provided the supper. The band was a celebrated American one, and its services, too, were given for the charity without any fee. The leader of the band received a letter of thanks from Queen Alexandra. The King of Spain and the Prince of Wales came to this ball, and decorations were worn. It was considered a great success. The Committee consisted of the Marchioness of Crewe, the Countess of Pembroke and Montgomery, the Countess of Ancaster, Lady Tree, and myself. The tickets were sold from 1 Carlton House Terrace, and they could all have been sold twice over. I was able to give the Queen's Nurses £1,000—quite a large sum in those days.

George's second daughter, Cynthia, was eighteen years of age when I married George. She had just left a school near Eastbourne, and when we moved to Carlton House Terrace she started working at the War Office, which she went on doing until she married Oswald Mosley.[1] The first ball given at Carlton House Terrace was

---

[1] Oswald Mosley (b. 1896), who succeeded his father as 6th Baronet in 1928, and is sometimes referred to as 'Tom' Mosley. He married Lady Cynthia Curzon, the second daughter of Lord Curzon, in 1920.

for Cynthia's coming out. I think it was the only ball there at which George was present since the one he had given before the war for Irene. He was ill at the time of Baba's coming-out ball, which took place at a much later date. Cynthia was a very lovely girl, she was fair, and George always said she looked the most Curzon of his three daughters. She was happy and unaffected, and my three children soon became devoted to her. I presented her at Court with real pride, she had so much of George. Her coming-out ball was a very delightful party.

I always took particular trouble to see that the flowers were lovely when we gave a big party. The hothouses and the gardens at Hackwood provided them, as a rule, to perfection. I also liked to have music in the background at a big dinner, and I used to engage Cassano's orchestra to play outside the room when we were dining. One of the problems which I solved was the question of cocktails before dinner. In those days, just at the end of the 1914 War, cocktails were considered rather an innovation where formal entertaining was concerned, but many of the younger people liked them, and they helped to make a party 'go'. I knew that it would have caused delays and complications upstairs if they had been handed round in the drawing-room before dinner, and so I decided to have a cocktail bar in a room off the hall, where our guests could have a drink before coming up to the drawing-room. The first time that I arranged this, I had it all done by Buck's Club, and men in white coats with cocktail shakers were stationed behind a bar in the room on the ground floor. George, making a tour of inspection before the party, discovered this and could not imagine what it was for, because I had forgotten to tell him about it. He said to one of the men, "Who are you?" and the man replied, "We're Bucks, my lord." This mystified George completely, and the man went on, "Will your lordship have a cocktail?" George then rose to the occasion, and asked, "What have you got?" A White Lady was suggested, and George had one, which he swallowed without comment, and I don't think that he ever had another cocktail in his life.

I also had an oyster bar on other occasions, and once it saved the day, as all the electric lights failed just before dinner when we were having a big party. The bar was crowded with our guests when the lights went out, and they had received their oysters—and the brief blackout was the cause of much merriment as practically the entire Cabinet and their wives were herded together happily eating oysters in the dark until the lights came on again.

Our big parties were not always formal, official affairs. Once I gave a very gay party for young people, choosing a day when George had to be at Oxford on University business. The Prince of Wales was there, and everyone thought it a very cheerful party and there were jokes about what George would say if he were present. Suddenly a dignified figure, leaning on a stick, ascended the stairs. I ran down to greet him with a kiss, and as he looked round at the gay scene he said in George's characteristic voice, "My dear girl, I don't call this a party, I call it a debauch!" But my guests were soon undeceived— it was not George, but Malcolm Bullock, and the little deception had been carefully prepared. The great Willy Clarkson, the theatrical costumier, with his preparations ready in one of the upstairs rooms, had made up Malcolm to resemble George. The speech was the sort of thing that we liked to think that George would have said, for he always played up at a party and delighted in acting his own public self, although in private he could be as gay as any school-boy.

When George heard this story on his return from Oxford he was immensely amused. Others, however, may perhaps have been shocked, for shortly afterwards we received an enquiry from the highest quarters asking if it was true that Malcolm Bullock had carried his impersonation so far as to wear George's Garter. Luckily I was able to answer that this venerable object had not been frivolously employed. Malcolm had worn a blue ribbon across his shirt front, and a theatrical star provided by Clarkson.

The Prince of Wales was always happier and more in his element at a party of this sort than at a more formal one. I remember an occasion when the Prince came to a large and rather important dinner and did not wear his Garter. George, who had on his own Garter, wrote to the Prince afterwards, pointing out that he thought it a little discourteous on his part. He received a charming apology from the Prince of Wales the next day.

There is something impressive as well as beautiful about the ribbon and the star of the Garter. Once, when we had a big party at which the King and Queen of Spain and the King and Queen of Portugal were present, and the Prince of Wales, George and I realized when talking it over afterwards that we had had six Golden Fleeces in our house that night—the Golden Fleece is, I believe, the premier Order of Chivalry in Europe. We felt that this was indeed something to remember.

We gave a coming-out ball for my youngest step-daughter, Alexandra, and a dinner party for about thirty guests before the ball. Whenever it was possible I always liked to begin with a dinner party, because then there was no question of an empty ballroom when the first few people arrived, which seemed to me a bad start that should be avoided if it could be. Unfortunately George was ill, and could not be present, and he said that Alfred must take his place as host. Alfred was only eighteen, and in his first year at Oxford.

The Prince of Wales, the Duke of York,[1] and Lady Elizabeth Bowes-Lyon were among our dinner guests. (The Duke of York's engagement to Lady Elizabeth had been announced not long before this.) I remembered to ask Lady Elizabeth to be kind to Alfred, as he would be taking her in to dinner. It was really delightful to see how gaily and skilfully she drew him out; and Alfred, who at that time rather disliked parties, told me afterwards how much he had enjoyed talking to her.

I remember thinking, as I looked at her at dinner, that my lovely step-daughter Alexandra looked like a gardenia. I had taken a lot of trouble in choosing her dress—I always found it a joy to help her in her choice of clothes—and this dress, of white lace and tulle, looked enchanting. Alexandra had a lovely face, like a cameo, with a magnolia complexion, and black hair which she parted in the middle and gathered into a bun at the nape of her neck. She had a perfect figure, though she was not tall.

I used the beautiful round green table of malachite, which could seat fourteen, for the principal guests at dinner. All the tables had large silver bowls of white roses, massed rather flat, with white tuberoses standing up amongst them. (They had been grown in the hothouse at Hackwood.) These white roses in a silver bowl looked especially effective on the deep green of the malachite table. My own dress was pale pink, over silver—made by Madeleine Vionnet of Paris—and with it I wore pearls, and a small tiara.

After dinner, before the guests arrived for the ball, one arrangement which I had made went slightly wrong, with the result that Alfred took the Prince of Wales and the Duke of York to the ladies' cloakroom by mistake. I had decided to change the cloakrooms, giving the ladies the larger one, with more light and looking-glasses, and leaving to the men the ground-floor cloakroom which had been allotted to the ladies on former occasions. Unfortunately I had forgotten to tell Alfred of this change of plan. However, I heard great peals of laughter coming from upstairs when Alfred had discovered his mistake and had met the ladies returning from powdering their noses. Spontaneous laughter, however ridiculous the cause may be, is always a good start for a great party, and this

[1] Later King George VI.

ball for Alexandra's coming-out was very gay and successful, and I think that everyone enjoyed it.

One big dinner at Carlton House Terrace was given under a most unexpected handicap. This was the dinner of farewell to the members of the London Conference[1] in May 1921—and the boiler burst in the kitchen an hour before the party was due to begin! The kitchen was a pond and full of steam too, and I shall never understand how the kitchen staff produced the excellent dinner that they did in the face of such difficulties. Everyone played up magnificently, and though I went round before dinner cheerfully warning all our guests to expect the worst, the result was exactly what it would have been if no mishap had occurred at all. I have Helen D'Abernon's word for this—herself a most proficient and critical hostess—and she afterwards declared that the dinner was excellent, that everything was extremely well done and that the house looked beautiful. This, from Helen, was praise indeed, and I shall always be grateful to my chef and the servants who paddled about in the kitchen and struggled in the steam and disorder to produce such a vast amount of well-cooked food—for it was a very large party. Most of the Ambassadors and their wives were there, and many members of the Cabinet—I remember the Prime Minister, Mr. Lloyd George, arriving late from the House of Commons—and many distinguished Frenchmen, including Marshal Foch and General Gouraud, the Military Governor of Paris.

After every party was over, when all the guests had gone, George and I always went back to the drawing-room and talked about it, sitting side by side on a sofa. We told each other about the conversations that we had had with our respective neighbours at dinner, we laughed at the jokes, praised our charming and entertaining guests and—being only human!—had a comfortable little grumble about the dull ones, and enjoyed our party all over again as we talked about it. We always said that this was the best part of our parties.

[1] The London Conference of April 1921, dealing with reparations. The 'London Ultimatum' then issued declared that military action would be taken by the Allies if Germany defaulted, and eventually led to the occupation of the Ruhr.

CHAPTER XI

King George and Queen Mary

VERY soon after we were married we were commanded to spend a weekend at Windsor Castle with King George V and Queen Mary. It so happened that just before this visit took place, the news had been received of the death of one of the King's cousins. The other guests who had been invited to the Castle for the weekend had all been put off because the Court was in mourning; but the King wished to see one of his Ministers, and for this reason our visit was not cancelled.

We were given lovely rooms overlooking the Long Walk and the splendid view beyond it of Windsor Park over the noble avenue of trees which exists no longer. We were delighted to realize that Lady Minto and Lady Desborough were in waiting. They were both great friends of ours, and this of course added greatly to the pleasure of our visit. Shortly after we arrived Queen Mary sent for me, and I went to her sitting-room. She was very gracious and talkative, and put me at my ease at once by taking me to the window of the room and saying, in the most charming way, "Look, you can see your old home, Burfield, from here." She also said, "I have often heard about you from my sister-in-law—I know you are old friends." This was Princess Alice, wife of Lord Athlone, Queen Mary's brother. And then, while we were talking, the Queen showed me some lovely Chinese rugs on the floor of this room, and said: "Lord Curzon gave me these, on his return from India. I like them so much."

(I have before me now the letter which Queen Mary wrote to George, to thank him for one of these rugs. It was written from Windsor Castle on August 23rd, 1915.

"Dear Lord Curzon,

You must have a wonderful memory for colour, for the lovely little Chinese rug looks perfectly charming in my Wedgwood Room, in the space in the window as you suggested. I am most grateful for your kind and acceptable gift and send you my warmest thanks. The rug is an exquisite bit of colour and gives me great pleasure.

"Believe me,

"Yours very sincerely,

"Mary R.")

To return to my conversation with the Queen that afternoon at Windsor—she said to me, a little later on: "Come and see the room which I am having done up for the Maids of Honour—it has just been redecorated, and I should like to show it to you—I am sure you will be interested. But don't say anything to the King about it, because he thinks that I ought not to have anything of this sort done in war-time. I really had to have it done, however, because my poor Maids of Honour had no sitting-room of their own."

At dinner that night I sat next to the King, and he was perfectly charming. He talked to me at great length about the great Delhi Durbar, and told me about the visit to India of his uncle and aunt, the Duke and Duchess of Connaught, and of the Durbar at which they were present. He said, more than once, what a wonderful showman Curzon was. I must confess that this conversation made me a little nervous at times, because the King had a rather loud voice and what he said was certainly audible to everyone else at the table, which was not a large one. I had been married for only a short time then, and I was naturally anxious that my husband should not think that I was discussing him.

The news of the King's bereavement had been so sudden that we had received no warning about Court mourning. I was wearing my only black evening dress, which I had just brought back from Paris, where I got all my dresses, and it happened to be a dress made by Callot in the very latest fashion. It was rather short in front, and had a long pointed train. This made the King laugh very much. I was made to turn round in front of him, and he laughed and said: "How ridiculous! Off the ground in front, and all that trailing behind on the floor!" However, His Majesty was kind enough to assure me that I looked charming in it. After dinner the Queen took up some crochet work. It was a large white woollen shawl, and when I admired it she said, "I am told that this pattern is called the idiot stitch." The Queen made a great many of these warm, useful shawls, and I believe that she sent them to hospitals, for the babies.

The next morning the King took me to see a piece of ground where potatoes were growing, and told me that it was his own potato patch. When I asked him if he really did the work himself, he answered: "Of course I do. I dug it all—just look at my hands!"

We had luncheon in the family dining-room, and I was interested to notice that we all had napkin rings. King George and Queen Mary kept most conscientiously to the economy measures that they had decided to adopt for the duration of the war as an example to their people. At luncheon and at dinner they drank nothing but water. Prince George had arrived for luncheon, wearing naval uniform. The King, looking at the Prince's jacket, remarked: "Just look, his sleeves are too short *again*. He outgrows all his clothes so fast, and it is such an expense."

On Sunday morning we attended Morning Service in the private chapel of Windsor Castle, and in the afternoon we were asked what we would like to do, and when we were offered a carriage George was delighted to accept because he was suffering from his poor back, and he said that he would love to take me for a drive. We were given an open carriage and a pair of fine horses, and thoroughly enjoyed our drive through Windsor Park on a lovely sunny afternoon, with the early spring sunlight behind the bare branches of the trees. I knew it all so well because when I was living at Burfield I used to ride there almost every morning with my little sons.

The next time that I went to Windsor was for the funeral of the Duchess of Connaught, in March.[1] We travelled to Windsor in a special carriage with Mr. Arthur Balfour, Lord and Lady Salisbury, and Lord and Lady Lansdowne. I was deeply impressed by the service in such a wonderful setting, for I had never been to a funeral service in the lovely St. George's Chapel before. It gave me a shock to see the coffin disappear so suddenly through the special opening in the floor, descending on the mechanism provided to lower it into the crypt. The music was beautiful, and heart-breakingly sad. We were still at war, and most of us had suffered the loss of someone very dear to us. George sat in his Garter Stall, and I sat in a seat directly in front of him. Everyone was in Court mourning, and all the ladies had long black crape veils over their faces.

I only knew the Duchess of Connaught very slightly, but George had a real admiration and affection for her, since she and the Duke of Connaught had stayed with him in India for the Durbar, and they had become friends.

The first time that King George and Queen Mary honoured us by dining at Carlton House Terrace they were accompanied by Princess Mary. Among the other guests we had invited were a number of young men to amuse Princess Mary, including Lord Spenser, Lord Lascelles, and Lord Northampton. After dinner when I went to Princess Mary and asked whom she would like brought to her, she answered at once, "Lord Lascelles," and they talked together for a long time. I always like to think that this may have been the beginning of their romance, for not long afterwards the

[1] H.R.H. Princess Louise of Prussia, whom the Duke of Connaught had married in 1879, died March 14th, 1917.

Lord Curzon, author and M. Aristide Briand at the Cannes Conference, 1922

The Eton and Harrow cricket match. Mrs. Ambrose Dudley, the author and
Marcella arriving at Lord's

Christening of Lady Cynthia Mosley's son, 1923

Standing: Sir Oswald Mosley, Marcella, Alfred and Hubert. *Seated*: Lady Cynthia Mosley, Vivian Mosley, the author, Lady Irene Curzon and Lady Alexandra Curzon

King and Queen announced that Princess Mary was to marry Lord Lascelles.

This dinner was an elaborate function, and required a great deal of careful planning of every detail beforehand. The seating arrangements were greatly simplified by a table of precedence which George, with characteristic thoroughness, had provided for me. Our dinner table, adorned with masses of lovely dark red roses, did look very impressive, and all the beautiful Robert Adam silver from Kedleston, and the gilt service, were used. We had a good chef; and our butler was a treasure, and quite understood that dinner had to be served completely within the hour. We knew that the King and Queen did not care for very long dinners, and in any case it always seemed to us that an hour was quite long enough to linger over dinner, since the men spent an additional half-hour over coffee and liqueurs.

Cassano and his band played outside the room during dinner. We used the ballroom for this dinner, and it had to be in use again very shortly afterwards for a little entertainment. I had to give a good deal of thought beforehand to organizing this, as of course every trace of dinner, every crumb, had to be removed in a very short time and chairs arranged for the entertainment. However, when I had planned it all and given the necessary instructions I never gave it another thought, and happily it all went exactly according to plan.

We had George Robey to give us two or three of his best sketches, and Leonora Hughes and her partner Maurice to dance for us. They had flown over from Paris for the night. She looked lovely in a beautiful dress which Vionnet had made for the occasion and danced like a piece of thistledown. This lovely little lady later married one of the millionaires of Buenos Aires. It was a pleasure to me to see her quite unchanged years later when I paid one of my visits to the Argentine.

George Robey had given his services so generously during the war that we thought it would be a nice gesture to ask him to appear before the King and Queen. I had one anxious moment during his performance, when he hesitated noticeably in the middle of one of his songs. I was afraid for an instant that he was going to dry up, but he quickly recovered himself and went on, and the song was a great success. He told me afterwards that he had suddenly realized that he was just coming to a line containing a joke about royal hats,[1] and had been obliged to improvise an alternative on the spur of the moment.

[1] The little toques worn by Queen Mary were unusual at a period when extremely large hats were fashionable, and they gave rise to much popular comment.

King George had a great sense of fun, and he enjoyed nothing
more than a simple, domestic sort of joke. I once amused him
enormously by telling him about a really ludicrous little bone of
contention between George and myself, and I never saw him laugh
so much. What had happened was this. George and I had dined with
Mrs. Ronnie Greville, and after dinner George had said to me that
he proposed to slip away and return home to deal with his all-
absorbing Foreign Office boxes. Later on, when I myself was going
away, Sir Robert Horne and Edward Rice, who were leaving too,
asked me to go with them to the Embassy Club. I had never been
able to persuade George to go to the Embassy or any other night
club, however correct, for he was firmly convinced that all night
clubs were sinks of iniquity, and was a little pained by the idea that
I enjoyed going to them occasionally. So I went with Sir Robert
Horne and Edward Rice, and the first person I met when I got to the
Embassy was Lord Salisbury. I could hardly have been more surprised if it had been the Archbishop of Canterbury. He was having
supper with his daughter-in-law, Lady Cranbourne. The next morning poor George had one of his bad back attacks,[1] and asked Lord
Salisbury to come and see him because he did not feel well enough
to go to the House of Lords that afternoon—he was the Leader of
the House of Lords and Lord Salisbury the Deputy Leader. I went
into George's room in the course of the morning to see how he was,
and found them talking. Lord Salisbury seemed almost to welcome
the interruption, and proceeded to ask me gaily how I had enjoyed
the Embassy Club the night before. George turned on me a look of
positive horror, and fairly gasped with dismay, "Oh, you didn't go
to the Embassy Club, did you?" I had to admit that I had. George
was decidedly shocked by the notion of his wife visiting what he
persisted in regarding as a low haunt, and I could not help thinking
it exceptionally funny that I should have been given away by Lord
Salisbury, of all people. Later, when Lord Salisbury had gone,
George said to me, partly as a joke but still with a lingering note of
disapproval, that he did not consider that I ought to be allowed to
have a latchkey. I was delighted with this delicious nonsense, and
gave him my latchkey then and there.

It was that night that we dined with the Londonderrys at
Londonderry House to meet the King and Queen. I sat next to the
King, and told him the whole story, knowing how much it would
amuse him. He was perfectly delighted with it. After dinner he

[1] At nineteen Lord Curzon developed curvature of the spine, for which he
wore a special brace, and suffered acute pain at intervals until the end of his life.

called George and said: "What's this I hear about Lady Curzon having her latchkey taken away? You will of course give it back to her at once." The King roared with laughter, and so did George, who said, "Yes, Sir, but please tell my wife that she really must not frequent these low haunts."

So I got back my latchkey. I always wanted to get George to accompany me to the Embassy Club, but I never succeeded. However, after that I had his full permission to go there, and I often did. My latchkey remained in my possession.

Queen Mary will always have a very special place in my heart. As all the world knows, she not only looked a queen, but she was a queen in every sense of the word. My admiration and affection for her date from the time of my first visit to Windsor Castle. I had quite expected that it would be stiff and frightening, but her gracious charm and friendliness made it all delightful, and I had enjoyed every minute of it.

When the 1914 War was over, and the evening Courts and Presentations had started again, I, as the wife of the Foreign Secretary, had to attend every function, and, in that capacity, to perform certain special duties.

Before the entry of the King and Queen I had to be standing by the great doors leading to the throne room with the Marshal of the Diplomatic Corps. I still feel the thrill of excitement which the roll of drums and the National Anthem gave me as the royal procession entered the throne room. The great Officers of State, the Lord Chamberlain—Lord Sandhurst—and the Lord Steward—Lord Farquhar—in their Court uniform, their staves of office held before them, walked in backwards, facing the King and Queen. Queen Mary, a glittering apparition in a silver dress, many diamonds and a high diamond tiara, wearing the blue ribbon of the Garter, and moving as if on wheels, looked magnificent.

As soon as the King and Queen had taken their place on the dais, my train would be taken from my arm and spread. I would make three low curtseys at the entrance of the throne room, take a few steps forward with the Marshal of the Diplomatic Corps holding my hand, which he would release while I made three more curtseys —then a curtsey to the King, a curtsey to Queen Mary, and another curtsey to the King as he took my hand to help me up on to the dais. There I would stand until the ladies of the Diplomatic Corps had passed. I would then step down from the dais, curtsey again to the King and to the Queen, and walk to my seat near the dais, where I had to remember not to sit down until all the Ambassadors and the other gentlemen of the Diplomatic Corps had passed, because the King and Queen were still standing.

I enjoyed these Courts, and I was delighted when the King congratulated me on the way I had carried out my duties.

I remember that Queen Mary usually wore diamonds and pearls —I seldom saw her wearing coloured stones. The tiara that I liked best was a magnificent diamond one with large pear-shaped pearls that seemed to hang inside the wide band of diamonds and slightly shook as she moved. She often wore white, or cream, dresses, beautifully embroidered with pearls and diamonds, and of course long trains to match. I remember one dream of a dress of cloth of gold. Queen Mary wore masses of jewellery in a way that no one else could have done. On her it never looked too much. I have attended many Courts and evening parties at Buckingham Palace, and I have seen most of the beauties of their time pass before Queen Mary—and I found that in comparison with her they seemed colourless and almost insignificant.

Queen Mary thoroughly understood the art of dressing, and I would not have wished it changed in any way. The lovely soft mauves and blues that she wore were always perfect for Ascot and all the outdoor functions, and so were her charming toques. How well I remember her wonderful appearance at my step-daughter Cynthia's marriage.

Dear, beloved Queen Mary was always very kind and gracious to me. I received a lovely present from her every Christmas, from my marriage to George, in 1917, until her death. Her first Christmas present to me was a large photograph, in a lovely pink brocaded frame, which arrived with a note in which she said that if I would rather have a different coloured frame to suit my room would I please let her know and it would be changed. Of course I would not think of changing it. After this first Christmas, besides my wonderful Christmas present each year, I received as well a new photograph of Queen Mary, thanking me for my own small Christmas gift to her. She used to write her thanks on the back of these smaller, unframed photographs.

I have a wonderful collection of jade boxes, small figures, and other pieces in jade which Queen Mary gave me, because she knew that I collected jade for my Chinese room at Hackwood, which I later removed to Bodiam Manor. Among her other presents were small exquisite scent bottles, small boxes and little animals encrusted with precious stones, the work of Fabergé, the famous Court Jeweller of St. Petersburg.

I was surprised to learn from King George himself that, in spite of a lifetime of public appearances in every part of his kingdom, he was still sometimes disconcerted by the concentrated gaze of vast crowds. He told me this after the wedding of Princess Mary, when George and I had been commanded to dine at Buckingham Palace. I had to drive to the Palace alone because George had had to go to the Foreign Office first, and come on in his own car. The Mall was absolutely packed with people, vast crowds surging round the Palace hoping to see the Royal Family make further appearances on the balcony. My car crept along at a snail's pace through the crowd, and everyone turned and stared at me because at the moment there was nothing else to stare at. I had never had this experience before, and I found it frightening, although of course I knew that it was quite unreasonable to feel alarmed by the friendly stares of a most good-humoured crowd. Still, I found it unnerving to be surrounded by thousands of faces, and all of them looking at me. In the course of the evening I confided my feelings of temporary fright to the King, and he said: "I know exactly what you mean. Throughout my life I have found it disconcerting to be surrounded by a very large crowd. *All those eyes*, fixed on oneself!"

King George was always amiability itself on the many occasions when I was next to him at luncheon or dinner, very easy to talk to, and most good-humoured. Once, without realizing it, I tried his patience very high. It was at luncheon at Buckingham Palace, and I was wearing a hat with a long, narrow feather which stuck out at one side—as it happened, the side next the King. Queen Mary was on his other side—they always sat next to each other—and after luncheon she said to me: "Do you realize that your feather kept on brushing the King's head while you were talking to him at luncheon? I must say that I think he bore it with remarkable patience, because as a matter of fact one of the things that he can't bear is having his head touched."

I was on a visit to the Argentine at the time of King George's Jubilee. I remember my surprise, and delight, at receiving the King George Jubilee Medal, which had been sent in the Foreign Office bag to our Ambassador, for him to hand on to me. I have been told, by a friend who was present, that King George, after the drive through London with Queen Mary on the Jubilee Day, was overwhelmed by the tremendous enthusiasm of the people every-where. He said, with tears in his eyes, "I had no idea that the people thought so kindly of me."

The King had just recovered from his long and dangerous illness

when my husband's fatal illness began. I remember writing to thank
him for one of his many kind letters of enquiry, and sending him a
message from George—saying that just as he (the King) had been
spared to get well and carry on his care for his people, so he (George
Curzon) was certain that he also would live to see him again, and,
he hoped, to be of use to his King and his country. Throughout his
life my husband thought of himself as serving the King—not the
Prime Minister or the Conservative Party. This stately message is
typical of his feelings for the Throne.

When King George died I was invited to attend his funeral at
St. George's Chapel, Windsor Castle. As I sat there in my deep
mourning and my black veil—no longer in the place which I had
formerly occupied directly in front of George's Garter Stall—I
grieved deeply for the King, who had always been kind to me, and
who had seemed to be so much a part of my happy life with my
husband who had died ten years before. I had a very real pain in my
heart, and I grieved for the passing of an era.

The cortège was hours late in arriving, because the funeral procession in London, through vast crowds of mourning subjects, had
taken far longer than anyone had anticipated. At last we heard the
boom of the distant guns, and looked towards the great doors and
waited for them to open. It was a moment of intense sadness. The
doors were thrown open, and the royal cortège slowly mounted the
steps at the West End of the Chapel. The clank of swords was audible
through the muffled notes of the Funeral March. As always, Queen
Mary was dignity personified as she walked behind the coffin.

The day was cold, and dark, and overcast, and we had waited
for hours in St. George's Chapel, which is very cold in winter. It was
a severe test of physical stamina, and many people in the congregation returned to London in a state of collapse, caused partly by sorrow
and partly by cold and exhaustion.

CHAPTER XII

An Adventure

IN the early autumn of 1921 I spent five weeks at Langenschwalbach, in the Rhineland, in order to take the cure there. The following extracts from my letters to George describe my impressions of it all. They begin on August 30th with a description of my journey.

"I arrived at Cologne at 6.5. a.m., where I was met by three smart British officers (I don't know any of their names), also a secretary of Mr. Robertson who had come to travel with me to Coblenz. We had a wonderfully comfortable car only used by the British High Commissioner when he goes up and down the line. We left Cologne at 7.25 a.m. and arrived at Coblenz at 9.15. Mr. Robertson[1] met me at the station and took me to his house for breakfast. His wife is a very nice little cheerful American of about 32, quite simple and unaffected. The house of the High Commissioner is charming. We had breakfast in the garden as it was such a lovely morning. Then Mr. Robertson motored me here through the most divine scenery, very much like Switzerland, beautifully timbered—no trees cut down like poor England. What fools we are in England when we think of Germany as being hard hit by the war. I have never seen a more prosperous looking country—roads *perfect*, inhabitants very fat, well clothed and shod, they spend money like water. Of course this may only be in the Rhineland where all the Inter-Allied troops are spending so much money, which must of course help to prosper Germany. It was a two hours' motor run from Coblenz here. Mr. Robertson stayed and lunched with me—when he left I felt very much that I was really in for a dull time. . . ."

". . . I think I have lost a stone already and I have only had 3 mud baths and 2 iron ones. I must have 15 mud baths and 12 iron before my cure is finished and I am only allowed to take one bath a day. Oh, darling, I am lonely—no one to talk to, and I read all day until my eyes ache. My days are beyond expression in dullness. I have my

---

[1] Malcolm Arnold Robertson (1877–1951), who was created K.B.E. in 1924. He was British High Commissioner on the Inter-Allied Rhineland High Commission 1920–21.

breakfast at 8, then walk to get my glass of water at 9 o'clock, walk for ½ hour afterwards, then this mud bath at 9.30. This bath is the most disgusting thing you can imagine—very thick, black lumpy smelly mud, one sits on hard things like very hard hot bricks. I lie in this filth for ½ hour, then I get into a hot bath of iron water which is called the cleansing bath—but it isn't!—for 10 minutes, then walk home and go to bed for 2 hours, with hot mud poultices. I get up at 1 o'clock for lunch, and then another ½ hour's rest on a long chair. Don't you feel sorry for me?"

". . . It is such a comfort to get a letter from you every day. I am afraid you must be having a very dull time at Kedleston all alone, but I would gladly change places with you. . . ."

". . . Only a week today (Sunday) since I arrived here, and yet if I were asked where I had spent the summer I should feel inclined to say at Schwalbach! . . . I thought of you this morning reading the lessons in the beautiful little Church and wished so much that I were there to take part in that perfect little service. I had a mud bath instead of going to church. There is a little English church here, but of course it is shut. . . . It is beginning to get much colder here, I am sorry to say. I dread the long cold evenings. Dinner is at 7 o'clock, as a great concession to me I dine at 7.30 and then sit about in a big fur coat until I am glad to go to bed at 9.30. It is indeed lonely not to have a single soul to talk to. There is a Mrs. Ronnie Hamilton staying at another hotel, and I walk with her in the afternoon. . . . I had a very happy letter from Marcella yesterday. They seem to be all enjoying themselves at Clovelly in spite of having very cold rainy weather. Patsy Ward, Irene, and Miss Swinton are staying there. As you know, the children will return to Hackwood on the 17th. I enclose a cutting from a German paper, about you. I believe it is called Lord Curzon's cushion. They say they thought you looked, or sat, very tall at the last Conference in Paris: they then noticed that you were sitting on your map. They wondered if you were afraid of it being stolen, even in such exalted company. I suppose it is really meant as a hit at the French. What a lot of work you will have done at Kedleston by the time I see it. I always love hearing of all your labour, so do tell me about it."

"I am sorry to have missed writing to you yesterday. I was really much too ill . . . however today I am much better. . . . You say in your letters I don't tell you how I pass my day. I thought I had given you every boring detail. You know my breakfast is at 8 o'clock, then a most delightful walk of 20 minutes through a lovely wood with linden trees meeting over my head, rather like Hackwood's beautiful 'Cathedral'. Then a glass of water at 9.15. The water is full of iron so one has to drink it through a glass tube very slowly. Then on for another ten minutes to my mud bath. I pay 5 marks extra and get what is called the Salon de luxe, the mud is in a huge copper bath. I often wonder how Germany has all of these copper baths left. (In the Mud Bath House there must be about 100, and in the Iron Water Baths, 200.) The mud which you get into is black and so thick that I almost lie on top of it. I started with the temperature at 41, I now have it at 44. I must get down leaving only my head out and the two palms of my hands turned out. How I wish you could see me—I could easily hold a reception as I am quite clothed in mud. After half an hour of mud I get into the cleansing bath for 10 minutes, then the same lovely walk home. . . . I dine sometimes in my room and sometimes in the restaurant at 7.30. I never dress for dinner as no one does. . . . I have never spoken to a soul except the Dr., the Hotel manager, and Mrs. Hamilton. I wish you could just see the class of people that surround me—Germans of almost the peasant class. Most of the French people are in the best villas. I often see them at the Waters, but they also look very common and stare me out of countenance. There is no English Chaplain here, and no English Consul. Next week if all goes well I shall hire a car and go for some drives as the weather is quite perfect and still warm. . . ."

". . . Such excitement this afternoon—they told me there was a parcel for me at the Customs House. I at once sent for it, I had to pay 25 marks for it (sounds a lot but fortunately it is only 2 shillings). When I saw it I knew it was your grapes. My maid and I opened the box—alas, to find a white fermented pulp, and the whole room still smells of sour wine! You must not send any more, darling, as you see it takes so long on the way. The box was quite beautifully packed and had not been tampered with in any way; it arrived on the 10th—what day was it sent?"

". . . Mr. Robertson came to see me again yesterday, he brought me some partridges that he had shot the day before, also some lovely flowers from his garden. He leaves for England on Saturday. I am to have his official motor here while he is away, which will be a great joy. I will of course pay for petrol, chauffeur's keep, and garage of

car. Mr. Robertson has been most kind. Will you write him a little
letter of thanks for all his thought for me. . . . I think we shall have
to come and live here—my hotel bill including bedroom, bathroom,
sitting-room, maid's room and both our meals came to £7. 0. 0.! I
pay only 17/6 a day for rooms and board! Of course the food is
beyond words bad. It makes my mouth water to think of my lovely
lost grapes. . . . How good you are to write me such dear long letters.
I can't tell you what a joy they are to me. . . . This morning came a
letter from Edgar D'Abernon[1] saying he had arranged with you to
come and see me. He says he will appear in a motor on Tuesday
evening and stay for 24 hours. He says he hears that Schwalbach is
reserved exclusively for what is falsely called the weaker sex, and
wonders if he will have to don a domino or petticoat! It will be nice
to see someone from the outside world."

". . . I enclose a bath ticket which will show you what I look like
when I get out of the mud bath. I am just like Tar Baby. (I wonder
if you have read *Brer Rabbit*?) After the mud the woman attend-
ant pours about 8 small pails of water over me to get the mud off
before I get into the cleansing bath . . . soon I shall be half way
through my fourth week. I have received your letter—your delightful
letter, darling—how natural and how touching is all that you write.
How well you know the way to the heart of your Gracie. 'Back
Number', indeed! These abilities, and charms, the only ones worthy
of yourself, will last for ages and never wither. I enclose a letter I
received this morning from Mrs. Moon. I am really rather worried
about the water at Hackwood, I am so afraid of the drains going
wrong. Don't you think it should be seen to at once? . . . I brought a
lot of books with me—don't you remember, I had a wonder-box
packed by Hatchards? I have read *The Tragedy of Lord Kitchener* by
Esher, with which I was rather disappointed. I have also read
Letters to Nobody, Fleetwood Wilson, all about India—mostly about
the big game hunting there. I have just finished Harold Nicolson's
Life of Paul Verlaine which he makes most interesting—this is the
young F(oreign) O(ffice) Nicolson you know. I have also read *The
Dark Geraldine*, which I did not like, *Good Grain*, Emmeline Morrison,
fairly good, and *The Blue Vase*, Lady (A.) Scott—such a good
detective story, you must read it. I read at my meals as the waits
are so long, and in this way get through such a lot."

[1] Edgar Vincent, Baron D'Abernon (1857–1941), who was created Viscount
D'Abernon in 1926. He was British Ambassador in Berlin 1920–26, and originated the idea embodied in the Pact of Locarno in 1925.

". . . No letter from you today, and it is cold and raining. Poor, poor Gracie! Yesterday afternoon I motored to Wiesbaden, one of the oldest watering-places in Germany, formerly the capital of the Duchy of Nassau, and now the chief town of the Prussian district. It is surrounded by orchards and vineyards, and is a most attractive and, for the most part, well built town. A number of handsome streets with houses and villas of very ugly German architecture. To me, it is most extraordinary to find a people living in this beautiful country for which nature had done everything, so absolutely devoid of taste. Their houses, their clothes, their manners! The women too should be good-looking, they all, or mostly all, have quite lovely complexions, beautiful hair, and good teeth—and yet no one could call them good-looking. I think it must be their want of grace."

". . . I have so much to tell you that I hardly know where to begin. I am sorry to have missed two days in writing. . . . I knew Edgar D'Abernon wrote yesterday telling you of my terrible adventure of Monday evening. Darling, it was the *most* awful experience of my life. I started out for my usual solitary walk at 5.30, a perfect evening but rather cold. I walked for miles through the woods, they are too lovely at this time of the year with the leaves just turning, and the ground covered with purple heather. For some time I kept to the well known beaten track, but I then thought of penetrating more into the woods and making a détour and returning home by a different route. To make a long story short, at about 7.30 (I could just see the time by my wrist watch) I began to realise that I was lost! It was then getting dark very fast. I was *terrified*. It became so dark that I could not see the little bridle path on which I was trying to walk. It is impossible to describe all I felt—to be alone in a dense, dark *German* forest, and to think that I should have to pass the night there, was almost *un*thinkable. I kept on walking all the time, as I was too frightened to rest for even a moment for fear I might faint. There were no sign-posts, and even if there had been, I had no matches and could not have read them. The hills are very steep, with deep precipices at places. I was afraid of falling and spraining, or breaking, my ankle. I stopped at intervals, and called my loudest, only to be answered by my own echo. I think, darling, I must have walked *many, many* miles. The doctor had complained to me the day before of how the wild boar had come down from the hills—the very hills I was in—and dug up his potatoes! Of course I thought I heard them grunting all around me. I really did see one in the end but it ran away from *me*! I was also in great fear of walking on snakes. I have since been told that they never come out at night because it is so cold. I soon became almost desperate. I prayed hard to be found. I also remember pleading in my prayer, 'My worst fault is only my extravagance.' I also prayed hard for the moon to come out. At about 9.30 the moon did show itself, and I then climbed up a very steep hill to have a survey of all the country. To my great joy I espied a high road on to which I clambered, not knowing in the least where it led. I went on walking (frozen to the bone, I only had on a thin silk coat and skirt) for miles. I finally could go no farther, so sat down on a stone almost exhausted, when—Oh, joy!—I thought I heard a dog bark. I shouted, and after much more shouting on my part I was answered by some German voices, which turned out to be a rescue party from the hotel consisting of: the hall porter, the head-waiter, my English chauffeur, a French chauffeur, two dogs (wolfhounds) and my maid. Even after they had heard and recognized my voice they lost much time in finding me, as I was on a road on the high top of the mountain, while they were still in the valley. Everyone is puzzled to know how I got up there, nor can I explain. This all took place at about 10.30, we then trudged home. I arrived home about 11.30, *so* tired, cold, and footsore. . . . I had been walking from 5.30 till 11.30! My maid then told me all she had done. When I did not appear for dinner (at 7.30) she became alarmed and told the proprietor of the hotel that I had not returned. A nurse remembered having passed me at six o'clock on my way up the mountain. Three men from the hotel (the same who eventually found me) were sent in search. They were gone for an hour and a half, only to return and say that I could not be found. My poor maid and everyone in the hotel became seriously frightened. The hotel manager went at once to the Colonel in charge of the French troops here. He gave the command to 50 of his soldiers to look for me (Black men!) and they started forth with bugles and torches! I once heard the bugle, and shouted in answer, but to no effect. I have since been told, they heard a faint noise or cry in the distance but thought it was an owl or some other night bird! There were also 2 German police with their dogs searching for me. When I had returned to the hotel the difficulty was to let all who were still out on search know, and to call them back, so they sounded the Reveille in Barracks. This caused great excitement in the town. It was rather amusing to hear them asking, 'Has the lady been found?' while I walked in their midst quite unnoticed. At the sound of the Reveille heads were thrust out of windows asking what had happened. The poor things no doubt thought, another war. The French officer just answered in the most off-hand way, 'It is all right, you can sleep in your beds.' Result of my evening walk:—1,000 marks to French soldiers; 1,000 marks to German police; 1,000 marks to hotel servants; great fright to poor Gracie! With the help of my maid I wrote a letter to Colonel Steck to thank him. I will be so pleased if you will also send him a note of thanks. I enclose his letter to me, and also his card. He poor man was terrified for fear his black men might have dragged me into the woods and assaulted me. I believe the Germans almost hoped that this had happened! They are so eager for grievances against the black troops. I have been told many harrowing tales since my escapade of people who have been lost in those self-same woods and never found; and one poor lady last year got lost and her body was only found three months later, although searches had taken place for weeks. I will write tomorrow and tell you all about Edgar D'Abernon's visit. Good-bye, darling. . . . I hope you are glad I was found."

". . . I greatly enjoyed Edgar's visit. He arrived on Tuesday at teatime. I took him for a long walk and showed him where I started off for my adventure of the previous evening. We dined here and as I was still very exhausted I went to bed early. On Wednesday morning I had my usual water, and mud bath, and two hours' rest. Then we motored to Wiesbaden, where we had an excellent lunch— what a treat good food now is to me! We then went to see a French exhibition that has just been opened, of quite good Empire furniture and *objets d'art*. The French held their exhibition as a kind of propaganda, hoping to do good to French trade, but the Germans had boycotted the whole exhibition, which is beautifully done—not a soul to look at it! We then motored on to Frankfurt, about an hour's run—a very ugly big dirty manufacturing town. We were met at the hotel by our Consul as Edgar had asked him to arrange to take us over the Weinburgs' racing stables and stud, just outside of Frankfurt. I found this rather tiring and most disappointing, as things are not done anything like so well as with us. I had expected much greater perfection. We returned to the hotel at Frankfurt where we had tea. I then left Edgar at about 6.30 (his train was 9 o'clock from Frankfurt to Berlin) and I arrived here at about 9.30. It took ages motoring home in the dark over very bad roads. Edgar was in wonderful form. One cannot help liking the old thing. He is much thinner, and his clothes *more* untidy, and looking as if they had been handed down by a giant. I do not think he is looking at all well. It is a great mistake when a big man of his age tries to get down

so much weight. . . . They are most anxious for me to go to Berlin to
stay with them for a few days. I should very much like to see the
place. I asked the doctor and he said if I did not do too much it
would do me no harm. It is only a night's journey from here. . . .
Thank you so much for your letter which I received this morning—
but you had not finished it! I am delighted with your plan for the
Lower Hall. It seems to me you will be able to fit in quite a number
of things from the Collection. . . . I am sure we could use some in the
large hall at C.H.T. It would be such a joy to *live* with some of those
lovely things—of course I only mean the ones you will still have left
over, after using as much as possible at Kedleston. All our big
entertaining is at C.H.T., and I think I have already explained
about your Delhi Trumpeter things to King George, King of the
Belgians, King of Spain, King of Sweden, Prince of Wales, Crown
Prince of Japan, and all the statesmen in Europe! Let me know,
darling, if you think anything could be done. . . ."

"I am *so* glad that it is all settled that you do not go to America.
The doctor had told me that I must on no account go, and I hated
the thought of being without you for so long. I also fear a failure of
the Conference,[1] and am very glad you are out of it. Edgar
D'Abernon thought the three—A.J.B., Bonar Law (if he goes?) and
Lord Lee a splendid combination. He also said he thought it would
be a very wise step if they took some member of the *Opposition* with
them, such as Asquith, or Crewe,[2] as this would clear the Government of the *entire* responsibility, and would be a good thing for the
Press and public. Also if things went very badly the Opposition man
could be made the scapegoat? Edgar came here direct from (Lord)
Crewe, so doubtless he heard the idea discussed there. He also tells
me that Peggie is going to America. . . . I am glad you did not have
to go to Scotland. I have had no letter from you today, and no
papers for a whole week—so I am indeed cut off from the world. . . .
You ask about Hackwood. I thought we had decided to keep it open
if there is no Autumn Session. Miss Chapman has joined Marcella
there, they are to come to London for one day a week for different
lessons. . . . Well, darling, you can't complain that I don't write long
letters to my beloved husband. I hope you really read them. . . ."

[1] The Disarmament and Far Eastern Conference at Washington, November 12th, 1921–February 6th, 1922, between the United States, Great Britain,
France, and Japan. It resulted in the Washington Treaty for the limitation of
naval armaments. Great Britain's delegates actually were Balfour, Lord Lee of
Fareham, Sir Auckland Geddes, Lord Beatty, and Lord Cavan.

[2] See note 2, p. 196.

"Two days without a letter, and still no papers! . . . I am longing
to know the estimate for the Blue room at C.H.T., I think the plan
sounds quite charming. As you know I wish the room to be quite
simple. I spoke with the representative of the firm when he came to
take measurements, and we both agreed that the Vitrine should
be between the windows, to balance the room. Of course I mean to
keep those lovely chairs, and thought of putting them on either side
of the fireplace, where they will be much more seen than in their
present position. Col. Ryan came to see me to-day. He takes Mr.
Robertson's place while he is on leave—such a nice little man, he
has a D.S.O., and I should think is much more intelligent than Mr.
Robertson. Very rare to find a good soldier so intelligent.[1] He tells
me he has left the Army and is now under the F.O. It is a divine day
here, although cold. I am just going for my solitary drive, feeling so
forgotten and neglected.

"It is bitterly cold here, and as I have only brought thin summer
things I count the days until I can get away. It is so cold I can hardly
hold my pen. I get a tiny little fire in my sitting-room in the evening.
I have one of those funny German stoves made of tiles. I don't
like them because you cannot see the fire. . . . The photographs you
enclosed of myself were taken by a little man who used to follow me
everywhere when I lived at Windsor and take snapshots of me for
the papers. He wrote to me so often that I at last allowed him to
come, and he took them in the ballroom at C.T.H.—they are only
newspaper photographs, that is why you have not seen them. . . .
Please send me Baba's Paris address, as I will go and see her, and
take her out to lunch with me. . . . Of course, darling, I look forward
to taking up my duties at Kedleston. It is really the kind of life I long
for and love. I really suffer from having *too* much in my life. I sometimes long for less reponsibility. Anything I do darling, you must
admit I put my whole heart into. . . . I hope you are not disappointed
in Sir Percy Loraine.[2] I enclose what I think *such* a nice letter from
him in answer to mine of congratulations on his new post. He is the
best *young* man I have met. . . . I was so glad to receive your letter
of the 27th this morning and to know that you now understand all
that I went through in my terrible adventure. Here I am looked on as
almost a *heroine*. They were so surprised to find me, apparently,
so *un*frightened and without tears, as they had expected to find a
hysterical woman almost unable to walk. . . . You did not understand

[1] George, who had had trouble with the Army in India, thought that all
soldiers must be fools.(*G. C.'s own note.*)
[2] Sir Percy Loraine, 12th Bt. (*b.* 1880), British Minister to Persia 1921–26.

my letter about the case with the Herald's coat. I did not really
admire it, I much prefer the lovely picture from the Gallery there
instead. I only wished to point out the attention which anything
connected with your Viceroy days always attracted from our most
illustrious guests.

"The doctor came to say good-bye to me today. When the
season here is over he goes to Frankfurt and is doctor in a big
hospital there. I shall be almost the last person to leave this horrid
hole. The hotel is more than half closed down—one is waited on at
table by the same woman who makes one's bed! However I must
admit that I feel so much better than when I arrived. I walk miles
every day, and am a little thinner . . . the pain in my knee is quite
gone . . . on Monday I motor to Frankfurt and take the 9 o'clock
train and arrive in Berlin about 8 o'clock the next morning. . . ."

"Here goes my last letter from Schwalbach. I have had to change
my plans . . . tomorrow I motor to Coblenz where I lunch with
Col. Ryan and then motor to Cologne, where I get a train at 10 in
the evening for Berlin . . . I shall send this letter to C.T.H., as you
tell me that you go there on the 4th. How pleased all the farmers at
Kedleston must have been to have you call on them. I always admire
the Kedleston Inn Farm. I think it will have to be my Dower House
some day! I shall be anxious to know if White the gardener has
given you any new plans for the Pleasure grounds. What a lot we
will have to talk about when I do return. Do write me some political
and F.O. news to Berlin. I am really rather embarrassed when I am
supposed to know and don't!"

"Here I am, having arrived an hour ago. My first impression of
Berlin is a gloomy one, as it is pouring with rain. The Embassy is
charming, and shows Helen's[1] good taste in every way. It is much more
attractive than the Embassy in Paris. I had a very long and tiring
day yesterday. I left Schwalbach at 10.30 by motor and lunched at
Coblenz with Col. Ryan and his mother Lady Ryan, and afterwards
motored on to Cologne where we arrived at about 5.30, dined with
Col. Ryan and his sister and Belita Hollway, and took the train
here at 10 o'clock. I am feeling very tired as I did not sleep at all
well in the train, so forgive stupid letter. I was met at the station by
young Hay, and found old Edgar waiting for me with whom I had
breakfast. I have not seen Helen yet, it is not yet 9.30! I am going to
rest until lunch time. I found letters waiting for me from Mother and

---

[1] Helen, Lady D'Abernon, wife of the British Ambassador.

Eton, Fourth of June : Marcella, the author and Alfred

A formal occasion

Marcella, but none from you! The sun is coming out. Now I am
here I am rather unhappy as I have no smart clothes with me. I
shall say I am too ill for a big function."

"Two letters and the papers this morning. Last night the dinner-
party here was a huge success. I enclose a list of the guests.* I sat
between the Foreign Secretary (Mr. Rosen) and the Swedish Minister (Count Essen). I found Mr. Rosen most charming. He speaks
English, and I almost forgot he was a hateful German! He is a very
great admirer of yours. He was in Persia for some time, and tells me
your book on Persia is the *only* book worth reading.[1] He also says he
has often to write articles about Persia and always uses your book as a
text-book. He reads most of your speeches and asked me to send him
a copy of your last published speeches! Altogether a very clever man.
I am to lunch with them tomorrow. Tell it not in London, or I shall
be called pro-German! I was to have gone out tonight with Edgar and
Helen to a play, but I have a horrid cold so I am going to bed
instead."

*"*Enclosure* :—   British Embassy, Berlin.
          Grace, dearest, You may just like to know who dines
to-night. You have the German F.O. on one side the Swede on the
other.

Ly. Curzon.	Soler. Sp. Amb.
Selves. 2.	Della Faille. Belgian
Essens. 2. Swedes.	Minister.
Rosens. 2 F.O.	Dressel. American High
Castellane. 1	Commn[r].
Laurent. Fr. Amb.	Kilmarnock
	Addison.
	Joscelyn Hay."

                                                    H.

"Thank you so much for two dear letters received this morning.
I am sorry to say I have no news to give you as I am still in bed with
such a horrid cold. It *is* bad luck as there is so much that I longed to
see. How strange that the whole of my five weeks at Schwalbach
I should never have a cold, when I was really *roughing* it, whereas
here, in all this magnificent luxury and wonderful comfort, I got one at
once. I do wish you could see Helen and Edgar. I think they are both

[1] *Persia and the Persian Question* (1892).

                                                    I

too wonderful in every way. Helen is, I think, looking more beautiful than ever, unless it is that my eyes have seen nothing but monstrous German women for so long. She makes the most perfect Ambassadress, and one is proud of her. You would not recognise the Helen of many cross moods we knew in England. She is always smiling and anxious to please, and most gracious to everyone. She has learnt to speak German, and I believe she loves being here. They seem to entertain a great deal, unless it is only because I am here. Everything is quite beautifully done. Helen says she likes to make the Germans feel that *we have won the war*! All I can say is that it is a thousand times better in every way than the Embassy in Paris, in the Derbys' time or at the present time. I have decided to leave on Sunday. . . ."

CHAPTER XIII

Some of Our Guests

MY duties as the wife of the Secretary of State for Foreign Affairs[1] included a vast amount of entertaining. We gave dinners and luncheons at Carlton House Terrace for visiting statesmen, and for foreign Royalties and Heads of States, and also for the members of the Government and of the Diplomatic Corps. All these parties are interesting to me to remember—some of them were delightful, a few were rather heavy going, and all of them were memorable for some reason or another. I have always liked giving parties, taken trouble over it, and then enjoyed the parties myself. On looking back, I remember a great deal of pleasure, and a few *contretemps* which make me laugh when I think of them.

The first really large party which we gave at Carlton House Terrace, when it was not even fully opened before the end of the war, was a dinner to the Prime Minister (Mr. Lloyd George) and the Dominion Prime Ministers, in June 1918. I can't think how we contrived to have such a big, formal party when the house was not by any means in proper order, and the war-time rationing was so strict. Unfortunately I can't recall the details of what we gave this great gathering for dinner. (I hope it was not one of the meatless days that used to occur two or three times a week in those times. Game from Hackwood and Kedleston was luckily always available.) However, the war-time difficulties must have been overcome somehow, because it was generally considered to have been a successful party. As well as all the Prime Ministers our guests included the Salisburys, the Crewes, the Selbournes, the Winston Churchills, the Archbishop of Canterbury, Lord Crawford, Arthur Balfour, John Morley, Lord Bryce, Lady Desborough, Lord Robert Cecil, Mr. H. A. L. Fisher, Mr. J. M. Barrie, Sir Henry Newbolt, and many others.

When the 1914 War was over, and a new German Ambassador was appointed to the Court of St. James's, I had to receive his wife when she came to make her call. (The wives of newly accredited Ambassadors always call on the wife of the Foreign Secretary at once.) I did not look forward to this, as it seemed to me still rather early days, after all our sufferings in the war, to begin social relations

---

[1] Lord Curzon was Foreign Secretary October 24th, 1919–January 23rd, 1924.

again. However, Frau Stahmer arrived, and greeted me with a strong American accent, and I immediately exclaimed, "Oh, I am so pleased to find that you are an American!" To this she replied emphatically, "I was born an American, but my heart is pure German." I felt that perhaps this was rather a *gaffe* on my part, and so I sent her a little note afterwards, explaining that I was an American myself, which always made me eager to meet a fellow-countrywoman.

At the first big reception that we gave for Members of the Diplomatic Corps, the Stahmers were avoided by everyone, and left alone with each other. Nobody would say a word to them, their isolation was quite noticeable, and common politeness as their hostess obliged me to spend some time talking to Herr Stahmer, and then sitting with his wife on a sofa. I must say that I did not much enjoy doing this, but of course one owes a duty in one's own house to evidently unpopular guests—they have been asked to the house, and they must be entertained at least to some extent. I did my rather reluctant best for them—and afterwards I was criticized for this elementary politeness, and people said that they supposed I must have pro-German sympathies, after seeing me make conversation to the Stahmers when I would far rather have talked to anyone else in the room.

One of the parties that I can never think of without smiling was the dinner that we gave for the Shah of Persia, in 1919—the late Ahmed Shah,[1] a very roundabout and solemn young personage. The principal guest invited to meet him was the Duke of York—afterwards King George VI—and others were the Stamfordhams, the Derek Keppels, Lady Pembroke, and Lady Anglesey. A day or two before the dinner, the Shah had sent me a Persian Order with a beautiful diamond star, and I had duly obtained permission from Buckingham Palace to accept it. We soon discovered, however, that the Shah had hoped to be given the Order of the Garter, which his father had received, and that he was greatly disappointed when he found that it would not be given to him. (The reason for this was a decision, taken not long before, that the Order of the Garter must henceforward be restricted to Christendom, and that non-Christian Sovereigns were not eligible to receive it.) It was evident that this disappointment had cast a gloom over the Shah's spirits when he dined with us. He was very solemn at dinner, and afterwards, in the

[1] Sultan Ahmed Shah (1898–1930), who succeeded his father in 1909, when the latter was compelled to abdicate, and was himself deposed in 1925 and succeeded by Riza Khan Pahlavi.

drawing-room, he rather unexpectedly asked for tea. A tea-tray with an enormous silver teapot was brought up for him, and he drank cup after cup. I watched, fascinated, as he half-filled each cup with sugar—his tea must have been practically syrup. When he left the house, a most unfortunate incident occurred in the hall, just as he was going away. The orchestra which I engaged to play on these occasions was placed in the hall, and, acting on my instructions, was playing the Persian National Anthem as the Shah went down the stairs with George. I was following just behind the Duke of York. When he got to the last step of the stairs, the poor Shah suddenly stumbled, or tripped, and fell down flat in the hall— indeed, flat is not at all the right word, as he was so very rotund, and positively *rolled* before George could get to his assistance. It was really an irresistibly funny sight, and the Duke of York and I were hard put to it to restrain our merriment as we watched from a few steps higher up the stairs. George kept on giving us severe glances over his shoulder as he hurried to help the Shah to his feet again. The Duke of York and I did our best to look suitably solemn and sympathetic, but it was not easy. The Shah, poor man, was terribly upset, when George had righted him and smoothed him down, because he said it was an extremely unlucky omen for the ruler of Persia to fall down when the Persian National Anthem was being played. Sometimes in after years when I met the Duke of York, when he had become King George VI, he used to say to me with a chuckle, "I shall never forget your party at Carlton House Terrace when the Shah fell down the stairs!"

In the early part of the same winter—1919—we gave a luncheon for M. Venizelos and Field Marshal Lord Allenby—a most interesting occasion. A dinner party that we gave at this time was for the King and Queen of Portugal and General Pershing, the Commander-in-Chief of the American Forces. This seems to me, in retrospect, rather an odd choice of guests to meet each other, but no doubt George had good reasons of his own for wishing them to be invited to the same party. A luncheon at this time which I remember with pleasure—and also a shade of regret!—was one which we gave for the Emir Feisal, son of King Husein of the Hejaz. Conversation with the Emir Feisal had to be carried on through his interpreter, as he did not speak English or French. He was a man of great charm and fine presence, and gave an impression of keenness and ability which made itself felt even through the tiresome barrier of interpretation. In the course of luncheon he asked me if I would accept a gift of some of his famous white Arab horses—he said that he had heard that I was fond of riding and that I owned racehorses and was interested in racing. I instantly thought how lovely it would be to have the white Arabs at Hackwood, and I was about to accept with the greatest delight, when suddenly I noticed that George was frowning at me and making unmistakable signals to indicate that I must refuse. I realized just in time that the wife of the Foreign Secretary must not accept such gifts from the rulers of other countries, and so I hastily changed my eager expression to one of grateful regret, and, through the interpreter, conveyed an apologetic refusal. I got the impression, from his smile and the twinkle in his eye, that the Emir Feisal fully realized how reluctant I was, and how disappointed. I learned afterwards, with some envy, that he had given them to the Duchess of Portland!

Early in 1920 we had a very big dinner for the Prince of Wales and the Members of the Peace Conference who were assembled in London. Princess Helena Victoria and Lady Patricia Ramsay were the other royal guests on this occasion, and, as well as our Prime Minister Mr. Lloyd George, the foreign representatives at the Conference included Maréchal Foch, General Weygand, Marchese Imperiali,[1] Cambon,[2] Miller[3] and Hymans[4]—and masses of other people whose names have less historical importance. I have only a general impression that this party was a success and that I enjoyed it.

In December 1920 we gave a small and very pleasant luncheon for the King and Queen of Denmark. To meet them we had the Lyttons, the Londonderrys, the Churchills, the Imperialis, the Marquis de Soveral, and Lord Farquhar.

One of our parties that I remember being rather tedious and dull was a dinner that we gave for the Crown Prince of Japan, Prince Hirohito.[5] Princess Alice, Lady Athlone, came to this dinner, but even her great charm and natural gaiety could not quite help us to make it a success, because the Crown Prince and his suite imparted an atmosphere of ruthless dullness which nothing could overcome. His command of the English language was known to be excellent, but Japanese Court etiquette required that he should speak nothing but Japanese, and that every word that we said in reply to his trite

---

[1] Marchese Guglielmo Imperiali di Francavilla (1858–1944), of Italy.
[2] Jules Cambon (1845–1935), of France.
[3] David Hunter Miller (1875–1932), American lawyer, legal adviser to the U.S. Commission, who collaborated in drawing up the final draft of the League of Nations Covenant.
[4] Paul Hymans (1865–1941), of Belgium.
[5] Emperor of Japan from 1926.

questions through the interpreter should be repeated to him in Japanese. This made the conversation extraordinarily slow and also slightly absurd, as we all knew perfectly well that he had understood everything that we had said in the first place, before the interminable interval while the interpreter painstakingly translated, and the Crown Prince listened with a fixed and wooden grin. It was all as different as possible from the really necessary interpretation done for the Emir Feisal who had listened with such an alert and interested expression and who obviously could almost read our replies from our faces as we spoke. With the Crown Prince of Japan it was quite otherwise, and if his demeanour was correct at the Japanese Court, it was certainly very dreary at Carlton House Terrace. Later, he sent me a gift, contained in an elaborate Japanese casket. When I opened the casket, I found inside it an object wrapped up carefully in a beautiful scarf of fine white Japanese silk. The object was a photograph of himself! I couldn't help regretting that it was in order for me to accept this not very exciting little gift (although I did rather like the scarf)—whereas I had had to refuse the wonderful present of the Emir Feisal's beautiful white Arab horses.

Another party of ours that I look back on with a slight feeling of regret is a luncheon we gave for the King and Queen of Portugal— because it ended in a most unfortunate mishap. At the end of luncheon our butler was lighting cigarettes with a lighter which gave rather a big flame. It was apt to flare up when it had just been refilled, and I had already warned him to be very careful when using it. On this occasion it suddenly flared up when he was lighting the Queen of Portugal's cigarette, and in a flash it had caught her veil and the brim of her hat. I was busy talking to the King of Portugal and did not see this happen, when I was suddenly interrupted by Maud Cunard saying urgently to me, across the table: "Gracie! The Queen of Portugal is on fire!" I looked round quickly, and I was so surprised that all I said was, "Oh, so she is!" The smouldering parts of the Queen's hat were rapidly extinguished by the butler, and she was soothed by George, but her eyelashes were decidedly singed, and she went straight off to an oculist directly after luncheon in order to make sure that no harm had been done to her eyes. Luckily she found that all was well.

Years afterwards, I most unfortunately gave some slight offence to the King and Queen of Portugal, through no fault of my own. It was after George's death, on the occasion of my daughter's coming-out Ball at Carlton House Terrace. I had a big dinner party first, to which the King and Queen of Spain came. The King and

Queen of Portugal did not dine, but were invited to the Ball. Just after dinner, the Queen of Spain had a severe attack of nose-bleeding, and I took her to my room and stayed with her until she recovered. Naturally I could not leave her, and unfortunately the King and Queen of Portugal arrived while I was still upstairs with the Queen of Spain and so could not receive them on their arrival. They were, understandably, a little hurt by this omission; and although, as soon as I was free to go downstairs to my guests, I did my best to put matters right, it was certainly a little difficult to explain that the Queen of Spain was there first because she had been asked to dinner!

The Queen of Spain had a wonderful presence, and dressed beautifully. She often wore a magnificent parure of turquoises set in diamonds. I have never seen another set of jewels like them, and they were extremely becoming to her very English form of beauty. We gave a big dinner for the King and Queen of Spain in the early days at Carlton House Terrace—a very delightful party when the other dinner guests included the Spanish Ambassador and Madame Merry del Val, the Pembrokes, the Londonderrys, the Crewes, the Cromers, the Ribblesdales, the Ancasters, the Churchills, the Cranbournes, the Duchess of Portland, Arthur Balfour, the Duke of Westminster, Lord Beatty and Lord Hardinge. As I went to receive the Queen of Spain when she arrived, I realized with a flash of horrified recognition that her dress was a replica of the one I was wearing myself. Both were made of white and silver brocade, by Worth of Paris, and they were absolutely identical. I had to make a hurried excuse a moment or two later, and rush up to my room and change with lightning speed into something else. Luckily the maid I then had was quick and resourceful and equal to any emergency. I reproached Worth afterwards about this, and he candidly admitted that he had thought it safe to make identical dresses for the Queen of Spain and me, because he knew I was unlikely to go to Madrid, and forgot that the Queen of Spain might very well dine with me in London.

The King of Spain was always very gay and cheerful and the best of good company. Nothing ever damped his flow of high spirits. Years afterwards when I was living very quietly in the country because events in the Argentine had obliged me to curtail my expenses, I met the King of Spain at a luncheon in London. He said he had not seen me for ages, and asked where I had been. I said, "Well, Sir, since I lost my fortune I have lived very quietly and seen nobody." To this he replied gaily, "But that's nonsense—I lost my fortune too, but I still go about and see my friends and enjoy myself!"

The Prince of Wales was a frequent guest of ours at Carlton House Terrace in the early twenties. It was evident that he did not enjoy the formal dinners and receptions, and was far happier at the purely frivolous parties that I gave occasionally for my step-daughters and other young people. Even at these parties he was put out by the least suggestion of formality. At the coming-out ball that we gave for my second step-daughter Alexandra, George was suffering from one of his bad back attacks, and I had to see the ball through without him. When the time came to go down to supper, I went to the Prince and made my little curtsey and said, "Supper is ready, Sir." He looked quite taken aback, and answered: "Oh, must we go down now? I didn't think we would have to be so formal." I must say I found this a little disconcerting. However, he came down to supper, and was charming.

In writing about the parties that we gave, and the many distinguished and interesting people whom we entertained, I am able to refresh my memory from my wonderful autograph book. This charming book, bound in dark blue leather and beautifully tooled in gold with great artistry, was a present from George soon after our marriage. Our guests wrote their names in it at Carlton House Terrace, and at Hackwood, and at Montacute, and I took it with me sometimes when I knew that I was going to meet persons of historic importance. In this way I have in my book the signatures of the 'Big Four' in Paris, when I joined George there—Georges Clemenceau, Woodrow Wilson, Orlando, and D. Lloyd George. One page, dating from that time, has nothing on it but the name Foch, in a bold handwriting—that was written when we lunched with him in Paris. There is one even bolder—a huge, conceited scrawl at the top of a page—which was inscribed by Mussolini when he came to lunch at Carlton House Terrace. Some people I knew used to send their autograph books to be signed, simply for the sake of a famous signature, which could hardly be refused. That I have never done, and my beautiful dark blue book contains nothing that was not written in one of our houses, or at least in my presence, when, if I was not a hostess, I was one of the guests.

At weekends, and at other intervals between our parties in London, we entertained at Hackwood—delightful summer house parties, and big shoots in the autumn and winter. My autograph book reminds me of the many guests whom we received there.

I first met Princess Marina of Greece in Paris, when she was at a finishing school kept by a delightful Russian lady, Princess May Madjeska. My daughter Marcella was there at the same time, and in fact she shared a room with Princess Marina for about a year and a half. The Princess was a lovely girl, and grace personified—it was always a joy to watch her playing tennis, or dancing—and she was natural and completely unspoilt. She often stayed with us at Hackwood later on, and was always a delightful guest. I had the pleasure of taking her to her first Ascot from Hackwood, with my own daughter. Her parents, Prince and Princess Nicholas of Greece, were staying at Hackwood that week, but they, like George, did not accompany us because they shared his lack of interest in racing. They used often to visit us, with another beautiful daughter, Princess Olga, afterwards Princess Paul of Serbia. (George very much liked and admired Prince Paul, whom he thought very able and charming.) I have a vivid picture in my mind of a weekend party at Hackwood, and of George and Princess Nicholas of Greece sitting together on a sofa in the saloon, when lovely little Jean Norton floated through the room with the Aga Khan trotting heavily and purposefully after her. George looked up in some surprise and said, "Am I to understand that the Aga Khan is really in pursuit of Mrs. Norton?" They were playing a favourite house-party game called Sardines, and this glimpse of it greatly puzzled George—as well it might.

I was a guest at the wedding of Princess Marina and Prince George, afterwards Duke and Duchess of Kent, and later on I was privileged to dine with them in Belgrave Square. I was charmed with the way in which the young Duke took his responsibilities as a host, when he told me at dinner that he always saw the chef himself and discussed the arrangements for their parties; and he added, with delightful pride, "I also discuss with Marina what dress and jewels I advise her to wear." I am thankful that I have this memory of their youth and happiness, which ended so tragically when our gallant and youngest Prince met his death in an aircraft in the last war. The courage and grace with which the Duchess of Kent has continued to play her part for England has won the admiration of all of us.

We had a weekend house party at Hackwood in the spring of 1919 for the King and Queen of the Belgians and Prince and Princess Arthur of Connaught. I remember that Princess Arthur talked constantly of operations—she had done splendid work in a hospital during the war, and had even taken an active part in the work in operating theatres. Up to a point this conversation was of course very interesting, but when it tended to become too gruesome —there was one grim little anecdote about amputating a finger—I found that I was always trying to divert it to less distressing subjects.

Among the other guests we had at this party were Prince Napoleon[1]
and his wife Princess Clementine—not a very lively couple, but perhaps they were part of George's collection of Napoleonic relics—
the Duke and Duchess of Wellington (which seems a little tactless),
and Lord Charles Beresford. Dear old Charlie Beresford, everyone
loved him, and he always said just what came into his mind without
a moment's reflection. His wife, to whom he was devoted, used to
make up in a rather obvious way, and on one occasion when he was
walking down the steps of the Royal Yacht Squadron Club at Cowes,
he saw Lady Charles approaching and said merrily, "Here comes
my little frigate in a fresh coat of paint!" The Winston Churchills
stayed with us at Hackwood, and Winston spent a lot of time with
his easel painting in the grounds—their beauty charmed his painter's
eye. Indoors, his conversational powers were tremendous. I remember one evening when he stood on the hearthrug with his back to
the fire and held forth with terrific gusto. Afterwards, when we had
all gone upstairs, George said to me, "Really, Winston talks too
much—no one else could get a word in, and I never had a chance to
speak, in my own house, all the evening!"

Smuts was a guest whom we very much enjoyed. The first time
that he came he complained that the Hackwood drive was so long
that he thought he must have lost his way, and almost told the
chauffeur to turn round, because he could not believe that they would
find the house at the end of it.

The King and Queen of the Belgians were often our guests at
Hackwood. At one house party that we had for them they met George
Grahame.[2] The King took a great fancy to him, and hinted to my
George that he would be very acceptable as our next Ambassador in
Brussels—a change was almost due. So George decided to send
George Grahame to Brussels, an appointment which otherwise he
might not have got. George always said that he felt sure that the
King of the Belgians simply wanted to have another man in his
capital as tall as himself. The King and Queen of the Belgians
stayed at Hackwood before Cynthia's marriage to Oswald Mosley,
with Princess Alice and Lord Athlone, the Londonderrys, the
Marquis de Soveral, Sir Hedworth and Lady Meux, and other
guests. King George and Queen Mary and King Albert and Queen
Elisabeth came to the wedding at the Chapel Royal, St. James's,

[1] Prince Victor Napoleon (1862–1926), grandson of Jerome Bonaparte and
son of Plon-Plon.
[2] Sir George Grahame (1873–1940), Minister Plenipotentiary in Paris 1918–
20, and Ambassador to Belgium 1920–28.

and it received a tremendous amount of publicity, partly on account of the Royal wedding guests, and partly because of Cynthia's wonderful appearance as a bride. The newspapers called her the Bride of the Year, and the Lily Bride—and indeed she did look quite lovely.

CHAPTER XIV

Our Everyday Lives

GEORGE and I, when we were apart, had the old-fashioned habit of writing to each other every day, or very nearly. However, except for my cure at Langenschwalbach, and for the trip that I made to South America in 1923, we were not often separated for more than a few days at a time, and not many of the letters that we exchanged on these occasions have survived. I still possess a few, and these I have inserted in their proper places in this book, because I think that letters can give a better feeling of what was going on at the time than the most vivid recollection can do.

When Parliament was in session we lived at Carlton House Terrace, and usually spent the weekends at Hackwood—sometimes at Montacute, and occasionally with friends. From time to time I went to Paris to see my dressmakers, and George spent some weekends at Kedleston, alone or with Mr. A. S. G. Butler,[1] the architect, attending to the improvements there. There were occasions when George was abroad at a Conference, when I would probably join him for a few days in the course of it. Apart from these separations, the routine of our life was seldom interrupted. George's eldest daughter, Irene, lived in a house of her own in Leicestershire, and Cimmie, the second daughter, was married to Oswald Mosley. Baba, the youngest, lived with us. My little daughter Marcella was in the schoolroom, and my sons came to us in the holidays from Eton, and later from Oxford, in the Vacations. It was a life packed with activity, domestic and social and official, and a very strenuous one. Looking back, I believe that I thoroughly enjoyed it. I remember being extraordinarily tired sometimes, but I also remember the gaiety and the fun, the happiness of watching my children grow up, and the pleasure that I received from entertaining for my step-daughters, and making all the arrangements for Cimmie's wonderful wedding, and bringing out Baba. It was a happy household, and one of the tiny details of our arrangements that stays in my memory was the regular delight—for us a purely domestic one!—of the Lord Mayor's Banquet. At this annual festivity husbands and wives are

---

[1] Arthur S. G. Butler (*b.* 1888), noted for his country houses, churches, etc., who has also published books, including a study of *The Architecture of Sir Edwin Lutyens* (1950).

always seated next to each other, and it was almost the only occasion every year that George and I had the treat of a *tête-à-tête* dinner. We used to save up scraps of gossip for each other, and little matters of mutual interest, for this occasion, and when the night came we were full of miscellaneous news and points to be discussed, beginning with the turtle soup and not finishing until the Banquet was ended— we enjoyed it like anything.

In March 1922 George went to Paris to attend the Conference which had assembled to discuss the evacuation of Anatolia by Greece. I remained in London, and the following are some extracts from the letters I wrote to him while he was away:

". . . I was delighted to hear from you this morning. What long hours of Conference you are having. But what a comfort that it is all going so well. . . . Maud Cunard was my only visitor today. She came to me from a reception which she said was more like a funeral than anything else. She also told me that she had dined with Winston and that he had said the one post he longs for is the F.O.! We must not let him have it! . . ."

". . . I am always made happy by the arrival of your dear letter about 11 o'clock every morning. I am disappointed though to read in today's letter that your leg and foot are again causing so much pain—of course due to overwork. Poor you! Such long hours of Conference. . . . Yesterday Nora Musgrave, Sigrid Loeffler and Mother came to see me. Nora was delighted at having at last let Edenhall for 20 years . . . and Mother was delighted with her spring cleaning! I wrote to Baba for her birthday and also about buying some of her clothes before leaving Paris. . . ."

Later that spring George was laid up with a bad attack of phlebitis, which caused him much pain and was aggravated by insomnia. He had to stay in bed, at Hackwood, for some weeks. During that time I had to go to Paris for a few days, with my son Alfred, and wrote these letters to George while I was away:

"May 15th, 1922.   Ritz Hotel, Paris.
I am longing to know if you had a better night last night—I hope with all my heart that you did. As I said in my telegram we had a wonderful crossing. Alfred and I sat on deck, and it was a perfect afternoon. I was met, as usual, at every place, and the journey was most comfortable. Sir Milne Cheetham[1] met me at the Paris station

---

[1] Sir Milne Cheetham (1869–1938), Minister in Paris 1921–22.

with Moss. There was a huge crowd at the station as Carpentier[1]
came from England with us—he was given a great reception. I
found the usual flowers awaiting me from M. de Castellane, Aga
Khan, and Charles Mendl. I dined downstairs with Alfred—the
usual Sunday crowd. Lots of people came to talk to me—Mr. and
Mrs. Vansittart (he is looking much better and tells me he is in the
doctor's hands here), Maggie Greville, Mrs. Loeffler, Mendl and
Castellane. I came to bed early and left Alfred downstairs to dance a
little. Irene telephoned to me this morning to ask if she could come
to lunch today. I have already received a number of invitations but
I shall refuse them all as I want to get my work done as soon as
possible and get back to my poor ill Boy. The weather here is perfect
but I still feel very tired. My rooms are nice but noisy as they look on
the Place Vendôme. . . ."

"Tuesday.   Ritz Hotel, Paris.
I was delighted to receive your telegram yesterday, saying you
had had a somewhat better night through sleeping in my comfy bed.
How glad I am. I also received a letter from Baba last evening written
on Sunday evening after having dined with you, in which she says
you seemed so much better and that you were very cheerful. How
wise I was to come away! I told Nurse I was sure you would be much
better without me. Irene lunched with Alfred and me yesterday.
She is looking very well, and is thinner. She returns to London
today. The Ritz was crowded for luncheon. I saw King Manoel of
Portugal, Prince and Princess Christopher of Greece, the Duke and
Duchess of Portland, Bell Herbert, the Duchess of Roxburgh, and
lots of Americans. Alfred dined last night with Charles Mendl and
went to a play—I dined alone in my sitting-room as I was so
tired.
"I enclose a letter I received yesterday from Mr. Vansittart. His
doctor came and gave me an injection—it does not hurt in the least,
and I shall have one every day while I am here, and the great thing
is that I can go on with the treatment in London as he has an understudy there. I do hope, when he goes to London at the end of the
week, you will let him come and see you. He is a charming man. I
am sure his treatment will do you more good than all those stupid
English doctors. I know your leg will take a long time. Dr. Holmes
told me so before I left London.
"Your dear letter has just arrived—also the one about the key.
Alfred gave the key to Baba before leaving, so she has *two*. Please

[1] Georges Carpentier, the French boxer.

ask her for mine, will you. Alfred is in bed today with a bad cold.
He coughed all night so I asked the doctor to see him this morning
and he has put him in a plaster and says he will not be able to go to
the country until Friday at the earliest. This morning I had a letter
from Hubert's Dame at Eton telling me that he is in bed with bad
glands. My worries seem to be unending. I do hope, darling, that
the new doctor will be a success. . . ."

Enclosure.
"May 15.   British Embassy, Paris.
Dear Lady Curzon,
             I asked Dr. Lesueur this morning to ring you up about .
lunch time and he said he would be at your disposal this evening
between 5 and 6 if you cared to see him. I hope you will: I'm sure
he'd do you good. I've also written to Lord Curzon about a dozen
pages by tonight's bag, urging him to give this a trial in London.
(Lesueur goes over on Friday.) I hope that if you're satisfied after
talking to Lesueur you'll back the idea up. I do really think it's a
marvellous thing and a dozen injections might really make all the
difference to Lord Curzon and be the turning point. I'm not superstitious but there is sometimes a fitness in things. I've put my heart
as well as my back into working for him for two years and it would be
so 'right' if my own experience in this also turned out to be the best
service I could do him.
                              Yours very sincerely,
                                Robert Vansittart."[1]

   In spite of every treatment, however, George's leg remained
very painful, and finally he went, in July, to Orléans to do a cure
there. I wrote to him about the return journey to England at the
end of the cure.

"August 1st, 1922.   1 Carlton House Terrace.
   I am so disappointed and unhappy to know that you are
still so far from being well. My poor darling, you have had a terrible
time—just think of five months of suffering! It seems so very unfair.
I will do all in my power to help you when you return at the end of
the week. I only hope you won't find Sunday a bad day to travel, as
you know it is the day before the Bank Holiday. Philip is most
anxious for you to go for the night, or as long as he can persuade you

   [1] Robert Vansittart (*b.* 1881), created Baron Vansittart in 1941. He was
secretary to Lord Curzon during his tenure of the Foreign Secretaryship 1920–24.

Author on board R.M.S.P. *Andes*

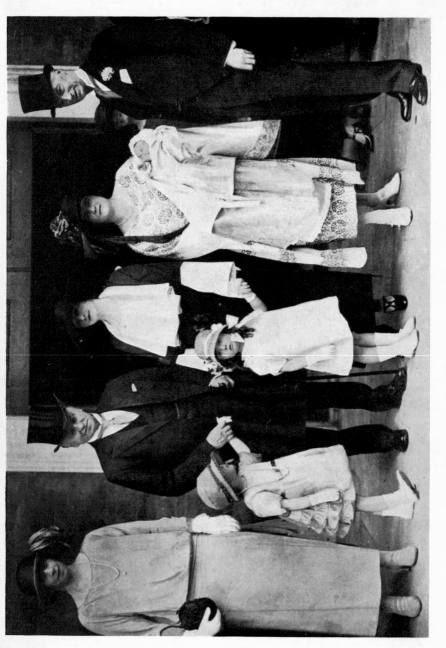

Christening of The Hon. Frank Curzon's son

Lady Linlithgow, Lord Curzon, the author, Hon. Mrs. Frank Curzon with infant son, Hon. Frank Curzon

to stay at Lympne, on your arrival. He would send a car with me to meet you—he would also of course take in Nurse for the week-end or longer. I would go to Lympne the night before and see that your room was in order with good blinds to keep the light out. You need not come down to dinner unless you wish. I saw A.J.B. at lunch with Maud yesterday. He is going to Lympne if you go, and says he could talk to you there, as he leaves London on Saturday for good—he says he would hand over the F.O. to you there. Will you send me a telegram as soon as you receive this, saying what you would rather do. I go to Hackwood tomorrow, and I shall return in time to meet you at Lympne, London, or what ever you decide to do. . . . Baba is at Hackwood, but goes this week end to Sandwich to the Spender-Clays. Hubert goes today to Hackwood from Eton. You will be glad to hear that Fox has found your links in an old shirt in the wardrobe in your room also the waistcoat buttons in a white waistcoat. I must close this to catch the bag. . . ."

I had forgotten this detail of the lost links and waistcoat buttons until I re-read this letter; I feel sure that George must have been much annoyed at finding himself abroad without any—unless his man had packed a spare set—for he always dressed for dinner, and very much disliked dining in his day clothes. He was anything but a dandy, and indeed he wore his clothes until they were quite shabby and I had to persuade him to order new ones, but the one thing that he made a point of was bathing and changing before dinner, no matter how busy his day and his evening. It was part of his personal frugality and Spartan upbringing that made him grudge the money spent on his own clothes—he would pay ten thousand pounds for a picture, but nothing would induce him to buy a new dressing-gown. But he quite enjoyed new things to wear if he hadn't felt self-indulgent about buying them—I remember giving him a smart dark blue silk bed-jacket with braid froggings across the front, so necessary for him as he was often in bed with a bad back and used to receive a lot of visits there, and he was quite proud of this elegant garment and asked his visitors to admire it. He looked his best in evening dress, because he loved everything ceremonial. In his robes as Chancellor of the University of Oxford he looked really magnificent.

I accompanied George on many occasions when he went to Oxford in his capacity of Chancellor. When he was going to make a speech at Oxford he never prepared it until we were in the train, but worked on it during the journey from London. I remember the

K

carriage littered with papers that he was consulting, and sheaves of notes for his speech, and the scramble to collect them as we arrived at Oxford Station. On one occasion I was present at a function at the Sheldonian Theatre, when George found that the Latin speech usually prepared for the Chancellor had gone astray. He spoke extempore in Latin, and there was so much giggling, and eventually roars of laughter, that I began to wonder if they could possibly be laughing at him. I was told, as soon as the speech was over, that it had been full of brilliant Latin jokes, which had caused all the laughter. I do not understand Latin, and it did not occur to me that it was possible to be actually amusing in a dead language! I accompanied George on the delightful occasion when an Honorary Degree was accepted by Queen Mary, and walked in the splendid, dignified procession from Balliol to the Sheldonian, through the 'Broad' lined with dense throngs of undergraduates. A photograph of both of us which George especially liked was one taken as we were standing together on the steps leading up to Hall at Balliol.

I shared almost all of George's many interests, especially his concern with the improvements to our various houses and his passion for period furniture and works of art. He loved to discuss these things with me, and indeed I learned a great deal from his excellent judgment. I was, of course, deeply interested in his political career, and a day never passed when we were together without a long talk about his current anxieties and difficulties and hopes. I think he found it helpful to talk to me as it eased his mind of some of his worries to tell me about them. He also very much enjoyed the harmless gossip of the day, and we spent many a happy half-hour laughing over some silly story that was going the rounds, and George's comments were always so elaborately expressed and yet so pungent that they often made me laugh. I remember one comment on the marriage of a man we knew—"I am told she has a colossal fortune, but a calamitous appearance." No one could be dull in conversation with George.

I had a few interests of my own which George did not share. Playing golf was one, and riding another—these of course were made impossible for him by his bad back. Still, he took a great interest in the golf course at Hackwood; and eventually, and almost in spite of himself, he became interested in my racing. He had never cared for racing. Every year, on Derby night, we dined at Derby House to meet Queen Mary, because on that night the King entertained the members of the Jockey Club at Buckingham Palace—George was always put next to Queen Mary and they used to talk about old furniture. I only remember George going to a race meeting once in all the years I knew him, and that was on one occasion when I persuaded him to come with me to Ascot. We were greeted by King George with roars of laughter as we went up the stairs to the Royal Box, and the King exclaimed: "Curzon at Ascot! I can scarcely believe it!" George answered, quite amiably: "Oh, really, Sir, when I have made the effort at last, must I be laughed at for my pains? Just look at my clothes and the trouble I have taken—buttonhole and all!"

My interest in racing dated from the early days of my first marriage, in the Argentine. I have always enjoyed it, but I did not become an owner until a few years after I married George. One day I bought a racehorse. It was called Lulworth Cove, and I bought it from the Duke of Portland, at one of the sales; of course it was bought for me by an agent acting on my behalf. When the Duke of Portland learned that I was in fact the purchaser he was rather worried, and told me that if he had known that it was I who was concerned he would have sold me a better horse. However, he need not have worried, because Lulworth Cove won a race at Ascot, to my great delight. He beat the King's horse. I happened to be standing with King George V as this race was being run, and he, following with his race-glasses, said to me, in surprise, "What's this horse, coming up and overhauling the rest?" I said, "It's my horse, Sir." Lulworth Cove came in first, after an exciting race, and the King was the first to congratulate me.

George was a little taken aback, to begin with, by my venture into ownership, but quite soon he was reconciled to the idea, and he even took some trouble to verify and to provide me with the ancient Curzon racing colours of brown and pink, which date from the early eighteenth century. He had never taken the least interest in racing, but after a while he became really concerned with the success of my horses, and sometimes he used to tell me that he had seen the result of a race, when I had a horse running, on the tape at the Carlton Club. I used to feel really touched when he told me this.

My horses were trained with Vandy Beatty, at Newmarket, and by Walter Nightingale, at Epsom. I was on the whole reasonably successful during my time as an owner, but whenever I had a good win I invariably bought another horse with the proceeds, and when I lost I just stood the loss, and so it is not easy to make a fair estimate of my Turf profits and losses. The most important race I ever won was with Arctic Star, a half-brother of the famous Brown Jack. I owned Arctic Star in partnership with Sir Matthew Wilson, and won the Cesarewitch in 1928, but as Arctic Star ran in Sir Matthew's colours, my half-share of the ownership was not generally recognized.

We used of course to stay with our various friends in the country from time to time—not very often, because we had our own week-end house parties at Hackwood and Montacute, and the little time that George could spare from his innumerable preoccupations he liked to give to the improvements at Kedleston which meant so much to him. However, I remember several enjoyable visits to the houses of our friends. One of the first of these was a delightful one to the Salisburys at Hatfield. George adored this wonderful Elizabethan house. He told me that he had many happy memories of the time he had spent at Hatfield in earlier days, when he was Under-Secretary for Foreign Affairs in the great Lord Salisbury's Administration. (It was from that post that he had been sent by Queen Victoria to be Viceroy of India before he was forty.) I remember asking him which of all the great houses in England he would choose to show to a distinguished foreigner as representing our best: and he immediately answered, "Hatfield." As an alternative, I suggested Knole, the beautiful home of the Sackvilles, and he said although he greatly admired Knole and thought it magnificent, Hatfield came first in his opinion because it was so typically English, a perfect example of all that was best in the English tradition: only in England could such a house be found, and he felt that it had partly acquired this feeling from the character of the family that owned it. He added, "I have always wished that there were more Cecils in the world."

Our fellow guests at this party at Hatfield were the Duke and Duchess of Portland, the Desboroughs with their daughter Imogen (afterwards Viscountess Gage), Lord Richard and Lady Moira Cavendish, Arthur Balfour, Evan Charteris, Edward Rice, and others whose names I cannot now remember. This was my first meeting with Edward Rice, who was later to marry my daughter Marcella. (At this time she was still a child in the schoolroom.) George and I were given rooms in a part of the house close to the Chapel, and I remember very well the strong sense of the supernatural that affected me each night, and the feeling that there were ghostly sounds and movements close at hand.

Another visit which we paid in the early days of our married life was to Lord and Lady Bute at Cardiff Castle. Here we were the only guests, and poor George was kept fully occupied in making speeches on the progress of the war as a member of the War Cabinet. I had never before heard him speak from a platform, and I was thrilled when I realized how well he could speak when he was being heckled.

The interruptions seemed to put him on his mettle, and the worse the heckling, the better he spoke. I remember his first meeting in the town of Cardiff. At the beginning he got what I think might be considered a rough reception, but as he went on he was listened to with attention and with real appreciation, and when he had finished there was great applause. It was all entirely different from his speeches in the House of Lords—the only ones I had heard at that time—and I thoroughly enjoyed it. We rushed from one meeting to another, and for some reason we never seemed to have anything at any meal except sandwiches and champagne, presumably because of the war-time difficulties of those days. George returned to London quite exhausted.

I remember an enjoyable visit that we paid to the Duke and Duchess of Devonshire at Chatsworth, where many of our fellow guests were those whom we had met at Hatfield—nothing could have been more agreeable. Chatsworth is so vast that one takes quite a lot of exercise in merely going from one room to another. I well recollect feeling quite worn out, although I had been greatly interested, after being shown round the enormous stables by Lord Spencer for one whole morning. Here we were given rooms on the ground floor, opening out of the great hall which was full of innumerable statues, and so I had none of the eerie sensations that I had experienced from the nearness of the ancient Chapel at Hatfield. It was a delightful party. One of the days that stays in my memory was a drive to Hardwicke. The Duchess had made Hardwicke most beautiful. She now lives there. I think it is the most lovely and romantic house I have ever seen. Built originally in the midst of unspoilt green country, it is to-day entirely surrounded by coal mines. Even the trees are black, and the Duchess complained of the difficulty of having anything kept clean.

At the end of our visit, George and I motored back to Kedleston, on a perfect morning, with the countryside looking a dream of loveliness, and for the first time I admitted the beauty of Derbyshire. I remember the Duchess of Devonshire telling me when I was first married to George, "Once you have lived at Kedleston, you will find the southern counties cramped and small."

I remember another cheerful house party at Blenheim Palace, given by the Duke of Marlborough to celebrate his sixtieth birthday. He said that the last time he had had a birthday party had been when he came of age, and he thought that it was time that he had another one. It was an excellent party with a splendid ball which I very much enjoyed.

Of course our lives in London, as long as George was Foreign Secretary, were largely taken up with official duties of various kinds. The burden of these duties weighed heavily on George, especially as he had so many other interests which he never relinquished, however great the pressure of work—he was always writing at least one book, and making plans for Kedleston, and corresponding with innumerable people on all kinds of subjects, and visiting Oxford, and attending meetings of the trustees of the National Gallery, and bidding for treasures at Christie's—there was no end to his activities, and never enough time in one day for all of them. The best contribution which I could make towards easing the strain of overwork was to make sure that all our official parties went smoothly and successfully, and this I tried to do to the best of my ability. George disliked official entertaining, but I enjoyed it all, in various ways, and there was always some fun to be got out of every social event, however solemn and formal. I have always believed that if you take a gay and cheerful view of things, other people are more likely to share your view than not.

In 1922 King George V honoured me with the Grand Cross of the British Empire. When I went to the Investiture to receive it at his hands, I had no idea whether I ought to kneel down to receive it or not; nobody could tell me, for I was the first lady to receive this grade of the Order. So when I came before the King I asked him, in a discreet murmur, which seemed the only sensible thing to do, "Do I kneel down, Sir?" The King replied loudly and emphatically, "Certainly not!" I was wearing a wide-brimmed hat—big hats were in fashion then, and I suppose I never considered the fact that the sash of an Order has to be put on over one's head. The King, in great good humour, negotiated the obstacle of my hat most skilfully, manœuvring the dark red silk sash over it without in the least disarranging my injudicious headgear, and I felt that he was almost chuckling as he did so. The first time that I went to Court after receiving this decoration, I simply could not remember exactly how the King had put it on—I could only remember the hat, and the King's amusement—and so I called out to George to come and advise me when I was dressing. George came into my room from his dressing-room, and said, taking up the sash, "Oh, you wear it over the left shoulder, of course." George was accustomed to wearing the Garter ribbon, which is the only Order worn over the left shoulder— all the others being worn over the right one. It was really very unobservant of both of us not to have realized this, but of course I assumed that George was right and thought no more about it, whereas for once his eye for detail had been confused by a personal habit. So I went to Court with the sash of my Order worn over the wrong shoulder. The King, and Queen Mary, and all the other members of the Royal Family tactfully refrained from making any comment—except Lord Lascelles, who could not resist coming up to me at supper and saying, with an amiable smile, "Lady Curzon, you have got your G.B.E. on the wrong way round!" I was a little taken aback by this, but it was too late by that time to worry about it, as I explained to him—I could not, at that stage in the evening, unpin my star and rearrange the whole thing—and he cordially agreed.

I remember one of the staff of the American Embassy of those days coming up to me at a Court after the presentations had taken place, and saying enthusiastically, "I was just tickled to death to see you—an American—standing there on the dais with the King and Queen of England!" I was not exactly overjoyed at this remark, but there seemed to be nothing I could say.

George, with his bad back, found the long hours of standing at Court very exhausting, especially after he had had the attack of phlebitis in his leg and knew that standing always made it worse. He hit on the brilliant idea of having his court sword made into a sort of shooting-stick, with a blunt ferrule on the point of the sword, and a hilt that divided into two and formed a seat. After that, when he went to Court he could sit on it, to the great relief of his painful leg.

CHAPTER XV

Our Own Houses

K EDLESTON is a wonderful house—indeed, it is more than a mere house, it is a small, perfect palace, one of the master-pieces of Robert Adam (who completed the building begun by James Paine). I could well understand why George adored it, and how its pure, classic beauty had made such a lasting impression on him from his childhood. And yet, much as I admired it, I never felt the affection for it as a house that I felt for Hackwood, or for Montacute. I always thought that it needed a warm sun to bring its frozen beauty to life. The vast, splendid Hall, the long galleries, the tall, cold rooms with their great windows looking out over the Derbyshire dales, would have come into their own under a hot blue sky with strong sunlight to warm them. If only it had been built at Genoa or Naples! The delicate pale colours that make the interior of Kedleston so lovely—the pink Derbyshire alabaster of the huge columns in the Hall, the grey-blue of the hangings in the State-rooms —seem to add to the feeling of lifeless perfection in that cold Northern light. Like so many houses of the great classic mid-eighteenth-century period, it stands in isolated beauty, surrounded by grass, and remote from the warmth and colour of flower gardens and flowering trees and shrubs—all these are at some little distance from the house —and there is something a little cheerless about its perfection, both outside and within.

George had loved Kedleston so much, ever since he could remember anything, that eventually it became one of the ruling passions of his life. He realized, however, that it had some disad-vantages—for one thing, it was almost excessively large. (Doctor Johnson had crushingly observed, after visiting it, that "It would do excellently well for a town hall.") Although George's own habits were spartan enough, after growing up in those classic, comfortless surroundings, he was determined to make it really habitable accord-ing to twentieth-century notions of comfort. He looked forward most eagerly to the time when it would be our principal country house, after the lease of Hackwood had expired. He made the most elabor-ate plans for new bathrooms and electric lights and central heating and telephones, and everything that could bring it up to date without affecting its essential character. As a child he had lived with his parents and his brothers and sisters in what was called the family wing, but now the State-rooms were being brought back into use.

I contributed some of my own ideas to this process of modernization—the difficulty always being to secure comfort without sacrificing a single detail of Robert Adam's unified design. For instance, in the great drawing-room the enormous windows had never had any curtains because the architraves of pink marble were an essential part of the scheme and must never be hidden. I suggested that curtains of grey-blue chiffon velvet, to match the damask on the walls designed by Adam, should be hung *inside* the architraves and looped up with invisible cords by day, and let down behind the marble surround to cover the cold glass panes by night. This idea of mine was duly carried out, and was a great success.

The State bedroom was a noble room, with the same blue damask hangings woven originally to Robert Adam's design for all the State-rooms, and a superb bed hung with the damask, and headed with a great needlework design consisting of a huge C surmounted by a coronet and surrounded by mantling. Many of these hangings—even then more than a hundred and fifty years old—had become very fragile and were in danger of falling to pieces when the rooms were in use again. I had the most fragile of them covered with the finest and most transparent chiffon of exactly the same colour. This preserved the fabric, and prevented the risk of tearing them when they were touched, and when it was done the chiffon was practically invisible. This delicate operation was carried out with great skill by workers from the Royal School of Needlework. George was delighted by these practical suggestions that I made, and relied on me to plan all such renovations while he devoted his own spare time to his vast schemes for new plumbing, electric wiring, and central heating.

There are fascinating tales and legends about Kedleston, handed down through the nine hundred years that the Curzons have lived there in various houses built on the same site where the Kedleston of Robert Adam now stands. It is said that the Young Pretender, in his dash to the South, spent one night there with his loyal followers. Out of respect for the lady of the house he departed the next day because he learned that she was about to have a baby. Nevertheless, he took all the horses from the stables.

George was passionately concerned with the plans for the renovation of Kedleston, which he had entrusted to Mr. A. S. G. Butler, the architect. Very often while I was entertaining parties of our friends at Hackwood he would go to Kedleston by himself, for a day or two, to keep an eye on the progress of the work there, and to make sure that nothing whatever was done without his final approval—which was given only after the most meticulous tests. He went into every minute detail of the plans, down to the last bath-tap and electric-light switch. He even used to get into the new baths—lined, first of all, with copies of *The Times*—in order to discover if they were the right shape from inside. His improvements involved installing in this vast house more than 3 miles of piping, and he took endless trouble to ensure that each electric-light point was in the right position in every room. Rearranging the books in the library was another thing that occupied him, and he arranged for the expert repair of every piece of furniture that needed it. Almost all the furniture, at any rate in the state-rooms, had been designed by Robert Adam.

George was just as much concerned with the alterations and improvements to the gardens and pleasure grounds, and he used to fret when bad weather prevented him carrying out the changes which he had planned. He wrote some letters to me in the spring of 1924 which show his anxious preoccupation with his scheme for planting, and the keen personal interest which he took in the whole management of Kedleston. (I must explain that at this time he was about to engage a new agent, as Mr. Pelham, who had managed Kedleston for many years, was retiring. Someone had told George that the new agent, whom he had practically engaged, was a Roman Catholic.)

"March 9, 1924.   Carlton House Terrace.

It is a very fine day tho I have not been out, so I trust that your party has been a success both Saturday and today. I have been at work on my book. I see pretty clearly that I shall not be able to get away this April for our tour of Spain—as with a new Agent at Ked quite ignorant coming on April 7, with the Museum cases requiring to be installed in April, with all the planting which has been hung up by the shocking winter and none of which has yet been done, requiring to be taken in hand unless we are to lose another whole year—for nothing can be planted after April—I realize alas that it is out of the question and that we must take our holiday later. We will have it some time, but this Spring it is clearly impossible. . . . If you are staying on at H——d I will come down any night you like to see my darling wife."

"March 11, 1924. Ked.

It is icy cold here and snowing hard, so I can do nothing and all planting is out of the question. I only hope it is better with you at Hackwood. I wonder if you have been or are going to the Zoo to see the wire cages. Pelham says it will be most difficult for any Agent here who is a Catholic; as he has to manage the Church Schools and Council at Mulginton and Quarndon, etc. as my representative. I shall hear tomorrow what are the facts and am very doubtful if he turns out to be a R.C. whether I ought to keep him. For in that case he will have begun by deliberately deceiving me. Pelham told him all about the Church duties he would have to perform and he never said a word about his own faith. It is all most annoying. Butler is causing me infinite trouble."

"March 13, 1924. Ked.

It turned fine yesterday and I had a splendid day planting in the pleasure grounds—completed the beds in the long walk going up to the wood. I am much relieved also at hearing that the new Agent is *not* a Catholic. Daffodils coming up everywhere. I suggest that next Friday afternoon (after a meeting I have in the City that day) we go down to Montacute till the following Monday or Tuesday. Then on Monday April 3 I must come down to Ked. to say good-bye to Pelham who leaves on Saturday the 5th. It would be very sweet if you would come down then till Monday 7. I think you accepted to dine with the Massereenes on April 8, after which I presume you will want to go to Paris. One of my best workmen here, a very fine old fellow called Copertake, who has done all the tree felling with me in the pleasure grounds during the last two years, died suddenly yesterday of cancer in the stomach. I am going over to see his poor widow who is also very ill. I hope you are having a happy time. I come up on Tuesday by train reaching London at 5.45 p.m. Hay (from the London Parks) comes down about planting the new flowering trees on Monday."

Another fine old servant at Kedleston was Voss, the head gardener. The Voss family had been gardeners at Kedleston for generations, and George used to say that the Vosses had probably been there as long as the Curzons. Among the many improvements which George planned was a new rose garden specially for me. We were both very fond of roses. After his death I made frequent visits to Kedleston, taking with me his favourite red roses to the Memorial Chapel. Dear old Voss would meet me at the door of the Chapel with the keys, and I used to go down to the vault to put my roses on

George's coffin. The coffin rested on a bier in the middle of the vault, and, like the coffins of past generations of Curzons, was covered with red velvet and studded with gilt nails. The other coffins were on shelves at each side.

On one of these visits, when I had arranged my roses and was about to leave, the electric light fused and I found myself suddenly in the dark. The vault was not really an alarming place, when lighted; it was lined with white marble, and seemed full of peace. Indeed, to me it was a sacred place—but even so one would not wish to be left there in total darkness. I felt my way to the opening of the stairs, praying not to come in contact with any of the coffins, and climbed up. When I came to the top, Voss, who was waiting for me there, exclaimed at once, "Oh, my lady, what has happened?" I suppose my face must have been very white.

Once, when I was paying one of my visits to the vault, I noticed in an empty space on one of the shelves a postcard with something written on it in George's handwriting. (He had a habit of using postcards for making notes and memoranda, and always used a thick blue pencil for making these notes.) I looked at the postcard, and on it was written, 'Reserved for the second Lady Curzon'. That is a thing I have never forgotten. It is a long time since I played the Bess of Hardwicke part that George envisaged for me, moving from one to another of four splendid houses, and I am touched when I think that he took care to ensure that I should rest at last in the Kedleston vault.

George had no country house of his own when he returned from India, as his father, old Lord Scarsdale, was then alive and was living at Kedleston. So George took Hackwood on a furnished lease, assigned to him by Lord Wilton, who had it on a long lease from Lord Bolton. When this lease expired, and I renewed it, that Lord Bolton had died. His successor, who scarcely knew what the house contained, came to inspect it, and decided to remove for his own use much of the furniture. So it was necessary to refurnish the house to a large extent. Of course it already contained many beautiful things that belonged to George. His own room on the ground floor, where he worked when he was there, was hung with red silk damask, and had a big eighteenth-century writing table and other charming possessions of his own in it. The fine tapestries, and the lovely chandeliers, all belonged to George too. George's knowledge and judgment of antique furniture and silver—and of course above all of pictures—was really remarkable. (The only branch of this sort of knowledge that did not interest him much was old china—he used to say that he had never had time to master the intricacies of all the china 'marks' which a connoisseur has to recognize.) Having grown up among the Robert Adam treasures at Kedleston, he had early developed an appreciation of lovely things, and had cultivated his critical sense by sheer hard work and intensive study. Experts and dealers respected his judgment, and he was never deceived by a fake, or at fault when 'dating' a work of art. In every-day matters of what is called 'taste', however, we did not always agree. For instance, he preferred the look of a thick, dark tablecloth to the perfect surface of satin-wood or mahogany, and insisted on concealing many a charming table with a heavy cloth and then displaying books and portfolios of prints on it. Although he adored the perfect beauty of the State bedroom at Kedleston, he never thought of having anything done to his own bedroom at Carlton House Terrace, which remained with an ugly brass bedstead and a shabby Edwardian flowered wallpaper until I had it done up for him, as a surprise, when he was away from home. He was delighted with the result when he returned, but later he complained that the mattress on the fine new bed was unbearably flat and level, whereas the old one had had a nice comfortable hollow which fitted him exactly!

I really loved Hackwood best of all our houses. It had been built in the late eighteenth century on the site of an earlier house, in a stately and formal design, and architecturally it was not nearly so important or so perfect as Kedleston or Montacute. Still, I liked it best. The stone had a warm look, and the rooms were welcoming and gracious. It always seemed to me the ideal place for country entertaining. Perhaps it is the recollection of all the delightful house parties I had there, the gaiety and the good talk, the pheasant shoots in lovely autumn weather, the varied fun at every season of the year, that makes me think now that it was perfect. The gardens were lovely, and I made many improvements while I lived there. Among others, I made a large aviary, for all the macaws I had brought back with me from South America in 1923.

Montacute is a gem of a house, a marvel of typically English beauty in a lovely, tranquil setting. I have many happy memories of it. This Tudor building made a fascinating contrast when we went to it from Hackwood, or from the Palladian purity of Kedleston or Nash's Regency taste at Carlton House Terrace. We did not spend as much time at Montacute as we did at our other houses, because when George inherited Kedleston he soon became occupied with his improvements there, and I always preferred Hackwood for entertaining. However, we had several large house parties at Montacute—three very successful ones in the summer of 1919, I remember —and we used quite often to go there for a few days by ourselves to enjoy its peace and beauty.

We moved so often from one of our houses to another, and our lives were so busy and strenuous, that I made every arrangement to ensure that these moves were made with the minimum of packing and trouble. There was a housekeeper at each house, and housemaids; so that only the downstairs servants—kitchen staff, and menservants—had to accompany us. Each house was kept fully stocked with linen, and with silver—George possessed masses of lovely silver, and I had, of course, my own, so fortunately there was enough for all the four houses. I arranged that we should leave spare sets of all our small personal requirements in each house—brushes and combs and tooth-brushes and dressing-gowns and such things— so that there was very little to think of when we made a sudden move from one to another.

As well as the four houses that we lived in, George possessed Tattershall Castle in Lincolnshire, and Bodiam Castle in Sussex, both historic buildings which he had bought in order to preserve them. Tattershall, built by Lord Cromwell at the end of the fifteenth century, is a square brick castle and stands tall and lonely in the flat Lincolnshire landscape. It contains the famous stone chimney pieces that George saved, in the nick of time, from being exported to America, and restored to their original positions. I shall never forget the occasion when I had to dash up there on polling day during a General Election in order to vote! George insisted on my exercising my vote there, because he thought the Conservatives would have a narrower margin in that constituency than in the others where I was entitled to vote. Tattershall, like Bodiam, was left by George to the National Trust in his Will. It interested him greatly, but it never charmed him as Bodiam did. George loved the whole atmosphere of Bodiam, with its many rounded towers reflected in the moat, standing in one of the loveliest of the valleys in the Sussex Downs. He felt that it brought back the Age of Chivalry to him, and he almost expected to see knights in armour, or trains of long-robed ladies on their palfreys carrying falcons on their wrists, coming out of the great gate of the Castle. I could well understand this, because I had had the same feeling myself ever since the first day I saw it. When he bought the Castle, George bought Bodiam Manor as well, a pleasant, sunny house of no particular style or architectural merit, which for a long time was occupied by one of his sisters.

When the last war was nearing its end, and George's sister, to whom he had lent the Manor for her life, had died, I took the Manor on lease from the National Trust. George had only bought the house and grounds for fear that it might be built over, which would spoil the view from Bodiam Castle. At that time he wished to have part of the Castle restored as a Dower House for me. Later, we both decided against this, although the architect's plans had been drawn up. I lived at Bodiam Manor for ten years with my son Alfred. After his marriage two years ago I thought it too isolated a house in which to live alone, and so I handed it back to the National Trust. My greatest regret was parting from the perfect picture of the Castle from my bedroom window. I had grown to love this divine view, knowing it well at all seasons, in snow, cloud and sunshine, and in moonlight too—its beauty was breathtaking always.

Bodiam Manor was an ugly house, but I made it very agreeable inside, and it had a charming garden. The only real feature of the house was its unusual large early Victorian winter-garden, where I took pleasure in growing Marechal Niel roses and tall camellia plants that almost touched the glass roof.

Hackwood, however, will always remain my favourite among our houses. Long after George's death I had the pleasure of showing it to Queen Mary, and of finding that she shared my appreciation of its charm. A few days before leaving for a visit to the Argentine in 1933, I received a quite unexpected message from Windsor Castle saying that Queen Mary intended to visit me at Hackwood on a certain afternoon—it was the 22nd of April—that she wished it to be a private visit and would stay to tea. Queen Mary had never been to Hackwood in the days of our rather lavish entertaining in George's lifetime. I was now living there very quietly, with only my elder son, Alfred, with me. I was grateful for this kind and gracious thought, and indeed it touched me very much.

When she arrived she brought the lovely Duchess of York, and Lord Harewood with her. The Queen went all over the house, and showed the greatest interest in everything, especially the pictures and the very beautiful Grinling Gibbons carving. (Of course her knowledge of antiques and *objets d'art* of every sort was outstanding. She and George used to have long and absorbing discussions on these subjects.) I remember that at one point during our tour of the house Alfred was rather shamed, when the Queen asked him about a large bust that stood in the entrance to the saloon. It had never occurred to him to wonder whom it represented; however, he took a quick look at the side-whiskers and guessed—"Lord Palmerston." But the Queen, whose memory was remarkable, corrected him. "I think you are mistaken," she said with a smile. "That bust is the Tsar Alexander the Second—we have one like it at Windsor."

When the Queen, the Duchess of York, and Lord Harewood had seen all over the house, they made a tour of the gardens, and the park. I showed them George's wild garden, which he had planted himself; the cockpit, which had been forgotten for generations until George verified its existence and restored it to something like its original condition; and the amphitheatre, which was in a beautiful natural setting, with perfectly kept grass banks—this had been one of George's special and favourite features of Hackwood. I showed them also the great avenue of trees which we used to call the Cathedral, because the branches met overhead and made a lofty vaulted roof of green, so that it was like walking down a vast aisle between the smooth straight columns of the tree-trunks.

We also visited Polly Peachum's Arbour. Polly Peachum was the nickname of Lavinia Fenton, an actress who created that role in the first production of *The Beggar's Opera*. The Duke of Bolton, owner of Hackwood, had made her his mistress, and later married her. The actress who died a Duchess made a great impression in the eighteenth-century countryside, and is still remembered at Hackwood. 'Polly Peachum' is said to have given plays in the amphitheatre.

When we had finished our tour of the grounds we visited the ruins of Basing House at Old Basing. Queen Mary was much dismayed when, on our return journey to Hackwood in her car, we ran over a little lamb which must have strayed through the fence. She expressed her distress, and then added, in a most practical and consoling way, "Still, you will be able to eat it." When we arrived back at Hackwood the Queen looked as cool and charming after all our rambles as she had when we started, whereas I was rather exhausted, felt hot and untidy, and was horrified to discover that I had a laddered stocking.

My younger son, Hubert, had arrived in time for tea, and it was a pleasure to see how easily and quickly the Duchess of York made these two young men forget their shyness. She said to me, in her charming way, "We are all concerned to know where you are going to live when you leave Hackwood." The Duchess of York's friendliness and natural graciousness of manner endeared her to everyone. She had come to many parties at 1 Carlton House Terrace as Lady Elizabeth Bowes-Lyon, and was always a favourite guest.

Before leaving Hackwood, Queen Mary asked me if I had a piece of plate which had been given to George by the King and herself

Author with Lady Alexandra Curzon

At the National Gallery, 1924
Lord Curzon, the author, Lord Lansdowne, and Lady Lansdowne

after their visit to India, when they were the Prince and Princess of Wales and George was Viceroy. I showed her this magnificent piece of silver, which we used to call the Prince of Wales' Cup; and I pointed out to her another splendid piece, which had been given to George by the Duke and Duchess of Connaught at the end of the Delhi Durbar. It was made in the form of a pilgrim's bottle, with massive silver chains. Both these cups were more than three feet high, and used to stand on tall pedestals in two corners of the great dining-room at Hackwood.

When Queen Mary said good-bye, she added, "I hope that we don't kill any more of your livestock on the way home."

CHAPTER XVI

Conferences

I ACCOMPANIED George to Cannes[1] when the Meeting of the Supreme Council was held there in January 1922. I was present at the historic luncheon party at the Cannes golf club at La Napoule which ruined the career of M. Briand. It looked, and was, an absurd party to find lunching at a golf club. All the men wore dark suits and stiff collars, and some of them wore patent leather shoes. As far as I remember, Miss Stevenson[2]—Mr. Lloyd George's secretary—and I were the only ladies present, and neither of us was dressed for playing golf. At luncheon I sat next to M. Briand, and afterwards I watched while photographs were taken— the famous photographs which showed him swinging a club and addressing a golf ball under the beaming supervision of Mr. Lloyd George. These photographs were eagerly published in all the French newspapers, and the French public, already suspicious of M. Briand as a subservient ally of England and of the English Prime Minister whom they detested, turned against a politician who made himself ridiculous in such frivolous circumstances at such a grave moment. That his teacher was Lloyd George of course made things ten times worse. The oddest thing about it all seems, in retrospect, that on this famous day no member of the party actually played golf. They were only playing at playing, but Mr. Lloyd George and M. Briand, clowning in order to amuse the Press photographers, managed to change the course of French history. M. Briand returned to Paris, was overthrown by M. Poincaré almost at once, and George had to hasten to Paris, travelling by day as he could not sleep in a train.

Towards the end of that year the Lausanne Conference[3] took place. We agreed that I should not accompany him, but that I should

---

[1] The Conference of Cannes, January 6th–13th, 1922. This was a meeting of the Supreme Council of the Allies to consider the reparations question on the lines laid down at the London Conference of December 1921. The conference ended prematurely when Briand was attacked in the French Senate and Chamber for his supposed subservience to Lloyd George, and resigned on January 12th.

[2] Frances Louise Stevenson, who in 1943 married David Lloyd George and is now Frances, Countess Lloyd George.

[3] Conference between the Allies and Turkey, November 20th, 1922– July 24th, 1923 (with an interval February 4th–April 23rd, 1923), which resulted in the signing of a Peace Treaty.

join him at Lausanne for about a week, a little later on. The following are some extracts from the letters I wrote to him there from London:

"Nov. 25th, 1922.   1, C.H.T.
    . . . I have to thank you for a dear letter every day this week. I must try and tell you of all my doings. Wednesday night, I dined with Maud Cunard to go to the first night of *The Lady of the Rose*. When I arrived I found the only other woman was Ivy Chamberlain! However, she seemed very pleased to see me. The three men of the party were Lord Granard, Sir Frederick Ponsonby and a young boy called Captain Jenkins. Maud had the Royal box, and the box opposite was occupied by Lord Birkenhead[1] and his family, and he, to my horror, came in to visit our box! I heard Maud say, 'Hello F.E.,' so I took great care not to turn round. He then leant his two arms on the back of my chair and remained there in full view of the whole theatre (which was crowded with friends) for an entire Act. His wife was watching the proceedings from her box with opera glasses and laughing the whole time. I feel sure he did the thing out of pure bravado. Maud was told the next day by Locker Lampson who was in F.E.'s box that when he returned to his wife he burst into tears and said, 'Lady Curzon cut me!'
    Thursday night I dined with Maggie Greville—quite a pleasant party. I sat between the Duke of Sutherland and Lord Hugh Cecil —Lord and Lady Milner, Sir Esmé Howard, the Walter Guinnesses, the Bonham Carters, Sir Robert Horne—with whom I just shook hands—and Sir George Younger. I told Violet Milner I would give her away, as she asked when we arrived in the hall if you were there? I answered that she couldn't be reading the papers!

    "Nov. 27th, 1922. I sent you an unfinished letter on Saturday as I had to rush to catch the train to Basingstoke where I was going for the night. I told you about Maggie Greville's dinner, from which I went on to Muriel Beckett's dance. I could not dance as my foot gives much too much pain. I thought it a stupid party so came away early. Friday afternoon I had a tea party for about 30 people. I think it was a great success, as people arrived at 4.15 and stayed until 6.30!

    [1] Frederick Edwin Smith, Earl of Birkenhead (1872–1930), often referred to as 'F.E.' He had been Lord Chancellor under Lloyd George 1919–22, and had supported the continuation of the Coalition. He was, therefore, very bitter against those who brought about its fall in October 1922. Among the latter had been Lord Curzon, who had felt it impossible to support the Coalition any longer in view of the differences between himself and Lloyd George on the conduct of foreign policy.

although I had no music or entertaining. I had the Spanish Ambassador and Madame Merry del Val, the German and Madame Stahmer, the Brazilian (his wife is also away), the Italian (whom everyone thought so charming, his wife has not yet arrived), the Swiss Minister and Madame de Paravicini, the Chilean and Madame Edwardes, the Duchess of Portland, the Duchess of Sutherland. The Duchess of Devonshire was coming but had to go to bed with a bad chill. Lady Salisbury came early to help me. And Lord and Lady Cromer, Lord and Lady Shaftesbury, Peggy Crewe, Maud Cunard, Sir John Hanbury-Williams, Mr. Monck and Mr. Vansittart. I had a buffet tea in the Empire room and we just talked in the big drawing-room. I went to the opening of Parliament which I thought a wonderful sight. The House of Lords was packed. I did not go in the afternoon as it was Marcella's birthday and she had one or two friends in to tea. I hear F.E. made a clever speech with two or three stings in it. I went to the Duchess of Sutherland's reception which I did not think well done. Poor Bonar looked as if he had not shaved for days. He looked more like a Labour P.M. than a Tory one. On Saturday I lunched with Maud and sat between the Spanish Ambassador and Lord Buckmaster.[1] Lord Buckmaster told me that he and all his party were very much annoyed at having F.E. sitting on the Opposition Bench, as he says we are back at Party Politics and he supposes F.E. still calls himself a Conservative. . . . I have just returned from lunching with the Paravicinis, a huge party in my honour. I hope to get to you in time for lunch on Sunday the 3rd. . . . Let me know if I can take you anything. Shall I take out a valet? Your horrid man has not turned up yet. . . ."

The 'horrid man' was the temporary valet who was immortalized by Mr. Harold Nicolson in his story 'Arketall'. He was dismissed for dancing, drunk, at a gala ball at the Beau Rivage Hotel at Ouchy with one of the lady visitors. Before departing he hid all George's trousers.

"November 28th, 1922.   1, C.H.T.
    . . . So pleased to hear by your dear letter received this morning that everything is still going so well. Your valet came here yesterday, he only stayed for 20 minutes, he was paid his wages only, as you advised. I dined last night with Lady Meux. Lord Derby took me

---

[1] Stanley O. Buckmaster, Baron Buckmaster of Cheddington (1861–1934), who was created a Viscount in 1933. He belonged to the Liberal Party.

in to dinner and it was such an amusing party—bridge afterwards—
I will tell you all Lord Derby told me when I arrive on Sunday. He
is quite the most conceited man I have ever met. Baba spent the
week end at Cliveden with Nancy Astor, who had a party for Lloyd
George and Mrs. Lloyd George! They must have been surprised to
see Baba, as you know they (the Ll.G.s) heard Nancy attack me
about you. I lunched today with Maud Cunard and sat between
the French Ambassador and Lord Peel. I heard much praise of
you. . . ."

"Nov. 29th, 1922.   1, C.H.T.
    . . . I was so glad to get your letter this morning. I go to Paris
tomorrow by the 2 o'clock train and will go on to you on Saturday
night. . . . Last night I dined with Lord Granard—tiny party and
we went on to a play afterwards. To-day I had a small luncheon party
here of the Spanish Ambassador and Madame Merry del Val,
Italian Ambassador, Lord Charles Montagu, Col. Walter and Lady
Evelyn Guinness, Maggie Greville and Lord Ancaster. I leave Paris
at 8.35 p.m. and arrive at Lausanne at 8.2 a.m. on Sunday. Will you
send somebody to meet me and my luggage. I am so happy at the
thought of so soon seeing you."

"Dec. 1st., 1922.   Hotel Ritz, Paris.
    I was so pleased to find your letter on my arrival here
last night. I had a very good crossing and a most comfortable
journey. I was met as usual at all the change places. I have my old
comfy rooms in the courtyard. Charles Mendl lunched with me
today, and Lord Hardinge came to see me at 5.30 and has only just
left, 7 o'clock. He seemed in very good form and told me all the
Paris news. He said he had not written to you as there was nothing to
tell you—he says there is nothing for him to do in Paris as you are
doing all the work at Lausanne. He seems to think it a great pity
that the meeting of the Prime Ministers is taking place next week in
London as he thinks the French are sure to be disappointed with the
result, and then it will have a bad effect on your Conference. Alice
Hubbard has been in to see me. I am to lunch with her tomorrow.
She has told me of a wonderful new doctor at Lausanne whom we
must both see. I am dining in my rooms this evening as I am rather
tired. How much I look forward to seeing my darling on Sunday. . . ."

I joined George for a few days at the Hotel Beau Rivage at
Ouchy-Lausanne at this time, when the Conference had already

lasted for some weeks. (It lasted for nearly three months altogether.) I was delighted to find George so well and so happy when I arrived at Lausanne. Everything was going well with the Conference at that time, and I had never seen him in a more cheerful mood, I enjoyed every moment of my short visit.

I was present at an imposing banquet given for Ismet Pasha[1] at the Hotel. I found him most difficult to talk to—as, indeed, George also found him, in Conference—but I did my best; and after the banquet, I even danced with him.

George was lucky in having a very congenial Staff at Lausanne. He saw a great deal of Harold Nicolson, and also of Vita, who was at Lausanne with Harold, and they both became great friends of George's. George had a high opinion of Sir Horace Rumbold, who had come to Lausanne from his post in Turkey. Surrounded by people on whose judgment he could rely, and whose company he enjoyed, he was in excellent spirits.

After the banquet for Ismet Pasha, the next event was a luncheon given for Mussolini—a much smaller affair, but far more cheerful. I found Mussolini both interesting and amusing. He spoke little or no French, but we managed at luncheon to converse quite satisfactorily—he spoke Italian, and I spoke Spanish, and although we could not either of us *speak* the other language, we were able to understand each other fairly easily, and the amusing tangles of these two similar Latin tongues made conversation at luncheon very cheerful and gay. Mussolini had quite a good presence—although short, he had a rather fine head, and he had the manners of a courtier. His conceit and his vanity were beyond belief. He told me that he intended to pay a visit to London, and that before he did so he would learn English—he said that he could easily learn it in two weeks. The day after the luncheon party he called, and before calling he sent me the largest basket of flowers I have ever seen.

Later, he did pay a visit to London, and lunched with George at Carlton House Terrace. I happened to be away at the time, and on his return to Rome he wrote to me in English—perfect English— telling me how sorry he was to miss seeing me while he was there, and explaining that he wished me to know that he was proud of having learned English before his visit. I don't suppose for a moment

---

[1] Ismet Inönü, Turkish statesman, known in early life as Ismet Pasha (*b.* 1884). He was Kemal Atatürk's chief of staff in the war against the Greeks 1921–22, defeating the Greeks twice at Inönü, which he adopted as his last name. First Prime Minister of the new republic 1923–37, he signed the Treaty of Lausanne in 1923, and was President of Turkey 1938–50, when he became Leader of the Opposition.

that he had written the letter himself—it must have been written for him—but he remembered his boast to me, and such was his vanity that he had to write to make it good. I wonder how he would have got on in English if I had been there, and he had been obliged to prove his boast in conversation!

"Dec. 11th., 1922. Ritz Hotel, Paris.

. . . I sent you a telegram this morning saying I had arrived up to time and had a very comfortable journey. Thanks to you I had a berth to myself, as the Guard gave my maid another compartment. It has been a damp, horrid dull day here, and I miss the bright sunshine of Lausanne. I have been shopping all day. I had lunch in my sitting-room, I have seen no one. They telephoned from the Embassy to know how long I was staying in Paris. I hear Charlie Hardinge goes for good on Saturday. The London Conference[1] seems to be going well, at least so this morning's papers thought. I shall eagerly look to see what to-morrow's papers have to say about Austen Chamberlain's apology in the House. I hope the gang of 'Dirty Dogs' will leave you alone for a bit.[2] I hope you are feeling better, and how much I hope your Conference is going better. I have a feeling it is going to be a success and you will get the great recognition you well deserve. I have sent my maid to the station to meet Marcella and her Governess—they should arrive at any moment. It will be a great pleasure to have my little daughter with me. It is the first time she has ever been away with me. . . . I am so glad I went to Lausanne. I really loved my week with you, in spite

[1] The London Conference of December 9th–11th, 1922, on reparations. It broke up, as had the London Conference of August 7th–14th, 1922, with the French and the rest of the Allies still in disagreement on the settlement of the problem.

[2] The affair of the Gounaris letter. Demetrios Gounaris (1866–1922) was Prime Minister of Greece 1920–22, but as a result of the revolution of October 1922 was impeached and executed for high treason. In an effort to save himself he had produced a letter written to Curzon on February 15th, 1922, in which he pointed out the increasing weakness of the Greek position, the increasing strength of the Turks, and said that unless arms and financial help were forthcoming Greece would have to withdraw from Asia Minor. On December 3rd, 1922, extracts from this letter were published in the *Sunday Express*, and questions were asked in Parliament, both in the Commons and, by Birkenhead, in the Lords. Lloyd George, who had been Prime Minister at the time, and the rest of the Cabinet, denied having seen either the letter or Curzon's reply, and it momentarily seemed that Curzon had failed to perform his duty in informing his colleagues fully as to the Greek situation. Further investigation, however, conclusively proved it was the memory of the Cabinet members which was at fault, and that both letters had been duly circulated to them. General apologies to Curzon and the Foreign Office staff involved followed.

of not being well. I am so happy to think of you in your charming rooms and to know that you are being well looked after—as I do feel all your Staff try to do their best for you. . . ."

"Dec. 12th., 1922.   Ritz Hotel, Paris.
    ". . . I was so pleased to receive your dear letter, and to know that you miss me a little. I am glad to know that you went for a drive with Sir Walter Tyrrell. Marcella and her Governess arrived last evening. Marcella is looking much better. . . . The only person I have seen as yet is the Queen of the Belgians, who asked me to go and see her at her hotel (Meurice). I found her looking very well, better than I have ever seen her. She was most anxious to know how you were. Do write to her, as she does so long to hear from you. She seems very frightened that we are going to break with France—and was much worried that the London Conference came to nothing. She tells me that the next meeting will take place in Paris, not Brussels. She also said that poor Belgium needed the money so badly that they would have to stick to France.
    How pleased I was to see the great Ll.G. had to apologize to you and the F.O.—but I have not seen a paper about the apology from F.E. in the House of Lords. I think Ll.G. is still playing a dirty game and trying to make *you* share the blame about Greece—I hated his apology. I think the whole thing is a deep plot which only his brain would conceive. . . ."

"Dec. 13th., 1922.   Hotel Ritz, Paris.
    ". . . You have not mentioned receiving any of my letters—and I have written every day. It was an effort for me to get up this morning as I was so enthralled reading the English papers vindicating you. I almost felt sorry for the 'Dirty Dogs', as they have made fools of themselves. Marcella and I had lunch with Alice Hubbard to-day. The Hotel is very dull, full of rather uninteresting Americans. Charlie Hardinge came to see me this evening. He did not have much to say of interest beyond that he did not think Bonar Law's Government would last long! He said he thought you were doing wonders. I wish you would tell me how all is going on at Lausanne. You do still hope to come home for Christmas? . . ."

"Dec. 15th., 1922.   Hotel Ritz, Paris.
    ". . . Here goes my last letter from Paris, as we leave to-morrow. I wonder how I shall get on, as Lord Hardinge is going by the same train. I did not tell him I was going, as he did not ask me! Moss

came to see me to-day to say he was sorry he would not be able to help me as he would have to be with the Ambassador; he added, "As your Ladyship knows, he does not like me to help you!" I am really glad to see Charlie Hardinge[1] leave Paris—he has *no* gratitude. I hear he expects to be at your place in the F.O. if Ll.G. ever gets back! He would not say a word against Ll.G. when he came to see me. As you know Lord Crewe is coming here in time for the Conference on Jan. 2nd.,[2] and Eddie Derby has lent him his flat! How like him to try to get the Crewes under obligations to him at once. I hear Lord Crewe cannot go to the Embassy as it will not be in order. I lunched with Mendl to-day, he had Baron and Baroness Weddell (they want to give a party for you if you come to the Conference in Jan.), B. de Castellane, and Helen D'Abernon—not looking well, she tells me that Edgar had gone to London to see you. I asked if he did not know that you were in Lausanne? Helen told Charlie Hardinge that she envied him going home for good. She does not look happy.

Mr. and Mrs. Hudson were also at Mendl's party, they are here at the Embassy. . . . Also Ian Malcolm—he goes to England to-morrow. Darling, the letter from *The Times* you sent me was the one I had sent to you! All the papers are at last doing you justice. I am proud of you. I am congratulated every day wherever I go, on your big successes. You really have brought off a big thing. I wonder how soon you will know your plans. It will break my heart if you don't get home for Christmas. . . ."

"Dec. 20th., 1922.   1, C.H.T.

". . . I wrote such a short note this afternoon, I must now try and give you all the news. The Anglesey Ball was a great success—I stayed until 2! As you know I dined there for it. I sat between my host and the Spanish Ambassador. It was all quite beautifully done and there must have been about 300 at the ball. I danced with Sir Robert Horne![3] He is just off to America—he says on business. I wonder if you will think I should not have danced with him. I told him I only spoke to him as he had not been quite so bad as the other 'Dirty Dogs'—he seemed delighted with this! Everyone here says he is coming back into the Government. He let me see that he wants

[1] Charles Hardinge, Baron Hardinge of Penshurst (1858–1944), British Ambassador in Paris 1920–23.

[2] The Paris Conference of January 2nd–4th, 1923, at which Bonar Law made a last attempt to prevent the French from occupying the Ruhr in order to enforce reparations payments.

[3] See note, p. 192.

to. Lord and Lady Birkenhead were also there, and I cut them with great pleasure. . . . I talked for some time to Lord Winterton, who told me many things about the Lyttons and India. Old Horace[1] also talked to me (what gay men!) and said, "It breaks my heart to have to sit across the House from dear George." I told him I did not think it made much difference where he sat. I was surprised to see Lord and Lady Milner at the Ball. They were both full of your praises. Violet said she was going to write to you. . . . To-day I lunched with Maud and sat between Sir George Younger and Sir Filson Young (editor of the *Saturday Review*.) Sir George Younger[2] had just returned from a week end at Hatfield with the Salisburys. He left poor Jim in bed. He thought Salisbury's speech in defence of you very feeble, but said, "Poor Salisbury is very afraid of F.E.'s sharp tongue and does not dare say much." He also said that the only way to treat F.E. is with studied politeness, as it was the one thing he did not understand, and was completely disarmed and could not make his rude retorts. Sir George Younger also told the whole table that if poor Bonar's health gave out you would be the only other possible P.M. I asked him what about Austen Chamberlain coming back. He nearly jumped out of his chair and said Austen would *never* get into this Government, and the country would not stand him at any price. He said, "Curzon must get known in the country on his return— they *want* to know him,"—all this Filson Young endorsed. Filson Young said he sent Vansittart a good copy of the caricature of you in his paper last week—I hope it was sent on to you. I enclose a cutting from to-day's *Morning Post* of Sir George Younger's speech and the nice things he said about you. I also talked to Lord Buckmaster after lunch at Maud's, and he said they were going to have a meeting about the House of Lords' Opposition, as they could not tolerate having F.E., Duke of Marlborough, Lord Astor, Lord Farquhar, Lord Midleton, and Lord Lee sitting with them! He said you will have an easy time, as they will never agree with F.E., or back him in anything. . . . I am afraid you will never wade through this long letter, but I had to get up to date with all my news. . . ."

"Dec. 23rd., 1922.   Hackwood.
    . . . This is to wish you a very, very merry Christmas. I hope you will at least have a day of rest. I arrived here with Marcella and Hubert in time for tea yesterday. Alfred, Mother, Dot and Ambrose

---

[1] Lord Farquhar.
[2] Sir George Younger, Bt. (1851–1929), who was created a Viscount in 1923. He was Chairman of the Unionist Party Organization 1916–23.

come this afternoon and Baba tomorrow. Hackwood is looking
wonderfully improved—the house, I mean. I think the new housekeeper is a Tartar but a very competent woman. The weather is
horrid—cold, wet, and blowing a gale. We all stay here until the
27th., when we go to London for the night and leave for St. Moritz
on the 28th. Alfred returns to Melton for the holidays. Baba joins
us at St. Moritz on the 9th Jan., she is waiting until then as she wishes
to go to one or two of the Hunt Balls. If you are staying much longer
at Lausanne I will settle the children at St. Moritz and run down to
see you for a night or two. What a lot of dinners and banquets you
are having. I know how much you hate this form of entertainment—
how glad you will be when they are over. Cim and Tom leave
tomorrow for the South of France, they have taken poor Adele
Essex's villa until the middle of February. The Queen has sent me a
Christmas present, a kind of French electric lamp, rather like the
clock and candlesticks that were on the mantelpiece in the Blue
Room that you sent to Kedleston. I sent her a nice book. Maud C.
sent me a very pretty diamond and jet hat-pin, Madame Merry del
Val a gold-topped scent bottle, Lord Londonderry a blotter, Evie
a green vase, Sir George Grahame an umbrella, Mrs. Loeffler a
very pretty belt, and Sir John Lavery a print of his painting of the
House of Lords. I opened your present before I left London—what
lovely mirrors! Darling, a thousand thanks—I long to go to Montacute to hang them in my sitting-room. How too dear of you to have
thought of my Christmas present before you went away. I did not
bring them here as I was so afraid they would get broken. They are
just what my room most needs to lighten the oak panelling. I have
been hanging them in my mind's eye ever since I opened your
parcel.

I did as you asked me and got presents for Mother, Dot, Ambrose,
and my children, from you. I will tell you about them in my next
letter. Baba was delighted with your cheque. Again Dearest with all
wishes for a merry Christmas—but please not too merry without
me! . . ."

"Dec. 30th., 1922.   Palace Hotel,
                                                           St. Moritz.

. . . It was such a joy to be able to speak to you last night. I
think you still sounded as if you had a cold. I was also delighted to
find a telegram awaiting me here, and a letter from you. I also
received another letter from you this morning. I am sorry you must
take that long tiresome trip to Paris, but I can understand the P.M.

needing you. I do wish things were more promising. However all the world knows you have done wonders in any case. I saw no one before leaving London but the family . . . the only person on the boat we knew was Mendl—he of course went by another train to Paris. He told me the French were behaving very badly. I am rather sorry for poor Lord Crewe, I do hope he will be equal to the situation. All went well with us until we arrived at Zurich and I thought I would like to send a telegram to you. I asked my maid to send it; she, stupid woman, without asking how long the train would stop, got hold of Marcella—the maid without a coat or hat, and Marcella without coat or gloves—they left the train and rushed round the station looking for a telegraph office. When they returned to the platform the train had been gone for 3 minutes. I knew nothing of this or I would have stopped the train. I was dressing, and of course had not meant my maid to get off the train, but to hand the telegram to the guard. You can imagine my anxiety when I knew that Marcella was left behind, and with no coat! And then, what does the stupid woman do but hire a motor and try to catch the train! It is a wonder that they were not both killed. The motor cost £12 10s. 0d., and of course they had to get a train in the end. Hubert and I waited at Chur from 1 o'clock until 5, when they joined us. Marcella was none the worse, I am glad to say.

The weather here is not good, lots of snow but no sun. The Hotel is full of Argentines, alas! all of whom I know—some Hope and Torres cousins of the children's, the Moore-Brabazons, and that is all so far. I hope it does not get too smart as I long for a rest. I am looking forward so much to spending your birthday with you. I hope you do not leave Lausanne before the 11th. I wish my darling a very happy New Year and look forward to spending most of it with him. . . ."

"Jan. 1st., 1923.   Palace Hotel,
                                                St. Moritz.

. . . I send you all my fondest love and wish you ever so many happy returns of our anniversary. I am so sad not to be able to spend it with you. I received your telegram of good wishes today, telling me you had received my little anniversary gift of a card case. Just think, darling, we have been married six years—in some ways it seems so much longer, as I can't think of my life without your belonging to it. I am proud to belong to you, and as I look back I don't think there is much that I would wish to change since we met. Of course darling we have had our little disturbances—all mostly my fault—but I think the circumstances of our lives made this inevitable. At any rate it is now so long since we have been unhappy together that I feel we have reached our Harbour. I long for a letter from you telling me all about the happenings at Paris. I am afraid you will be very tired after your long journey. How horrid of the *Manchester Guardian* to attack you. I had hoped they were more just—Maud Cunard speaks so well of the paper. The weather here is horrid, snowing all day, we have not yet seen the sun. The people are beyond words terrible and I am not liking it very much. I shall put on skis for the first time tomorrow—I used to go very well on them years ago. . . ."

CHAPTER XVII

Death of Mr. Bonar Law. Mr. Baldwin's Government

IN May, 1923, I was in Paris for a short time. I wrote from the Ritz Hotel, where I was staying, to George, who was at Kedleston for the first part of the Whitsun recess. I was to join him at Montacute at the end of the week. At this time we had all realized that Mr. Bonar Law's health was giving serious cause for anxiety. He had been on a voyage in the hopes that it would do him good, but the hopes were not justified, and he returned a very sick man. He stopped in Paris on his way back to England while I was there—but I did not see him—and sent for Sir Thomas Horder[1] to give his opinion as to the prospects of his health enabling him to carry on the Government. I knew nothing of this, except the rumours about his illness, when I wrote to George at Kedleston.

"— May, 1923, Friday.   Ritz Hotel, Paris.
"My darling Boy,
        "I am so very sorry to have missed writing to you the last few days. You have been so good about finding time to write to me every day, I am all the more ashamed. I am so glad to hear all that you have to tell me from Lord Younger. I really feel you will be the next P.M., and so many people I meet here say you will. I hope you have better weather at Kedleston than we are having—it has rained for the last three days and is also quite cold. I must tell you about my dinner parties—I really am very gay and go to a party every night. If it were not for you, I would much rather spend the Season here, as London has grown stale for me. My first big dinner was at the Granards', where we sat down 35 at one long table in their quite lovely panelled dining room—lots of the smartest French, as well as Roxburghs, Maggie Greville, Peggy Crewe—Lord Crewe does not dine out yet. I dined at the Embassy on Wednesday night—a dinner party of 65, which was quite beautifully done, all arranged (I am told by Peggy) by Lord Crewe. A few more people came in after dinner and there was a small dance. Lord Crewe is looking very well, much better than before his illness, his hair raven black, quite pink cheeks, and he seems less deaf! They both seem to be a great social success. On Thursday night I dined at the American Embassy.

[1] Later Lord Horder, of Ashford (1871–1955).

We were about 18 at dinner, mostly French—rather a dull party, and not so well done as when the Wallaces were at the Embassy. On Friday night Dot and Ambrose gave a dinner party at the Ritz!—consisting of Hubert and me, Marquis de Castellane, Lady Michelham and Charles Mendl. Later Peggy called for me and took me to supper at a new Russian place, which was most amusing—our party being Lady Alington, Lord Alington, Mr. Eric Phipps (whom I like so much) and Mr. Rubinstein the musician."

"*Sunday*. I did not send this letter yesterday as I thought you would get it quicker if Hubert took it this morning. Last night I dined with Baroness Wedell. I always enjoy going there—they have all the most charming French people, and you know how delightful their house is. I lunch today at the Embassy and may go to the races with Lord Crewe and Peggy. Tonight I dine with Mendl who has a small party and we think of going to a theatre afterwards. Tomorrow night I dine with the Wallaces to meet the King and Queen of Portugal. (I hear they—the Wallaces—have bought the lovely house they had when he was Ambassador—you remember we dined there together.) On Tuesday I am to lunch with Sir Basil Zaharof, and dine that night with Marquis de Castellane. I return to my Boy on Thursday, and look forward so much to going to Montacute with him on Friday. Thank you so much for writing about my rooms for Oxford. I hope you were able to get me some. For my Ascot party I have so far got Eloise Ancaster, Marquis (and wife) de Polignac, Marquis de Castellane; I have written to Ava Ribblesdale, Lord and Lady Cromer, and the Carisbrookes, but have not heard from them yet. Would you approve of my asking the Aga Khan? He is staying here —and as his horses win so many races he would give me some good tips. But I will not ask him until I hear from you. He sends me the most lovely flowers. Let me know darling if there is anyone you would like me to ask.

"I was quite sure you would not like my picture. I hope Maud will really take it, she so often says things that she does not mean. Everyone who has seen it says that it is not good enough. . . . Thank you so much darling Boy for taking the things to the School of Needlework for Montacute. I think I have the green table cloth you mention put away with my things. Many thanks also for the Oxford letter about Hubert. I am sure you will be pleased with Hubert's trip. He returns to London this morning and to Eton tomorrow. I hope you will see him before he leaves London. If my Boy becomes P.M. I will not go to B.A. as I feel he will need me at home.

"This afternoon I go to tea with Madame Henessy. With fondest love darling Boy, and I hope you were pleased with the visit to Kedleston. . . ."

Later that week, just after I had posted my letter to George, Peggy Crewe came to see me. She told me that Mr. Bonar Law had spent the previous afternoon with Lord Crewe and her at the Embassy, and had told them that Sir Thomas Horder took a grave view of his illness and had advised a consultation with specialists as soon as he returned to London. He—Mr. Bonar Law—had made it clear to the Crewes that he feared that the result of the consultation would almost certainly be his resignation. The Crewes had found it a very pathetic and affecting conversation. Peggy came to tell me all this, because she felt that I ought to go back to England at once, to be with George, in the circumstances—she and Lord Crewe felt certain that he would be sent for by the King and was bound to be the next Prime Minister. I was surprised, and of course thrilled—I had had no idea that the crisis might occur so soon—and I felt very sorry for poor Mr. Bonar Law, whose illness was evidently worse than anyone had realized. However, I felt that George would almost certainly not want me to make a sudden change of plan in the circumstances, and, while Peggy was with me in my sitting-room at the Ritz, I put through a telephone call to him, and luckily was able to speak to him at Kedleston with very little delay—and he said, as I had expected, that I was not to alter my arrangements, but that we would go to Montacute at the end of the week as we had originally planned. Peggy then told me that Lord Beaverbrook was in Paris, and that he too was strongly of the opinion that George would be the next Prime Minister. She asked me to go with her to see Lord Beaverbrook, but I declined, as I felt that nothing would be gained by such a visit. I was always reluctant to become involved unofficially in anything that concerned Cabinet matters.

In due course I went back to England at the end of the week, as we had arranged. George and I went to Montacute together for a quiet weekend by ourselves. There was no telephone at Montacute —the absence of it was one of the things that George liked, and thought that it contributed to the remote, restful atmosphere there— and so we heard nothing until, on the morning of Whit Monday, he received a letter from Mr. Bonar Law, telling him that he had resigned for reasons of health. His letter ended with the words, "I understand that it is not customary for the King to ask the Prime

Author with Marcella

Author in her boudoir at Hackwood

Minister to recommend his successor in circumstances like the present and I presume he will not do so; but if, as I hope, he accepts my resignation at once, he will have to take immediate steps about my successor."

As may be imagined, that Whit Monday was a day of intense anxiety, speculation, and hope for George and me. Most unluckily, I had severe toothache and had to stay in my room, and George, feeling restless and excited, kept on coming in from the garden and talking to me about the political future. Late that evening the village policeman bicycled to the house with a telegram—it was a Bank Holiday, the post office was shut and the postman and tele-graph boy were off duty, but the urgency of the situation was realized and the policeman undertook to deliver this message. It was from Lord Stamfordham,[1] saying that he wanted to see George in London the next day.

George felt quite certain that this was simply in order to tell him that he was to be sent for by the King. He was full of hope and the most buoyant optimism as we travelled from Yeovil to Paddington. Our journey from Montacute to Carlton House Terrace must have been the most photographed one of our lives together. All the news-papers seemed to be sure that George was about to become Prime Minister. There were crowds, and camera-men, even at Yeovil station. At Paddington there were many Press photographers, and great crowds of onlookers who clapped and cheered as we walked to a taxi; when we arrived at Carlton House Terrace there were more crowds assembled, and more photographers. (My toothache had given me a swollen face, and I had no wish to be photographed that day; but it all seemed to add to George's happy optimism about the outcome of the journey, and he was most willing to stop, and stand smiling while the camera-men took their pictures.)

Lord Stamfordham came to see us at Carlton House Terrace—and the blow fell. The King had sent for Mr. Baldwin! He had taken this decision because the Labour Party was the official Opposition in the House of Commons, and had no representatives in the House of Lords; and so it was felt that a Conservative Prime Minister must not be a Peer. George's disappointment and distress, after so much encouragement to be hopeful about his great and life-long ambition to become Premier, was acute and painful. I was present when the news was broken to him by Lord Stamfordham, and George could not restrain his tears.

[1] Lt.-Col. Arthur John Bigge, Baron Stamfordham (1849–1931), Private Secretary to George V as Prince of Wales and King 1901–30.

It had been cruelly misleading for George that the message from Lord Stamfordham had contained no hint of this decision—a simple summons to come back to London had sounded so much more like a preliminary to being sent for by the King. I learned afterwards that there had been a meeting of certain members of the Cabinet, including Mr. Bridgeman, Mr. Amery, and others, on the night that Lord Stamfordham's message had been sent. This meeting had been attended by Arthur Balfour, and the tenour of the views expressed by everyone at the meeting was to the effect that a Prime Minister in the Upper House was a hopeless proposition in the existing circumstances. This view was subsequently conveyed to the King by Arthur Balfour; it turned the scales against George and in favour of Mr. Baldwin. We did not know this when Lord Stamfordham broke the news to George at Carlton House Terrace. George felt then that he had been treated unfairly—brought back to London without a hint that Mr. Baldwin had been chosen, and allowed to accept the cheers and the clapping of the public under a misapprehension. He was cut to the heart, and deeply distressed. I tried hard to induce him to realize that the issue must still have been in doubt when Lord Stamfordham's telegram was sent—I knew the King well enough to be certain that he was incapable of doing anything so thoughtless and unkind as letting George imagine that he was to be chosen when in fact the decision had gone against him. King George V was an exceptionally kind-hearted man, and would never have been so inconsiderate to any of his Ministers—and especially to George, whom he knew so well. I did my best to persuade George of this, and to get him to realize that there must be an explanation for the misleading message.

The next night we were to dine with Lord and Lady Farquhar in Grosvenor Square, to meet the King and Queen Mary—a long-standing invitation. George, whose health was always at the mercy of his emotions, was still too much distressed to feel able to dine out. He wanted me to decline as well, but this I said I would not do, as it would have looked as if we entertained feelings of resentment if we had both stayed at home. So I went alone to the dinner party, George having sent a message of regret that he was not well enough to accompany me. After dinner in the drawing-room, when the men came to join the ladies, and the King was asked whom he would like to talk to, he immediately sent for me. I went and sat in a low chair beside him, and he said straight away, "I suppose Curzon wouldn't come to-night because he didn't want to meet me?"

This was a difficult remark for me to answer. I tried to be tactful as well as truthful, and I answered, "He really is not well, Sir—he *is* very hurt and disappointed."

The King evidently understood this—he knew George very well. He gave me a comprehending look, and said, "But what can I do about it?"

I said, pleading as persuasively as I could for what I knew would pacify George: "Sir, won't you send for him to-morrow and tell him yourself your reasons for your decision? That I know would make all the difference to him."

The King looked almost relieved, and said that he would certainly do so. He then said to me: "Arthur Balfour told me that his uncle, the great Lord Salisbury, had found it very difficult to lead the Conservative Party from the House of Lords—and the Opposition then was the Liberal Party, with an equal representation in the Upper House. The difficulty to-day would be insuperable."

CHAPTER XVIII

Letters from Lord Curzon to Me

GEORGE was well known as a loyal colleague with a great sense of the obligation of Cabinet solidarity. During the Great War and in the long crisis of peacemaking he was willing to serve with statesmen of different political views, and he never stooped to secret intrigue. But though no one else ever heard him complain, he wrote to me with perfect freedom. That is why these letters may seem unduly critical. At that time his views were shared by many in the Conservative Party.

"Nov. 5. 1923. Foreign Office.
"My darling girl,
     "I have just come back from the Abbey funeral of Bonar. It was rather a sombre performance; and one could not help thinking that many of the congregation were wondering how poor old Bonar ever got there. I met Burnham[1] afterwards and asked him what the general sentiment on the subject was. He said that everyone knew it to be absurd; but that the Press had been stampeded by Beaverbrook who as soon as the breath was out of poor Bonar's body, turned on the full blast of the Rothermere cum Beaverbrook furnace and practically forced the entire Press into line. He concurred in thinking that in a month or two Bonar would be completely forgotten, and that in days to come people would ask who he was and how he ever got there. When we marched down from the Choir to the Nave— where a little casket containing his ashes (for he had been cremated) was let down into a small hole in the pavement, shaped like this— I found myself near the Prince of Wales. He fidgetted and looked about; never once turned a glance to the grave or the coffin, and showed himself profoundly bored with the whole performance. Of course cremation has the advantage of saving a great deal of space and thereby admitting of many future interments. But it has its ridiculous side. For a sham coffin was carried under a great white pall and deposited on a catafalque before the Sanctuary in the earlier part of the service and subsequently borne to the grave, where it was

---

[1] Harry Lawson, Viscount Burnham (1862–1933), owner of the *Daily Telegraph* and President of the Empire Press Union in 1923.

put on one side and disappeared, everyone knowing that there was no body in it at all.

"Last Saturday Philbrick took me down to Bodiam in your car, where I found the Manor House quite charming, well furnished, very comfortable and almost luxurious. It is indeed a delightful house. Geraldine was much better than I had anticipated and able to show me round. Her eldest daughter who is engaged is a very attractive girl, quite good looking and with charming manners."

"*Nov.* 8. I was so pleased my darling to receive your long telegram from Lisbon (also one from Vigo) and to know that you had been properly received there. I sent you a wireless on the Bay of Biscay. I hope you got that too. I will send another when you are in mid Atlantic and have wired in order to catch you at Madeira to-day. I envy you the sunshine and the palms. Here it has turned quite cold, for the first time. I shall think of you passing Tenerife, if you do. But maybe you do not go sufficiently far to the South.

"This morning I got a belated letter from the Crown Prince of Sweden[1] from Nancy Astor's house at Sandwich, thanking us both for the silver tankard which he greatly admired. He is going to stay a month here on his return from his honeymoon, and I suppose I shall have to invite him to lunch.

"Yesterday I had to go to meet the King of Sweden[2] at lunch at the Swedish Legation. After lunch he took me into another room, sat down and had a good $\frac{1}{4}$ hour, he would not speak to anyone else. Nothing could exceed his friendliness and courtesy, and he particularly asked about you. He said Europe was in the hands of a madman (Poincaré) and that all the nations were looking to me to pull them out. He implored me to take a strong initiative, whether France likes it or not, and said that otherwise Europe will be ruined.

"The last two days have been a whirlwind of negotiation and trouble in order to get the Imperial Conference to agree to a report (written by myself) on Foreign Affairs. The obstacle has been Mackenzie King, the Canadian, who is both obstinate, tiresome and stupid, and is nervously afraid of being turned out of his own Parliament when he gets back. Smuts has been a tower of strength in these

[1] Crown Prince Gustaf Adolf (*b.* 1906), King Gustaf VI from 1950, who on November 3rd, 1923, had married as his second wife Lady Louise Mountbatten, sister of Earl Mountbatten of Burma.

[2] Gustaf V (1858–1950), who succeeded to the throne in 1907.

pourparlers, and has been running in and out of this house with Hankey[1] 2 or 3 times a day.

"I go in every evening at 8 p.m. to the schoolroom and have a long talk with Marcella who is one of the sweetest things in the world, full of originality, humour and character.

"Alwar[2] asked to come to lunch and have a long and confidential talk about India, and he went half an hour ago. He says that Peel[3] knows nothing whatever and cares little about India, and that Reading[4] is a very weak Viceroy. He never reads a file or studies a subject, but has people in who state to him a case orally, just as though he were a lawyer in chambers, and then decides. He says Lady Reading loves the Viceroyalty, which her health has been good enough to enable her to enjoy, so much so that she was enabled to accompany her husband on a tiger shoot where she had the satisfaction of seeing him miss three tigers running.

"As to the prospect of a General Election there appear to be 2 currents in the Party; (a) for an early Election, (b) for postponement for as long as possible. I think that when Parlt. meets great pressure will be applied to bring about the former, and that it may be impossible to resist for long. This is what I have prophesied all along will happen.

"On the other hand I think personally that there is no excuse for plunging the county into the cost and turmoil of a General Election while the European situation is as it is. A Govt. that is on the verge of an Election is never strong and its action is discounted by foreign Powers. Neither do I think that Baldwin has any right to prejudice issues so great because he is personally in favour of a fiscal programme which he has made no attempt to think out.

"Burnham said to me: 'As you know we backed you (in the D.T.) for the Premiership against Baldwin, and every day is tending to show that we were right.'

[1] Colonel Sir Maurice P. A. Hankey (b. 1877), who was created Baron Hankey in 1939. He was Secretary-General of the Imperial Conferences of 1921, 1923, 1926, 1930, and 1937.

[2] His Highness the Maharajah of Alwar who, together with Sir Tej Bahadur Sapru, presented India's case when the position of Indians in other parts of the Empire was reviewed at the 1923 Imperial Conference: a resolution that "it is desirable that the rights of such Indians to citizenship should be recognized" had been passed at the 1921 Conference, although without the agreement of South Africa.

[3] William R. W. Peel, Viscount Peel (1867–1937), who was created Earl Peel in 1929. As Secretary of State for India he was head of the Indian Delegation at the 1923 Imperial Conference, and had opened the citizenship question with a general statement.

[4] Rufus Isaacs, Earl of Reading (1860–1935), created Marquess of Reading on his return to England after his term as Viceroy 1921–26.

"Nothing can exceed the cheerfulness, good temper and courtesy of Baldwin, except his impotence. At the Imperial Conference he never opens his mouth and leaves the entire lead to me.

"I have to stay in town this weekend for the Armistice celebration on Sunday. I have had enough of all these ceremonies in the Abbey—so many in the last few years.

"In return for Winston sending me vol. II[1] of his book, I sent him a copy of mine.[2] He has not even acknowledged it!

"That stormy petrel F.E.[3] is back. It will be interesting to see what he will do—torn between love for Winston on the one hand and of advocacy of Free Trade on the other.

"A.J.B.[4] was a pall bearer at Bonar's funeral. He looked frail and old, but walked all right, and had to stand a long time. So had FitzAlan,[5] but he said that he had been a different man since he had been treated by Chaussand. I have ordered *Weekly Times* to be sent to you to the various addresses. I will close this letter now and write another before the mail goes on Saturday. This is no. (I) in the series.

"Good night my sweet darling girl. I hope you have not been lonely or miserable on the voyage. Hubert will have been a great consolation to you. I hope too that the fruit and flowers turned out well. I think of you at all hours of the day and night and miss you more than I can say, for my life as you can well picture is one monotonous round of official duties.

"Love to Hubert and Mabel.

"Your loving

"Husbin."

"Nov. 9, 1923.   Foreign Office.

"My darling girl,

"I was equally surprised and enchanted when on going in to dinner last night alone with Sandra I saw a letter from you lying on the silver table in the hall. It had not occurred to me that Lisbon was so near.

"What good news about your passage through the Bay—and the flowers and the fruit.

"I have just come from a meeting of an International Institute where I had to propose a vote of thanks to the Prince of Wales. Lord

[1] Winston Churchill, *The World Crisis*, published in four volumes, 1923–29.
[2] *Tales of Travel.*
[3] Frederick Edwin Smith, Lord Birkenhead.
[4] Arthur James Balfour.
[5] E. B. Fitzalan-Howard, Viscount FitzAlan of Derwent (1855–1947), Viceroy of Ireland 1921–22.

Grey,[1] Devonshire,[2] the Prince of Wales and myself on the platform, all the Dominion Premiers there, and a very distinguished audience. I made what are called one of my new class of speeches and had them all in roars of laughter for $\frac{1}{4}$ hour.

"I then came down here (F.O.) and the Spanish Ambassador has just left the room.

"I fear the political outlook is stormy and bad. The papers have been full of reports of an immediate Dissolution, and accordingly, as Baldwin had told us nothing about it and appeared resolved to shirk the matter altogether at the Cabinet, I raised it at once, strongly deprecating a General Election immediately, as savouring of trickery at the expense of the Electorate and of our opponents, as fatal to the proper or resolute conduct of foreign affairs during the very serious foreign crisis through which we are passing, and as likely to lead to electoral disaster. The majority of the Cabinet were in my favour, but there was a strong minority (Lloyd-Greame, Chamberlain, Hoare, Sanders, Bridgeman, Worthington-Evans)[3] who were on the other side. The P.M. as usual did not utter—, but promised to think carefully over the matter before Parlt. meets next week.

"He has behaved in the matter, as I think, with great unfairness, and unwisdom. First, as I told you, he sprung his new proposals upon the Cabinet without the slightest warning. Moreover, it now turns out that he had arranged the whole business with the Conservative Caucus (i.e., the Party Managers) in advance.

"I said all the time, and it has proved true, that once he promulgated his plans, even in outline, a General Election could not be for long postponed.

"I have reason to believe that before this morning he had made up his mind to Dissolve next week, and would have done it—he may do it still, as it is the prerogative of the P.M.—but for the steps that I took this morning.

"I am afraid that he will end by ruining the Party. For if he goes

[1] Edward Grey, Viscount Grey of Fallodon (1862–1933), Foreign Secretary 1905–16.

[2] Victor C. W. Cavendish, 9th Duke of Devonshire (1868–1938), Secretary for the Colonies 1922–24.

[3] Respectively: Sir Philip Lloyd-Greame (b. 1884), President of the Board of Trade, who in 1924 assumed the name Cunliffe-Lister, and was created Viscount Swinton in 1935; Neville Chamberlain (1869-1940), Chancellor of the Exchequer; Sir Samuel Hoare (b. 1880), Minister for Air, who was created Viscount Templewood in 1944; Sir Robert Arthur Sanders, Minister of Agriculture; William Clive Bridgeman (1864-1935), Home Secretary, who was created Viscount Bridgeman in 1929; and Sir Laming Worthington-Evans (1868-1931), Postmaster-General.

Lord Curzon leaving Carlton House Terrace

Sketch portrait by Sargent

Portrait by Sargent

The author's mother, Mrs. Monroe Hinds

to the Country and comes back with a diminished majority or with none at all, grave will be his responsibility.

"I think myself that in view of what was said this morning he may begin by trying to postpone a General Election till January. But I also think that his hand will very likely be forced as soon as the Session begins (next Tuesday) and that it is quite conceivable that by the time that you receive this a General Election may be in progress.

"If that be—whatever the result I shall regard it as a most unforgiveable and unpardonable proceeding. Salisbury, Bob Cecil, Devonshire, Cave, Novar,[1] and the more experienced members of the Cabinet were with me.

"I have just detected St. Aulaire[2] in another dirty intrigue with Poincaré and Gwynne[3] of the *Morning Post,* to get at the P.M. behind my back in order to get rid of me or to defeat my policy. When St. Aulaire next asks to see me I shall absolutely decline. I cannot have anything to do with a man so perfidious and base.

"Well, I must stop. But I know that all this will interest you greatly.

"I hope, my darling girl, that the programme I sent you will be of use to you. . . . I shall constantly think of you and wish you success and you may be sure that I shall long for the day when you return; though whether you find me in or out of Office is a matter of the utmost doubt.

"All love and kisses from

"Your loving

"Boy."

"Nov. 10th, 1923.   1, Carlton House Terrace.
"My darling girl,

"Before I go to bed this Saturday night I will write you a line. Smuts came to see me this afternoon and he bore a sort of message from the Dominion Premiers with whom he had talked. It was to implore me on no account to leave the Govt. or retire from the F.O. He said that he and all his colleagues had been profoundly impressed by the feebleness of the P.M., who evidently knows nothing

---

[1] Respectively: James E. H. Gascoyne-Cecil, 4th Marquess of Salisbury (1861–1947), Lord President of the Council; Lord Robert Cecil (*b.* 1864), Lord Privy Seal, who was created Viscount Cecil of Chelwood in December 1923; Victor C. W. Cavendish, 9th Duke of Devonshire (1868–1938), Secretary for the Colonies; George Cave, Viscount Cave (1856–1928), Lord Chancellor; Ronald C. Munro-Ferguson, Viscount Novar (1860–1934), Secretary for Scotland.

[2] The Comte de St. Aulaire, the French Ambassador.

[3] Howell Arthur Gwynne (1866–1950), editor of the *Morning Post* 1911–37.

about anything except perhaps business and finance. They all realized that the only effective force in the Conference so far as the Home Govt. was concerned had been myself, and that I was P.M. in everything but name. He wanted to say for them that they entirely agreed with my policy in every respect, and were convinced of its strength and rightness and that their trust in leaving the country was in me. Coming here had been an eye opener to them and my exposition and defence of our Foreign Policy had been a revelation. All this coming from a man of the unemotional but sincere character of Smuts was a great stimulus and encouragement to me, because I work in such complete isolation, with a Cabinet who have neither knowledge nor courage, and who like all small men, make trouble to cover their smallness.

"Once again I had to write Baldwin's speech about For. Affairs for the Guildhall last night, and the only papers (*Morning Post* and the Northcliffe Press) who would have denounced it if made by me applauded it from his lips!

"This afternoon St. Aulaire asked to see me, and I had the utmost pleasure in declining. I am not going to see so venomous a snake.

"Carnegie[1] has sent me the most splendid account of your landing, etc. at Lisbon, which I send you with translation and pictures! You seem to have risen to the occasion in masterly style! Sweet girl.

"Now I must stop for to-night, as it is past 1 a.m. and I can take it up again later on. Good night my darling girl. You are ploughing away over the Atlantic and I hope sometimes send a thought to your husbin.

"Your loving

"Boy."

"Nov. 13. 7 p.m.   Foreign Office.
"My darling girl,

"I sent you off a telegram today by Marconi to tell you that the thing you most feared is to happen, and that there is to be an immediate Dissolution of Parlt., with a General Election on December 6.

"It has come about in the most unfortunate and unprecedented way.

"In an earlier letter I told you how at the Cabinet last week the great majority led by me were entirely opposed to a snap election. Baldwin undertook to think it over during the end of the week. I fancy that the Party managers were hard at him during that time on

[1] Sir Lancelot Douglas Carnegie (1861–1933), Envoy Extraordinary and Minister Plenipotentiary at Lisbon.

the ground that he would be unable to keep the party together in Parlt. in the forthcoming Session, and that we have a much better chance of winning with an unknown programme than with a detailed plan—and other considerations of a tactical description. Anyhow he opened the Cabinet this morning by telling us in a sentence that the King had agreed to an immediate Dissolution, that Parlt. will be prorogued on Friday, and that the General Election will take place on or about Dec. 6. There was I think a general feeling that he has gone so far with his preliminary steps that there was probably no other way out, and that a postponed Election would be fraught with even worse disaster. But I think the Cabinet were profoundly shocked and incensed at the way in which they have been treated, and at the recklessness with which the Govt. and the country, entirely contrary to the will and wish of either, have been plunged into a General Election by the arbitrary fiat of one weak and ignorant man. Jim Salisbury is talking of resigning, and I think will. He declined to attend H. of L. this afternoon. Derby[1] is furious, and says Europe is dominated by madmen—Poincaré and Mussolini— and England is ruled by a damned idiot (Baldwin). This is the man whom he assisted to put into power in May last and for whom he helped to turn me down. I wonder what all the men who clamoured for Baldwin then think now.

"Of course if we win by the same or an enhanced majority, he will be justified, although I expect that our tariff troubles will only then begin.

"But if, as seems more likely, we only get a reduced majority, or possibly no majority at all, what a weight will rest upon his shoulders. I think he will then be deposed from the leadership of the party.

"Actually I have to carry on during the Election as I suppose I shall be the only important member of the Govt. left in London, and Foreign Affairs will have to proceed. They were never in a worse condition, as we are on the eve of a break with France.[2] This is

---

[1] Secretary for War.

[2] The reparations issue. Claiming that Germany had deliberately defaulted on deliveries, France and Belgium had sent troops to occupy the Ruhr in order to extract payment by force, passive resistance by the Germans ensuing. Lord Curzon failed to persuade Poincaré to agree on an impartial enquiry, and on August 11th, 1923, sent a note explaining in detail the British viewpoint, which occasioned great indignation in Paris on its publication. In October Germany, under severe economic pressure, applied to the Reparations Commission for an investigation of her resources and ability to pay. This eventually led to the Commission's decision on November 30th to set up the Dawes Committee, which was to evolve the Dawes Plan, intended to adjust Germany's payments so as to leave her currency and general economy stable.

the moment that Baldwin has taken for this rash and unnecessary move!

"He told me after the Cabinet that Austen Ch. and Birkenhead are willing to back him, but think they will do so with greater effect if they are made Ministers at once. Probably they are right, and they will I should think be made Ministers without Portfolio. But here too a good many will think that F.E.'s co-operation in the campaign will be rather dearly purchased at the cost of having to take him back and embrace him as a long lost brother. Austen will be better received and will be more useful.[1]

"The first consequence of these proceedings has been that Asquith and Lloyd George are embracing and shedding crocodile tears on each others' shoulders and that the great Liberal Party is united!

"By the time that you get this, all will be over, and my feelings and prophecies will be equally out of date. I don't suppose there will ever have been an Election where the outlook was more obscure. Anyhow, I am prepared for the worst, and think it more than probable that you may come back to find an unoccupied but happy man.

"This afternoon came your wireless about the maid. What an amazing bit of bad luck, and how shocking of her and her people never to have let you know. I have written at once to Mme Edwards at your suggestion. I wonder what my poor girl will do after Rio, at Buenos Aires, and your return. I am indeed sorry. Perhaps if the operation be successful she may be able to join you again on the way back.

"The Abbey Service went off well on Sunday (Armistice Day) but the Dean[2] preached, as I thought, a very poor sermon. There was such a vast crowd outside that my car was absolutely stopped and I had to get out and walk across St. James's Park to return home.

[1] In 1921 Austen Chamberlain had become Lord Privy Seal and Leader of the House of Commons in the Lloyd George Coalition, but many Conservatives considered that he sacrificed too many of their principles, especially in connection with the 1921 settlement which established the Irish Free State. Consequently on October 19th, 1922, a meeting at the Carlton Club decided that the Conservative Party should leave the Coalition, and discarded Chamberlain in favour of Bonar Law. Naturally Chamberlain and his supporters (including Birkenhead) received no office in the Bonar Law, or the succeeding Baldwin administration. The breach was not closed until in Baldwin's second administration in 1924 Chamberlain became Foreign Secretary and Birkenhead became Secretary of State for India.

[2] Herbert Edward Ryle (1856–1925), Dean of Westminster from 1911.

There I met Lord[1] and Lady Scarbrough and the old girl was profuse in her praises of you and your beauty.

"I have not otherwise left the house or seen anybody outside.

"Walter Lawrence[2] called on Sunday. He said that if only I had called him in in May last, he would have made it all right with the King and he would have sent for me! He thinks that both King and Queen regard us both with admiration and respect, but me with a certain awe; but that we, or rather I, certainly have enemies in the entourage as he has heard them himself tell quite untrue and malicious tales about me.

"I shall go back presently and have my usual evening talk with Marcella. I have told her to go and buy the best guitar she can find as my Birthday present to her. She has been going out quite a lot to Kinemas, concerts, etc. and is as tranquil and as happy as ever.

"I hope my poor sweet girl is not suffering over much from the great heat. Here it is quite cold. I trust that your cabin is not stuffy so that you can sleep at night. I will post this tomorrow to catch Murray's boat.

"How I hope that you will be rewarded for your long and arduous journey and that everyone will combine to help you when you land.

"Lord Riddell[3] came to see me at F.O. just now. He says I am one of the most misjudged of men and he wants to write an article and put it right. I told him that I had not suddenly become another man at 64, that I had been the same all my life and had been known as such to all my friends, and that if the pressmen had ever taken the trouble to know me or enquire about me from those who did, they might have been spared the parrot-like repetition of a silly old tag and might have helped me in my career instead of hindering it by every means in their power.

"I am having sent you weekly not only the *Weekly Times* but your adored *Tatler* and *Sketch*—both this week equally bad."

"Nov. 13.

"On coming in this evening I found your dear letter of Nov. 6 posted at Madeira, but telling me about your visit to Lisbon. But the photo you spoke of was not enclosed. Anyhow I send you my

[1] Alfred G. B. Lumley, 10th Earl of Scarbrough (1857–1945), A.D.C. to George V.

[2] Sir Walter Lawrence, Bt. (1857–1940), private secretary to Lord Curzon 1898–1903.

[3] George A. Riddell, Baron Riddell (1865–1934), proprietor of the *News of the World*, etc.

batch from Carnegie.[1] He is a dull dog, but not the only one in the Service. Lisbon will certainly see him out."

"Nov. 14.
    "I am posting this to-day.
    "Long Cabinet this morning, with obscure members talking interminably about For. Affairs. The P.M. as usual sat there absolutely silent and saying not a word. It is heart-breaking serving under such a man. Bob Cecil as usual full of wild ideas. Jim Salisbury after saying yesterday that it was probably his last appearance turned up smiling.
    "It is all a huge gamble. If we fail Baldwin will have been guilty of one of the greatest crimes in history, and if it be so he will have sinned from a mixture of innocence, ignorance, honesty and stupidity—fatal gifts in a statesman when wholly dissociated from imagination or vision or savoir faire.
    "My book[2] continues to get the most amazing reviews and I don't suppose that any book in modern times has been more praised.
    "Goodbye my sweet Gracie my darling wife,
                                        "Your loving and devoted
                                                            "Boy."

"Nov. 15, 1923.   1, Carlton House Terrace.
"My darling girl,
        "I posted you two very long letters yesterday, Nos. 3 and 4. But I just add this, as another boat leaves I believe tomorrow, to say how pleased I was to get your telegram today about the Dissolution. I well know how anxious you must be and so are we all, and particularly at the way things have been done. The negotiations about Austen and F.E. have broken down because there were a number of the party who absolutely declined (and with very good reason) to let the latter come back; and as he and Austen stood together, the result has applied to them both.
    "I had a back attack in the night, I hope not a bad one, and have been in bed all the day. . . . I send you Mme Edwards' reply about the maid, and feel that you must be very miserable without her. I hope you may be able to pick up someone out there.
    "I send you the latest pictures of myself and am as always
                                        "Your very loving
                                                            Boy."

[1] See note, p. 186.
[2] *Tales of Travel.*

"Nov. 18, 1923.   1, Carlton House Terrace.
"My darling girl,
          "You should be at Rio to-day. I have sent you a telegram
there, and one to Bahia and Pernambuco and two wireless telegrams.
I hope you have had them all. I got your message from Madeira
brought home by the *Avon*. You seem to be having a royal reception
everywhere; and I got your wireless about the great heat and about
the General Election.
          "Of course every human being condemns it, except the Liberals
who are going to profit. Baldwin's foolish policy is a perfect Godsend
to them, since it has brought them together and given them a fine
playing hand. The Labour Party expect I am told to lose seats, but
I should think that the Liberals will win a good number, and hold
the scales in the next Parlt. Baldwin thinks he is going to maintain
his majority and even increase it. But I cannot believe that. Anyhow
I do not see how he can get a majority large enough either to carry
any big measure of Tariff Reform or to last for any considerable
time. Our people are all playing up as best they can. But they secretly,
indeed openly, grumble as they hate the commotion, the expense and
the risk. Why on earth B. should not have gone tranquilly on for the
next three years no sane man can say. His evil geniuses have been
the whipper-snappers of the Cabinet, Amery,[1] Lloyd-Greame,[2] and
I believe N. Chamberlain. They buzz about him night and day, and
he is lamentably weak. Great excitement has been caused by the
failure of the attempt to bring back A. Chamberlain and F.E. I
don't think B. handled it very well, though the version given in the
newspapers, that after he had agreed to accept them the Under-
Secretaries went and threatened B. with resignation, is quite untrue.
He came in here for an hour yesterday morning—as I have been
laid up with back attack—and told me the whole story. It was really
the preposterous demands of F.E. and Chamberlain who insisted
that when the Government is re-formed places should be found not
merely for themselves but for all who went out with them, including
even Crawford[3]—that broke down the settlement. Moreover, F.E.
incensed Baldwin by his cynical insolence, admitting that he had
done his damnedest during the last year to injure us in every way,
and was proud to have succeeded.
          "What a cad the man is! Moreover he has deeply angered all

----

[1] Leopold Stennett Amery (1873-1955), First Lord of the Admiralty.
    [2] Sir Philip Lloyd-Greame (*b.* 1884), later Viscount Swinton, President of the
Board of Trade.
    [3] David A. E. Lindsay, 27th Earl of Crawford (1871-1940), Minister of
Transport in the Lloyd George Coalition in 1922.

the thinking and serious people by his Glasgow Rectorial Address, when he ridiculed Idealism.[1] The women voters are said to detest him.

"Another thing that made B. cry halt was that just before they went to see him they were all lunching with Lloyd George!

"The latter has commenced making electioneering speeches of the old Limehouse type,[2] and will, I have no doubt, excel himself.

"My own belief is that Austen and F.E. will work as hard at the Election as though they had been Ministers.

"It is said that if Horne[3] were available the H. of C. men would take him for it will be their only chance of making peace with the Party and coming back. I shall probably have to go to the City and make a speech on For. Affairs as I did last time. Now just for the moment I am laid up with a back attack. It came on in the night three days ago. But I hope not a bad one. I have not been out since Thursday. I shall not go about making speeches,[4] partly because we are in a serious foreign crisis with France, and my duty is here— partly because, though I see not the slightest objection to putting on duties—just as all other nations do but ourselves—I think the moment chosen is calamitous, and even if B. wins and puts on his duties, I do not see how unemployment is going to be affected. All this is the result of the step taken by the King in May last. I wonder what Salisbury, Derby and Co. who turned me down then are thinking now!

"This afternoon Mackenzie King the Canadian Premier came

[1] In his Address as Lord Rector on November 7th, 1923, Lord Birkenhead had said, "The world continues to offer glittering prizes to those who have stout hearts and sharp swords."

[2] A reference to the speeches made by Lloyd George as Chancellor of the Exchequer at Limehouse and elsewhere, in defence of his drastic "war budget against poverty and squalor" introduced on April 29th, 1909: it had dismayed the City and the propertied classes.

[3] Sir Robert Stevenson Horne (1871–1940), Chancellor of the Exchequer in the Lloyd George Coalition 1921–22. On the fall of the Cabinet he retired from active politics, although continuing to represent Hillhead until created Viscount Horne of Slamannan in 1937, and became prominent in the City.

[4] This campaign, from which Lord Curzon excused himself on the ground of the demands of the delicate situation in Foreign Affairs, was fought on the dominant issue of the tariff. Baldwin wished to introduce Protection as a cure for unemployment, etc., but Labour and the Liberals (led by MacDonald and Lloyd George respectively) were united in support of Free Trade. This unity of opinion, however, extended no further, and Liberals and Unionists combined in some constituencies to oppose Labour. Baldwin's party was already divided on the Free Trade issue, and the confusion was worsened by the unexpected support given by Lords Rothermere and Beaverbrook to Lloyd George—a complete break with their traditional advocacy of Protection. It was suggested that Lloyd George, Churchill, Birkenhead, and Austen Chamberlain might form a Coalition.

in to say good-bye. He said that he had come to the Conference with a violent prejudice against me based on the newspaper pictures of the superior person. He said that he and the whole of his colleagues had been profoundly impressed by my courtesy and affability, knowledge of the subject and eloquence. He declared that in all their opinions this was the main souvenir of the Conference, and that in future he would follow everything that I did and said with intense interest and regard.

"I nearly sank into the ground with surprise and confusion.

"Oh! How those cursed papers have killed me for half a lifetime. I can never recover now.

"I am not very keen on having Bob Cecil in the H. of Lords. He asked Baldwin for a Peerage as his health will not permit of his fighting a General Election, and of course he could not be refused. He is a terrible nuisance to me in the Cabinet, talking interminably and always wrong about Foreign Affairs. However, in the H. of L. he cannot speak without my consent, and may even at times be useful.

"By the time my precious girl gets this she will be deeply plunged in her own affairs. Oh how I trust that you will find good counsellors and see your way through the maze. You must send me some private wires through Alston to say in a few words whether you are making good progress and are satisfied or disappointed. I trust that my summary of important points may be useful to you. It is 1.15 a.m., so good night my darling.

"Marcella is wonderfully well and retains her great charm. I go in and see her and have a good talk every day. You must tell me how the voyage suited Hubert. I hope he is not affected by the heat.

"On Friday, Marcella's B day, we are going to have a mild 'bust'. I am going to take her to see *The Little Minister* (her own choice) and have asked Mother, Dot and Ambrose to dine here and go with us.

"This morning a terrible thing happened. I was suddenly informed that —— (one of the domestic staff) had stopped the whole night here and slept with —— (one of the maids). He seems to have crept in at 8 p.m. last night and locked himself in her bedroom with her. Louise who was on the watch saw him creep out this morning. I saw Wyliman, Fox and Co., and all expressed the utmost horror and surprise that such a thing could go on in this house under their nose.

"The maid was packed off without a protest in half an hour, and

N

Marcella is being looked after by Louise. It is very lucky that (unfortunate as you have been) you did not take this little b——h with you—for conceive what she might have done on board ship.

"I have since written to Alfred telling him that on no account must he employ him again. And what a little brute the man must be to have acted in this outrageous way."

"5 p.m. I have just had the enclosed letter from Sidney Herbert to say poor Belle died peacefully early this morning. Poor soul she was a dear affectionate faithful friend and it is sad to see her life go out in this tragic gloom.

"I have been expecting a telegram all day from you at Rio. Perhaps one will still come. For I love to hear that all is well with my sweet girl.

"I send you Boni de Castellane's[1] first article about his married life. I call it disgusting, and hope that we shall never allow him in this house again. I expect the later numbers will be even worse.
                                   "Your loving
                                           "Boy."

"Nov. 20 1923.   1, Carlton House Terrace.
"My darling girl,
          "I have just got your telegram from Santos. I think mine to Rio, tho sent off on Saturday last, the day before you were due there, must have missed you and been forwarded to Santos. We heard by telegram and all the papers reported the big official party given to you there, and I have pictured you marching in with all your jewels on looking a queen of beauty. I must say I think you have been well done at each place, and there is something after all in being wife of a For. Sec.!

"I went out again today for the first time and made a speech at a lunch to General Harington.[2] He is a fine fellow. But I did not let

[1] Comte Boni de Castellane, French connoisseur, self-confessed spendthrift, and man-about-town of London and Paris. He married Anna, daughter of the American financier Jay Gould, and in his *Confessions*, published in book form in 1924, gave a full account of the breakdown of their marriage over the dozen years which preceded the case in the French courts which brought it to an end.

[2] General Sir Charles Harington (1872–1940), G.O.C.-in-C., Allied Forces of Occupation in Turkey 1921–23. After the defeat of the Greeks in 1922, the Turks demanded that they should evacuate E. Thrace. British troops at Chanak blocked the advance of the Turkish forces across the Straits in pursuit of the Greeks and a clash was imminent. In October 1922, however, Harington negotiated an armistice with the Turks which, after near breakdown, was signed at Mudania.

out that he had cold feet about once a fortnight at Constantinople, and that I was always applying foot warmers to his lower extremities.

"Julia has pressed me to look in for dinner tomorrow night, but I don't feel sure about going.

"F.E. and Austen C. spoke at a lunch today supported by A.J.B. and Derby. The latter, after damning Baldwin heartily last week, has now become his most ardent supporter, and he and F.E. are going to tramp Lancashire together and shout for protection which Derby at least has always condemned. The general opinion seems to be that Baldwin has done a very foolish thing, and that though we may be returned, it will be with a much diminished majority. However, the Party agents think differently.

"Mother, Dot and Ambrose come to dine and play on Marcella's Birthday—and I am going up to Ked at the end of the week, in order to stay.

"I have Lutyens'[1] plans for your garden, rather over elaborate I think.

"I find that a boat is going tomorrow, so I will send (6) and (7) by it.

"I do hope that when you get this you will have broken the back of your heavy work. I shall long to get a telegram from you.

"Thank God —— goes tomorrow, and another fellow comes in his place. He looks respectable and I hope is not a drunkard.

"I will send a wire to meet my darling wife in Buenos Aires, where I am sure you will be tremendously feted. You will presently begin to complain of the length of all these letters! But you asked for them.

"Love to Hubert.
"Your loving Boy."

"Nov. 22 1923.   1, Carlton House Terrace.
"My darling girl,
            "I am just back from the funeral service at St. Margaret's for poor Belle. Not many people, 50 or 60 I should think. As I came out I saw Charlie Hardinge[2] to whom I gave a lift in my motor. He said he was intensely happy in his idleness.

"I have just gained a considerable diplomatic victory over Poincaré, who wanted to play the fool, and seize more German

---

[1] Sir Edwin Landseer Lutyens (1869-1944), architect noted for his design of the Cenotaph, individual treatment of country houses, and his work in Hampstead Garden Suburb.
[2] See note 1, p. 169.

territory over the return of the Crown Prince[1] (who is a wretched creature not worth thinking about). The Campaign being on, and no Cabinet fortunately possible, I have acted by myself and for the first time in 8 months have forced Poincaré to give way. I said that I would break the Entente unless he agreed. Of course the F.O. Press Dept. is too stupid to take any credit for it; and I suppose I shall see in the papers that it is all due to the brilliant diplomacy of Bob Crewe![2]

"Last night I just went along to dinner with Tommy and Jubags and came back from the dinner table. I sat between Julia and Moyra Cavendish who looked like a young girl. A.J.B. was on the other side of Julia and quite happy, supremely indifferent as to the crisis, praising F.E. in one breath and L.G. in the next and living in an Empyrean of his own.

"Tonight my second small dinner for the Dominion Premiers takes place here—Bruce, Massey, Milner,[3] Baldwin and self. Our chef went to Paris the other day because his wife's mother was dying, she has since died and he has been away a week. Of course, —— was taking no steps to secure his return and I had to telegraph.

"In his place the Granards' chef came in (not *nearly* so good) and in his first three days gave me

"Noisettes.

"Tournedos.

"Custard!

"—— is beyond all conception incompetent and the servants treat him with contempt. We cannot keep him long.

"I was delighted yesterday to receive telegram from my darling wife from Santos. It would seem that my telegram to Rio which was sent off the day before you were due there, must have missed you and

---

[1] William (1882–1951), known as 'Little Willie', Crown Prince of Germany, and eldest son of William II (the Kaiser). On Germany's defeat he had fled to Holland, and on December 1st, 1918, renounced his rights of succession. On November 10th, 1923, however, he suddenly returned to his estates at Oels in Silesia, and the French Government wished to compel Germany to surrender him. Curzon persuaded Poincaré to give up the project, and the matter ended with the German Government's note which set out the renunciation of the ex-Crown Prince, and confirmed that the Kaiser would not be allowed to return.

[2] Robert O. A. Crewe-Milnes, Marquess of Crewe (1858–1945), British Ambassador in Paris 1922–28. He was a Liberal.

[3] Respectively: Stanley Melbourne Bruce (*b.* 1883), who was created Viscount Bruce of Melbourne in 1947, Prime Minister of Australia; William Ferguson Massey (1856–1925), Prime Minister of New Zealand; and Alfred Milner, Viscount Milner (1854–1925), whom Baldwin invited to accept chairmanship of a tariff committee: protection being rejected by the electorate the committee was never formed.

been wired to Santos. Anyhow I meant it to be there in time to greet you at Buenos Aires. I telegraphed last night though you are not due there till tomorrow.

"S. is going about making his old vulgar claptrap speeches exactly the same as twenty years ago, and Buckmaster has actually appeared on the platform with him! I offered to go and make a big speech in the City on Foreign Affairs. But Sir Reginald Hall,[1] the Tory organizer, seemed to be completely indifferent, as he wants the campaign run exclusively on Preference, so I have heard nothing more.

"Good-bye my darling girl . . .
"Your loving Husbin."

"Nov. 24 1923.   1, Carlton House Terrace.
"My darling girl,
        "There is I find another boat going today so I will pop in a hasty line.

"We endeavoured to make Marcella as happy as possible yesterday. We had lunch together, and then off she went to a Cinema, and then in the evening all the family dined here—Mother, Dot, Ambrose, Baba, Marcella and self, and we went on to see *The Little Minister* which was cleverly acted (Fay Compton and Owen Nares) and which we all (including even me) greatly enjoyed. . . . Marcella will tell you about her presents.

"I am going next week to take down a roll of Ivor Churchill's Chinese paper and see how it will fit the walls of your bedroom at Ked.

"We are all awaiting a telegram to say that you have arrived at B.A., and are rather wondering that as you must have landed yesterday morning, it has not come.

"You will be inundated with all my letters. But I know how a long way off one value news from home, so I have written an awful lot.

"Lloyd George is stumping the country in his best old-fashioned style, and is actually to support old Asquith on his platform. The latter's seat is said to be in some danger. Winston[2] also is having a hard fight at Leicester.

"What an unnecessary thing it all is. You will not find a single

---

[1] Admiral Sir William Reginald Hall (1870–1943), Principal Agent of the Unionist Party 1923–24.

[2] Churchill was to lose the seat at West Leicester to Pethick-Lawrence by over 4,000 votes.

person here who approves of the Election, or who does not condemn Baldwin for plunging us into it.

"Having won a very considerable victory over Poincaré in our latest diplomatic encounter of course I see it attributed in every paper to the courage and sagacity of Baldwin, who had no more to do with the thing than our butler, and to the admirable diplomacy of Bob Crewe! But so it is, and I am hardened to it now. Good-bye darling girl,

"Your ever loving
"Boy."

"Nov. 27 1923.   1, Carlton House Terrace
"My darling girl,
          "It has been bitterly cold here for the last 2 days and a dense fog in London. I have barely been out except to F.O. Marcella is very pleased with the little terrier which Chips Channon gave her and which capers about her schoolroom. My present was a guitar with which she is making progress. I see next to nothing of Sandra who is out all day. Where she goes I have no idea, as she never leaves word with anybody.

"We often think and talk of you in the golden sunshine and probably the great heat of Buenos Aires. . . .

"I have been having one of those dreadful bouts with bills. Wyliman has revealed that during July the cost of each person in this house, servants included, (for food alone) was £5 per week! And yet if they were on Board Wages they would get 16s. each per week. He admits that it is the most scandalous thing he has ever known, and he attributes it all to ——. No wonder we are becoming paupers!

"The Election goes on merrily or gloomily according to the outlook. It seems rather futile talking about the probable or possible result, since by the time that you get this it will be known. Besides, with the immense mass of voters particularly the women, no one has any idea of how it is going to turn out.

"Jim Salisbury has gone abroad, and the Free Trade Conservatives are sulky and silent, except E. Derby who goes about trying to prove that he is both a Free Trader and a Protectionist."

"Nov. 29. "There is a boat going tomorrow by which one can post today, the last but one before you leave B. Aires. I have been in bed for 2 days with back pain and also acute pains (but I think only muscular) on my right side. I think if I rest I shall get rid of them.

And there is nothing to tempt me outside, icy cold and very raw. You are well out of it.

"I have never had any acknowledgment from Paul of Serbia for the silver candelabra. I wonder if he ever got them.

"I hope you are going on well and seeing daylight in your puzzling affairs. . . . However you will soon be back. Nearly a month has already gone. We are all very lonely and desolate without you. It is as though the light had gone out. Good-bye, my dear sweet wife. May you be happy and successful.

"Your ever loving
"Boy."

CHAPTER XIX

More Letters from Lord Curzon to Me

"Dec. 2 1923   1, Carlton House Terrace.

"My darling girl,

"I was enchanted to get your letter from Pernambuco yesterday morning. But how terribly you must have suffered on the journey from heat, discomfort, and no maid. That wretched woman ought never to have taken the place. Evidently she was a confirmed invalid and it is cruel that you should be landed with the expense of her operation, maintenance and return journey. I will add a line about her insurance when I have got hold of Wyliman. He appears to be away. But I don't know if you would have been better off with ——, the other maid. For if she could take —— up to her room and sleep with him there before the whole house, what would she not have done on board? Servants nowadays are a perfect curse. The new chef tho' good at greasy French dishes does English cooking too abominably and his kedgeree, pancakes, meringues and soups are miserable. Moreover he is as extravagant as they all are.

"I send you a further instalment of Boni. What a little cad the man is. Also one or two articles of Rothermere's attack upon me. We consulted as to whether I should make any reply; but F.O., P.M., and all said Better not or he will have a great attack every day up to the Election. We have ascertained that three times a week he gets the material for his articles sent over to him from the Quai d'Orsay at Paris. It is noticeable that in the General Election, while of course the general Liberal and Labour cry is that the F.O. has made a mess of everything and let our prestige down, neither Asquith, Ll.G., W. Churchill or any other has dared to mention my name or to accuse me of anything. That is left exclusively to the *Daily Mail* and the *Evening News*. I am so used to it now that I have ceased to mind. But I doubt if any For. Sec. has ever had such a dead set made at him by journals professing to belong to his own party. However, they slate poor Baldwin equally; and I begin to think that there is no such thing as decency honour or gratitude in the Press of this country.

"Before next Sunday the Election will be over. Everyone seems to anticipate a much reduced Conservative majority, and you cannot find anyone to approve of Baldwin's mad plan of going to the country. He goes about making very honest straightforward speeches, while poor old Derby tries every night to loop the loop, as both a Free Trader and a Protectionist, and only makes himself ridiculous.

"Ll.G. is supposed to have done himself no good by his flippancy and abuse. But they say he expects to get back or at least to hold the scales. The worst of it is that even if we are returned, we shall probably be so weak that there will be another General Election in 6 months, perhaps earlier. In my own mind I believe that Ll.G. still hankers for a Coalition; he is very careful never to say a word against Birkenhead, A. Chamberlain and the remainder of the old crew. One thing is pretty certain, I think—that I shall not be in Office a year hence perhaps not in 6 months perhaps earlier—although you need attach no importance to the silly stories of my being jettisoned. After all, where would Baldwin be without me? And that he knows full well.

"When I last wrote, I was ill with back and other pains, and had to put off an audience with the King on Friday morning. At 10.45 a.m., when I was in bed, Stamfordham rang me up to say that H.M. proposed to come round at once and see me in bed! It was all I could do to stop him, i.e. the King. He said that the German Emperor went to see Lascelles in his pyjamas, and why should not he? He persisted in the offer. But I would not agree and said I would get up at any time and come round to the Palace. To tell the truth, I knew the King well enough to be sure that even though he came, in his great good nature, he would make a fine story of it afterwards. So eventually I prevailed and went to the Palace at 6 p.m. The little man was at the top of his form. He told me that he regarded the General Election as the greatest mistake; that he had protested against it to Baldwin and had even asked him to represent his views to the Cabinet (which I need hardly say Baldwin never did). Further he had left on record a minute of his conversation with Baldwin, so that he might be quit of any responsibility in the future. He then told me that he had proposed to make Bob Cecil a Baron (on his elevation to the House of Lords), whereupon he had received an indignant letter from Jim Salisbury who had insisted on his brother being made a Viscount! He also said that until last week he had never seen or met Bob Cecil in his life, and did not know him by sight! I stayed 50 minutes and then bowed myself out with profuse expressions of gratitude for the King's offer to come and see me.

"I see in the picture papers that Irene is appearing on the platform with Cim—both making Liberal speeches and attacking my Foreign Policy. Dear me, what next?

"Ava Long asked me to dinner, also Mrs. Ronny Greville. But I have declined both, as I do not feel much in the humour of dining out, and I do not enjoy dinner parties at all.

"Darling, I hope that my letters have told you all that you like to know. Certainly I have not stinted them either in number or length. I am rather hoping to get a wire from you before long to say what progress you are making. Marcella, Miss Murison and I had quite a pleasant lunch today, and I go in and have a talk with her morning and evening every day. Sandra is away somewhere in the country— I forget where.

"This will reach you just before Xmas when Hubert will hand you a little gift from me which I hope you may think pretty. I am sure you will hate being away from your children, at least two of them, and the family party at Christmas time. But you will soon be back amongst us all, and at least you will have escaped the presents to my ungrateful servants, and the tree!

"I will finish this tomorrow. In the meanwhile Good night my sweet angel. I long for your return. We all miss you terribly, and I in particular at this trying time. *Dec. 3.* Monday. *The Times* has an article this morning in which it thinks we may do better in the Election than has been generally anticipated, and that Baldwin may get a majority of 30 at the least, possibly 60. We shall see. But will the majority be enough to enable us to do anything substantial, or to last?

"I hope you got the *Weekly Times* and the picture papers which I ordered.

"And now to the post. Good bye my precious girl. A happy Xmas to you and Hubert and all love and blessings.

"Your loving
"Boy."

"Dec. 6 1923.   1, Carlton House Terrace.
"My darling girl,

"I am writing this rather at random, not knowing where it will go to—whether Santos or Rio. But I am making enquiries.

"The Election is going today throughout the country. Fortunately it is fine though very cold. Only 200 results will be given tonight, and I will send you a telegram about these tomorrow. We shall not know the remainder until Saturday morning when I will send you another wire from Ked. I don't at all want to go down there, as it is so cold. But I have to go and see a new farm bailiff and also to settle the site of the filtering beds on my property.

"Lutyens is coming to dine with me tonight to discuss his plans for your rose garden which I think are quite needlessly elaborate and would cost thousands.

"Butler the architect is going ahead with the house plans and seems very intelligent as well as enthusiastic.

"All sorts of voting cards have come for you from Basingstoke, Montacute, Tattershall and this constituency, but strange to say none from Kedleston or Bodiam! I have not troubled you with them as they consist mainly—on both sides—of the most barefaced lies and they would be hopelessly out of date when they reached you. It seems very strange that you should have votes in six places and I not one anywhere!

"Alice Keppel asked me to dine tomorrow, but I declined her, like Ava and Mrs. Ronald Greville, as I do not feel in the mood. Indeed I am leading the life of a hermit. *December 9.* Sunday night. I returned from Ked tonight and there I was delighted to receive the envelope from Rio with a letter from my darling girl. All the other enclosures I am handing or posting to the recipients. I wonder if you ever got my various telegrams sent while you were en route, either by wireless or to the ports.

"During the last 3 days I have sent you two about the Election, (1) showing the first day's result (2) revealing the catastrophe which exceeded my worst anticipations. You will have known all through that I deplored Baldwin's suicidal move which I thought injurious to every interest concerned. But that the punishment would be so severe no one foresaw.

"The Conservative majority is literally wiped out and our tenure of office which might have lasted for 3 years may not last 3 weeks or even 3 days.[1]

"Everything that I had prophesied in my speeches at the Cabinet in late Assembly has been realised or intensified. You have known for long how poor an opinion I had of Baldwin's fitness to be P.M., and now alas the world knows it too. I have not seen him since the Election as he is at Chequers and does not come up till tomorrow. Our Cabinet to decide what we do is to be on Tuesday, and there will be time to tell you the result before this mail goes.

"Of course he ought to resign and probably will. Then logically I ought to be sent for if another Conservative Minister is to be chosen, we being still by far the largest section of the House 250 and 190

---

[1] The state of the parties at the Dissolution had been: Conservatives 346 seats, Labour 144, Liberals 117, and Independents 8. In the new Parliament it was: Conservatives 258, Labour 191, Liberals 158, and Independents 8.

(Labour). Alternatively the King, if Baldwin resigns, might send for Ramsay MacDonald or Asquith as Leader of the Liberal Party. But neither could last, and indeed no Minister who is chosen can last except by a concordat of the other party or parties to keep him in until another General Election in the summer.

"I do not of course expect for one moment to be sent for, partly because the reason which debarred me in May last will be fatal still, and partly because the *Daily Mail* has succeeded in convincing many people that my Foreign Policy has been a failure and that I am a bitter enemy of the Entente whereas as you know all the Dominion Premiers implored me to go on and all I have done is to refuse to truckle at every stage to Poincaré. The usual newspaper stunt is going on about Derby, but I am not disturbed by that, and anyhow I would not serve under him.

"I feel so much your not being here. I have no one to talk to. Cave is coming to see me tomorrow, and I shall see Jim Salisbury. Bob Cecil is in Paris.

"All the crowd who kept me out before—Amery, Bridgeman & Co.—will of course do their best to keep me out now—all the more that they are smarting under the sense of their own crushing defeat.

"However all that I am writing now may be out of date and even foolish 48 hours hence. So I will stop now and wish my sweet wife good night.

"I long to hear how your affairs are prospering. I have only had one telegram since you arrived at B.A. and you did not allude to business.

"*Dec. 10.* Today Younger[1] and Jim Salisbury (who is suffering from giddy fits and is not at all well) came to see me here and Cave at F.O., and I went to see Baldwin at 3 p.m.

"The King has pressed Baldwin not to resign before Parlt. meets on Jan 8., because (1) he would have to send at once for Ramsay MacDonald, who at present has no mandate from the country (2) we are still the largest party in the House of Commons and have no right to resign until Parlt. has withdrawn its confidence.

"If then we are to wait for Parlt. to turn us out, there could be no point in putting in another Govt. for 5–6 weeks.

"The idea therefore is that we should continue till then, and the 2 sections of the Opposition in the Debate on the Address will then combine and move a vote of Censure and turn us out. In that case I shall cease to be For. Sec. a few days before you arrive in England and all your worst forebodings will have been fulfilled.

[1] Sir George Younger.

"We shall then go into Opposition and wait for Labour and Liberal to fall out and for another General Election to ensue.

"To all this have we been brought by Baldwin, who seemed quite cheerful today and unconscious of the terrible doom he has brought upon our Party.

"I will write again after the Cabinet tomorrow to say if they take this view. Alfred returns from Oxford tomorrow.

"You will have seen that W. Churchill, Mond,[1] Barlow[2] and Sanders[3] (the two latter Conservative Cabinet Ministers) all lost their seats or failed to be elected. The Duchess of Atholl[4] won a seat in Scotland. Tom Mosley[5] got in with a much reduced majority, 4000 odd instead of 7000 odd, supported by Cim and Irene who made Radical speeches!

"Wyliman has made enquiries and has ascertained that your maid is not covered by any Insurance Policy of ours. I am afraid she is a dead out of pocket expense. Too bad.

"I will close this now and make a separate letter of the Cabinet decision and what follows as I find I need not post till the 12th. What reams I have written you since you left Gracie. I hope you have not been bored. At least you will be able to drain the dregs of our official life! We must do our best to enjoy our holiday when it comes.

"But my God, fancy a Labour Minister in the Foreign Office!

"Your loving
"Boy."

"Dec. 11th 1923.   1, Carlton House Terrace.
"My darling girl,
          "Midnight. I have just received in a F.O. box your telegram transmitted by the Co. expressing your grave disappointment at the result of the Election. It is indeed heartrending and so unnecessary. This morning at Cabinet, which met to decide our course of action, Baldwin asked me as usual to lead off. I entered upon a

---

[1] Sir Alfred Mond, Bt. (1868–1930), who was created Baron Melchett in 1928. He was Liberal M.P. for Swansea 1910–23, and had been Minister of Health 1921–22.

[2] Sir Anderson Montague Barlow (1868–1951), who was created a Baronet in 1924. He was Conservative M.P. for S. Salford 1910–23, and had been Minister of Labour 1922–23.

[3] Sir Robert Arthur Sanders, Minister of Agriculture.

[4] Katharine, Duchess of Atholl, wife of the 8th Duke. She was Unionist M.P. for Kinross and W. Perth 1923–38.

[5] Sir Oswald Mosley was Independent M.P. for the Harrow division of Middlesex 1922–24.

reasoned argument to the effect that we had no right on Constitutional grounds to resign now, with the result of compelling the King to send for Ramsay MacDonald who is the leader of less than 1/3 of the new H. of C.; that it was our duty to take our fate from the House when it meets on Jan 8. Of course if they turn us out we shall go; and in almost every way it would be better for our party that they should; since it is only in opposition that a defeated party purges itself and recovers strength. And, as I am wiring to you tomorrow, it can only be by the combined votes of Labour and Liberal that we can be rejected. Whether this happens or not depends entirely on whether Asquith and Lloyd George are willing to see a Labour Govt. in power. It is reported that they abominate the very idea and that they are not unlikely to postpone the death blow until they feel that they can get more out of it for themselves.

"We shall see.

"Meanwhile, as soon as Mussolini, Poincaré and Co. have realized that our Govt. may go out, and Labour may come in, they are tearing their hair with disappointment and lamentation that they did not come to terms with us while they had it in their power. Bob Crewe in particular wires that this feeling in Paris is very strong.

"It is possible therefore that with this more accommodating spirit abroad, I may be able to clear the board of some of the worst obstacles during the next few weeks.

"I forgot to say that after my speech at the Cabinet every single member without exception followed and expressed his entire concurrence with what I had said. E. Derby put in a feeble bleat that he had thought that Balfour might be called in at this emergency; but he realized in view of the Cabinet's attitude that this was impossible.

"So we remain for the present and so does Baldwin. How far the Party as a whole condemns him for his ruinous tactics I cannot say. There seems to be a general tendency not to be down upon him and to say that though beaten he fought like a gentleman, which few others did. Our own Party won't have anything to say to Austen or to Birkenhead whose intervention in the Election, though much trumpeted in advance, did not have the smallest effect.

"When I went down to Ked. last Saturday I took with me a roll of the Chinese wall paper and hung it up in your bedroom. The 9½ panels will just do the walls (with a framework in the case of each panel) but they will certainly make the room look rather smaller, so I left the panel hanging up for you to see before you decide. Good night sweetheart. Your telegram says that things are moving slowly with your own affairs. I did not expect anything else. But at least you do not say that they are not moving at all, so I am hopeful that you may come away with good results.

"The papers reported that the President gave you a dinner last night and I am sure you will have had a wonderful reception everywhere, whether we are going to be turned out or not.

"After all we have had a good innings and could hardly expect to stay in for ever : though equally we could not expect the rope to be pulled tight by our own Prime Minister."

"Dec. 17. 1923.   1, Carlton House Terrace.
"My darling girl,
        "You will be very sorry to hear that our friend Willoughby de Broke[1] has died suddenly. He apparently overdid himself in the Election, caught cold, went to bed, had meningitis, and was snuffed out. I am very sorry; for he was an attractive whimsical creature with a good deal of personality and it was a pleasure to meet him.

"I was delighted to receive this morning your little letter from Montevideo in which you referred to your wonderful reception at Rio; and this evening by a coincidence, came a long extract from a Spanish newspaper at Rio, sent by Tilley, which I can manage to read fairly well and which describes your dress and appearance and diamonds and Order, your charm of manner and beauty of appearance and so on. Of course you are a rare combination for the purpose, being, apart from your official position, daughter of a former Minister to Rio and speaking Spanish perfectly!

". . . On Saturday after lunch I went next door for 10 minutes for the Dss. of Roxburghe to show me their house. It was all in curl papers, so that I could see nothing of the furniture or tapestries. She has a very nice big sitting room next to the library; and there is a fair drawing room upstairs. I did not care for the dining rooms. All is done in Lenygon style. But the house as a house is not a patch on this, tho enormous sums . . . were spent upon it, first by Mrs. Maddison Drummond, and afterwards by Horlick.

"There have been no political developments in these last few days. Tomorrow Asquith is to meet the Liberals and decide whether to turn us out at once or not. The day, if they do it, will be about Jan. 17 or 18—the day of Gracie's return. So that your privilege will disappear the day you land.

"Poor us!

[1] Richard Greville Verney, 19th Baron Willoughby de Broke (1869-1923), Conservative M.P. for Rugby 1895-1900, and author of *Hunting the Fox*, etc.

"Cave however says that Haldane[1] declared to him that Ramsay MacDonald does not want to come in just yet but would prefer to wait a bit. We shall see.

". . . I go to Ked. on Friday to distribute beef on Saturday and shall be there for a few days. It will be desperately dull, but there is plenty there going on in grounds and house, and must now go sharp ahead.

". . . I am going out this afternoon to buy your present for the Queen.

"I wonder how Hubert is going on. I expect the long sea trip has done him all the good in the world. Marcella is developing into a very sweet young girl, full of independence both of character and judgment. We talk daily about all sorts of things and I am devoted to the darling child.

"It is 1.20 a.m. and I must say good night to darling Gracie and stop.

"*Dec. 18.* The evening papers announce the engagement of Lady Carnarvon[2] only 8 months after C's death to Col. Ian Dennistoun. She is 47, he 42.

"Your loving
"Boy."

"Dec. 19 1923.   1, Carlton House Terrace.
"My darling girl,

". . . Today I dashed out and bought a really lovely present for the Queen. It was a genuine old Italian pietà (nearly double the size of the one I gave you for your room at Montacute) 2 Limoges enamels one in centre one above, framed in an Italian metal gilt frame richly chased, with a brass handle at the back. It will stand upright which yours will not. I send it tomorrow to the Queen.

"Tomorrow as it is Dot's birthday Marcella and I dine with your Mother. I have sent Dot a cheque as I have no time to hunt for a present.

"Asquith made his speech this afternoon, of unrelenting hostility to the Government. I expected nothing else; and he means to combine with Labour to turn us out. I expect it will be Jan 18, the day of your return: that will mean Ramsay MacDonald.

[1] Richard B. Haldane, Viscount Haldane (1856–1928), who was to become Lord Chancellor in MacDonald's 1924 Government.
[2] Almina, Countess of Carnarvon, widow of the 5th Earl who had been associated with Howard Carter in the discovery of the tomb of Tutankhamen, and who died in Egypt April 5th, 1923. In the same year she married Lt.-Col. Ian Dennistoun (1879–1938).

Marcella

Author and Mr. Henry Channon, M.P.

"To this Baldwin has brought us! Of course Asquith is thinking more about his own party than the country: for he expects Mac-Donald to come to grief before long and then the King is to send for him.

"Baba told me today she has been suffering from pain in her side and saw a doctor who said she has a 'grumbling appendix' by which I suppose he means what may develop into appendicitis if it is not looked after.

"She is going to spend Xmas with Irene and then go to Weston-birt (Holfords) and afterwards to Eloise for the Stamford Ball.

"You will be on your way back my darling when you get this. I do hope it will be with something achieved. I anxiously await any news about that.

"Of course I shall be head of the Opposition in the House of Lords, but I shall try to take things easily for a while.

"I long for your return as I have felt so much this long solitude at a very anxious time. It was bad luck for both of us.

"Your loving
"Boy."

"Ked. Sunday Dec. 23 '23
"My darling girl,
         "Just as I was going in to Church there came a pouch with your big envelope containing the most darling photograph in the world. I never saw a better. It is up before me now, and I am proud to think that that darling creature is my wife. As you know, I am devoted to her and miss her every hour of the day and long for her to come back. I handed over the other envelopes to Mrs. Aston and old Voss, whose voice trembled with emotion. Her daughter was not in Church, and we had a very scanty attendance and practically no choir, tho the snow, which was deep on the ground when I came down, had melted. It is very cold and a stormy wind.

"Before I left London on Sunday I nipped out and bought a sweet little pair of 18th century paste shoe buckles for Marcella, and a little gold box for Mother. Then I went to lunch with the King and Queen. I am sure that they asked me as a counter demonstra-tion to the infamous attacks which the Rothermere Press has been making upon me for months. I stayed for 1 hour & 20 minutes, and they talked at lunch (we three were alone) over every conceivable subject. She was delighted with your present and told me she had written herself to the Pernambuco address which I gave her.

o

"As Auckland Geddes's eyes[1] will not permit him to go back to America, I have appointed Howard,[2] who made every sort of excuse and did not at all want to go.—Really these diplomats in their selfishness are amazing. I am sending Rumbold[3] to Madrid since he is not alert enough for Berlin. I then offered Berlin, *faute de mieux*, to Grahame,[4] a promotion which he had done little to deserve. Would you believe it?—he refused on the ground that he was ill in bed and could not move to such a cold climate as Berlin. (Brussels is on the same latitude.) He thus threw out of gear the whole of my remaining plans which were Barclay[5] to Brussels, Granville[6] to Stockholm, and so on, besides adopting an attitude which is fatal to all discipline, and, as Crowe[7] told him, will prevent him from ever getting further promotion. As I have often told you, I felt that he was a mollycoddle at bottom with no real spirit of courage, and he has now conclusively proved it. He has done for himself irreparably with me, and I hope that you too will have nothing more to say to him. Crowe has been putting daily pressure on me to send Tyrrell[8] to Berlin. I have declined, since as I told you at Lausanne I found that Tyrrell's cleverness is all on the surface, and that his judgment is not sound. He more than once gave me away there, and his famous communiqué at Paris was the finishing touch. Old Edgar[9] will therefore remain undisturbed, and the new Govt. must find a successor to him.

"I gave away the Xmas beef yesterday but was a good deal annoyed because so much as a matter of course do all the cottage tenants now take the gift that they did not, except in a very few cases,

[1] Sir Auckland Campbell Geddes (1879–1954), who was created Baron Geddes in 1942. He was Ambassador to the United States 1920–24, being compelled to resign by serious eye trouble: he effected a marked improvement of Anglo-American relations.

[2] Sir Esmé W. Howard (1863–1939), who was created Baron Howard of Penrith in 1930. He was Ambassador to the United States 1924–30.

[3] Sir George Montagu Rumbold, 9th Bt. (1869–1941), Ambassador to Spain 1924–28.

[4] Sir George Dixon Grahame (1873–1940), Ambassador to Belgium 1920–28.

[5] Sir Colville Barclay (1869–1929), Envoy Extraordinary and Minister Plenipotentiary to Sweden 1919–24.

[6] Granville G. Leveson Gower, 3rd Earl Granville (1872–1939), Envoy Extraordinary and Minister Plenipotentiary to Denmark 1921–26.

[7] Sir Eyre Crowe (1864–1925), Permanent Under-Secretary of State for Foreign Affairs from 1920, who was at the head of the Foreign Office section in the later stages of the Lausanne Conference, at which peace was concluded between the Allies and Turkey.

[8] Sir William George Tyrrell (1866–1947), who was created Baron Tyrrell in 1929. He was Assistant Under-Secretary at the Foreign Office 1919–25, and headed the Foreign Office section at the Lausanne Conference in the earlier stages.

[9] Edgar D'Abernon.

take the trouble to come down to receive it, but sent tiny children instead, or asked their neighbours to carry back their consignment. Pelham was very angry.

"I authorised him to give your present of coal to the 2 —— ones, and the Xmas tree is standing in the Hall, waiting for the presents for the Sunday School children, which, although bought by Ellie and sent off days ago by Gorringes, have not yet arrived!

"I will go on with this later.

"I am so pleased to hear that Alston[1] has stood by you well and been of real use. It was good luck having an able man there instead of a duffer like ——, and in a letter to me he says that you liked the legal adviser he chose. . . . I think that during the forthcoming year we had better go slow—as we shall be out of Office—and try to pay off the accumulated debts, so as to make a fresh start.

"I think the picture of you too sweet—one of the best I have ever seen. I have a wedding anniversary present for you but more of that later. I hope you liked the old-fashioned buckle I sent.

"*Dec. 27.* I cannot find out from F.O. when the boat is going that should take this to St. Vincent to reach you there Jan. 10. So I am sending it up to be posted in good time.

"I got your telegram Xmas day my darling and was delighted with it. I hope you got mine—and little buckle.

"I also telegraphed as you asked to President and For. Min. Today you have left B. Aires and are probably just now dropping down the River. I do hope it is with work well done and a clean slate.

"How I long for you to come back. You have been away for nearly 8 weeks and so far I have only had 3 little skimpy notes.

"Contrast my enormous pile of M.S.!

"Icy cold. Deep snow. Impossible to get out.

"Your ever loving
"Boy.

"I send you a lot of newspaper cuttings about my supposed elevation to a Dukedom! But I have never mentioned it to a soul and I do not suppose there is any more truth in it than on previous occasions. After all what does it matter."

"Dec. 29 1923   Ked.
"My own darling girl,
            "To-day I received your happy telegram from Rio, which

[1] Sir Beilby Francis Alston (1868–1929), Minister to the Argentine Republic and Paraguay 1923–25.

contained the encouraging words that your visit has been really productive, and that you leave your affairs settled. I truly hope that this is the case, and that your long and trying journey has been justified.

"I got your telegram on Christmas morning, and I trust that you also got mine. I loved the beautiful old box that you left for me —sound and solid and masculine—just the thing for a man's table. I mentioned it in my Xmas telegram and I thank my sweet girl for her remembrance and gift.

"I wrote you a long letter addressed to St. Vincent having been told that a collier may be going out which would reach that place before your vessel arrives. But to-day I hear that there is no such ship, and so I have told them re-address it to Madeira whither also this letter will go. I am telegraphing also to Tilley[1] to tell him to tell you that while you will get a pile—at least 3 or 4—at Pernambuco, there will be nothing after that till Madeira, when you will indeed be nearing home.

"In some ways I envy you for having been away. For we have had a detestable winter so far—scarcely a fine day, always frost or snow or sleet. Here it is so cold and horrible that I hardly get out. Butler is here drawing plans for electric light, radiators, w.c.s and bells—of all of which there ought to be enough to satisfy the most exacting taste.

"In 2 or 3 days I go back to Town and Cabinets recommence to decide our attitude at the opening of Parliament. Asquith made what I cannot help thinking was a very ill advised and truculent speech, in which he seemed to gloat over the prospect of turning us out and letting Labour in. But the papers are pointing out that this is little short of treason to the State, and that he will meet with small consideration from us when Labour is turned out a little later on and he looks to us to support him—as he does—in forming an administration. Again there is something very arrogant in the leader of the smallest party in Parlt. thus claiming to create and upset Ministries and to dominate the State.

"My own impression—and so far I have been pretty right—is that the greed for office on the part of the Labourites and the desire of Asquith to show his power will be so great that they will combine to turn us out on or about the very day on which you get back to England and that this is your last State journey for some time— perhaps for ever, who knows?

"And to think that we owe all this to the weakness and folly of

[1] Sir John A. C. Tilley (1869–1952), British Ambassador to Brazil 1921–25.

Baldwin, Derby having backed him up throughout now says he has had enough of him and threatens to raise the standard of revolt in Lancashire! But we know what that is worth.

"This evening we had a Xmas tree in the hall for the Sunday School children, and I distributed your prizes, bought by Ellie—nothing like yours—and had races down the whole length of the lower hall for sixpences. Baba is at Westonbirt (Holfords) and goes on to Eloise for the Stamford Ball.

"Serge and Chips[1] presented Marcella with 2 more animals—little green parroquets which sit on a perch back to back and look profoundly miserable.

"I am rapidly getting to the end of my Indian book[2] and have only 1½ more chapters to write. I have received the most charming letters from outside people about my Travel Book,[3] which seems to be read everywhere. I never thought it would be such a success.

"Now I am off to bed as it is past 12.30 and after a hard day in and about the stables I am tired. We are bothered by the deer getting out of the Park in places where the fence is not finished. There are 10 out now, and they are going to have a shoot on Monday and get as many as they can. (They shot 4.)

"We shall all expect to see Hubert quite filled out and turned into a son of Anak, whereas if Gracie looks like her photograph on the deck of the *Andes* she will look the sweetest thing in the world. As for me I look more like a butler out of a place than ever, and am sure that when we are turned out I can easily get a good situation.

"Your loving
"Boy."

"Jan. 1. 1924.   Ked.
"My precious girl,
          "I have had 2 telegrams from you to-day, one for New Year and one for our anniversary. It is 7 years ago, and I would do it 1000 times over again. I hope my darling wife would do the same, tho perhaps she is more doubtful. I think we have had great happiness—if some trouble. But I don't think we need ever have any more of the latter again, and I at any rate am proud of and devoted to my sweet wife.

"How good to think that every day and hour brings you nearer.

---

[1] Serge Obolensky and 'Chips' Channon (Henry Channon, Conservative M.P. for Southend West from 1950).
[2] *British Government in India* (2 vols.), 1925.
[3] *Tales of Travel* (1923).

You are at Rio to-day, next at Pernambuco where you will get a pile of letters.

"The architect Butler is here and I have had a very tiring time for 4 days in going into every room and settling where are to be the electric light radiator and bells. This house is really not a single mansion but a sort of garden city or college with several houses.

"My cousin Sir Ernest Paget[1] has died, aged 82.

"Sophy (my sister)'s girl Hilda is engaged as are all my nieces, to an impecunious parson. It seems to be the fate of the family.

"I dread getting back to the greasy French cooking of the Granard's chef which I detest. Wyliman says he only came to us to fill a gap while Mrs. C.B. was away and means to go back to her. I should like to try the experiment of a really good English cook like Mrs. Owen.

"Weather here shocking. Good night my sweet girl. I post this on 3rd on returning to London. All my blessings for the New Year. The Political crisis[2] remains the same and is indeed insoluble. This is the price that we all have to pay for the utter incompetence of Baldwin and the madness of his selection by the King.

"I don't think you will like the Chinese paper in your bedroom here. It is terribly noisy and fussy for a bedroom. You want something much quieter in that small room."

"Jan. 2 1924   1, Carlton House Terrace.
"My darling girl,
        "I have just got back to town and had a sweet telegram from you. It seems that you cannot have got mine to Rio for our happy anniversary tho I telegraphed it from Ked 2 days before. I on the other hand received yours and am made happy by your loving remembrance.

"When I got back tonight I rushed up to see Marcella. One of her parroquets has died from over eating! The little terrier had to be taken away suffering from epileptic fits—the usual experience with pets! Alfred was in bed, but nothing the matter.

"Fox came in to say that Maurice has been in bed ever since I went away and the doctor says he has tuberculosis. He is to be taken

[1] Sir Ernest Paget, Bt. (1841–1923), who was chairman of the Midland Railway 1890–1911.
[2] The situation at the beginning of 1924 was without precedent. Both Liberals (Asquith) and Labour (MacDonald) having declared against coalition, Baldwin remained in office pending the confirmation of the verdict of the electorate by a vote in Parliament. On January 21st, however, MacDonald moved a vote of no confidence, in which he was supported by the Liberals, and himself took office.

to hospital tomorrow and must leave our service. You will I know be very much distressed. Fox will at once look out for another.

"Tomorrow there is a Cabinet to settle about the King's speech.

"This letter has to go tomorrow to catch you at Madeira. I will write next to Lisbon. Good night my darling wife drawing nearer and nearer thank God.

"Your loving
"Boy."

"Jan. 6 1924.   1, Carlton House Terrace.
"My darling girl,
     "I have just been reading a splendid letter from Alston to Vansittart in which he talks of your tact and charm and of the amazing success of your visit which he said has done more good to British interests in the Argentine than any royal visit could have done. I have never read such a tribute—and it makes me so proud of my darling wife who has so worthily supported the credit of our name. He says you charmed them all—from the President downwards—off their feet.

"*Jan. 9.* In reply to one from you I have wired to St. Vincent to tell you that Parlt. opens on Tuesday 15th (I have procured a ticket for ——) and that we are expected to be turned out on 17th or 18th—so that my darling girl when she lands will no longer be the wife of the For. Sec.! Of course if I can get down I will be at Southampton to meet you. But in the above conditions it may be impossible.

"I will wire to Cherbourg if I find that you touch there.

"I was today appointed Chairman of the Trustees of the National Gallery in place of Lansdowne who has retired.

"Bob Crewe has just been in for a final talk before he returns to Paris tomorrow. He will go on as long as he can and endeavour to keep things straight.

"Whether the new Govt. will keep on Edgar (who is also coming over) or replace him I cannot say.

"You will remember that one of the points upon which the King insisted most strongly in May last was that I could not possibly be both Prime Minister and For. Sec. as I had rather assumed. Rumour has it that Ramsay MacDonald is to combine both offices,[1] although he is to be Leader of the House of Commons—where his Party is in

---

[1] Owing to the unsettled position in Europe, and bad relations with France, MacDonald did combine the two offices. Other ministers included Philip Snowden (Chancellor of the Exchequer), John Robert Clynes (Home Secretary), Richard Haldane (Lord Chancellor), Lord Parmoor (Lord President of the Council).

a great minority—as well. This must infallibly break down in practice since no man could do the double work. Even with the House of Lords I should have found it difficult. But the idea of even trying was then scouted as ridiculous.

"I suppose that Haldane will be Leader of the H. of Lords. And who the other Peer Ministers will be God only knows.

"E. Derby gets back from Cannes tonight and has wired to come and see me at 10 p.m. about the passages in the King's Speech about Protection which he and I want to abandon. We shall have a tough fight over it in Cabinet tomorrow.

"When we have retired I rather expect that Baldwin will offer to resign the leadership of the Party, but that his friends will arrange for a meeting to re-elect him. They will not look at A. Chamberlain, Birkenhead is detested—Derby is not and never has been a serious proposition—and both are Peers. Since I was passed over in May last my chance is supposed to have been extinguished; tho as A. A. Baumann[1] former M.P. and now leader writer in the papers says their refusal to take me is incredible. It

(page missing)

"My darling girl, you have been very bad about writing to me— only three letters since you left, saying next to nothing. At Madeira you were going to write from Rio. At Rio you were going to post at Buenos Aires. At Buenos Aires the next post was going to contain a really good letter! Here it is Jan. 9 and I have not the dimmest idea what you have done during these 5 busy weeks, though a mail went once a week. And meanwhile I have written you sheets and sheets. I expect between 25 and 30 letters many of them 2 and 3 quarto 4 page sheets. Well well!

"Now I must stop and catch post. You will soon be back. Icy cold here, snow sleet and blizzard. I am afraid you may find it very cold and rough in the Bay of Biscay.

"The latest is that perhaps we shall not be turned out till a day or two.

"After your return.

"Your loving
"Boy."

---

[1] Arthur Anthony Baumann (1856–1936), editor of the *Saturday Review* 1917–21, contributor to the *Fortnightly*, etc.

CHAPTER XX

Our Last Two Years Together

IN the autumn of 1923 I went to the Argentine, accompanied by Hubert, who had not been well and who would, I hoped, benefit from the voyage. It was a business visit, in connection with my property there, and with a legal question that had arisen over my first husband's inheritance. It was while I was away on this trip that George wrote to me the letters which have been given in the last two chapters. He really enjoyed writing letters—especially, I think, to me, for he found it a good substitute for talking to me, and easing his mind of the burden of political worries and speculations before he went to bed. He wrote very much as he talked—long words and formal phrases came naturally to George—and yet they sometimes look over-elaborate in his letters, but they never did when he was speaking. George was a fascinating talker, and held one enthralled. I remember one occasion when I had to go alone to a great dinner party—I forget whose it was, but George had refused on the plea of pressure of work—and all through that evening I found myself regretting that I was not dining at home alone with George, because his conversation would have been so much more worth listening to. It never came out well on paper. However, George wrote me everything that was on his mind during the time that I was away in South America, and I wrote to him in return some letters that were all too few and too brief—as he makes plain in one of his last letters to me! (I lacked George's facility in writing letters, and never enjoyed doing it as he did, unfortunately.) Not all of my few and scrappy letters from this trip have survived, but I will quote from those that remain, and also from one to my Mother.

"Nov. 6th, 1923.   R.M.S. *Andes*, at Madeira.
". . . We are due to arrive at Madeira at 9.30 tomorrow morning, and Hubert and I hope to have a nice long day on shore. It is I think the nicest of all the ports." [I must here explain that I was so used to the voyage to South America that I thought of the ports of call en route in much the same way that people think of the hotels they dine or lunch at when motoring to Scotland.]
"I must tell you about our visit to Lisbon yesterday. We arrived about three in the afternoon, and were met by two motor launches

—one very smart Presidential one with two charming Portuguese Naval Officers (who spoke perfect English) on board. They made a most delightful speech of welcome in the name of the President (who had sent them) and presented me with a beautiful bouquet of flowers. They then took Hubert and me in their smart launch (we were much photographed) on shore, where we found a President's motor (very smart with footmen) at our disposal for the day. Our Minister then took charge of us. He had also come on board to meet us, with a launch, and a motor from the Legation, but I thought it more polite to make use of the President's one. He agreed that I was right to do this. . . . His wife is away in England where she has gone for Princess Maud's wedding. Lord Carnegie is a nephew of Sir Launcelot Carnegie and Sir L.'s daughter is to be one of the brides-maids. We drove first to see all the beautiful state carriages, dating from 1700 down to the one used by the late King. They are reputed to be the finest collection in the world. Then to the Legation where we had a rather dismal tea—only Sir L., a young Secretary whose name I do not remember and his sister. The house is quite nice—quite simple, but in good taste. It has belonged to our Government for over 50 years, but Sir Launcelot tells me that the furniture is all his. It has a delightful garden. . . . I see by the wireless news that poor old Bonar was given a very small funeral. I wonder if you were asked to be a Pall-Bearer. It is almost grotesque to think of old weary Bonar in state at Westminster. I see also that Winston has been asked to stand as Liberal candidate for Bonar's old seat. The Liberal Party seem to be getting very busy and having large meetings at the Albert Hall, with Asquith making speeches. Do please keep me posted with all that is going on—you know how interested I am. I enclose a horrible photograph the Lisbon papers published of me before I arrived. They publish that I am on my way to spend the winter at Madeira—no doubt that is why the President sent to welcome me to Portugal. Rather a sell for them. Please keep the cutting for me. . . ."

At Madeira I was met by the Governor, and enjoyed, as I always did, my day on shore at that charming little place with its flowers and its steep streets and its sunny cheerfulness. At this point on the voyage I had a stroke of bad luck, for the maid I had engaged for the trip became ill, and it turned out that she had known all along that she was threatened with an illness which might become serious and require an operation. I was very sorry for her, but also rather put out, as it involved me in a lot of expense and inconvenience, all because the selfish girl had concealed the state of her health for the sake of the excitement of the voyage. I wrote a rather grumbling letter to George about all this from Pernambuco.

"Nov. 15th, 1923.   R.M.S. *Andes*, Nr. Pernambuco.
     ". . . I have nothing but a tale of woe to tell you. I sent you a wireless a day or two ago to tell you how ill my maid is. She has been in bed ever since and the doctor says she must be landed at Rio to be operated on at once. I shall have to pay for the operation and for her room at the nursing home—it would be fatal to send her to the public hospital—and also for her return passage to London. Will you find out from Wyliman if she is insured. Darling, please pity poor me, in all this great heat with no one even to get things out for me. My cabin is so small and on the hottest side of the ship. Your wireless arrived this morning telling me you were going to have a General Election at once. By the time you receive this all will be over. Darling my heart just aches to be with you at this time. I am heartbroken to be out of it all. Please keep me posted as to all that happens. I can't bear to have you go out of Office! And also Boy darling if you are offered an honour of any kind, do take it. I am sure it would be best and it would please me. What a fool the P.M. is to have a General Election at this moment. I always knew old Asquith and Lloyd George would come together to fight an Election—nothwithstanding all they said to the contrary. How I dread my time at Buenos Aires. I shall only live for your letters, and looking forward to my return to you. Please forgive stupid letter. My cabin is so hot that I am writing on deck in the greatest discomfort and noise. . . ."

From Rio I wrote to my Mother. She was always especially in my thoughts at Rio, because she had met and married my Father there, and because her early descriptions of it to me as the most beautiful place she had ever seen remained in my mind each time that I went there, and I agreed with her in thinking this.

"Nov. 17th, 1923.   R.M.S. *Andes*.
"My darling little Mother,
     "I am so sorry not to have written before this but I told Marcella to show you my last letter to her. I am afraid this will be the last chance I will have for writing before Christmas. Tomorrow we arrive at Rio. We are to spend the night at the Embassy, where there is to be a large dinner party, and then a Reception at the Foreign Office in my honour when they expect over 500, the same evening. How strange life is, Mother darling. I like to think of my darling little

Mother having been married and spent so much of her youth there —and that I should return to the same place in a position also to be made much of. I will write and tell you all about it afterwards. This has been rather a dull voyage. We have had the usual sports and fancy dress ball. . . . I hope my children spend Christmas with you. I want to be able to think of you all together. . . ."

I enjoyed our visit of twenty-four hours to Rio very much, and, judging by the newspaper reports of the official Reception, it was evidently considered a great success. We stayed with Sir John and Lady Tilley at the British Embassy, which was then a house perched high on a hill called Sta. Thereza, from which there were the most glorious views over the lovely bay, and also to the mountains. After a dinner party at the Embassy we drove to the Palacio Itamarati— the Brazilian Foreign Office—for the Reception, which was very well done, and was followed by a great Ball. Earlier in the day I had learned from Sir John Tilley that there had been considerable mis-givings in Official circles about the Ball. He had been anxiously consulted about this, as the Brazilians were afraid that I should think dancing very frivolous! He had already told them that he was sure that I should like it, but they were still in doubt. I was very much amused by this, and assured him, as he had already assumed, that I should enjoy a Ball, and so he telephoned to the Ministry of Foreign Affairs and set their doubts at rest. It was a very good Ball, and I enjoyed both it and the Reception which preceded it—it was an especial pleasure to me, as I said in my letter to my Mother, to be received officially in the place where my parents had been married and had held their own official position. It seemed a strange but happy chance of fate that sent me there as the wife of the British Foreign Secretary. Slightly handicapped by the lack of my maid, I did my best to make a good appearance, and the letter from George when he had seen the reports seems to justify the efforts I made. I found it easy to feel at my best in Rio.

The next day I lunched at the American Embassy, with the American Ambassador, Mr. Morgan.[1] (He was the American Ambassador at Rio for a very long time, and everyone liked him— he was most popular.) Mr. Morgan had taken the trouble to look for, and to find, a dispatch written by my Father when he was Minister there, long before I was born. At luncheon he read the dispatch to the party, and I was charmed and touched by this

[1] Edwin Vernon Morgan (1865–1934), Ambassador Extraordinary and Plenipotentiary to Brazil from 1912.

gesture. I had a wonderful time at Rio, as the wife of the British Foreign Secretary, and the daughter of a former American Minister there.

At Montevideo I received a telegram from the British Minister at Buenos Aires, Sir Beilby Alston, saying that the President or his representative would be coming on board to meet me on my arrival at Buenos Aires; and he added that the ship would dock very early, but that no one would come on board to welcome me until later in the morning. Relying on this message, I was still in bed when, at an early hour soon after we had arrived, there was a knock on the door of my cabin, and I was told that *they* had come! My maid having been left at Rio de Janeiro to undergo an operation for appendicitis, I had no one to help me in this emergency. However, I did my best very rapidly, and Hubert and I soon made our appearance, and received a wonderful reception. Buenos Aires was the end of the journey I had undertaken in the interest of my children and my own affairs.

Once more I was greatly fêted. Sir Beilby Alston was a wonderful organizer, and made all the arrangements. Hubert and I had a splendid and exciting time. Señor Alvear,[1] the Argentine President at that time, was charming, and a gentleman (this is not always the case). Also he had a charming wife. A great Ball given at the Jockey Club remains a delightful memory, the Ball given in my honour by Señor Alvear. On arrival I walked with him up the beautiful pink alabaster staircase, which was celebrated for its magnificence, and at the top we stood while first the British National Anthem was played, and then the Argentine. I think the Argentine National Anthem must be the longest one of any country, it seemed to go on for ever. Many parties were given for me at our Legation, and the dinners and the receptions were beautifully done. I am always sorry to remember how hard Sir Beilby Alston worked to have the British Legation made an Embassy. When at last it became an Embassy, poor Sir Beilby had already been sent *en poste* to Rio de Janeiro. Before leaving Buenos Aires I gave a large Reception at the Plaza Hotel, to which the President, all the Government, the Corps Diplomatique, and a large crowd of other friends came.

It was known in Buenos Aires that I was collecting birds for my aviary at Hackwood. I was given many wonderful and rare ones, and when I embarked on my return voyage, I left Buenos Aires with twelve large cages of birds—and the flowers I received had to be distributed all over the ship as my cabin would not hold them.

[1] Marcelo Torcuato de Alvear (1868–1942), who was President 1922–28.

The Argentine people are very generous, and love giving presents. Hubert and I were both delighted to join the ship for home, as we were exhausted with so much gaiety, and such a strenuous send-off, although we had enjoyed it all. Even so, I thought that Hubert was looking better than when we left England.

In January 1924, George wrote to me, "I have just been reading a splendid letter from Alston to Vansittart, in which he talks of your tact and charm and the amazing success of your visit." This praise quite turned my head!

George came to meet the ship at Southampton, as he had promised in one of his letters that he would if he could possibly manage it. It was a joy to be met by him, and it reminded me poignantly of that other time when he had come to Southampton to meet me on my return from the Argentine, just before our marriage. Then he had been on the crest of the wave of his great political career—and now he was to be out of Office after seven years of ceaseless work and immense responsibility. I felt the contrast very keenly, and I knew that he was feeling it too.

In spite of the political disaster that had overtaken the Government, George was full of happiness at our family reunion. Only one thing happened that caused a little distress—I had brought back, among all the other birds that I had acquired in the Argentine, a specially fine macaw as a present for George. No sooner had I presented it to him than it promptly bit his finger to the bone!

After I had been at home with George for a few weeks, I took my children to St. Moritz for a short holiday. This is an extract from a letter that I wrote to him then.

"Feb. 13th, 1924.   Suvretta House, St. Moritz.
   ". . . I long to return, as I really no longer care for this life, but the children seem to love it. . . . The D'Albas have arranged a wonderful trip for us in Spain in April. The Duke is coming to stay with Lord Revelstoke the first week in March, and wishes to meet you and talk about the trip. He says we must take our motor. I am looking forward to it. I enclose a letter that I have received from Mrs. Vansittart. I think they sound rather disappointed about the F.O. I was told that someone had asked Harold Nicolson the other day how things were going on at the F.O., and he answered: 'It is as if Lord Curzon had gone to Kedleston for a few days.' I am also told that someone asked Mr. Humphries of Hatchard's (book shop) if your book was selling well, and he said it has sold better than Asquith's and Winston Churchill's together!. . . ."

We never made the trip to Spain. Before my return from the Argentine the Baldwin Government had fallen, and now that George was no longer at the Foreign Office he was more than ever absorbed by his plans for the improvements at Kedleston. The spring planting of trees and shrubs there needed supervision, and this made our travels in Spain impossible—as he explained in a letter to me which I have quoted in an earlier chapter.

Now that the Conservatives were out of Office I saw more of George than at any time since our marriage. It seemed quite strange to have him join me at the tea-table. We dined out more often, and even paid one or two country house visits.

I remember one of these that we both enjoyed, a Saturday to Monday at Lympne, the unusual, rather oriental house belonging to Philip Sassoon. Among our fellow guests were Lady Violet Bonham Carter, whom George considered the best woman speaker he had ever heard, Hilaire Belloc and his sister Mrs. Belloc Lowndes, and Mrs. Gubbie, who was Philip's cousin.

Philip was remarkably graceful, and I loved to watch him playing tennis. Once I told him that he reminded me of a black panther, and he answered, "Why *black*?"

We often motored down for the day to Bodiam Castle, where George was enthusiastic about the repairs and excavations which he was having carried out. He could now spare the time to address meetings of various kinds, and I heard him speak in the Albert Hall to a crowded meeting of the Primrose League, of which he was Grand Master. He even joined us when I took the children to the theatre. At the play he enjoyed himself as though he also were a child. Because for so many years he had been too busy to go to the theatre he found difficulty in following the conventions of the modern stage, and often he would ask me to explain the plot.

This was a George entirely new to me. But how obviously he missed the toil of Office!

During this time I attended two or three evening parties at Buckingham Palace, where I always encountered the Prime Minister, Mr. Ramsay MacDonald. He seemed to like talking to me, but perhaps he thought his frequent attendance needed an explanation. I remember that he once said to me, "I have to come to these functions, in my capacity as Foreign Secretary." I answered, "What an example for my husband, who never came." Why couldn't he admit that he came because he enjoyed the parties at Buckingham Palace—as we all did?

While George was Foreign Secretary, I had thoroughly enjoyed the little part I had played at the Royal Garden Parties. I would arrive in time to be at the side entrance to the garden at Buckingham Palace, near the door from which King George and Queen Mary would come. Before their arrival all the Diplomatic Corps would take their places, to be greeted by the King and Queen. It was my pleasant duty to be present at this Presentation.

I recall an unfortunate incident when I arrived wearing a large hat. As I walked down the terrace steps leading to the garden, a whirl of wind removed my hat and carried it away! Luckily, as I was always more than punctual, there were few to see my embarrassment. George never attended the Garden Parties; he could not have borne so much standing about, because of the weakness of his back.

I remember a luncheon at Carlton House Terrace in 1924 for the Crown Prince of Italy.[1] Both George and I were charmed with his delightful manner, his knowledge, and his appreciation of pictures. He was an extremely good-looking young man. It was with pleasure that we received the news of his betrothal to Princess Marie-José of Belgium, who, as a child, had spent some of the years of the First War at Hackwood. The two sisters of Crown Prince Umberto, Princess Elena and Princess Mafalda of Savoia, had also paid us a visit at Hackwood. They were both delightful guests, and charmed us all with their ease and grace.

The last Ascot party at Hackwood with George was larger than usual, and seemed to have a strong foreign element. Prince Serge Obelensky, the Aga Khan, the Marquis de Castellane, the Marquis and Marquise de Polignac, Lord and Lady Londonderry, Lady Ancaster, and Chips Channon were our guests. I remember being rather embarrassed each day as some members of the party were invited to lunch in the Royal Box at Ascot, but not Boni de Castellane. (I had sent the names of our guests at Hackwood to a member of the Royal Household.) Poor Boni evidently thought that perhaps he was not properly dressed for the occasion, as each day he appeared in a more elaborate costume, much to our amusement—finally wearing a long frock coat! It seems that the 'Powers that be' thought that Boni was divorced, which was not the case; on the contrary, he had spent years trying to get Rome to annul his marriage, for he was a Roman Catholic. I explained this to one of the King's Lords-in-Waiting, and Boni lunched with the King and Queen. His departure from Hackwood at the end of his visit was like a Royal one. Boni sent for each of our servants in turn, and gave them handsome

[1] Later Umberto II.

Author and Hubert setting out for Marcella's wedding

Wedding group at Carlton House Terrace after Marcella's marriage to Mr. Edward Rice

presents. He even sent for the chef, to congratulate and reward him. The staff talked for days of his generosity.

George and I spent a delightful Saturday to Monday with Violet Milner at Great Wigsell, near Bodiam, in Sussex. Violet was one of George's oldest and greatest friends. I remember his saying that Violet had a brain like a man's, and it was a delight to talk to her. She lived in a charming old Tudor house. Later, when I went to live at Bodiam Manor, she was my nearest neighbour, and we became devoted friends. During the visit with George, I recall sitting next to Rudyard Kipling at dinner. He proved to be an easy companion, and quite unspoilt. Rudyard Kipling died before his wife, and Mrs. Kipling at her death some years later left their charming little Tudor house, Bateman's, at Burwash, with one of the loveliest gardens in Sussex, to the National Trust. This was open to the public, and it was my delight to pay many visits to it, taking my guests from Bodiam Manor.

I had never flown; and when Sir Sefton Branker offered to take me up in an aeroplane, I accepted eagerly. I motored a short distance out of London to the aerodrome—I think it was Hendon—where I found Sir Sefton Branker waiting for me. I was rather surprised at the smallness of the aeroplane—an open one, with only two seats. I was strapped into the seat behind him, and I was thrilled by the beauty and the wonder of the flight through the air. At times I thought that my neck would be broken, and try as I would, I could not crouch low enough to be protected by the small screen in front of me. It was wonderful to see the sky where the ground should have been, and to realize that we were looping the loop—which we did three times! I returned home delighted with my new experience. The next day I was not well, and when my doctor was called, he found my heart missing a beat. He asked if I had received or suffered any kind of shock. I had certainly not felt the slightest alarm when flying, but George blamed the looping the loop, and, I fear, wrote to Sir Sefton Branker and reproached him.

George, as I have said already, was a deeply sentimental man, and he never forgot the dress I was wearing at luncheon with the Duchess of Rutland in Arlington Street when we first met—a dark blue voile dress, and a dark blue hat trimmed with bird of Paradise feathers. This luncheon took place on the 24th of June in 1915. Every year after our marriage, on the anniversary of the luncheon, I was asked to wear the dark blue dress and the hat, and George and I lunched alone together. However, I became rather bored with this dress and hat, and gave them to my sister. She was younger than I,

P

and as the fate of younger sisters is often to have the elder sister's dresses handed on to her, she did not mind. One day she came to a small luncheon party at Carlton House Terrace, wearing the dress and the hat (in which she looked charming). The footman handed me a little note from George, written on the back of the menu card, which said, "Gracie, how could you?" He had recognized the dress and the hat, and I had to take them back from my sister. I remember that the next 24th of June I again struggled into the dress, with some little difficulty—alas, I had grown stouter.

I remember a luncheon party, late in 1924, given by Philip Sassoon at his house in Park Lane. Amongst other guests were Austen and Ivy Chamberlain. Philip seemed to me to be making an unusual fuss of them. This was just after Baldwin had been returned for the second time. When I went home, I told George that I felt certain that Austen would be appointed Secretary of State for Foreign Affairs, and George answered, "You are too suspicious—Baldwin would never do such a thing to me." However, I was right. Austen went back to the Foreign Office, and George was appointed Lord President of the Council. I knew Philip—he seldom backed the wrong horse.

George spent a fortnight at Lou Sueil with the Balsans on the French Riviera a few weeks before his death. I was expected to join him there—I had promised to do so, but I had not gone, as I wished him to enjoy by himself a visit to Consuelo, a friend of many years' standing and also a friend of Mary, his first wife. As usual, he wrote me daily letters telling me of his delightful drives, and of the beauty and perfect taste of Lou Sueil, and of the kindness of Consuelo and her husband. I was disappointed to find him looking far from well on his return. Travelling was always a great trial for him. However, after a few days he seemed better.

He had an engagement to deliver an important speech at Cambridge, and by that time he seemed very well again. He was in high spirits. I heard him speak in the House of Lords in answer to a question by Lord Oxford, and he had never appeared in better form. The day that he went to Cambridge, I am glad to remember that I did a thing which our busy lives seldom permitted; I called for George and drove with him to the station and saw him off.

That night I was dining with Cecil and Alice Bingham, who had a big dinner party from which we were all to go on to a Ball given by Lord Brassey. Towards the end of the dinner I was called to the telephone to answer an enquiry from the Press—I was asked if George were ill, as there was a rumour that his speech at Cambridge would not be given. I said that I knew nothing of this, and that he had been perfectly well that afternoon. I felt very uneasy after this enquiry, but I did not telephone to Cambridge because I was sure that if George needed me I should have received a message from him, and I knew that if nothing was wrong he would have disliked receiving a fussy telephone call from me based only on a rumour from the Press. So I went on with the Binghams to Lord Brassey's Ball; and there I was again called away to answer similar questions about George from the Press. I went home then, thoroughly alarmed, and put through a call to Christ's College, where George was staying. I was told that he had had a sudden attack of illness, that a doctor had been called, and that George wished me to fetch him on the following day and take him back to London.

I left London at five o'clock the next morning in my motor, and was with George at Cambridge by breakfast time. I found that he had been suddenly taken ill while dressing for dinner in the house of the Master of Christ's, with whom he was staying. He had had a severe haemorrhage, but notwithstanding this, he had insisted that he must deliver his lecture. A doctor had been called, who declared that the attempt to lecture would have serious results, as he had lost so much blood. Then George submitted, with a reluctance that was only in keeping with his life-long fight against physical disability.

He was anxious to leave for London as soon as I arrived, in order to get the best advice and attention from his doctors at home. I shall never forget that drive. George was feeling very ill, and undoubtedly realized that this was an illness from which he might not recover. He was in great suffering, but he did not complain. He held my hand, and from time to time he spoke, slowly and thoughtfully. Once he said, "I know that I have not been a good man—but, on the other hand, looking back, I don't think I have been a very bad one." Later he said, "If anyone ever asks you if I believe in a future life, you can tell them that I most certainly do." His courage and his resignation were very moving and beyond all praise.

At six o'clock a consultation took place at Carlton House Terrace between Sir Bruce Bruce Porter and Sir John Thomas Wilson. They advised an operation, but decided, in order that he might be strengthened for the ordeal, to defer it for three days. Those days he spent in bed, making voluminous memoranda as to State and other papers in his possession, and in making additions to his Will. His brother Francis Curzon was with him while he did this, and I thought it best to leave them together. George wanted me to be present also, but it would have been too painful for me to hear him calmly discussing his testamentary arrangements.

The operation appeared to be successful, and for eight days he made a gallant fight, notwithstanding great weakness. He lay ill in my bed, for my big, comfortable bedroom was a better place in which to nurse him than his own small room. On Wednesday the 18th of March, serious symptoms developed—congestion of the right lung, and it seemed certain that this would prove fatal. Each time that the doctors had seen him, he used to ask me, after they had left, what they thought—and I used to try to reassure him, in the hope that such encouragement would help to give him strength. At last, however, I was told by the doctors that he was dying. They told me that I ought to tell him. Sir Thomas Horder said: "It is right that he should know. He is dying; he is a very great man, and it would be wrong to deceive him any longer. He should be told the truth, so that he may prepare his mind in his own way."

So I went back to George, who was very weak, and when he immediately asked: "What do they say? Am I going to recover?" I answered very gently, "Darling, I'm afraid you are very bad." He closed his eyes without a murmur, and repeated the Lord's Prayer aloud. Those were the last words he spoke. He held my hand until he lost consciousness on Thursday. He never regained consciousness, and on Friday morning, at half-past five, George died, still holding my hand. Baba and Francis were with him. I had scarcely left his bedside day or night for the whole fortnight.

At the time when this happened, and indeed for many years afterwards, I could not possibly have brought myself to describe these last, intimate scenes for publication. But I remember how his own closest friends came to see me, one by one, after his death—men of great wisdom and distinction, like Lord Salisbury, and Lord Crewe, and Lord D'Abernon—and how they all urged me to write down details of George's courage and faith during his last days, and, some day, to give them to the world. They said that I owed it to George to do so. And now, after thirty years, I find it possible to describe what was too personal and too sacred to write about at the time.

George's funeral was impressive and moving beyond words. It began with the Burial Service in Westminster Abbey, conducted by the Archbishop of York. The Pall Bearers were the Prime Minister, the Lord Chancellor, the Speaker, the Chancellor of the Exchequer, Lord Salisbury, Lord Oxford, Lord Birkenhead, and Mr. Ramsay MacDonald. The coffin, made from a two-hundred-year-old oak from

Kedleston and covered with an ancient pall embroidered with the Curzon arms in gold, rested on a bier surrounded by tall lighted candles, and the insignia of George's Orders—the Garter, the Star of India, the Indian Empire, the Victorian Order, and the rest— were placed on purple cushions at the foot of it, where my great cross of crimson roses also lay. Wonderful flowers sent in memory of George were piled against the chancel rails. The seats within these rails were occupied by representatives of the King, Queen Alexandra, the Prince of Wales, the Kings of Spain and Belgium, the Crown Prince of Sweden, and by many members of the Diplomatic Corps. The large congregation included almost all our friends, and large numbers of the general public. When the majestic Service was ended, the coffin was carried out to Chopin's Funeral March and a muffled peal sounded from the Abbey's great bells.

The coffin was taken by train to Kedleston, and George lay in state that night in the Great Hall at Kedleston. I arranged for an extemporized altar to be placed at the end of the Hall, covered with a crimson cloth, and the next afternoon the first part of the Committal Service was held there, conducted by the Archbishop of York and the Bishop of Southwell. It was attended by all the family mourners, by his Derbyshire friends and neighbours headed by the Duke of Devonshire, and by the tenants of the Kedleston estates. The Archbishop gave an address that was simple and most moving —he spoke not as the Primate speaking of a great Statesman, but as a clergyman mourning the loss of an old friend. Then the coffin was lifted by eight sturdy tenants and carried down the steps of the North Entrance and along a winding path in fitful spring sunshine to the little church, where the last prayers were said in the beautiful Memorial Chapel on which George had lavished infinite pains to make it perfect—so small that only the clergy and the members of the family could be present at this final moment. While the hymn "Now the labourer's task is o'er . . ." was being sung by the choir— surely no one ever deserved this tribute more than George—the coffin sank silently into the vault where all the Curzons lie.

CHAPTER XXI

After Years

AT the time of George's last illness, Marcella and her Governess Miss Murison were in Jerusalem. They had joined Ivy Chamberlain and her daughter Diane on a trip to the Near East. Imagine my anxiety when I received a cable from Ivy Chamberlain saying she had been obliged to leave Marcella and Miss Murison behind in Jerusalem because Marcella was too ill to travel, they were in the best hospital in Jerusalem, and there was no cause for me to worry. It was in fact a good hospital, but Marcella found her stay there a little trying. The hospital was run by Christian Missionaries who were trying to convert the Jews, but the doctor who attended her was a zealous Zionist, who bristled at his surroundings. This cable arrived two days before George's death, and so I could not go out to my daughter—who was only fifteen years of age. Miss Murison sent daily cables to me; and Marcella made a good recovery, and returned home two weeks after George's death.

Later that year I took her to Aix-les-Bains. I have written in another chapter about this visit, when we saw a lot of the Prime Minister and Mrs. Baldwin. Mr. Baldwin was always kind to me. He said that as long as he was in the Government, I was also, and insisted that I should keep my Diplomatic passport.

I had intended to spend that winter in India, with Marcella. George had planned a tour for me to make in India, as he wished me to see all that he had done in restoring and creating there. I had taken my passage, and all the arrangements had been made for me to go with Marcella on our return from Aix-les-Bains; but, on my way back to England, while in Paris getting clothes for Marcella and for myself, I received a telegram from my sister saying that my Mother was seriously ill. We returned to London, and I cancelled the trip to India. My Mother was dangerously ill, but she recovered in due course; by that time, however, it was too late for me to make new plans for the Indian journey.

It was a sad coincidence that the lease of Hackwood expired in 1926, the year after George's death, and the lease of 1 Carlton House Terrace came to an end only eighteen months later. I renewed the Hackwood lease. George had left to Kedleston most of his pictures, tapestries and antique furniture at Hackwood. In fact for some time he had been working with his lawyers to arrange that I should live at Kedleston, paying a rent to Dick (his nephew Lord Scarsdale), who he seemed to think would welcome this idea. If Dick did not agree to this, I was to take the Hackwood *objets d'art* to a smaller house at Derby, which belonged to the estate. I never liked this plan —but I felt it my duty to carry out, as far as possible, George's wishes. I asked Dick about leasing Kedleston from him, but the rent he suggested was far beyond my means and the upkeep would have been very costly. I was pleased—I had no wish to live at Kedleston without George.

In the end, most of George's collection of pictures from Hackwood, so much prized by him, were sold by Dick, his successor at Kedleston, to help pay Death Duties. Before his operation, George had agreed with his brother Francis that his effects from Hackwood should go direct to Kedleston—instead of to me for my life and afterwards to Kedleston—leaving to me the long lease and contents of Montacute, and also the lease and contents of 1 Carlton House Terrace.

I think this was a much better and easier plan in every way. When the time came, I renewed the lease of Carlton House Terrace, as I wished to bring out Marcella there. She was in Paris for the next two years at Princess Madjeska's wonderful finishing school. Hubert had joined the Life Guards, Alfred had gone on a world tour, Baba (Alexandra) was with me at Carlton House Terrace. George had died on Baba's twenty-first birthday. I always remember a sad little talk that I had with George before his operation, when he said, talking of the things that would happen if he died, "I feel certain that Baba will marry Major Metcalfe, A. J. B. will take my place as President of the Council, and Asquith will be Chancellor of Oxford." In some way these thoughts of George's became known to Margot Asquith. She came to see me and implored me to publish something in the newspapers to the effect that George had expected her husband to be the next Chancellor of Oxford. Margot was so persistent that I sought advice from Bob Crewe. He said that I must not allow it to appear that George was "dictating from the grave", as George would not have wished it. George had only been surmising the changes that he expected might happen.

Lord Cave was elected Chancellor of Oxford in succession to George, and that was the only one of George's three prophecies that was not fulfilled. Margot said no more about it—she was too impetuous and warm-hearted to bear resentment about anything. She and Lord Oxford were old friends of mine, and stayed with me on more than one occasion at Hackwood. I had known them well, long before I married George. Indeed, I have before me a letter which Mr. Asquith wrote to thank me for a book I had sent him, addressed to me at Trent Park in the early days when I first became friends with this most interesting couple.

"12 Sept., 1916   10, Downing Street.
"My dear Mrs. Duggan,
        I am much touched by your delightful letter and your most beautiful present. Thank you a thousand times. I am more than glad to believe that in these troubled and anxious days, I have found in you a new and true friend.

                              "Always
                                "Yr. Affect.
                                    "H. H. Asquith."

        Before my marriage, I had greatly enjoyed their luncheon parties at 10 Downing Street, and it was always a pleasure to receive the Asquiths at Hackwood. Margot was a fascinating but quite incalculable character—one never knew what she would do next. Her life was so full, owing to her remarkable vitality, that she was always taking short-cuts to enable her to fit more things into twenty-four hours than a day would hold. For instance, she used to write her 'bread-and-butter letter' in advance, on Hackwood writing-paper, and leave it behind for me when she left; and on one occasion, she added a postscript to say that she had taken with her all the flowers out of the drawing-room because she had a luncheon party in London that day and would have no time to get flowers on her return. During George's lifetime they did not visit us, because George was deeply offended with Margot for having published in one of her books some early verses of his without his permission. As the years passed, I had tried to induce George to forget and to forgive this cause of offence; and at last I had succeeded, and had persuaded him to agree to make friends with Margot again, just before his death—and, alas, he died before the reconciliation could take place.
        Baba's engagement to Major Metcalfe was announced, and the marriage took place, as Cynthia's had done, at the Chapel Royal, St. James's, by permission of King George V. Baba was a goddaughter of Queen Alexandra, after whom she was named. Hubert accompanied her to the Chancel, and I gave her away. She was a lovely bride. I love that beautiful little Chapel, full of sacred

Hubert John Duggan

Mrs. Baldwin addressing a meeting at East Ham on behalf of Hubert

Two of Queen Mary's Christmas cards

The author's grand-daughter and great-grandchildren
The Countess of Plymouth, Viscount Windsor, and Lady Emma Windsor Clive

atmosphere and overflowing with historic interest. I tried to make her wedding all that George would have wished. We had a Reception at Carlton House Terrace to which crowds of her friends came. Hackwood was given over to them for the first part of their honeymoon, before they went to Italy for the remainder. Later they left for India, as Fruity was to continue his duties with his regiment for a time. I missed Baba very much, we had become great friends and we had many tastes in common. She was only thirteen when I married George, and I had become devoted to her.

I paid many visits to Paris to see Marcella at Princess Madjeska's finishing school. It was always a pleasure to have tea with the young girls on Sundays, when they did the duties of hostesses. It was a delightful school and beautifully run in every way. I went to Paris to be with Marcella for her Confirmation, which took place there. She was fortunate in having many friends in Paris; she often lunched on Sundays at our Embassy, where Lord Crewe was then Ambassador, and Peggy Crewe was most kind in taking her out.

I was counting the days until she returned home. My life at that time was rather a lonely one, I was not yet out of mourning and did not see a great many people. One of my few distractions was racing. I shared Jeanne Clayton's house at Newmarket for the meetings there—she was a delightful woman, and her house was always a gay and happy one. On looking back, those were the only Newmarket meetings that I enjoyed, although I had a house of my own there later.

Much of my time was spent in supervising the refurnishing and redecoration of Hackwood. I made a new golf course, and reorganized the shoot, which was a good one. Major Eric Mackenzie was my Comptroller, he thoroughly understood the shoot and ran it well. I often had many of the best shots in England to shoot—Harry Stonor, who was a pleasure to watch, I would choose to stand by him as often as possible; Simon Lovat, another excellent shot; Lord Edward Montagu, Scatters Wilson, and many others. One Sunday an amusing thing happened, when Harry Stonor (a devout Roman Catholic) and Lord Londonderry were taken by mistake by my chauffeur to the wrong churches. Harry Stonor was taken to the Old Basing Parish Church, where the Service was so 'High' that it was some time before he noticed the mistake; Lord Londonderry however was under no misapprehension whatever when he found himself in the Roman Catholic Chapel, and dashed out again immediately, furiously muttering something which was probably, "To hell with the Pope!" I always invited ladies to these shooting parties, but I

remember only one who shot, Mary Blandford—and she was a good
shot too. At times I thought that my guests expected too much. One
man arrived with a valet, a chauffeur and two loaders—four
servants brought by one guest! I had a certain amount of trouble
with the Master of the H.H., who always seemed to want to bring
the hounds over just before my most important shoot. Unfortunately
both my boys enjoyed hunting more than shooting. After dinner at
these parties we played bridge. I often looked back with sad longing
to the Whitsuntide parties of other days—the brilliant talk, and the
wit, when George and I had Ettie Desborough, Winston and
Clemmie Churchill, Arthur Balfour, Evan Charteris, Harry Cust,
Edgar and Helen D'Abernon, and Julia Maguire as our guests—but
then I was always a much better listener than a bridge player.

Some of the parties at Hackwood that I remember with the
greatest pleasure were given for Hubert. Alfred was abroad, and
Marcella not yet out. Hubert had among his friends a great number
of young beauties. They were all the 'lovelies' of the day. I recall his
Colonel, Sam Ashton, speaking of these beautiful girls as 'Hubert's
Beauty Chorus'. I have never seen a greater bevy of beauty. I can
see them now round the long dining-room table. The first that comes
to my mind is Lettice Lygon, the eldest of Lord Beauchamp's
daughters; she was tall, graceful and very fair, a truly lovely girl—
she made me think of a Fairy Princess; Diana Fellowes, also beautiful; Mary Ashley-Cooper, a special favourite of mine, with such
delightful manners; Diana Bridgeman, lovely, with outstanding
charm; Bridget Parsons looked golden and had a good wit. I think
Hubert's especial favourite was Daphne Vivian, who was delightful
to look at and the best of company. I don't think you would find such
beauty, charm, and finish or distinction amongst young ladies in any
other place but England.

The young men I remember at these parties were Charlie
Cavendish, Richard Sykes, Hugh Lygon, Chips Channon, and
Philip Yorke.

Alfred preferred bachelor parties; the friends he liked to have at
Hackwood were Robert Byron, Gavin Henderson (now Lord
Faringdon), and Evelyn Waugh; one or two of my women friends
would make up the party.

Alfred loved travelling, especially in eastern Europe. I remember
that in 1925 he and Robert Byron accompanied Gavin Henderson
in a great motor tour from Hamburg, by way of Berlin and Inns-
bruck, to Florence and Rome. Then they went on by Naples to
Durazzo, across the Adriatic to Patras in Greece, and after a stay in

Athens home by Yugoslavia, Budapest, Vienna, Strasburg, and Paris. At that time the roads in Yugoslavia had not been repaired from the damage of the First War, and he told me that one day between Skoplye and Belgrad they took eleven hours to go sixty miles.

A few years later Alfred went with a friend to Mount Athos, and nearly every summer he visited Greece or European Turkey. He spent one summer in Constantinople, helping as a volunteer in the excavations conducted by St. Andrews University in the Hippodrome. Alfred was away from home a great deal, but my last visit to the Argentine was in his company. That voyage was now so familiar to me that I felt I could recognize every wave between England and the River Plate, but it was a new experience to travel alone with Alfred, and it was fun to show him all the familiar sights. In Buenos Aires Mr. Leslie, Manager of the Pacific Railway, invited us to accompany him and Mrs. Leslie in his special train on an inspection of the whole line. It was a wonderful trip, lasting a week; we slept in magnificent wagon-lits, and the rest of the train was made up of special cars and dining cars. The hills of Cordoba, in the northwest, were a beautiful sight after the endless Argentine plains, but the experience I remember best was dawn at the Mar Chiquita. This is Spanish for the 'Little Sea'. Actually it is a wide lake, the home of enormous flocks of wildfowl. As the sun came up great troops of flamingoes rose on the wing, until it seemed that the glow of sunrise was being repeated in every quarter of the sky. The whole world was a rosy pink.

Marcella came out in 1926, and earlier that year she and I had both been very busy doing voluntary work during the General Strike. She had made great friends with the Baldwins when we were at Aix, and they sent for her to go and work at 10 Downing Street, which she did every day while the Strike lasted, sorting letters and addressing envelopes. My work consisted in running a canteen for lorry drivers who were doing night driving. I seemed to spend the whole night frying sausages, and getting my hands burnt by the hot spluttering fat because the sausages were always exploding, until a kind lorry driver exclaimed in surprise, "*Prick* them, Miss—*prick* them!" So I received my first lesson in cookery.

Seldom have I given an entertainment that gave me so much pleasure and satisfaction as the coming-out Ball for Marcella. We had a large number of guests for dinner, including the King and Queen of Spain, the Prince of Wales, as well as many of Marcella's contemporaries. I had the usual arrangement, six or seven tables holding ten, in the large dining-room, Cassano's band played outside the room during dinner. I had taken a lot of trouble and the house looked wonderful. A big marquee had been built on the terrace overlooking the Mall, with a good floor for dancing. The Gobelin tapestry from Hackwood was hung round the walls of the marquee, and the beautiful silver chandeliers (four of them), also from Hackwood, were hung from the ceiling. A raised platform or dais with comfortable chairs was at one end of the marquee, and at the other, a large opening on to the terrace, where chairs, and many flowering shrubs, growing in tubs, were arranged. To enter the marquee guests had to descend three or four steps from the red room. At the base, on each side of the steps I had enormous blocks of ice covered with water-lilies from Hackwood. (It was a warm evening.) The beauty of this ballroom was delightful.

The greatest appreciation came from Winston Churchill, who had come on from an evening Court at Buckingham Palace. Clemmie had attended the Court with him, and, being tired, had gone home. Winston was so impressed by the beauty of the scene that he went home, found Clemmie in bed, and said that she must get up, and not miss this lovely Ball. He returned bringing Clemmie with him.

Ambrose's band played in the marquee, and the upstairs drawing-room had been turned into another ballroom, where Cassano's band played. He played mostly waltzes, by request, and there were to be seen most of the older guests who preferred the waltz.

My lovely Marcella was eighteen . . . at home with me. . . . She looked, and was, all that a mother could wish. Her white lace and tulle dress, with garlands of white roses, seemed perfect for her.

Marcella's first Season in London was a gay one for me. I loved taking her to all her parties—chaperonage still existed then. In fact I don't think Marcella went out even in the daytime without her maid, or someone in attendance. No doubt the present-day young girls will laugh at this, to them, ridiculous custom. I presented her at Court—feeling very proud of her—and we had a young party at Hackwood for Ascot. I remember Princess Marina staying with us for this Meeting, and how delightful she always looked. Marcella also went with me to Newmarket. It was such a joy to have my lovely daughter with me. However, she did not share my love of racing, and I think she only went to these two Meetings.

I gave other small dances for her that Season as well as her coming-out Ball. I often arranged to have two dinner parties on successive nights at Carlton House Terrace. It simplified the household and staff arrangements in many ways, and the masses of flowers sent from Hackwood to fill the house would stay fresh for two parties; also, the lovely silver from Kedleston was used only for parties, and so it was convenient to have it out for two nights in succession. On one of these occasions, I had invited a young party, consisting entirely of Marcella's friends, for the first night, and had asked older people to the dinner that I was giving on the second night. To my great dismay, Mrs. Arthur James, who had been invited for the next party, arrived at the first, just as we were going in to dinner. Someone had to be sacrificed in order to save the situation, and so I went over to my daughter, whose perfect nature and perfect manners I could always rely upon, and said, "Grannie is not very well, darling, and wants you to dine upstairs with her." Marcella never demurred, although my Mother was not even in the house, but went away smiling—and I put Mrs. Arthur James in her place at dinner, between two charming young men. Venetia James told me afterwards that she had never enjoyed a dinner party so much! She never realized her mistake—or perhaps it had been a mistake on the part of my secretary—but she was a very shrewd hostess when she entertained in her own house in Dover Street. I remember a Ball that she gave there, when I felt disinclined to dance, and went down to supper early with a man with whom I happened to be talking. Venetia had arranged that I should go to the second supper, but just before the guests began to go down to this, she came to me and said, "You need not go down to supper, Grace, because you have had it already—I saw you!"

I doubt if my secretary had made a mistake over Venetia James' invitation, but she certainly made one when I was sending out cards for a rather frivolous party at Carlton House Terrace. The late Lord Rosebery received one, and told me that he had been quite mystified on being bidden to a party of mine, with the words 'Fancy Dress— Comic' written across the corner of the card!

I remember another Ball when the question of going down to supper had an amusing sequel. This was a Ball given by the late Duchess of Norfolk at Norfolk House in St. James's Square. I happened to be talking to an old friend of ours, Chips Channon, and went in to supper with him to finish our conversation. The next day I received a politely apologetic note from the Duchess of Norfolk regretting that she had not seen me in time to arrange for me to be taken in to supper! This apology reminds me of an occasion when, during George's time as Foreign Secretary, I went to an evening party at one of the Legations. I had arrived in good time, and was sitting with the other guests, when, after what seemed a long delay, our host, the Minister, announced that the entertainment could not begin until Lady Curzon arrived. I had to catch his eye and tell him gently that I was there! After this episode George always arranged that I should be accompanied to these parties by someone from the Foreign Office, who would make it clear that the wife of the Foreign Secretary was duly present.

Marcella became engaged to Edward Rice at the end of her first Season. I persuaded them to wait until after her nineteenth birthday for their marriage, and I admit I was sad at the thought of losing my lovely daughter so soon. In the early spring we spent some weeks in Paris choosing Marcella's trousseau. Her wedding dress and the bridesmaids' dresses were made by Madeleine Vionnet. Marcella's dress was of the traditional white satin, with a very long and truly magnificent train of cloth of silver covered with white chiffon embroidered with white lilies and pale green foliage. It was carried by four little pages, Michael Cecil, Simon Warrender, Nicholas Mosley and John Godley, who wore white satin 'Cavalier' suits with lace ruffles and each had a red rose on his coat. There were six bridesmaids—Diana Bridgeman, Catherine Willoughby, Esmé Glyn, Betty Grosvenor, Rosalie Willoughby, and Cynthia Burnes, and they wore dresses of white tulle over silver tissue, with wreaths of red roses, and carried sheaves of long-stemmed red roses of the same colour. The wedding at St. Margaret's, Westminster, was one of the most beautiful I have ever seen, the weather was perfect, and the whole world seemed to be smiling on my young daughter's marriage. Canon Carnegie officiated. Sir Thomas Beecham's wedding present to Marcella was an offer to bring the London Symphony Orchestra to the church and to conduct the wedding music—the first time that this had ever taken place. Seldom can such a feast of music have been equalled at a wedding. Before the ceremony Sir Thomas conducted the Slow Movement from Beethoven's Second Symphony, and Schubert's Unfinished Symphony—and as the bridal procession left the church the orchestra played the Wedding March from Lohengrin and the March from Meyerbeer's *Le Prophète*. The church was decorated entirely with white flowers and red—lilies and white lilac, and masses of red roses that filled the air with fragrance. Patrick Rice, Edward's brother, was his best man. Hubert brought Marcella to the church, and I gave her away, and when we all went into the vestry to sign the Register, I was escorted by Lord Balfour, who was one of the witnesses, as were the King and Queen of Portugal, Princess Alice, and Prince Paul of Serbia.

1 Carlton House Terrace was perfect for the Reception. A big marquee had been built on the terrace overlooking the Mall, where stood the buffet, and a rather wonderful wedding cake. The flowers here were the same as those in the church—red roses, and lilies in groups. The wedding presents were on view in the ballroom. I welcomed the guests at the top of the stairs, and they went on to the drawing-room to congratulate Edward and Marcella. My daughter's wedding was as perfect as I could make it, and I look back on it with a mother's pride and love.

History repeats itself. Marcella's lovely daughter Caroline followed her own mother's example and became engaged to Other (Lord Plymouth) at the end of her first Season, and married in the early spring at the age of nineteen. Caroline was also a most lovely bride, and she wore Marcella's beautiful lily-embroidered train for her wedding. She has made me proud of being a great-grand-mamma to a boy aged three and a baby girl of one year.

Marcella's marriage left a great gap in my daily life, but my sons' interests absorbed me, and in those days there was still plenty of gaiety. I remember a wonderful Fancy Dress Ball given by the Duchess of Sutherland. I was idly discussing with Gabriel Wolkoff what we should all wear, when he said, "I can see you as a white peacock," and designed for me a most beautiful dress and head-dress, which I had carried out to his design and wore at the Ball. The back of the dress was covered with real, long, white peacock feathers, and the effect was remarkable.

It was soon after this Ball that two of my younger friends, Chips Channon and Serge Obelensky, urged me to give a Fancy Dress Ball at Carlton House Terrace—but a comic one, not stately fancy dress, they insisted. I thought it quite a good idea, and once I had sent out the invitations I entered into the spirt of the thing whole-heartedly. My guests came in every imaginable—or unimaginable —costume. Serge and Chips and various other young men wore the white robes and hoods and masks of the Ku-Klux-Klan, and with a concerted movement they all suddenly swooped upon Madam Merry del Val and carried her off—to her most evident delight. Edie Londonderry came as Circe—her nickname—followed by a company of her friends dressed as various birds and animals. I received my guests, dressed in some rather ordinary fancy dress— Egyptian, I think—and half way through the evening I went upstairs to a room where the clever Mr. Clarkson was waiting to transform me into a Negro Parson. My face was blacked, I wore a skull-cap to simulate baldness, a black suit and big masculine shoes, and from then on I mingled with my guests and even danced with them without any of them ever penetrating my disguise. Only my step-daughter Cynthia Mosley identified me—I danced with her, and suddenly she whispered "Gracie!" in my ear with a grin, but she did not give me away to anyone else. It was an amusing and odd experience to find myself for once in the position of an invisible hostess. (This was the party to which Lord Rosebery had been asked by mistake, much to his own mystification.)

At about this time my son Hubert was married to Joan Dunn, the youngest daughter of Sir James Dunn. Their wedding took place at St. Martin-in-the-Fields.

Racing continued to be one of my principal amusements. I always enjoyed the Goodwood Meetings; to begin with the weather was generally good, we could wear summer dresses and the men lounge suits. There was an air more of a large garden party than of a race meeting, the course lovely and green; lunching in the different tents or rooms was always fun. The London Season would be over, and we felt we would not have to return there, which was a relief by the end of July. I used to rent a house for the Meetings, and on one occasion the late Lord Derby stayed with me. I had rather a large party, and I remember the house had but few bathrooms. Lord Derby told us at dinner that he had gone to have his bath, having been told the bath was ready, when to his great surprise he found a black baby in it! My maid was ill, and I had engaged a maid who had been in my service, and who had left me to get married. She could only come to me on condition that she brought her baby. I don't think the baby was black—a little dark, perhaps.

I have never been able to solve the mystery of why she had chosen to place her baby in Lord Derby's bath. This story ran through Goodwood Meeting and caused much amusement.

My son Hubert was anxious to enter Parliament as a Conservative, and, as always happens, he was expected to prove his merit by tackling a difficult constituency to start with. He was given East Ham, with the naturally hopeless task of ousting Miss Susan Lawrence.[1] He flung himself enthusiastically into this exciting, though losing, battle, and I backed him up to the best of my ability, as at this time his marriage was on the point of breaking up and he relied upon me to provide a domestic background in the electoral

---

[1] Susan Lawrence (1871–1947), Labour M.P. for East Ham North 1923–24 and 1926–31, and Chairman of the Labour Party in 1930.

campaign. I took a furnished house in East Ham—a nice, funny little house full of aspidistras—and I took my French maid with me, and we had Hubert's batman, and I had my Rolls-Royce and the chauffeur. We lived on hampers of food from Fortnum and Mason's, and I canvassed while Hubert was touring the constituency making speeches. Of course he did not win, but it was an enjoyable fight, and a far rougher one than any nowadays. One night, when we were leaving a meeting, a man came up to me when I was in the car and asked me to shake hands. I put my hand out of the window and he twisted my arm as hard as he could—I thought he had broken it.

Hubert having won his laurels at East Ham, where he had secured more Conservative votes than any Candidate had done before, he was rewarded by being sent as Candidate to Acton, then held by a Socialist but with a less vast majority than Miss Susan Lawrence's. Again I helped him in every way that I could—I even spoke for him, and ordinarily I am not good at public speaking and am most reluctant to do it, but at this time I found that the words came quite naturally, because of my great enthusiasm for my son's gallant efforts. We imported a bevy of beautiful young women to work and canvass in the constituency, and some of the results were quite amusing. I shall never forget a man who shouted, "Make that hussy go away from my door!"—pointing to lovely Diana Cooper standing, canvass-card in hand, on his doorstep. To my great joy, Hubert was elected, defeating the Socialist and winning the seat for the Conservatives. I think I have never felt prouder in my life. My pride in Hubert was overwhelming, and I even had a great sense of personal pride when people used to say, "Here's the Candidate's Mother." His striking good looks, charming nature, and excellent brain were indeed a combination to be proud of. Alas, I lost this splendid son eleven years ago—he died on active service during the Second World War.[1]

In 1931 a statue of George, erected by public subscription, was unveiled by the Prime Minister, Mr. Baldwin. The site is in Carlton House Terrace, opposite No. 1, our former London house; and the sculptor was Sir Bertram Mackennal,[2] who achieved a good likeness of George, although I regret that George was not wearing his Garter robes, but the robes of the Star of India. I think that George would have chosen the Garter robes, but I never saw the statue until the unveiling ceremony. I gave a large luncheon party at Carlton House

---

[1] Hubert Duggan (1904–43), M.P. for Acton 1931–43, died on active service as Captain and Adjutant in the Life Guards, October 1943.

[2] Sir Bertram Mackennal (1863–1931), the Australian-born sculptor.

Terrace before the unveiling, to most of the members of the Government, the Ambassadors, and many of George's old friends, including Bob and Peggy Crewe, the Salisburys, the D'Abernons, Evan Charteris, and the Desboroughs. I was a little shocked when Mr. Baldwin said, on his arrival, "I hope you will not expect a speech from me, as I have had no time to prepare one." I said, "But of course, Prime Minister, I do expect a speech." He then asked to be shown into another room, and hurriedly wrote a good speech. Mr. Baldwin was not famous for formal oratory, but he could compose a graceful tribute on the appropriate occasion.

CHAPTER XXII

George

I WISH I could find words to give the readers of my Memoirs a true picture of George—the man I knew. No one was ever indifferent to him; he was loved, or disliked.

George had a lovable and most complicated character. He was not an adaptable man. A man of the very highest intelligence himself, he was not always tolerant of others less gifted. He was easily hurt, and equally easily pleased. I always knew at once, without being told, just what he had experienced at his last Conference, or Cabinet Meeting. I prize above all others a letter of his from Lausanne, in which he writes: "I wonder if you have read the wonderful tributes to me in the English newspapers, *Daily Telegraph, Daily Mail, Evening Standard* and many others? I have suddenly been discovered at the age of 63. I was discovered when I was Viceroy of India from 39 to 46, then I was forgotten, traduced, buried, ignored. Now I have been dug up, and people seem to find life and even merit in the corpse."

George's friends, and indeed the public, have often wondered why he stayed in Office when he was being treated with little or no consideration at 10 Downing Street. I feel it is my duty to record that much of his willingness to remain in Office at that time was due to me. I had seen how very unhappy he had been when out of Office, and how greatly he minded not being what he called 'of use'. I quote from one of his letters to me. "Politics, as we have so often remarked, are a dirty game and the mud which others stir seems to settle with an almost malignant monotony on me. As you know, I would never have swallowed what I have done or consented to take office again, were it not that you so strongly wished me to do so, and that I am always urged and indeed expected to do the big thing." Again, at a later date, he wrote to me, "Politics are a sorry game, and your difficulty will be to keep me in them at all."

George was not the self-satisfied and conceited man that people who did not know him were apt to think. In one of his last letters to me from Lausanne, he wrote: "I do not think I will ever be Prime Minister, nor am I *fitted* for it. The chances against a success here are so great that my shares will go down."

No personal words about George would be complete without

243

a reference to his unique courage and endurance, the counterpart to his buoyant spirit. For George was *gay*. His gaiety of mind was always specially in evidence, when our two families were still at home, at dinner at Hackwood. He would keep us all amused, talking to Alfred and to Hubert of Eton and, later, of Oxford; Irene, Cimmie, Baba, and even on special occasions little Marcella—we were all enchanted by his wit and good talk. No one who saw him then could ever have called him pompous, overbearing, or a 'superior person'.

Of all the great dinner parties of which I have written in these pages, the perfect family parties at Hackwood will always hold the first place in my memory, and they make, for me, the most treasured and true picture of George.

Others have written fully, and at great length, of George's characteristics—but they were writing about the Viceroy of India, the Statesman, the Chancellor of Oxford, or the traveller, the connoisseur, and the author. They knew him, and they described him, in one of the many parts that he played with such distinction, in the life of his country and his age. I believe that I owe it to his memory to describe him as an individual, as a human being, as the man whose entire confidence I proudly enjoyed for so long.

There were, of course, many characteristics which George the public figure had in common with George the man at home. I think the chief of these was his brilliant mind. I was always conscious of his sparkling intellect, even in the most ordinary domestic circumstances. His command of language moved and thrilled me when I used to listen to him in the House of Lords, and it delighted me just as much at home even when he happened to be talking about rose trees or roast beef. His mind was so quick, he had a delicious sense of humour, and the long words and the fine, rolling phrases that he used on the most trivial occasions were always deliberately calculated to be effective and amusing—they were a constant source of pleasure and fun.

George in public life was dignity personified; and this dignity was perfectly natural, it was not assumed, and he never shed it at home because he was incapable of doing so. And yet his keen sense of fun enabled hm to laugh at himself and at his own dignified bearing, as for instance when he wrote to me (in a letter quoted in an earlier chapter), ". . . I look more like a butler out of a place than ever. . . . " This was a joke of very long standing, because he had once been mistaken for a butler at some party by one of the guests, and nobody enjoyed the mistake as much as George did. Some writers have implied that he was pompous, but that was anything but true—his sense of humour was far too strong. And, because his dignity was natural and not assumed, he never minded doing things which many men in his position would have thought undignified, such as carrying some treasure in an untidy paper parcel. And yet—he objected to my little daughter pushing a doll's perambulator along Carlton House Terrace! Truly he was a man of fascinating contradictions.

Although he was so unpredictable in many ways, George was superbly reliable in all social matters. He was a brilliant guest, and a most unselfish and considerate host. He always volunteered, when we were discussing the plans for a dinner, to take in the dullest dowager, and he would exert himself as much to amuse her as he would have done for a clever woman or for a beauty. His instinct for hospitality was very strong. He spent the last two years of his life planning every detail of comfort for the guests whom he hoped that we would receive at Kedleston.

George was extraordinarily sensitive. In spite of his dignity, his calm, his effortless command of language, he was terribly touchy and easily hurt by criticism and what he fancied were slights in public life. Equally, he was greatly moved by praise and congratulations, and by every sign of confidence in his work—these things affected him as deeply as criticism did. He was intensely emotional, and his emotions were constantly aroused by praise or blame in his public life. The one thing that he could never be was indifferent. He used sometimes to say, and to write to me, "After all, what does it matter?"—but he never meant it. *Everything* mattered to George. That was the secret of his extraordinary vitality in spite of all his ill-health and recurring attacks of pain.

The emotional side of George's nature was always in evidence in our private lives. He attached tremendous importance to all our anniversaries—birthdays, our wedding anniversary, and even, as I have described before, the anniversary of the occasion of our first meeting. This simple, affectionate outlook was one of the most delightful aspects of our life together. Often and often, at very big dinners at Carlton House Terrace, George would write a few words on the back of a menu card and send it to me by a footman, and I would quickly glance down and read a line or two of loving praise and admiration—such an enchanting thing for a wife to receive from her husband in the midst of a great gathering. And who else but George would have thought of sending those encouraging little messages from one side of the table to the other?

George was a perfectionist, and that is always a difficulty in domestic life as well as in public affairs. He complained often, and at length, of everything that was not exactly as he wished it to be. His own old servants were naturally put out by this tendency to criticize their work continually. They were aggrieved, they grumbled, but they stayed with him—they never left him. He commanded loyalty, and received it. I think they respected his terrible thoroughness—however much they may have grumbled, they were impressed by the Secretary of State for Foreign Affairs who found time to inspect the jam cupboards at regular intervals. He inspired affection in them as well as respect.

Having drawn my own picture of George, as he was at home, I feel that it should be completed by quoting from those who spoke the final words about his public life.

Mr. Baldwin, addressing the House of Commons after George's death, spoke as follows:

"He died as he would have desired, and as we should all desire to die—in harness: a harness put on by himself in youth, and worn triumphantly through a long life—a harness which he never cast off until his feet had entered the river. It may well be, when we look back on that life of devoted service to his country and of a perpetual triumph of the spirit over the flesh, that in some place on this earth, early on that Friday morning, may have been heard the faint echo of the trumpets that sounded for him on the other side."

Mr. Baldwin had gone to Bunyan for his model, and had succeeded in conveying the very atmosphere of simple beauty associated with the *Pilgrim's Progress*.

"It was my chance to see him," Mr. Baldwin said, "when he suffered great disappointment—at the time when I was preferred to him as Prime Minister, and at the time when I had to tell him that he could render greater service to the country as Chairman of the Committee of Imperial Defence, than in the Foreign Office. Each of these occasions was a profound and bitter disappointment to him, but never for one moment, when he had faced the facts, did he show by word, look, or innuendo, or by any reference to the subject afterwards, that he was dissatisfied; he bore no grudge, and he pursued no other course than the one I expected of him, of doing his duty where it was decided that he could best render service. This is true greatness, and of such stuff was Lord Curzon made."

One of George's oldest friends, Dr. Cosmo Gordon Lang, when Archbishop of York, paid a wonderful tribute to him in his simple, moving address in the Great Hall at Kedleston at the Burial Service. He began by referring to their friendship of over forty years' standing, and then recalled the magnanimity and greatness of spirit and of mind with which George had prepared for his life of devoted and unstinted service to his country and the Empire. He revealed that at the close of his Viceroyalty George had told him that in what he had tried to do he had been sustained by a passion for justice for the people of India. The Archbishop continued:

"We remember the courage with which he conquered pain and the courage with which he conquered the trials and disappointments appointed for him, especially in later years, when circumstances denied to him that highest place in the State which seemed to us all the natural crown of a life-long and honourable ambition. He felt the disappointment bitterly, but he refused to allow it to affect his devotion to the service of the country or his loyalty to his colleagues and the cause for which he stood. We can remember how loyal, constant and generous his friendship was, how he leaped forward to greet old friends and rejoice in the play of talk and the flowing over of rich humour. It is of the man himself that we think here in his old home. He had a gift for joy and his later years were crowned with a great joy. I know I am treading on sacred ground in the presence of her to whom we offer most full and respectful sympathy, but I cannot forbear saying I shall never forget the words he wrote to me, full of joy and pride, at his marriage. He had one great sorrow, and I shall never forget the impression given of the depth and sincerity of his spirit and almost passionate emotion, and the revelation of the almost amazing simplicity of his religious faith. The memory of that revelation of his religion can make us humbly content that in passing he will not find himself a stranger in his Father's house. Faults and failings there may have been in that forceful, vital, masterful personality, but they were of the kind we can leave trustfully in the pardoning and perfecting hands of God."

In these tributes to the greatness of George's character and achievements there is no reference to the wonderful generosity of his gifts to the National Trust of Tattershall Castle and Bodiam Castle, or to the painstaking research and expert supervision which he gave to their restoration. George's brilliance was so many-sided that it would have been impossible to touch on every aspect of it in a single speech or address. It remained for our old friend Harold Nicolson to record the knowledge, the hard work, and the loving care which George had devoted to restoring these two splendid Castles, a great Englishman's gift to the people of England—and this was done in a speech made at the unveiling of a plaque to the memory of George at Bodiam in October 1952:

"We are here, on this autumn afternoon, to attend the unveiling of a memorial to a famous statesman and a munificent benefactor. Lord Curzon lives in history as the most imaginative of Viceroys; as a Foreign Secretary who, by his force and vision, preserved his country and the world from a quite unnecessary war; as a man who, but for the accident of birth, would have been Prime Minister of Great Britain. In the thoughts of his countrymen, he survives as the last of our great line of Proconsuls, as a man who, by the power of his intellect, the astonishing range of his scholarship and memory, his rare capacity for extensive and intensive industry, rendered for almost half a century immense services to the Empire and the State. The legend will long linger of a man of excellent pride, of exalted ambition, of unequalled accomplishment, who throughout his life battled undefeated with constant ill-health and physical suffering, and who, when deprived by mischance of the supreme guerdon of a great career, had the modesty, the simple sense of public duty, to place his prestige and services at the disposal of younger and less experienced men.

"Lord Curzon assuredly was a formidable figure, cast in a Roman mould of imperial dignity. Yet these his lapidary qualities were illumined and softened by beams of a warmer sun. He was an emotional man, deeply sensitive to the sorrows and misfortunes of his fellow men. Above all, perhaps, he was a romantic, for whom the age of chivalry was not outworn, and who in the beauty of art and nature found solace and refuge from the turmoil, the rancour and the disillusion of political life.

"In India he will long be remembered as the Viceroy who aroused the Indian peoples to a sense of pride in the beauty of their own architecture and antiquities and who encouraged them to preserve and to embellish the rich heritage bequeathed to them by their own past.

"On his return to this country his veneration for the legacy of former ages induced him to devote his unsurpassed energies to preserving for posterity places of beauty that might but for him have been denuded or destroyed. In 1911 he rescued Tattershall Castle in Lincolnshire and restored to it at his own cost the beautiful architectural features which were about to be dispersed. In 1917 he acquired Bodiam, which shone for him, to quote his words, 'as the most romantic and the most fairy of English castles', and determined that 'so rare a treasure should neither be lost to our country nor desecrated by irreverent hands'.

"Into the restoration of Bodiam he flung all his passion for beauty, all his unequalled attention to detail, all his unswerving persistence. He drained the moat, he repaired the foundations, he restored the fallen battlements, and, fully occupied though he was by his governmental responsibilities, he devoted months of research to a careful examination of the origins and construction of this building and to writing the book which will for ever remain the classic work on the lovely castle where we stand. He was able to disprove many depressing legends. He showed that it was untrue, as some had said, that Bodiam was a mere folly, erected, but uncompleted, in imitation of the Château de Derval in France. He showed that it was untrue that it had been pulled down in the reign of Richard III, but that it had merely been 'slighted' during the Civil War. He showed that it was untrue that it had always been uninhabited and proved that men and women had lived here in splendour, if not in comfort, through four centuries. It was not the fabric only that he restored: he gave back to Bodiam its very soul.

"There was a moment when Lord Curzon toyed with the idea of rebuilding the interior of the castle and living there himself, or making it a Dower House. He was restrained from this project by observing what Viollet-le-Duc had done to Pierrefonds and Carcassonne. He decided that 'what would have been an interesting architectural experiment might have degenerated into an archaeological crime'. 'Perhaps,' he wrote—and his words are memorable—'perhaps in preserving and dedicating the remains of the Castle to the public for all time, I may have rendered a rather better service both to sentiment and learning.'

"Today, Ladies and Gentlemen, owing to Lord Curzon's vision, munificence and public spirit, Bodiam is vested in the

National Trust, who, with the help of the local committees, will preserve it reverently as a national possession, as an adornment to this country and island, and as a memorial to a magnanimous humanist.

"Lord Curzon's latter years were gladdened by the devotion, the companionship, and, if I may say so, the serene beauty, of one who shared his love of Bodiam and who, in her widowhood, has come here to live within sight of the sombre, somnolent, towers which he loved.

"It is my privilege, as representing the National Trust, to invite you, Lady Curzon, to unveil this tablet in memory of your great and generous husband."

I feel that these tributes to the character of a very great man form the best conclusion to the Memoirs of his wife.

The idea of writing my Memoirs first occurred to me long ago; and at that time I received, and accepted, the very best possible advice upon the subject. When I had not long been a widow I was sitting at dinner beside King George V, and I mentioned to him that I was thinking of writing my Memoirs. The King said to me: "Lady Curzon, don't do that yet. It is sure to stir up controversy. Wait for twenty-five years."

I have waited for thirty.

INDEX